BEHIND
the
SCENES

Books by Jen Turano

APART FROM
THE CROWD

BEHIND
the
SCENES

JEN TURANO

BETHANYHOUSE
a division of Baker Publishing Group
Minneapolis, Minnesota

© 2017 by Jennifer L. Turano

Published by Bethany House Publishers
11400 Hampshire Avenue South
Bloomington, Minnesota 55438
www.bethanyhouse.com

Bethany House Publishers is a division of
Baker Publishing Group, Grand Rapids, Michigan

Printed in the United States of America

Library of Congress Cataloging-in-Publication Data
Names: Turano, Jen, author.
Title: Behind the scenes / Jen Turano.
Description: Minneapolis, Minnesota : Bethany House, a division of Baker
    Publishing Group, [2017] | Series: Apart from the crowd
Identifiers: LCCN 2016037746| ISBN 9780764230103 (cloth) | ISBN 9780764217944
    (trade paper)
Subjects: | GSAFD: Love stories. | Christian fiction.
Classification: LCC PS3620.U7455 B48 2017 | DDC 813/.6—dc23
LC record available at https://lccn.loc.gov/2016037746

Scripture quotations are from the King James Version of the Bible.

Cover design by Jennifer Parker
Cover photography by Mike Habermann Photography, LLC

Author is represented by Natasha Kern Literary Agency

17 18 19 20 21 22 23   7 6 5 4 3 2 1

For Dr. Robert Turner
Because every big brother needs
to have a romance novel dedicated
to him from his adorable,
yet occasionally annoying, little sister.

Love you!
Jennifer

CHAPTER ONE

MARCH 1883—NEW YORK CITY

Pressing her nose against the glass of the carriage window, Miss Permilia Griswold felt her stomach begin to churn as she took note of the throngs of people lining Fifth Avenue. Even though darkness had descended over the city hours before, the lure of witnessing New York society trundling down the street in their fancy carriages, on their way to Mr. and Mrs. William K. Vanderbilt's costume ball, was apparently enough of a spectacle to keep people out and about on a chilly spring night.

That her father's carriage was still blocks away from their destination of 660 Fifth Avenue and yet crowds were pressed three deep in and around the sidewalk, gave clear testimony to the importance of this particular ball and to the interest New Yorkers had for its highest society members.

Even though Permilia was included on the invitation list for the most important societal events in the city, she'd not grown up within the cosseted inner circles of society, which exactly explained why her stomach was churning.

She was uncomfortable in social situations, had yet to master all the rules that went with being a member of New York society, and . . .

"You're fogging up the window, Permilia, which is obscuring my view and making all the people outside our carriage appear to be little more than ghosts wobbling about. It's a most unnerving sight."

Tearing her attention away from a crowd she could see perfectly fine through the merest trace of fog on the window, Permilia settled it on her stepmother, Ida Griswold. "Forgive me, stepmother. That was most inconsiderate of me." Turning back to the window, Permilia began swiping at the mist with a gloved hand, stopping midswipe when Ida suddenly took to *tsk*ing.

"A lady must never use her glove in such a common fashion," Ida said, her words having Permilia's hand dropping into her lap. "And"—Ida's gaze swept over Permilia's form—"you've taken to slouching again. On my word, if you'd simply remember to maintain a proper posture at all times, I'm quite certain you wouldn't find yourself cast in the troubling role of wallflower season after season."

Swallowing the sigh she longed to emit, Permilia forced a smile instead. "Contrary to the prevalent thought of the day, I'm not a lady who feels as if my life has been ruined simply because I've obtained the somewhat undesirable label of wallflower."

"Of course your life has been ruined," Ida countered. "You're twenty-something years old, have never taken within society, nor have you ever attracted the devotion of a gentleman. Why, even your own stepsister doesn't care to spend time in your company."

"I believe that has more to do with the fact that Lucy and I have nothing in common than my tendency to slouch upon occasion." Permilia switched her gaze to her stepsister, Miss Lucy Webster, who was sitting ramrod straight on the seat opposite her, staunchly ignoring the conversation as she waved to the crowds gathered along the street.

Leaning forward, Permilia looked out the window Lucy sat beside. The crowd on Lucy's side of the street was obviously enjoying Lucy's waves, given the cheers they were sending her stepsister's way. Permilia couldn't say she blamed them for their enthusiasm.

Lucy had been chosen to perform in one of the many quadrilles Alva Vanderbilt had planned for the evening. And because Lucy was to be in the Mother Goose Quadrille, she was dressed to perfection as Little Bo Peep and looked absolutely delightful. Her honey-colored curls peeked out from under her cap, and her figure was shown to advantage with the low-cut neckline of her gown, her rather bountiful charms accentuated by the diamond necklace she was wearing. That Lucy had perfected a royal wave, moving her hand back and forth exactly so, had the corners of Permilia's lips curving up.

"It is such a shame that your father is still out of the city and couldn't attend this ball, dear," Ida continued. "He would have enjoyed seeing you looking so well turned out tonight."

Permilia's lips stopped curving at once as she settled back against the carriage seat. "I may have a propensity to slouch upon occasion, stepmother, and to not adhere to every society rule, but even you must admit that I'm always well turned out. Modesty aside, I do believe I possess a distinct flair for fashion."

Lucy immediately stopped her waving. Turning a head that sat on a remarkably graceful neck, she pinned Permilia beneath the glare of an emerald-green eye. "How can you make the claim that you're always well turned out? You purchase your clothing from stores that cater to working women and have less than desirable locations."

"True," Permilia said with a nod, the motion setting the large diamond tiara Ida had insisted she wear shifting around on her head. "But there's absolutely nothing wrong with the fashions I find in those shops. I enjoy shopping in out-of-the-way places, searching for designs that have a unique style. Besides, the owners of those shops need my money far more than the owners of the fashionable shops do. I, for one, am proud of the fact I have an eye for thrift."

She gestured to the sparkling white gown she was wearing, one that had tiny paste jewels sewn throughout the folds of the fabric, lending the garment an icy appearance. "My snow-queen ensemble was designed by an innovative woman who works in a little shop in a slightly questionable part of the city. And while I did pay Miss Betsy Miller a rather dear amount for my gown, as well as for the fur muff I had her design to complement the gown, the price I paid would have doubled if I'd sought out the services of a more esteemed establishment."

"Not patronizing the tried-and-true establishments of society is considered beyond peculiar, and that right there is exactly why you haven't taken with the fashionable set," Lucy argued. "Your father, my stepfather, is one of the wealthiest gentlemen in the country, which means you have absolutely no reason to be frugal. It's downright embarrassing when you're seen lurking around the poorer sections of town, and it lends clear credence to the idea that you're undeniably odd."

Permilia lifted her chin. "Simply because one comes from wealth does not mean one should abandon one's thrifty principles. Besides, Miss Miller, the woman I hired to create my costume, needed the funds she earned from me because her rent was past due and she was worried about being kicked out on the street."

Lucy's mouth gaped. "You had a *conversation* with this woman?"

"Of course I did. It's always seemed rather silly to me to be standing around having your measurements taken while not enjoying the company of the woman taking those measurements."

Permilia lifted her chin another notch. "And before you dissolve into a fit of hysterics—something your expression clearly suggests you're about to do—know that I have no intention of abandoning my habit of speaking with whomever I choose. Furthermore, I also have no intention of abandoning my frugal ways, even if those ways embarrass you upon occasion."

Lucy's forehcad puckered. "Your oddness is exactly why I have yet to acquire a suitable offer of marriage. I have no idea why you have to continue on with your stingy and peculiar attitude when that attitude is ruining my life."

"You've been extended five completely acceptable offers since you made your debut two years ago," Permilia shot back. "And since you and I barely acknowledge one another when we're out and about in society, I really don't understand how you can claim that I'm the one ruining your life. If you ask me, your disenchantment with the gentlemen who've cast their attention your way has more to do with your air of displeasure toward life in general, which, in my humble opinion, is a direct result of your unfortunate sense of entitlement and a condescending attit—"

"That will be quite enough, Permilia," Ida interrupted. "As is so often the case when we're trying to gently point out some of your more glaring faults, you immediately try to misdirect the conversation by throwing nasty accusations Lucy's way. She, I must say, has just made a most valid point regarding your position on wealth."

Ida began fiddling with a diamond bracelet that encircled her gloved wrist. "Possessing abundant wealth is not meant to be a burden, but meant to be fully enjoyed. Surely you must realize that by clinging to your parsimonious ways, while doing absolutely nothing to hide those ways, you're sabotaging any slight chance you may still have to take within society. You also diminish the chances of attracting the notice of a suitable gentleman, something your father hopes may still happen."

She released a breathy sigh. "Your father isn't growing any younger, Permilia. His hard work will be for naught if you don't find a worthy gentleman to bring into the family who has the business mentality needed to take over your father's many endeavors."

As Ida launched into another lecture, this one concerning the sad state of Permilia's social ambitions, Permilia shifted against the seat, being careful to maintain her posture as she did so. A second later, her thoughts began to wander, a direct result of having heard the lecture Ida was in the midst of delivering numerous times in the past.

It wasn't as if she'd intended to land herself on the fringes of society, but in all honesty, she'd never aspired to travel within society in the first place. She'd always believed she'd walk through life at her father's side, helping him run his many mining ventures and eventually taking over that running in the end, even though she was a woman.

Being a member of the fairer sex had never been an obstacle for her growing up, probably because she'd not been exposed to women much in her youth, her mother having died of a horrible fever when Permilia had been only two years old. That unfortunate death had left her with only a father to care for her. Since George Griswold had never wanted to leave Permilia in the charge of a nanny or female relative while he'd traveled to grow his investment opportunities, he'd taken her along with him. That had provided Permilia with a vagabond lifestyle, filled with adventures, wonders, and a great deal of dirt, especially when she'd spent time in the mines.

Her schooling had come at the hands of a tutor, not a governess. And, while learning the feminine graces had been woefully neglected, she'd received an education worthy of any man, something she'd always assumed she'd put to good use when she was given the honor of managing the family business.

That assumption had come to a rather abrupt end when her father met, and then married, within a remarkably short period of time, the widowed Mrs. Ida Webster, a formidable lady one learned rather quickly not to cross—and a lady who staunchly believed a woman's place was in the home, not traveling around the country participating in . . . business.

From the moment Ida had exchanged vows with Permilia's father, Permilia had found herself taken firmly in hand and taken firmly out of the mining world by her new stepmother— a circumstance her father, traitor that he'd apparently turned, heartily approved.

Ida, regrettably, came from a long line of Old New Yorkers, fondly referred to as the Knickerbocker set, and as such, she was accustomed to traveling in the highest society circles. That meant that the idea of her acquiring a stepdaughter with no societal interests was not to be tolerated, hence the reason Permilia was introduced to society at the ripe old age of nineteen.

That introduction had not seen Permilia gliding across the ballroom on the arm of one gentleman after another, but had, instead, seen her banished—and banished rather quickly, at that—to the wallflower section.

Her stepmother had not been pleased with what she proclaimed was a very sad state of affairs and had spent the ensuing years—of which there'd been quite a few—pondering the reason Permilia had not taken within the fashionable set. Ida had come up with a remarkably extensive list to explain Permilia's deficiencies, including Permilia's age, her intellect, her height, her unusual red hair, her lack of social graces, and . . . well, the list went on and on.

Since Permilia preferred to maintain a cheerful attitude, at least most of the time, and since contemplating the many deficiencies Ida kept compiling became somewhat depressing after a while, she'd taken to skulking around the edges of ballrooms, far away from her stepmother's caustic tongue. That skulking had, surprisingly enough, led to a most intriguing opportunity and had provided Permilia with a much-needed distraction as she was forced to attend one society event after another.

She had great hopes, though, that she'd someday be able to abandon her distraction—once her father came to his senses and allowed her to return to the mining life she'd been intending to live, not the fluffy world of—

"What about Mr. Rutherford?" Ida asked, the question effectively pushing any other thoughts Permilia might have had straight out of her head.

"Are we speaking of Mr. Asher Rutherford, the owner of Rutherford & Company department store?" she asked.

"Indeed we are." Ida gave a single nod. "I heard from none other than Mrs. Templeton that you've been seen speaking with that particular gentleman . . . twice."

Lucy let out a hiss of obvious outrage, a sound Permilia was fairly certain young ladies were not actually supposed to make—and that Ida unfairly ignored. "You've held conversations with Mr. Asher Rutherford?"

Permilia shrugged. "I'm not entirely certain haggling with the gentleman over the price he was trying to extort for ice skates at the impromptu booth he'd erected in Central Park can truly be considered holding a conversation with the man."

Two bright spots of color darkened Lucy's pale cheeks. "You *haggled* with Mr. Rutherford—one of the most eligible gentlemen in society?"

"He wanted over five dollars for a pair of ice skates." Permilia crossed her arms over her chest. "It was highway robbery." She smiled. "He eventually took three dollars and some change from me—a sum I felt was more in line with what the skates were worth—which allowed me to enjoy a lovely day on the ice with my very good friend, Miss Wilhelmina Radcliff."

Ida began mumbling under her breath, something about a *hopeless cause* and she was at her *wit's end*. When her mumbles finally trailed off, she set a determined eye on Permilia. "What was the conversation about the second time you spoke with Mr. Rutherford?"

"I must admit I find the idea that your friends are tattling on me fairly disturbing, but the only other time I can actually recall speaking with Mr. Rutherford was at Wilhelmina's engagement ball. It was not a conversation that had much meat to it. In fact, if memory serves, I believe we spent some time discussing the weather—a subject that you've stressed is a perfectly acceptable topic for polite conversation."

"You could have brought my name into your conversation," Lucy chimed in. "Mr. Rutherford is certainly a gentleman I'd *welcome* receiving a proposal from."

Permilia opened her mouth but was spared a response to that nonsense when the carriage began to slow to a stop.

Ida leaned forward, looked out the window, and drew back. "Smiles at the ready, my dears. We've reached Mrs. William K. Vanderbilt's new home at last. Given that there appears to be an entire swarm of curiosity-seekers waiting to greet us— and take note of what we're wearing, no doubt—we certainly shouldn't disappoint them."

Lucy raised a hand and adjusted her diamond necklace, situating the diamond pendant to better draw attention to her charms right before she lifted her head. "I'll do my very best not to disappoint them, Mother." With that, she slid across the seat right as the door opened. Taking the hand a groom extended her, Lucy hitched a charming smile into place and stepped out of the carriage in a flurry of satin and lace.

Holding up a hand that sufficiently stopped Permilia from scooting toward the door, Ida turned a stern eye on her. "I don't mean to come across as a nag, dear, but do try to be friendly to the gentlemen tonight, especially Mr. Rutherford, if you happen to cross his path. Although, from the sound of it, you may have burned that particular bridge."

"I have no interest in Mr. Rutherford, and besides, it sounded to me as if Lucy holds him in great esteem. It would hardly improve our sisterly relationship—or stepsisterly relationship, to be more exact—if I pursued a gentleman she desires."

"A lady never pursues a gentleman," Ida countered, her words at complete odds with the advice she'd just given Permilia. "As for Lucy and Mr. Rutherford . . . well, he has chosen to dirty his hands in trade, probably horrifying his dear mother in the process. Because of that—and because of the promise I made to my first husband before he died his tragic death concerning Lucy and her future prospects—she will only marry a gentleman who has no scandal tarnishing his name, one who truly upholds the Knickerbocker beliefs Lucy's father held in such high regard."

"Does *Lucy* know about that promise you made to your first husband?"

Ida looked a bit disconcerted before she lifted her chin. "As I was saying before we got distracted from the subject at hand, your father is very anxious to see you well settled, and this is the last society event of the season. You won't have another opportunity to mingle with gentlemen until we travel to our cottage in Newport for the summer, and that's ages away."

She waved a hand Permilia's way. "As I mentioned, you're looking very well turned out tonight, so do try to take advantage of that, if only for your father's sake. And remember, a smile can be a powerful weapon when it comes to attracting the attention of a gentleman. I suggest you put that advice to good use tonight, and hopefully, we'll have good news to tell your father when he returns home at the end of the week." With that, Ida scooted forward on the seat and stepped from the carriage.

Lingering behind, Permilia absently checked her fur muff, making certain the stash of dance cards she'd obtained—covertly, of course—from a Vanderbilt servant a few days before were still firmly tucked inside, along with numerous small pencils. Withdrawing her hand after she'd established that her supplies were in fine order, she began inching ever so slowly toward the door, not exactly certain she was anxious to face the crème of society who'd been invited to Alva Vanderbilt's first society ball.

Her inching came to a stop, though, when Ida's voice drifted through the open door. "Permilia, you're trying my patience. Don't make me come back in there and prod you along."

Shoving aside the thought that her life had been far less complicated before she'd acquired a stepmother, Permilia headed for the door, knowing there was no help for it but to stumble through the evening as best she could.

CHAPTER
TWO

Pausing midway through the carriage door with her hand extended, Permilia realized there were no Griswold grooms waiting to help her to the sidewalk. Glancing around, she found the grooms in question assisting the coachman as he tried to get Lucy's Little Bo Peep hook unstuck from the top of the carriage. Unwilling to wait for assistance because there was still a long line of carriages waiting to deposit their riders, Permilia jumped lightly to the red carpet covering the sidewalk, straightening her tiara when she felt it wobble on her head.

Pretending not to hear Ida's clucks of disapproval over what was apparently another blatant disregard for the social graces, Permilia lifted her chin. She then made the grave mistake of casting a quick look around.

What she saw had her freezing on the spot, unable to move so much as a single muscle.

People—and what could only be described as a throng of them—were assembled at least ten deep along the sidewalk, some even standing in the very midst of Fifth Avenue, each and every one of them craning their necks as they seemed to gawk Permilia's way.

Being a lady unaccustomed to people gawking at her, especially since she spent most of her time unnoticed at society events, she found herself at a complete loss as to what was expected of her next. Fortunately, she was spared further scrutiny when Ida sidled up next to her, whispered a sharp reminder to smile, took a painful grip of Permilia's arm, and towed Permilia along the red carpet. Lucy soon joined them, gliding along at Permilia's side, waving to the crowds as if it were an everyday occurrence for her to walk along on a red carpet.

What seemed hours later—but had in actuality been only minutes—Permilia stepped into a well-appointed entranceway, keeping her smile firmly in place as Ida handed their formally engraved invitations to the butler. Once he bowed them forward, Permilia found herself steered down a long hallway by a Vanderbilt footman dressed in maroon livery.

To her relief, when they reached an ornate fireplace with a fire crackling merrily away in the very midst of the hallway, Ida dropped her hold on Permilia's arm.

"I've just seen a few of my friends, so I'll leave you here, Permilia. Do try to remember what I've asked of you this evening, and do try to remember that smiling while keeping one's mouth firmly closed is a great asset when trying to draw the notice of gentlemen." She actually shuddered. "Gentlemen are not keen on ladies who are too intelligent, and I'm afraid that's exactly how you come across when you speak on even the most mundane of topics."

Turning to Lucy before Permilia could bring up the fact that she never seemed *able* to talk to most society gentlemen, her tongue becoming tied whenever she was in their company, Ida gave her daughter a lovely word of encouragement regarding the quadrille she was to perform later that evening. Patting

Lucy's cheek, Ida then hurried away, joining a group of society matrons gathered at the foot of a grand staircase.

"I'm off to the third-floor gymnasium to meet up with the other Mother Goose participants," Lucy said. "Please refrain from participating in anything that may cause me embarrassment, but do feel free to bring my name up in conversation if you happen upon that lovely Mr. Rutherford again." She tapped her Little Bo Peep hook against the marble floor. "He's a very handsome sort, rumored to be beyond wealthy, and . . . just think of the access to all the latest fashions and accessories a lady would have if she happened to gain his affections." With that, Lucy sent Permilia a nod, turned on her dainty heel, and with her skirts swishing in a very becoming manner—a move Lucy had perfected while watching herself in a mirrored wall—she disappeared into the crowd, leaving Permilia all alone.

Delighted to be left to her own devices, and anxious to view every nook and cranny that was permissible to view in Alva Vanderbilt's extravagant home, Permilia fell into step behind a group of exquisitely dressed guests who were climbing up the grand staircase. To her amusement, she found herself in the midst of kings, queens, milkmaids, pirates, and even a few brightly colored insects here and there. Trying to put names to all the costumed guests surrounding her, she reached the second floor and edged as discreetly as possible behind a lush fern, peering through the fronds as guests streamed past her. Sticking her hand into the fur muff, she pulled out one of her many dance cards along with a small pencil. Jotting down the names of some of the guests she recognized, along with the costumes they were wearing, she found her dance card filled with scribbles in a remarkably short time. Feeling as if she'd gotten a great start on her mission for the evening, she stepped away from the fern, stuck her dance card back into the muff, looked up, and found—to her very great surprise—an attractive gentleman smiling her way.

Not being a woman who ever attracted the attention of the gentlemanly type—what with the whole stigma of being a wallflower and all—Permilia wasn't exactly certain what one was supposed to do when a gentleman sent a smile in her direction.

Inclining her head ever so slightly in return, she was dumbfounded when the gentleman apparently took that inclination as an invitation to approach her, but before he had the opportunity to join her, she turned on a sparkly heel and bolted after a crowd of guests being led down the hallway by a man who seemed to be the underbutler.

Ignoring the curious looks sent her way when she slipped into the midst of the crowd, she turned her full attention to the underbutler, hoping that he'd be generous with information about the grand house, especially the second floor they were now viewing, which Permilia soon learned was the living quarters of Mr. and Mrs. Vanderbilt.

Fanning a face that was still a little heated over her almost encounter with a smiling gentleman, Permilia soon found herself distracted from her flustered state of mind by the underbutler's knowledge of the new Vanderbilt house. To her absolute delight, when she followed the man through a door framed with elaborate moldings, she found herself smack-dab in the middle of Alva Vanderbilt's boudoir.

Knowing this was a place very few people would ever get to see, she tried to drink everything in, especially the bathing chamber that came complete with a large marble tub and risqué paintings hanging from the walls. Additional paintings of the risqué sort were prevalent in the bedchamber as well as in Alva's private sitting room. Ducking into a shadowed corner to make a few notes on another dance card, she tucked that card back in the muff, but lifting her head, she found that while she'd been distracted, the underbutler had led everyone else out of the room. Not wanting to be found all alone in a place she shouldn't be alone in, she hurried out of Alva Vanderbilt's private quarters, quickly catching up with the crowd.

Falling into step with society members who were all attempting to maintain an air of nonchalance, even though it was likely the majority of them were practically bursting with the extravagance of the evening, Permilia followed them up another flight of stairs.

When she reached the top of those stairs, she discovered herself in the midst of a gymnasium that had been turned into a delightful tropical forest. It was filled to the brim with ferns and flowers that the underbutler explained had been fashioned under the watchful eye of renowned florist Mr. Charles Klunder. As Permilia moved away from the tour, she heard whispers speculating that the display must have cost more than most men earned in a year . . . or ten.

Pushing aside the discomfort that idea evoked, Permilia began strolling as casually as she could, slowing to a stop when her attention was drawn to a gentleman dressed as a dashing Richard Coeur de Lion. To her utmost confusion, that gentleman sent her a very warm smile right before he sent her a rather roguish wink.

Unable to recall a single time when she'd received a wink, Permilia felt heat begin to travel up her neck.

Knowing full well she'd be inattentive to her mission at hand if she continued to draw such unexpected attention, Permilia pulled her gaze from the winking gentleman and, as discreetly as possible, looked over the front of her gown, surprised to discover that everything seemed to be in proper order. Not one button was undone, nor was her neckline askew, which made it even more confusing to understand the attention that kept being directed her way.

Lifting her head, her gaze returned to the winking gentleman and found him now heading her way, carrying two glasses of what appeared to be champagne.

That sight had any thought of proper decorum vanishing straightaway. Abandoning all the many rules her stepmother had drummed into her about walking in a slow and dignified manner, Permilia spun around and dashed away into the crowd, earning more than a few raised eyebrows but thankfully losing the smiling-and-beverage-carrying gentleman in the process.

Needing to find a place to collect her scattered thoughts, Permilia breathed a sigh of relief when she spotted some large ferns. Hurrying their way, she disappeared into the fronds.

What she found on the other side of those fronds had her skidding to a stop, unable to help but smile at the sight that greeted her.

Sitting on what appeared to be an overturned log and looking more forlorn than usual were two fellow wallflowers—Miss Gertrude Cadwalader and Miss Temperance Flowerdew.

That they did not appear to be pleased to be in the midst of Alva Vanderbilt's ball was certainly an understatement. Taking a step closer to them, Permilia suddenly found herself at a complete loss for words when she got her first good look at Gertrude.

She didn't know Gertrude well, even though she'd frequently sat beside her at one society event or another over the years. The reason behind that lack of familiarity was a direct result of the unspoken rules wallflowers were expected to adhere to at all times.

One of the most important rules was that wallflowers did not converse with each other . . . ever.

Thankfully, that particular rule had finally been broken when a fellow wallflower, Miss Wilhelmina Radcliff, had required assistance in trying to evade the attention of Mr. Edgar

Wanamaker. The evading tactics had not exactly gone off as planned—especially since, instead of avoiding Mr. Wanamaker, Wilhelmina was now engaged to the man. But the antics of Wilhelmina and her Mr. Wanamaker had made it possible for Permilia and Gertrude to become friends. Permilia found the unexpected friendship to be very lovely indeed, seeing as she'd not made any friends since she and her father had moved to New York after living a somewhat nomadic existence for years.

Nevertheless, even though she had formed a friendship with Gertrude, she had yet to understand Gertrude's unusual sense of fashion. Though she always dressed in a rather peculiar manner, tonight, well, Gertrude had simply outdone herself.

Gertrude's golden curls were gathered together in two unevenly matched bunches on either side of her head. Brightly colored feathers were stuck into the bunches, and then more feathers—ones that appeared to be from a chicken—were attached to wings that had been sewn onto the back of her blue-and-green-striped dress. Additional feathers had been glued, and not glued very well, all over the fabric of Gertrude's skirt.

"I'm a peacock," Gertrude said before Permilia had a chance to recover her speech.

"Of course you are."

Gertrude grinned. "I know I don't look anything like a peacock, Permilia, but Mrs. Davenport, the lady I'm paid to be companion to, fancies herself a somewhat artistic sort. One of the conditions of her hiring me on as her companion was that I needed to agree to allow her to pursue her artistic nature by styling me in whatever manner she saw fit—or . . . 'as the muse strikes,' as she so quaintly put it."

Resisting the impulse to grab a dance card from her muff and write down that intriguing piece of nonsense concerning one of society's established matrons, Permilia summoned up a smile instead. "Perhaps the muse will stop striking."

24

Miss Temperance Flowerdew—another wallflower, but one who rarely spoke—let out what almost sounded like a laugh, until her eyes widened. She gulped in a breath of air and immediately settled into silence again.

Releasing a laugh of her own, Gertrude caught Permilia's eye. "While I can always hope that Mrs. Davenport will decide she's not an artistic sort, for now, since she pays very well for my company, I've learned to avoid mirrors at all costs." Gertrude patted a spot beside her on the log. "You're welcome to join us if you'd like."

Feeling a rush of affection for her new friend, Permilia moved to the log and took a seat. "May I assume the two of you plan to spend the entire ball hidden behind here?"

"I should think not," Gertrude said even as Temperance began nodding. Reaching over to Temperance, Gertrude patted her hand. "We can't stay here all night—especially since I've come to the conclusion that this cozy nook may have been created to offer couples seeking out a bit of privacy a place to . . . well . . . do whatever it is couples do when they go off searching for a secluded spot."

Temperance stopped nodding, turned a bright shade of pink, and got to her feet, shaking out the folds of what appeared to be some sort of servant costume. "I'll get in all sorts of trouble if anyone comes to the conclusion I'm hiding away back here in order to have a clandestine meeting with . . . a gentleman."

For the briefest of moments, Permilia simply stared at the woman who'd just strung an entire sentence together. "Get in trouble from whom, pray tell?"

Temperance shuddered. "It would be for the best if I didn't answer that, but I do appreciate you asking." With that, she spun around and rushed away.

"You don't suppose her cousin, Mr. Wayne Flowerdew, is abusive toward her, do you?" Gertrude asked.

"I'm afraid I don't know much about Mr. Flowerdew, nor about Temperance, for that matter," Permilia began. "I've heard the rumors that she's a poor relation, taken in by her cousin after her parents died a few years back. I've also heard that the Flowerdew family was fortunate in that they were vouched for by a very respected New York Knickerbocker matron who saw them accepted into New York society two years ago without much fuss."

She pursed her lips. "It's been clear to me for some time now that the Flowerdews place little value on Temperance. Her sole purpose in attending society events seems to revolve around her being at the ready if Wayne Flowerdew's daughter—the very fashionable, yet quite nasty, Miss Clementine Flowerdew—needs assistance with anything. Why, I've seen her called away from the wallflower section numerous times over the past two years in order to sew a button back on Clementine's gown, search out glue to reattach a heel that had come off Clementine's dainty shoe, and once . . . I watched Temperance hold a parasol over Clementine's head in order to keep the sun away from her cousin's pale complexion as they strolled around Central Park."

Gertrude gave a shake of her head. "And here I thought I had a difficult time of it being a paid companion to Mrs. Davenport, who isn't always pleasant, but at least there's only one of her, and—"

Whatever else Gertrude had been about to say got lost when there was a loud shriek and then a thud. A second later, one of the pillars that had been brought in to lend the gymnasium an ancient-Roman feel, and one that could be seen from their hiding place since it reached almost to the ceiling, began to teeter.

Not hesitating, Permilia moved into motion and burst through the foliage she'd been hiding behind. Her gaze took in the sight of Temperance lying on the floor, obviously a victim of an overly long hem, before she switched her attention to the pillar Temperance had apparently bounced against. To her horror, that pillar no longer simply teetered but began to topple, sending the plants on top of it cascading to the ground.

Dashing forward, she put her shoulder against it, praying that would be enough to set it to rights again.

To her dismay, the pillar turned out to be far heavier than she'd anticipated. As her feet began to slip out from underneath her, she called a warning to the guests closest to her, right before she completely lost her balance and slid to the floor. Lifting an arm to cover her face, she squeezed her eyes shut and braced herself for the pain that was certainly to come.

CHAPTER
THREE

Pausing in the midst of a conversation he was enjoying with some delightful young ladies, all of whom had obtained their lady-in-waiting costumes from his store, Rutherford & Company, Mr. Asher Rutherford blinked as what could only be described as a catastrophe-in-the-making began to unfold right before his eyes.

A decorative pillar was teetering in a most concerning manner, the teetering sending some of the potted plants adorning the top of it tumbling to the ground.

As the first plant hit the marble floor, guests scattered every which way, but amidst all the scattering, a lady dressed in a shimmering gown of white darted out from behind a clump of ferns. To his disbelief, she charged right up to the pillar that was now *tilting*, not teetering, and placed a slim shoulder against it, one that certainly wasn't strong enough to stop the disaster about to happen.

When her feet began sliding against the polished floor of the gymnasium, he immediately found the incentive to move, rushing forward and reaching the pillar right as the lady lost her balance. Meeting the falling pillar with a shoulder of his own, but one that was certainly broader than the lady's, he shoved with all his might, sending the pillar on a different course, one that didn't have it grinding anyone into the ground. When it hit the floor, it broke into numerous pieces, the sounds of the pieces tinkling across the marble floor overly loudly in a room that had grown remarkably quiet.

Silence settled over the gymnasium as a few leaves from the potted plants drifted through the air, until a lady standing near him—one who was sporting a most unusual hairstyle and wearing, curiously enough, what appeared to be chicken feathers attached to a wide swath of her costume—began clapping enthusiastically as she beamed a bright smile his way, her actions having the entire room bursting into applause.

Being a gentleman who'd never been uncomfortable with attention, Asher smiled and presented the room with a bow. As the applause began to fade away, he directed his attention to the rash young lady who'd certainly had good intentions but had behaved in a manner at distinct odds with her innate feminine nature. That young lady was still lying on the floor, her face almost entirely hidden beneath a gloved hand.

Leaning toward her, he took in the sight of well-coifed red hair that was a most unusual shade, given that it was mixed with a good deal of gold, and . . . it was a shade he'd only seen on one lady before.

His smile dimmed ever so slightly as he realized that the lady stretched out on the floor in front of him was none other than Miss Permilia Griswold, a lady he wasn't overly familiar with, but who evoked rather unusual emotions in him all the same.

Those emotions ranged from annoyance, exasperation, frustration, and even to grudging respect—all of the emotions, curiously enough, having come about during the *two* times he'd found himself in her company.

The first time he'd spoken to her had been in Central Park, providing skates—at a price, of course—to the many New Yorkers who'd braved the elements in order to enjoy the beauty of a snow-blanketed day. Miss Griswold had arrived at the park in the company of Miss Wilhelmina Radcliff, recent fiancée to his very dear friend, Mr. Edgar Wanamaker. Before he'd been able to do more than greet Miss Radcliff, though, Miss Griswold had begun to take him to task over what she'd felt were inflated skate prices.

Being a gentleman who made it his business to know the worth of every object he sold—and the worth of the service he extended to his customers that went with that object—he'd found himself at a complete loss for words when first presented with Miss Griswold's argument. He'd rallied quickly, though, when she'd begun haggling with him like a common fishmonger. But before he'd been able to claim a victory—and the exact amount of money he was asking for the skates—Miss Griswold had somehow won the day, handing him the exact amount of money *she* felt the skates were worth.

Before he'd had the presence of mind to protest, he was watching her stroll away, swinging her ill-gotten gains by their laces and whistling a far too cheery tune.

The second time he'd run across the oh-so-annoying Miss Griswold had been at Edgar Wanamaker and Wilhelmina Radcliff's engagement ball. Asher had been determined to let bygones be bygones, but when he'd attempted a polite conversation with Miss Griswold—talking about fashion, which he'd always found to be a most innocent topic and one normal ladies seemed to enjoy—Miss Griswold had gotten her back up. She was clearly irked that he'd had the audacity to question where she'd purchased her delightful gown, assuming that she'd had a renowned designer create it for her.

Sparks had practically flown out of Miss Griswold's brilliant blue eyes as she'd lifted a well-formed chin. She'd then informed him in a frosty voice that she rarely frequented renowned designers, finding that they charged prices that were far too steep for her.

When he'd made the grave mistake of pointing out that her father was one of the richest men in America and therefore those costs shouldn't truly concern her, her cheeks had turned an agreeable shade of pink right before she'd turned on her heel and stomped away from him, returning a mere moment later to make some unexpected remark about the weather. She'd then muttered something about her stepmother and trying to remember all the rules, before she'd turned back around and left his company without another word.

Their conversation had been more than peculiar, but now, with the memory of how vocal Miss Griswold *usually* was around him fresh in his mind, Asher bent closer to her, his gaze sharpening on her inert form.

Because Miss Griswold was not emitting a single sound—a concerning situation if there ever was one—alarm immediately replaced the annoyance his memories had evoked.

Realizing he needed to get her out of the crowd circling around them, Asher bent over, scooped Miss Griswold into his arms, and straightened, letting out a grunt when she began flailing about in his arms, quite like a fish out of water. Taken by surprise, his hold on her slackened, which caused Miss Griswold to tumble right out of his arms and back onto the floor.

Kneeling beside her with an apology on the tip of his tongue, Asher leaned toward her . . . but reared back a second later when Miss Griswold pushed herself to a sitting position. The apology he'd been intending to make was all but forgotten as he watched her rub an elbow that would surely sport a bruise come morning before she lifted her chin, caught his eye, and blinked a time or two.

31

Bracing himself for the wrath he was certain was soon to come, he was surprised when instead of taking him to task for dropping her so unchivalrously to the ground . . . she smiled at him.

Curiously enough, a smiling Miss Griswold was a lovely sight indeed, her smile having the unexpected result of lodging his breath in his throat, a circumstance that took him by complete—

"What a delightful surprise to discover that you, Mr. Rutherford, are the gentleman who saved me from a most gruesome death" were the first words to come out of Miss Griswold's now rapidly moving mouth.

The warm sensation he'd begun to feel in regard to her lovely smile disappeared in a flash. "You're surprised to discover *I* saved you?"

Miss Griswold gave a nod, the motion sending the large tiara she wore on her head listing to the left. "Indeed, especially since, as I was bracing myself to be crushed in a most horrible fashion, I found the presence of mind to ask for a touch of divine intervention, and . . . the good Lord above apparently sent *you* racing to my rescue."

"You asked for a touch of divine intervention?"

She reached up and made short shrift of setting her tiara to rights. "I'm sure you would have done exactly that if you'd been facing a gruesome demise."

"Perhaps, but . . ." He paused and caught her eye. "I must admit I can't recall a single time anyone's ever admitted to asking for divine intervention in the midst of a society event."

Pursing her lips, she seemed to think about that for a long moment. "I suppose you're right about that, Mr. Rutherford. But don't you find it somewhat peculiar that when people gather, say, at church, matters of divine intervention are expected, but when they gather outside of places specifically relegated as places of worship, the topic of God or anything relating to Him seems to become rather uncomfortable?"

"I would imagine that's because people are cautious, especially members of New York society, about offending those within their social circles. And talk of religion—along with politics, of course—can be a somewhat slippery slope to navigate."

Miss Griswold's eyes widened. "Ah, I imagine that's exactly what my stepmother was trying to warn me about a month or so ago when we were discussing my appalling lack of conversational savviness."

She leaned forward and lowered her voice. "You may very well find this to be surprising, but I'm apparently woefully deficient when it comes to conversing well with members of polite society. Truth be told, more often than not, I find myself completely tongue-tied whenever in the midst of the more fashionable set, and if I'm not tongue-tied, I seem to always broach a subject that would be best left not broached."

Asher lowered his voice as well. "May I assume then, especially since I've not experienced the whole tongue-tied business when I've been in your company, that you don't find me worthy to be considered a member of the fashionable set?"

"Don't be absurd, Mr. Rutherford. You own what is certain to become the most fashionable store in the city. If you're not considered a member of the fashionable set, I don't know who is."

With that, Miss Griswold pushed herself to her feet, seemingly unconcerned with the notion that young ladies were expected to allow a gentleman—if one was available, which he certainly was—to assist them to their feet after they'd taken a nasty plummet to the ground.

Deciding Miss Griswold would most certainly not appreciate recommendations of the etiquette sort, especially from him, the gentleman who was responsible for her nasty plummet to the ground the second time, Asher began rising to his feet as well. A second later, he found himself taken aback when Miss Griswold thrust a dainty hand his way, seemingly unconcerned yet again with the idea that ladies never, as in ever, initiated an act that would consist of them hauling a gentleman to his feet.

Not wanting to offend her, and also not wanting to draw more attention than they were already drawing, Asher took the hand and soon found himself standing right beside her.

"Quite frankly . . . " she began when he found his feet, "now that I consider the matter, it is rather curious that I'm able to speak freely with you." With that, along with a nod, she began dusting him off in a remarkably no-nonsense sort of manner.

The feel of her hands brushing, patting, and smoothing him out took him by such surprise that he found himself at a complete loss for words. He simply stood still as a statue while she continued her dusting, finally finishing her task when she plucked a few leaves from the billowing sleeves of his costume.

"There, you're looking dashing again, which further establishes the idea you're a most fashionable sort, especially considering . . ." She stepped back and gave him a quick once-over. "No one but a fashionable gentleman would dare step outside his house these days wearing . . ." She gestured to his costume, her gaze lingering on the purple frock coat that just happened to be trimmed with gold braiding. "Well, all that."

His eyes narrowed as he tried to discern whether or not she'd just insulted him. "I've seen many a gentleman this evening dressed far more outlandishly than I'm dressed."

"Indeed, as have I. But they, Mr. Rutherford, aren't nearly as adept at pulling off the look—yet another clear indicator that you are a staunch member of the fashionably elite."

"I suppose this is where I'm expected to say thank you?"

Her brows drew together. "There's certainly no need for that, since I was simply confirming what you along with everyone else in society knows. You're a well-established member of the

34

stylish set, which—" she blew out a breath—"truly does make it a bit of a puzzle that I'm able to speak so freely around you."

"Do I remind you of someone you're close to? Your father, perhaps?"

Taking a step away from him, Miss Griswold began looking him up and down before she, surprisingly enough, laughed.

It was not a delicate, tittering type of laugh, but a laugh that came from what seemed to be her toes and drew the notice of everyone standing in their vicinity.

"I think not, Mr. Rutherford, especially since my father started out in life as a mere miner, building his fortune through backbreaking work that involved a lot of dirt." She shook her head. "He's not one to wear anything other than the most boring of garments, no matter that my stepmother longs to see him dressed more stylishly." She sent a pointed look to the thick stockings that covered his calves, an item that had been required in order to truly look the part of an aristocrat from the Regency period. "He'd never wear those, not even to a costume ball. Although . . . allow me to say that you do seem to have surprisingly well-turned-out legs."

Asher swallowed a laugh. "Thank you, Miss Griswold. I've not had that particular compliment extended to me before, but . . . since we've ruled out some of the more logical explanations regarding why you're not devoid of words in my presence, perhaps—since you've proclaimed an admiration for my, er, legs—your admiration extends to my entire person, and . . . you hold me in great affection."

"No, that's not it," Miss Griswold said without the slightest hesitation.

Somehow that set Asher's teeth to grinding, but before he could contemplate why her immediate denial of holding him in any affection set his teeth on edge, she blew out a breath. "I suppose a reasonable explanation will occur to me sometime in the wee hours of the night. But since I can't puzzle out why I'm comfortable around you just yet, and I'm certain you've much better ways to spend your evening than standing around puzzling over my ability to speak to you, I do believe this is where we part ways."

A wave of disappointment took him by surprise over the thought of parting company with her, until a solution to that disappointment sprang to mind.

"You haven't allowed me the honor of filling in a spot on your dance card."

Instead of sending him the expected response to that request, Miss Griswold hugged the fur muff attached by a string to her left arm closer to her as she began backing away from him.

"That's very kind of you, Mr. Rutherford, but I assure you, there's no need to dance with me."

"There's every need," he countered, nodding to the muff. "May I assume you've stashed your dance card in there?"

"You should assume nothing of the sort."

"Hand it over."

For a second, what seemed to be clear panic flickered through her eyes, but then she shoved a hand in the muff, pulled out her dance card, looked it over, bit her lip, and then shoved the card back into the muff, pulling out another one a second later.

"How many cards do you have in there?" he asked when she apparently took issue with that card as well, tucking it securely away before pulling out yet another dance card.

"A few," she mumbled as she glanced at the card in her hand, dropped it back into the muff, gave the muff a shake, and then froze on the spot as the shake sent several dance cards, all of them maroon in color, falling out of the muff and to the floor.

"Allow me." Asher bent over and scooped up the cards. Straightening, he squinted at the handwriting scrawled all over

36

them. "Why have you written what appears to be descriptions of what the guests are wearing, Miss Griswold?"

Miss Griswold held out her hand, and when he placed the cards into that hand, she took a moment to tuck the cards back into the muff, then sent him a rather strained sort of smile.

"I enjoy scribbling down little details at all the society events I attend, Mr. Rutherford. It makes for a pleasant way to pass the evening and will allow me to remember those evenings when I'm at my last prayers and perusing my old journals." She inclined her head. "I do thank you for all of the assistance. However, since I've just recalled an urgent matter that I simply must address, if you'll excuse me, I hope you enjoy the rest of the ball."

Before Asher could do more than gape at Miss Griswold, she lifted the hem of her delightful skirt ever so slightly and exposed a shoe that seemed to be made out of hundreds of glass beads, giving the shoe a frosty appearance. She then spun on that shoe and dashed straightaway into the crowd, not bothering to speak so much as another word to him.

CHAPTER
FOUR

Having never before experienced anything as peculiar as a lady fleeing from his presence, Asher found himself riveted by the sight of Miss Griswold disappearing into the crowd, her shimmering gown sparkling in the light cast from the many chandeliers dangling from the high ceiling.

When the shimmering disappeared from view, it struck him that he'd not been given an opportunity to put his name on even one of her many dance cards. Finding that to be a most unacceptable turn of events, he started across the gymnasium floor, determined to track her down again.

When he reached the other side of the gymnasium, however, his plan came to a rather abrupt end when he was waylaid by a charming young lady dressed as a lady-in-waiting to Marie Antoinette.

Being a gentleman who firmly believed manners were what made a man, Asher took the arm of Miss Claudia Lukemeyer, strolling with her across the gymnasium as she chatted about everything under the sun. After they'd been strolling for a good few minutes, she finally broached the purpose for her seeking him out—that purpose being she desired his company as an escort for the dinner that was to be served at two in the morning.

Since he'd not yet promised to escort a lady in to dine, Asher took a moment to assure Miss Lukemeyer that he'd be honored to dine with her, earning a charming smile from her in response. Then, after adding his name to the dance card dangling from her wrist, promising to partner her in the Ticklish Water Polka, he delivered her directly into the midst of a gathering of her friends, promising her he'd join her in the ballroom when it was time for their scheduled dance.

Dodging the numerous quadrille dancers who were lining up to go down to the ballroom in order to begin their performances, Asher made it to the middle of the room before his plans for tracking down Miss Griswold were interrupted yet again by another young lady. This young lady, Miss Stillwater, was a long-time acquaintance of his who spent an exorbitant amount of money in his store. The fact that Miss Stillwater was friends with exactly the right people in the city made her a lady impossible for Asher to ignore, even if her attitude was far more acerbic than he enjoyed.

Taking hold of Asher's arm with a gloved hand covered in diamond bracelets, Miss Stillwater pulled him over to a group of fashionable New Yorkers, all of whom greeted Asher cheerfully and all of whom launched into a barrage of questions, wanting to know the true story behind the falling pillar and Asher saving a woman from certain death.

After putting to rest some rather outlandish ideas regarding why the pillar had fallen, the most outlandish of those ideas being a cloak-and-dagger murder plot with some unknown guest as the intended victim, Asher finished his story by assuring everyone that Miss Griswold had not suffered any life-threatening injuries and was fully expecting to enjoy all the festivities the evening had to offer.

That remark, unfortunately, started a completely different conversation, one that had all of the ladies contemplating exactly what enjoyment a wallflower could have at a society event.

"I do believe, my friends," Miss Stillwater drawled, "that we may soon have an answer to that particular question since it does seem as if two wallflowers are even now heading our way." Her lips curled. "Shall I do the honors and ask them to join us?"

"That may very well be their intention, since they seem to be walking directly toward us in a determined manner," another lady said as she took to waving her hand in front of her face, quite as if the mere thought of wallflowers joining them was enough to fluster her.

As titters ran through the crowd surrounding him, Asher looked around and found that two ladies were, indeed, approaching them, both of whom were certainly not members of the fashionable set, and one of them he recognized as the lady who'd been the first to applaud his saving of Miss Griswold.

Upon closer inspection, he recognized that lady as Miss Gertrude Cadwalader, a lady who often accompanied Mrs. Davenport, a wealthy society matron, to Rutherford & Company.

Unwilling to allow the two wallflowers to approach without support while Miss Stillwater and her associates sent looks of amusement their way, Asher stepped forward, earning a hiss of disapproval from Miss Stillwater in the process, one he staunchly ignored. Stepping right up beside Miss Cadwalader, he took hold of her hand and brought her fingers to his lips.

"Miss Cadwalader, how lovely to see you this evening, and may I say that your costume is most unique. Why, I don't believe I've seen another soul dressed as a chicken."

Miss Cadwalader, to his very great surprise, sent him a cheeky grin even as she retrieved her hand. "I'm a peacock, Mr. Rutherford, not a chicken, although I'm not surprised you're confused. Mrs. Davenport created the costume I'm wearing, but when she ruined all the peacock feathers she'd purchased by applying a wee bit more glue than was recommended, she learned that there were no more peacock feathers to be found in the city. That circumstance forced her to put her incredibly creative imagination to work—and I'm afraid chicken feathers are the result of that imagination."

"I'd forgotten Mrs. Davenport fancies herself a bit of a designer" was all Asher could think to say to that.

Miss Cadwalader's brow furrowed. "I thought she discussed her designs with you often, as in weekly, when she visits you at your store."

Asher's brow furrowed as well. "Mrs. Davenport may have mentioned her designs a time or two over the past year or so, but . . . we certainly don't discuss her ideas frequently."

Muttering something he didn't quite catch under her breath, Miss Cadwalader squared her shoulders and sent him a faint smile. "Well, no need to worry about that now, Mr. Rutherford. Truth be told, Miss Flowerdew and I have purposefully sought *you* out because we need your assistance." She tucked a broken feather that was drooping on the side of her head back behind her ear before she nodded to the lady accompanying her. "Have you ever been introduced to my friend, Miss Temperance Flowerdew?"

"I'm afraid I've never had the pleasure." Asher nodded to Miss Flowerdew, a young lady who was wearing a ratty-looking costume, apparently one that had once been worn by a real servant, given the grease stains attached to it. Reaching out a hand with the intention of placing a kiss on a glove that also seemed a bit stained, he stopped midreach when Miss Flowerdew suddenly thrust her hands behind her back even as she dipped into a graceful curtsy. Presenting Miss Flowerdew with a bow instead of trying to take a hand that was no longer available, he couldn't help but notice that her cheeks were beginning to turn somewhat splotchy. Those splotches had him returning his attention to Miss Cadwalader in the hopes of sparing Miss Flowerdew additional discomfort.

"You mentioned something about needing my assistance?"

Miss Cadwalader nodded. "Indeed, although I willingly admit I'm not certain it was wise of me to approach you, given the questioning you'll most definitely be in for after you return to your friends." She glanced over his shoulder to the friends in question and gave a shudder.

Knowing full well his exchange with Miss Cadwalader and Miss Flowerdew was being closely observed by Miss Stillwater, along with the society members with her, Asher didn't bother to turn but kept his attention squarely centered on Miss Cadwalader, who'd begun to develop splotches quite like the ones Miss Flowerdew was sporting.

Reaching out, he took hold of her hand and gave it a squeeze. "There's no need to worry on my behalf, Miss Cadwalader. I assure you, I'm more than capable of dealing with my friends."

Sending him a look that held a great deal of skepticism, Miss Cadwalader lifted her chin. "Very well, but do know that I'm only seeking out your assistance because you saved Miss Griswold earlier, which has brought me to the conclusion that you, Mr. Rutherford, are a gentleman a lady can rely on to help if a situation demands an . . . intervention, if you will."

"Someone needs an intervention?"

"Indeed, and not just any someone, but Miss Griswold again. She's been cornered on the far side of the gymnasium by a man dressed as what I'm going to assume is some obscure literary figure, given the sheaf of papers he's clutching, along with a pen, although I have no idea what literary figure he's supposed to be.

"Because Miss Griswold is not comfortable mingling or conversing with gentlemen of society—a circumstance that I blame her stepmother for, what with all the rule nonsense that woman is constantly throwing her stepdaughter's way, along with a good dose of criticism—I'm afraid being cornered is not a situation Miss Griswold knows how to handle well." She gave a sad shake of her head. "There's no telling what might happen if someone—as in you—doesn't intervene. At the very least, I would bet half of the chicken feathers that adorn my costume that Miss Griswold will inadvertently insult this unknown gentleman, causing her all sorts of trouble with that gentleman and with her stepmother in the process."

"Shall I assume time is of the essence, then?" he asked, extending Miss Cadwalader his arm. She immediately accepted the arm and nodded. He turned to offer his other arm to Miss Flowerdew but thought better of it when she began edging ever so discreetly away from him.

Having apparently decided that the whole time-is-of-the-essence statement he'd made had definite merit to it, Miss Cadwalader pulled him into motion and across the ballroom floor at a pace that earned them a few raised brows, and left her a little winded if he wasn't much mistaken.

Finding himself on the opposite side of the gymnasium within a remarkably short period of time, he came to a stop a few feet away from where a gentleman had, indeed, cornered Miss Griswold.

Temper he hadn't been expecting slid over him when he took note of the clear trace of panic in Miss Griswold's eyes. His temper increased when he realized that the gentleman, a man he wasn't acquainted with, was crowding Miss Griswold so effectively that her back was actually pressed up against the wall behind her.

Dropping his hold on Miss Cadwalader's arm, he strode forward, edging his way directly between Miss Griswold and her obvious tormentor. Taking hold of her arm, he pulled her away from the wall and past the man he didn't bother to acknowledge.

43

"Are you all right?" he asked, steering her over to a corner that was devoid of guests, lending them some much-needed space.

"I'm fine, Mr. Rutherford, just a little ruffled. I'm not used to such determined attention, you see."

"He didn't harm you in any way, did he?"

Her lips curved. "I'm not a lady who would allow a gentleman to physically harm me. And I'm perfectly capable of fending off unwanted advances, having learned how to defend myself through the diligent tutelage of numerous guards my father employed over the years. I simply thought that employing those defense strategies in the midst of a ball might be frowned upon by our esteemed hostess, Mrs. Vanderbilt."

"You were taught how to defend yourself?"

"Indeed I was, although I do prefer using a pistol to my fists." She smiled. "Pistols are far more effective, especially since one has only to brandish one to avoid most skirmishes."

He sent her what he knew had to be a weak attempt at a smile. "I suppose I should be thankful, then, that we're in the midst of a ball and you have no pistol available to you, otherwise Mrs. Vanderbilt's guests may have just witnessed a shooting."

"Why would you believe I don't have a pistol with me at the moment?"

Even though he was beyond curious as to where the lady had stashed a pistol, especially since it didn't appear one was in her fur muff, given that it wasn't an overly large muff and was currently stuffed with dance cards, Asher deemed it prudent to return to the conversation regarding the mysterious man who'd insinuated himself far too arrogantly into Miss Griswold's company. "Did you happen to catch that gentleman's name?"

"He told me he was Mr. Rice, but"—Miss Griswold shook her head—"I got the most curious feeling he was lying about that."

"Too right he was," Miss Cadwalader said as she rejoined

them, stopping directly by Miss Griswold's side. "That man is none other than a reporter from the *New-York Tribune*."

Miss Griswold blinked. "A . . . reporter?"

"Shocking, I know," Miss Cadwalader began. "Miss Flowerdew and I just happened upon my employer, Mrs. Davenport, who was in a dither because she recognized the man monopolizing you. She then disclosed to me that he's a renowned reporter, sent out on missions that require a bit of stealth."

Miss Griswold's brows drew together. "How in the world would Mrs. Davenport have access to that type of information?"

Miss Cadwalader shrugged. "I'm not actually certain, although Mrs. Davenport has proven herself to be rather adept at knowing things of a slightly interesting nature. Because of that, I have no qualms believing that man is exactly the reporter Mrs. Davenport proclaimed him to be."

Looking around, Asher found the man they were discussing now edging up to a gathering of chatting ladies. "I do believe you're right, Miss Cadwalader, especially since, now that you've pointed out the man's occupation, I think he may very well have been the reporter the *Tribune* sent to Rutherford & Company to cover a story about the new tea shop I'm in the process of opening."

"But what is a reporter doing here at the Vanderbilt ball?" Miss Griswold pressed.

"Mrs. Vanderbilt invited him, and he's not the only one," Miss Flowerdew said, speaking up for the first time.

Asher, along with Miss Griswold and Miss Cadwalader, turned to Miss Flowerdew, who was now looking as if she might be regretting drawing attention to herself, given the two bright spots of color that were staining her cheeks again.

"There are numerous reporters here tonight?" Miss Cadwalader asked.

"I'm afraid so," Miss Flowerdew said. "That right there is

why I was cautioned by my cousin—who was cautioned by the well-respected society matron who introduced my family into New York society—that I needed to be on my best behavior tonight in order to spare my cousin's family any undue embarrassment."

Miss Griswold stepped right up next to Miss Flowerdew. "Why would your cousin caution you about that?"

"My cousin is very careful with the family reputation," Miss Flowerdew began. "And rumor has it that the reporters who might be mingling around this ball are doing so in order to sniff out stories of a . . . scandalous nature."

"Good heavens," Miss Cadwalader whispered, turning a rather sickly shade of green. "It's no wonder Mrs. Davenport was in a dither if she learned that information as well. Honestly, if there truly are numerous reporters running amok, well, it could prove disastrous for . . ."

She stopped talking and nodded all around. "If you'll excuse me, I really do need to go have a chat with Mrs. Davenport before the ball officially starts and everyone gets distracted by all the dancing."

With that, she turned and hurried away, Miss Flowerdew following her a second later.

"What in the world do you think that was about?" Asher asked Miss Griswold, the only lady left in his company.

"I'm sure I have no idea. But if you'll excuse me, Mr. Rutherford, I do believe the quadrille dancers are now beginning to make their way to the first floor, which means the ball is about to officially begin. My stepsister is to perform in the Mother Goose Quadrille, and I would hate to disappoint her by missing it." With a curtsy, Miss Griswold began to head past him, sending him a quirk of an eyebrow when he reached out and stopped her progress by taking hold of her arm.

"You haven't allowed me to secure a dance with you yet,"

he said, remembering the reason he'd been determined to seek her out again in the first place. "I noticed that Mrs. Vanderbilt is offering a Go-As-You-Please Quadrille after the special quadrilles have been performed, and I'd be honored if you'd agree to dance the first general dance with me this evening."

"While I appreciate the gesture, Mr. Rutherford, do know that there's absolutely no need to offer to partner me."

Moving closer to her, Asher lowered his voice. "Are you unfamiliar with the steps of the Go-As-You-Please Quadrille?"

To his surprise, Miss Griswold sent him an honest-to-goodness rolling of her eyes. "Come now, Mr. Rutherford, surely you must know that asking a lady if she's deficient as a dancer is not proper in the least. But to answer your question, I'm somewhat familiar with the steps. If you must know, I was trying to give you a means to escape your obviously kind but somewhat rash offer, since I'm certain there are numerous ladies you'd much prefer to dance with."

"Why would you assume I don't prefer to dance with you?"

"I'm a wallflower, Mr. Rutherford. That means society finds me peculiar, an attitude you've witnessed firsthand since I recently charged directly out of your company with barely a by-your-leave. I know full well that fashionable society ladies don't charge away, and you, my dear sir, are known to associate with only the most fashionable of ladies."

She looked out over the crowd before releasing just the tiniest sigh. "However, since you have honored me with your offer, and I've been told it's considered churlish for a lady to refuse a dance, just one of the items my stepmother enjoys lecturing me about on a far too . . ." Her voice trailed away as her eyes widened before she . . . smiled.

It wasn't a sweet smile, nor was it a flirtatious one, but a smile more along the lines of a calculating one, something that had him taking a step away from her.

Miss Griswold didn't seem to notice as she stuck a hand in the muff, pulled out a dance card, looked it over, stuffed it back into the muff, and pulled out another one. Giving it a quick glance, she nodded and thrust it in his direction—but then drew it straight out of his reach before he had an opportunity to take it from her.

"Before you sign your name to this card, you and I need to come to an understanding, or rather, you need to agree to a condition before I can agree to dance with you."

"You have a *condition* in order to accept a dance with me?"

Miss Griswold nodded. "It's not a difficult condition, and it's not one you should reject out of hand, something your expression clearly suggests you're considering." She drew in a breath and quickly released it. "My stepmother, Mrs. Griswold, is becoming . . . annoying in regard to my lack of gentlemanly attention. So if you could find it in that heart of yours to agree to stroll ever so casually in front of her as we make our way to the dance floor, allowing her to see me in your company, I'd be ever so grateful. And if we could abandon the formality between us and begin to address each other by our given names, especially as we saunter slowly by my stepmother, I would be forever in your debt."

The very idea of Miss Permilia Griswold being forever in his debt was curiously intriguing and had him nodding his head before he could stop himself. "I see no reason not to abandon our formality, especially since it does seem as if we're becoming friends of a sort. It would be my pleasure to address you as Permilia, and you, of course, must call me Asher in return."

"Wonderful, and you'll try your very best to call me Permilia, in a somewhat carrying tone of voice, when we pass my stepmother on our way to take our place for the quadrille?"

Something that felt very much like caution settled over him, replacing the sense of intrigue he'd been feeling just a moment

48

before. "Aren't you concerned this sauntering and using an informal attitude between us will result in a misunderstanding with your father? I've heard stories regarding his proficiency with a gun, and I'd hate to be on the receiving end of that proficiency if he comes to the conclusion I've behaved in an untoward manner with his daughter."

"Of course I'm not. Besides, my father knows I'm more proficient with a gun than he is. He also knows I'd never tolerate a gentleman behaving in an untoward manner with me in the first place and am perfectly able of settling such a situation without my father stepping in."

Asher frowned. "Your father is rumored to be an expert marksman."

"Indeed."

Refusing to wince, Asher smiled instead. "You're a very unusual lady, Miss Griswold, er, Permilia. But since you're also somewhat frightening—and I mean that in the most complimentary of ways—I think it might be prudent to agree to your conditions."

"How delightful," Permilia exclaimed as she thrust her dance card his way again, actually allowing him to take it from her this time.

Adding his name to not one, but two dances, he lifted his head, finding that while he'd been distracted with the card, Permilia had become distracted by something over his shoulder.

Turning, he discovered a young lady, one he'd never seen before, inching her way toward them, holding a small pad of paper in her hand, along with a pencil. That the paper did not seem to be part of her outfit, given that she was dressed as Joan of Arc, was a bit confusing, as was the scowl Permilia was now sending the woman.

"Do you know that lady?" she asked.

"I'm afraid I don't."

Lifting her chin and not waiting for him to escort her, Permilia began marching toward the lady in question, stopping in her tracks almost before she'd gotten a good march going when the lady did an about-face and bolted straightaway, disappearing into the crowd with a clank of chainmail.

Marching her way back to his side, Permilia crossed her arms over her chest. "I think we may very well have just witnessed another reporter, and one who seemed far too curious about the two of us."

"Are you suggesting we may very well find references to us in print in the next edition of a paper or two?"

"I would love to be able to say no, but . . . that does seem a distinct possibility." She blew out a breath. "I can't help but wonder what Mrs. Vanderbilt was thinking, purposefully inviting members of the press into the very midst of her ball."

Asher handed Permilia her dance card. "She was evidently thinking that the times need to change. Society has never wanted the press to witness our little frivolities, as can be seen by the outrage that descended on society when the column Miss Quill's Quality Corner first began appearing in the *New York Sun* two years ago. That column, I'm afraid, is soon to be considered quite charming, especially since Miss Quill has always kept her columns to descriptions of what society is wearing and what is to be glimpsed design-wise behind the closed curtains of our homes."

Permilia's pale cheeks turned a shade paler. "Do you honestly believe that the reporters skulking amongst us at this very minute are going to report on more salacious tidbits than what Miss Quill reports on?"

"I'm afraid I do, especially since Mrs. Vanderbilt is a lady determined to secure her position within society once and for all. She's almost done just that by securing Mrs. Astor's approval, along with throwing a ball that will be remarked upon for years. However, if she obtains the admiration of the masses, she'll be more powerful than Mrs. Astor in the end."

"How . . . disturbing," Permilia whispered, her obvious distress having Asher moving closer to her.

"I doubt you have anything to worry about, Permilia, especially since I'm quite certain these reporters are attempting to sniff out matters of a scandalous nature. You don't appear to be a lady prone to scandal, so I'm sure the reporters will give you a wide berth. It is interesting, though, now that I think on it, that the reporter from the *New-York Tribune* singled you out to question."

"He probably discovered I'm a wallflower, and everyone knows that wallflowers are normally deprived of attention. That situation, if I were to hazard a guess, probably led the man to believe that I'd be only too happy to disclose any information, or observations, I might have had at my disposal."

Asher smiled. "I'm sure if that truly was the case, you delivered the man a crushing disappointment instead of the gossip he was evidently trying to gather." He looked over her shoulder and nodded. "But since it does appear as if the guests who are performing in the quadrilles are beginning to quit this room, shall we join them as they make their way to the first floor and watch them perform in what is certain to be an impressive affair?"

Permilia, to his surprise, shook her head. "I'm afraid I have a matter of a rather pressing nature to attend to, Asher, so if you'll excuse me, we'll meet again in the ballroom for the—" she looked down at the dance card in her hand—"Go-As-You-Please Quadrille. Although . . ." She lifted her head and narrowed her eyes at him. "It appears as if you've claimed two of my dances this evening."

"You do want that stepmother of yours to cease with her lectures, at least for the immediate future, don't you?"

"Well, yes, of course, but . . . two dances with me seems a bit much when you and I both know your offer to dance with me can only be considered a charitable endeavor."

"What an interesting manner of thinking you have, Permilia, but believe me, my offer was not a charitable endeavor at all. It was the result of a true desire to take to the floor with you."

Permilia's nose wrinkled. "You're not in need of additional investors for that fine store of yours, are you?"

A quirk of his brow was his only response to that nonsense.

Blowing out another breath, she allowed her shoulders to sag. "Of course you're not, and it was quite rude of me to suggest differently."

"I won't argue with you there."

"I did warn you that I don't have the gift of conversing well within polite society, but even for me, that was an uncalled for remark, and I do beg your pardon."

"Apology accepted, Permilia. And allow me to say that there very well may be hope for you yet with that whole not conversing well in polite society. Most members I know in that society don't have the ability to apologize—something you just did, and very prettily at that."

Sticking the dance card back into the muff, Permilia shook her head. "Which doesn't speak well of society as a whole, but thank you for accepting my apology." She smiled. "Now, since we've gotten that out of the way, and I do promise to try harder not to insult you in the future, I need to take my leave of your company. I'll meet up with you in the ballroom before our quadrille begins." With that, she turned and walked away, drawing the attention of more than a few gentlemen as she walked.

Unwilling to dwell on why that attention set his teeth to grinding, Asher moved back into the midst of the crowd and was soon joined by two young ladies, both of whom he knew full well would never consider insulting him, unintentionally or not.

Extending an arm to each of them, he pushed aside the surprising disappointment he felt over Permilia having abandoned him and walked from the gymnasium, anticipation running through him as he wondered exactly what type of extravagances he was soon to witness as Mrs. Vanderbilt officially opened her ball.

CHAPTER
FIVE

Permilia was rapidly coming to the conclusion that attempting to eavesdrop in the midst of a ball where twelve hundred guests had assembled was not a feat to be undertaken by the faint of heart.

Add in the pesky notion that she was continuing to attract unexpected attention from a wide assortment of gentlemen, and the task she'd originally thought would be fairly straightforward in nature was turning out to be nothing of the sort.

Quite honestly, she was now of the belief that Alva Vanderbilt's ball was a disaster in the making, especially because her position as a mysterious society columnist might very well be put into jeopardy before the night was complete.

Everyone knew that positions of a mysterious nature were only good for as long as the person embracing a mysterious attitude remained, well . . . mysterious.

The attention she kept drawing was making it difficult indeed to proceed with her business in a covert manner. That meant her job with the *New York Sun* might very well be terminated since her status as a confirmed wallflower was the very reason she'd been given the responsibility of the society column in the first place.

Wallflowers, as everyone was aware, tended to fade into the background. That right there was exactly why she'd been wooed by one of the editors at the *New York Sun*. He had believed Permilia would be able to obtain information for her column under the cloak of anonymity she wore at every society event she attended.

Now, however, after discovering that Alva Vanderbilt had invited members of the press into what should have been the hallowed midst of her ball, Permilia couldn't help but feel as if her position was soon to be obsolete.

Reporters, unlike Permilia, were not affiliated with society, and as such, they would not need to spend nearly the amount of time she did gathering information in a clandestine manner. They would have the luxury of traveling at will about an event, scooping up delicious tidbits for their respective papers with relative ease. They also didn't have to face the daunting threat of reaping extreme displeasure from society if their true identities became known.

Permilia, on the other hand, knew full well she'd be condemned as a traitor, banished from society for all time—which was no reason to get caught even if that idea was tempting—and embarrass her family no small amount if she were to be found out.

Even though she wasn't what anyone would call fond of her stepmother or stepsister, she certainly didn't want to cause them embarrassment or, worse yet, hurt Lucy's chances of forming a suitable alliance with a society gentleman in the future.

"The Hobbyhorse Quadrille is about to begin," a young lady standing on the other side of the Greek statue Permilia had chosen to lurk behind said. "My goodness, but I am curious to see the costumes for this particular quadrille. I've heard no expense was spared in the creation of them."

Edging as casually as she could from behind the statue, Permilia adopted what she hoped would be taken as an innocent attitude, allowing her gaze to wander over the crowd milling about while keeping an ear turned in the direction of the lady who'd been speaking, Miss Martha Norton.

That Miss Norton was always apprised of information Permilia needed for her column, such as the names of the most fashionably dressed at any given event, or better yet, where they'd acquired their fashions for those events, was reason enough for Permilia to remain in that lady's direct vicinity.

True to form, Miss Norton did not disappoint, even though she did begin moving forward, making it more difficult for Permilia to maintain an air of nonchalance as she trailed after her.

"Miss Edith Fish's portrayal of the Duchess of Burgundy is quite lovely, and do make certain to take note of the real sapphires, rubies, and emeralds attached to the front of her gown," Miss Norton continued even as her steps slowed considerably, quite as if she couldn't navigate talking and walking with any momentum at the same time. "I do have to say, in my humble opinion of course, that one of the most delicious gowns here tonight is being worn by none other than Mrs. Cornelius Vanderbilt II. She's dressed as the 'Electric Light' and her entire gown lights up, as well as the torch she's carrying." Miss Norton let out a charming laugh. "I would be rather nervous to wear a gown that lights up, fearing it would catch on fire at some point in the evening."

Miss Ann Greene, the young lady Miss Norton was strolling beside, shook her head. "I don't believe the lights are dangerous, Miss Norton. From what I've been told, Jean Philippe Worth installed batteries in Mrs. Vanderbilt's skirt, and that's what powers the lights. Batteries, from what little I know of them, aren't supposed to catch on fire."

Pulling a dance card from the muff, Permilia looked around,

saw that no one seemed to be paying her any mind, so jotted down the words *electric dress*, knowing her readers would adore reading about such a novelty and not wanting to forget about the dress with all the excitement of the night.

She didn't need to make a notation about Miss Norton being the source of her information because she never wrote about anything of a scandalous nature, or included snippets of gossip—or rather, she *almost* never included gossip in her well-received newspaper column, Miss Quill's Quality Corner.

She had done exactly one column during her two years working for the paper in which she had delved into a bit of fiction that had a distinct ring of gossip to it—fiction that had been needed in order to spare her friend Miss Wilhelmina Radcliff undue scrutiny by society for getting caught in a less than scandalous, though tenuous, situation. That situation could have very well seen Miss Radcliff ostracized from society and without the income her position as a society secretary provided. So Permilia published an article that had been more of a fairy tale than an actual article. That fairy tale had lent Miss Radcliff's situation a sense of romance, not scandal, thus sparing her the wrath of society.

Other than that one time, though, Permilia strove to report only the most innocent of details regarding society and the people who moved within it. Her readers enjoyed learning about what society members were wearing, the foods they were consuming during their eight or more course meals, the different wines that were served at those meals, and what their large homes looked like behind the windows always curtained against the curious regard of what they considered the riffraff of New York.

Miss Quill's Quality Corner had allowed that riffraff—although they were nothing of the sort—to see into the world of the socially elite, while providing her with a sense of purpose as she traveled from one society event to another. Her column also provided funds for a charitable endeavor she'd become involved with years before, an endeavor she, and she alone, funded.

Oddly enough, she'd come to enjoy crafting her articles, even though she knew full well she was simply biding her time with her writing until her father came to his senses and allowed her back into his business.

"I'm not certain I understand Miss Kate Strong's costume. Is that a stuffed cat on her head?" Miss Norton asked, her question prompting Permilia to tuck her dance card back into the muff as she looked around for a lady wearing a cat on her head.

"It is a cat's head," Miss Greene replied. "And I believe she chose her outfit because of how everyone calls her Puss, although . . . it's not a costume I would have chosen, especially not with what appear to be real cat tails sewn to her gown." Miss Greene gave a delicate shudder. "Quite frankly, I think wearing a dead cat on one's person is somewhat gruesome."

Standing on tiptoe, Permilia searched the crowd for the cat lady but abandoned her search as a collective gasp echoed around the ballroom as music began, signaling the official start of the ball. A mere moment after the first notes played, dancers dressed for the Hobbyhorse Quadrille cantered into view.

For the briefest of seconds, Permilia forgot all about her column as she watched the Hobbyhorse Quadrille unfold right before her eyes.

Permilia's stepsister, Lucy, had mentioned that the costumes for the Hobbyhorse Quadrille were made out of real horsehides and had taken over two months to make. But, even knowing that, Permilia had not been expecting the attention to detail that had gone into creating the look for this particular dance.

The ladies were dressed in scarlet coats, white satin vests and breeches, paired with patent leather boots, gold spurs, and riding crops. They were riding around the room astride their hobbyhorses, which turned out to be none other than their gentlemen partners.

Life-sized horse heads had been placed over the gentlemen's heads and attached to their waists, while what truly did appear to be real horsehides draped over the rest of their bodies. Their feet and hands were covered with embroidered hangings—the embroidery having been done in a pattern that looked exactly like horse legs.

As they galloped about, the guests broke into applause, the sound bringing Permilia back to her situation at hand.

Knowing her readers would expect nothing less than a detailed article, explaining in depth exactly what the Hobbyhorse Quadrille entailed and who the society members were who'd been privileged enough to dance in it, Permilia fought her way across the crowded room. Taking cover behind another fern, she couldn't help but feel grateful to Alva Vanderbilt for her extravagant decorations. Those decorations were providing Permilia time after time with exactly the right hiding place to complete her mission for the evening, especially since the fronds of the ferns were remarkably easy to peer through without undue notice being sent her way.

After watching the Mother Goose Quadrille, in which Lucy had looked quite charming as she'd glided about the room, Permilia then enjoyed watching the Dresden Quadrille. That dance had the dancers garbed all in white, evoking thoughts of Frederick the Great and lending the lady dancers the look of porcelain dolls, a look that was mesmerizing, if rather unsettling.

Scribbling her observations down as quickly as she could, even though she wasn't certain she did justice to the Star Quadrille since her view had become blocked by a large number of guests who'd moved in front of her, Permilia realized she'd gone through fourteen dance cards. The only card she had left to her was the one Asher had written his name on in order to claim not one but two dances, and for some reason, and one she didn't want to consider too closely, she was reluctant to besmirch that particular card with her notes.

Realizing she was in need of more dance cards, but dreading the very idea of having to seek out the Vanderbilt butler in order to procure those cards since he was more than a little intimidating, Permilia stepped out from her hiding place.

She found herself freezing on the spot a moment later, though, when her gaze was caught and then held by a dashing-looking gentleman dressed as a swashbuckling pirate—a gentleman who was smiling far too charmingly back at her.

He didn't have the look of a reporter about him, considering his costume seemed to be of a quality that most reporters would find far too dear to possess. But he wasn't a gentleman she'd ever seen before, that circumstance a cause for concern since she'd made it her business over the past two years to acquire the names and intricacies of all the members of society.

Information about dashing gentlemen was always required of a successful society columnist. And the very idea that she had no inkling as to the identity of the man directing his smile her way was troubling.

Knowing the only way to remedy that situation was to approach the man, even though that idea made her rather queasy, Permilia lifted her chin, took a single step forward, and then found herself incapable of further movement since her nerves seemed to take that moment to get the best of her.

Fortunately, the dashing gentleman evidently took her single step as an encouraging sign because he began to walk her way. Resisting the urge to bolt in the opposite direction, one that wasn't all that difficult to resist since her feet seemed to have become stuck to the floor, Permilia tried to summon up a smile, hoping that she wasn't actually grimacing at the man instead.

She'd been told by Ida on more than one occasion that gentlemen did not care to spend time in the company of ladies who spent their time grimacing.

Coming to a stop directly in front of her, the gentleman presented her with a very impressive bow, sweeping his pirate hat off his head in the process. He then straightened, put the hat back on his head, and reached for her hand. Bringing it to his lips, he placed a kiss on her knuckles as he caught and held her gaze.

Being a lady who truly was unaccustomed to such attention, and finding that attention to be completely unnerving, Permilia felt her cheeks begin to heat as she floundered for something to say, something that wouldn't have her embarrassing herself or, heaven forbid, her family.

Unfortunately, not a single witty thought fluttered to mind, nor did a single sound pass through her lips when she opened her mouth. Luckily, the man still holding her hand didn't appear to notice her dilemma as he began speaking.

"My dear lady," the gentleman said, "I do hope you will take what I'm about to disclose in only the most complimentary of ways, but I've been longing to speak with you ever since I saw you walk through the entranceway. You bewitched me in that moment, and I would have approached you then, but I lost you in the crowd. I have been desperately searching for you ever since, longing to make your acquaintance."

Permilia opened her mouth, discovered she was still unable to utter so much as a single word, but was spared the embarrassment of an uncomfortable silence descending over them when the gentleman continued with his flowery speech, as if he had yet to notice his audience was suffering from a certain case of muteness.

"I can only pray that you'll honor me with a dance or two this evening, as well as disclose your name to me or else I fear I will descend into a state of deepest melancholy, unable to . . ."

The rest of the gentleman's speech got lost when a loud

clearing of a throat interrupted him right before another gentleman joined them—a gentleman Permilia found herself, oddly enough, relieved to see.

"Ah, Mr. Slater, I see you've made the acquaintance of my very dear friend, Miss Permilia Griswold," Asher said as he ever so casually took hold of Permilia's hand and began tugging it away from Mr. Slater, who seemed somewhat reluctant to let go of it, that troubling situation resulting in a brief tug-of-war erupting between the two gentlemen.

Just when Permilia thought she was going to be parted with her hand for good, Asher won the day—doing so, if Permilia wasn't much mistaken, by stepping ever so discreetly on Mr. Slater's square-buckled shoe. Asher then tucked her arm into the crook of his, going so far as to give it a reassuring pat.

Mr. Slater, to give him his due, only let out the slightest hint of a grunt when Asher stepped off his foot, right before he beamed another charming smile Permilia's way and inclined his head.

"It is a true honor to meet you, Miss Griswold. And since your astonishing beauty has apparently caused Mr. Rutherford, a gentleman I readily admit to not knowing well, to forget his good manners, allow me to extend you my name. I'm Mr. Eugene Slater."

To Permilia's complete horror, when she opened her mouth to acknowledge Mr. Slater, the only sound she seemed capable of making was a squeak, a less than acceptable response if she'd ever heard one.

To her relief, Asher immediately came to her rescue again.

"Miss Griswold freely admits, at least to those close to her, such as myself, that she has not been blessed with the gift of conversing easily with strangers, Mr. Slater. Since it does appear as if Mrs. Vanderbilt has included far more guests than the usual four hundred tried-and-true members of society, I'm afraid Miss Griswold finds herself placed in an overwhelming situation tonight. That being said, I'm certain she's absolutely delighted to make your acquaintance."

Permilia managed a nod in Mr. Slater's direction, ducking her head a second later as she felt heat settle on her cheeks.

She'd always been a lady who blushed easily, but she was fairly certain she wasn't blushing because of Mr. Slater's attention. If she were honest with herself, she was blushing simply because Asher had just extended her one of the sweetest kindnesses she'd ever been extended.

She'd never felt at ease in social situations, bungling introductions left and right when she'd first been presented to society. That bungling had only increased the more diligently she'd tried to be accepted into the fashionable set, her failures giving Ida one opportunity after another to voice the many disappointments she suffered due to the extent of her stepdaughter's deficiencies.

No one, however—not her father, stepmother, Lucy, or anyone else she'd met over the many seasons she'd been out—had ever taken the time to stand beside her and explain her peculiarities away in such a matter-of-fact manner, as if turning mute simply because one was introduced to a person was an everyday occurrence and didn't merit the slightest bit of condemnation.

The very idea that the person to have done such a thing was Mr. Asher Rutherford was certainly surprising and lent credence to the idea that she may very well have been wrong about the man—especially the part where he was unlikable, churlish, and argumentative all the time. Although . . . she had actually enjoyed a few of their skirmishes, especially the ones centered around his products and what he was charging for those—

"I've always found ladies who are shy and modest to be quite compelling," Mr. Slater said, his words jolting Permilia back to the situation at hand, where she still, unfortunately, seemed incapable of uttering the most basic of words.

"And while I would never care to distress you or make you uncomfortable, Miss Griswold," Mr. Slater continued, catching her eye, "I promise that if you agree to honor me with a dance tonight, I'll do everything in my power to put you at ease."

Unfamiliar as she was with any attention from gentlemen, yet now finding herself the recipient of two gentlemen paying her marked attention, Permilia felt her lips curve into an unexpected smile. Drawing in a deep breath, she felt actual words begin to form in her throat, but before she could get a single one of them past her lips, Asher squeezed her arm and spoke for her yet again.

"I'm afraid you're in for a disappointment tonight, Mr. Slater, since all of Miss Griswold's dances have already been spoken for."

Mr. Slater's smile faded right before he set his sights on the dance card Permilia had forgotten she was still clutching in her hand, the one Asher had signed his name to, and the one that had numerous dances still waiting to be claimed. Lifting his hand, he quirked a brow her way. "May I see your card?"

"I'm afraid there's no time for that, Mr. Slater," Asher said, plucking the dance card straight out of Permilia's hand before he stuck it in one of his jacket pockets. Tightening his grip on Permilia's arm, he sent Mr. Slater a jerk of his head that might have been his attempt at a nod. "I believe the musicians are preparing to begin the music for the Go-As-You-Please Quadrille, a dance Miss Griswold has already promised to me. That means we'll need to bid you a good evening."

Mr. Slater, instead of stepping aside to allow Permilia and Asher to get on their way, actually took a step toward her, blocking the direct path to where the dancers were, indeed, now gathering.

"While it appears you have no dances left unclaimed, may I dare hope you've yet to promise your company to anyone for dinner?"

Permilia initially thought she'd misheard the gentleman. Lifting her head, she caught Mr. Slater's eye, and the intensity in that eye convinced her he truly did seem determined to spend time with her. Clearing her throat as her thoughts began to whirl with how to agree to dine with him in a manner that would allow him to believe she possessed at least a touch of sophistication, her thoughts faded straightaway when Asher cleared his throat.

"I do hate being the bearer of distressful news, Mr. Slater," he began. "But while Miss Griswold finds conversing with strangers uncomfortable, dining with one is downright disastrous for her, given that she suffers from a constricted throat throughout the meal, which does make her prone to, well . . . choking. Since I'm quite certain you don't want to be the cause of Miss Griswold's untimely demise, I'm sure you'll understand why she simply can't sit down to dine with you."

With that, and leaving poor Mr. Slater with his mouth gaping open, Asher tightened his grip on her arm and urged her into motion, hurrying her into the crowd before she had the presence of mind to stop him.

Chapter
Six

Jostling his way across the crowded ballroom, Asher suddenly found it somewhat difficult to jostle—that difficulty a direct result of Permilia deciding, for some curious reason, to begin dragging her unusual sparkly heels. Realizing that the scraping noise he was now hearing was coming from the vicinity of her feet, clear proof she truly was reluctant to continue forward, he brought them to a complete stop. Lifting his head, he caught her eye and waited to discover if she'd recovered her ability to speak.

"Honestly, Asher," she began a mere second later, "I simply cannot recall a moment in my entire life when I've been so thoroughly embarrassed. Why, I'm quite certain that Mr. Slater must find me to be a complete ninny right about now."

Finding himself remarkably pleased by the notion that Permilia did seem to be completely comfortable speaking in his presence, although uncertain as to *why* he was so remarkably pleased, Asher gave her arm a squeeze. "I'm sure he simply finds you to be extremely modest and shy, qualities I do believe the gentleman appreciates in a lady since he did mention something about those qualities earlier." He smiled. "And *my* modesty aside, I thought it was quite brilliant on my part to spare you from having to sit down to dine with the man by inventing a malady that gave you the perfect excuse to refuse his offer."

"Forgive me, but to refresh that obviously faulty memory of yours, I was not *given* the opportunity to refuse him since you took it upon yourself to *do* so in my stead. Furthermore, while I do appreciate what I'm fairly certain was your attempt at chivalry, I'm not convinced your excuse was entirely brilliant, considering you told him I suffer from a constricted throat. That is not exactly considered a malady, and the idea that Mr. Slater is now under the impression I suffer from such an unusual condition makes me seem even more peculiar than I actually am."

Asher's smile faded straightaway. "You didn't *want* to dine with Mr. Slater, did you?"

She narrowed her eyes. "It hardly matters now since that gentleman is most likely counting his blessings, thankful that he was spared the horror of having to dine with a madcap woman who suffers not only from muteness, but an inability to eat a meal in polite company as well."

"When you put it that way, you do come across somewhat like a lunatic."

She released what sounded exactly like a snort. "All thanks to you."

Unused to ladies snorting at him, and having no idea how to appease this particular lady since she was quite unlike any lady he'd ever met before, Asher did the only thing that sprang to mind, that being summoning up another smile. "On the bright side, though, being thought a lunatic has a certain amount of charm to it in an unusual sort of way."

Another snort was her first response to that. "No, it doesn't, and I'll thank you to not bring up the word *lunatic* again, if you please. While I don't mean to come across as churlish because you did intervene on my behalf, something the good Lord alone knows how infrequently occurs in the world I now reside in, I can't help but be a touch disgruntled with you."

Asher blinked. "Why in the world would you be disgruntled with me?"

"You lost me the very rare opportunity of actually sitting down to dine with a gentleman who is not at his last prayers. That, unfortunately, is a condition I fear most of the gentlemen who are pressed into service to escort me in to dine at every society event suffer from."

She heaved a resigned-sounding sigh. "It would have been a nice change of pace to dine with Mr. Slater, a gentleman who seems to possess a bit of an adventurous spirit, given that he was dressed as a pirate."

"I'm dressed as an adventurous aristocrat." He winced when he heard what sounded exactly like a touch of animosity in his tone, although why he was suddenly feeling less than amiable toward the world at large he couldn't actually say.

Permilia began rubbing his arm in a rather soothing type of way, quite like one would do with a cranky child. He could not claim to be soothed, more along the lines of embarrassed over his less than manly behavior, but—

"Well, of *course* you are looking exactly the part of an adventurous aristocrat," Permilia said, giving his arm another rub. "And forgive me if this comes out a little forward, but you make a very dashing aristocrat as well. However, *you* did not ask me to dine with you, Mr. Slater did. Although . . ." Her lips pressed together for a brief second as her eyes turned wide. "Good heavens, that certainly didn't come out the way I intended, and I do hope you understand that I wasn't attempting to secure your company for dinner this evening."

Asher's collar suddenly felt rather tight. "Of course I understood what you meant, Permilia. But I must now beg your pardon for not requesting your company for dinner in the first place, and for losing you a dinner partner because I, regrettably, didn't think the matter through as thoroughly as I should have done. I truly thought you wouldn't be interested in dining with the man since you were incapable of speech, but it was beyond rude of me to have made such an assumption without seeking your opinion on the matter first. As the situation stands, I'm afraid I've already promised Miss Claudia Lukemeyer my company for dinner tonight, which means . . . you'll be dining with someone not of your choosing."

"Thank goodness," Permilia breathed before her eyes widened another fraction. "Not that I'm suggesting I wouldn't have enjoyed your company, but . . ."

She drew in a deep breath, slowly released it, and then nodded. "Miss Lukemeyer is a lovely young lady, and I'm certain she'll make a wonderful dinner companion for you. And I've never heard a peep regarding her being anything other than proficient at maneuvering around the silver."

Asher's brows drew together. "I don't believe I've ever been partnered with a young lady who is anything *but* proficient with the silver."

"Then it's fortunate indeed that you aren't sitting down to dine with me, because I'm constantly misusing the soup spoons. Although, in my defense, they do look remarkably similar." Her forehead furrowed. "In all honesty, I've never been given an adequate explanation as to why a person is required to use a different utensil for every dish served. In my humble opinion, one fork, one spoon, and one knife should be more than sufficient as far as utensils are concerned in aiding a person with his or her meal."

Hearing a few notes of music coming from the direction of the orchestra, Asher pulled Permilia into motion, turning to catch her eye as he did so. "While I cannot claim to disagree with your point regarding the silverware, it might be wise for you to not voice that particular point to anyone else. We in society do enjoy clinging to our snobbish ways, and it won't benefit your position within this particular society to voice opinions that differ from the tried-and-true beliefs of the times."

"I don't really have a position in society that can be harmed overly much," she said in a remarkably cheery tone. "And as I mentioned before, since I'm normally escorted to dinner by members of the more elderly set, most of my partners are hard of hearing, so there's little to no danger of offending them even if something of a questionable nature does manage to slip past my lips."

"I thought you were jesting about dining with elderly gentlemen."

Permilia's shoulders drooped as she slowed to a stop. "I'm afraid not. Although"—she regained her posture as if she'd suddenly recalled ladies were not supposed to slouch—"occasionally some well-meaning society matron will send the wallflower table a few younger gentlemen to sit with us, but I don't particularly care for gestures motivated by pity. I've never enjoyed being on the receiving end of pity since it allows the person extending the pity to adopt a superior attitude."

Asher tilted his head. "I don't enjoy pity either, but surely there must have been a few times over the past season or so where you were invited to dine with a gentleman not at their last prayers or offered as a pitying gesture."

Permilia gave a breezy wave of her hand. "I'm afraid not, but there's no need to look so horrified. I've grown quite accustomed to my position within society and am perfectly content to fade into the background." Her hand fell back to her side. "I must admit that whole fading into the background approach hasn't gone exactly as planned this evening, though, what with all the unexpected attention gentlemen keep casting my way."

She leaned closer to him, lowering her voice to a mere whisper, which had him leaning even closer to her in order to catch her every word, since the violinists had now taken to warming up their instruments. "I thought at one point my buttons on the front of my gown must have come undone, which would have explained the bewildering attention, but . . . that didn't turn out to be the case, since each and every one of my buttons has remained securely fastened. If you must know, I'm now at a complete loss as to why tonight of all nights gentlemen have taken to noticing me. I've never attracted attention at any of the other society events I've attended, and believe me, there have been many over the past few years."

Staunchly pushing aside the image Permilia's words had conjured, one that had buttons popping free from buttonholes that just happened to reside on Miss Griswold's delightful gown, Asher straightened and took a step back, considering her for a moment. His gaze traveled from the top of Permilia's sparkly tiara nestled in her unusual curls down to the tip of one of the shimmering slippers barely peeking out from the hem of her gown. Lifting his head, he smiled. "I don't know why you're questioning the reasoning behind attracting so much attention this evening. You make quite the picture dressed in that enchanting bit of froth you've procured for your costume, and . . . have you done something different with your hair? Because, well, it looks very lovely indeed."

Permilia, instead of sending him the expected smile of appreciation over his compliments, began tapping her delicate shoe against the floor beneath her feet. "I've done nothing different with my hair this evening. And while my gown is indeed enchanting, it's not nearly as lovely as the gown I wore to Mrs. Astor's last patriarch ball. I can assure you that I received not so much as a second look from any of the gentlemen attending that event, yourself included."

Asher's collar immediately took to feeling somewhat tight again. "You were at Mrs. Astor's patriarch ball?"

"Of course I was. My stepmother insists I attend all the important events, especially since she and my father are seemingly still optimistic that I'll eventually secure the interest of a suitable gentleman."

"Then you should be very happy that you seem to be attracting a lot of attention of the gentlemanly type this evening."

Permilia's lips thinned. "I never said *I* wanted to secure the interest of a suitable gentleman. I said that's what my stepmother and my father seem to want. However, that's neither here nor there. The burning question for me at the moment is . . . why am I attracting so much attention this evening?"

Asher glanced around at the throng of guests surrounding them, all of them exquisitely dressed and all of them seemingly enjoying the night of their lives. He smiled when a perfectly reasonable explanation flashed to mind and returned his attention to Permilia. "This Vanderbilt ball isn't like any of the other society events you've attended. As we spoke about before, a large number of the guests here tonight do not travel within the highest levels of society, even though many of their fortunes are greater than most of those residing in the upper realm of our world."

Permilia's eyes began to sparkle. "What a brilliant deduction, Asher. That's exactly why I'm garnering so much attention. Those gentlemen are members of the *nouveau riche*, as Mrs. Astor would call them, and as such, they have no idea that I'm a wallflower."

She tightened her grip on his arm and began speaking in a voice that was little more than a whisper again. "While this is a rather abrupt change of topic, I'd like to return to the subject of Mr. Slater, if you wouldn't mind."

Having no idea where Permilia was going with her questioning, or why she'd taken to whispering again in the first place, since it wasn't as if Mr. Slater was a scandalous topic, Asher bent closer to her, catching something about Permilia wanting to know what Mr. Slater did for a living. Before he could respond to her question, though, he found himself completely distracted when the most delicious scent tickled his nose, a scent that seemed to be originating from the base of Permilia's throat, and a scent that was beyond tantalizing.

It was a blend of vanilla, citrus, and something he couldn't define, but it suited Permilia even though it clouded his senses. Dipping his head, he allowed himself the luxury of breathing in the scent more deeply while resisting the temptation to place his nose right up against the white skin of her neck, a delightful spot if there ever was one, and one she'd evidently spritzed ever so lightly with perfume.

A not-so-subtle elbow to his ribs had him straightening, shaking his head in order to dispel the fog that had descended over him. Taking a step away from Permilia, he found her watching him with a look in her eyes that clearly suggested she was now of the belief he'd lost his mind.

"What in the world are you about, Asher?" she demanded, her words taking a few seconds to sink through the haze that continued to cloud his thoughts.

"I'm pondering my response" was all he could muster up to say.

"Do you usually descend into a dazed and confused condition when you ponder?"

Not believing it would benefit him in the least to reply to that type of nonsense, he tugged down the hem of his waistcoat, using the time it took for that action to gather his scattered thoughts. When he felt as if he'd achieved a small measure of success with the gathering, he lifted his head. "Mr. Slater's in mining—copper, I believe, although he might have interests in other minerals as well."

He was not expecting the unusual response those words had over Permilia.

One second she was regarding him as if she was certain he'd lost his mind, and then the next she was beaming a lovely smile his way and looking at him as if he'd just extended her a most savory treat.

"Is he really?" she breathed right before she took a very firm grip on his arm and began sailing forward, pulling him along beside her.

"I do wish I'd known that about the man when he first walked over to me, because I certainly wouldn't have made such a cake of myself," she said, her strides increasing with every step until they were practically galloping across the room. "I've never lost my ability to speak with industrialists before, and learning Mr. Slater is in mining, well . . ." She turned her head and smiled at him. "I know how to speak mining."

"I didn't realize mining was a language," he said, a remark she completely ignored as she craned her neck and began scanning the crowd, likely looking for Mr. Slater—an idea that set Asher's teeth to grinding again.

"Do you suppose he's a gentleman possessed of a sense of humor?" she asked, wheezing ever so slightly as she tugged him along, dodging numerous guests.

"I'm not well acquainted with Mr. Slater, Permilia, but before you chase after the man, may I remind you that we are supposed to be on our way to line up for the Go-As-You-Please Quadrille?"

Permilia stopped in her tracks. "Goodness, you're right, and . . . I do believe the orchestra has finished warming up, which means the quadrille is about to begin, but . . ." Her voice trailed away to nothing as her shoulders sagged.

The sagging had him moving closer to her but then stopping abruptly when he recalled he had completely lost his ability to think the last time he came too close to her. "If you're concerned about the quadrille steps, you shouldn't be. I've been told I'm a very good dancer, which means I'll not allow you to stumble."

Permilia wrinkled her nose. "I'm a perfectly adequate dancer, Asher, thank you very much. It's not as if we're about to dance one of the more difficult quadrilles, and . . . if you neglected to notice, Mrs. Vanderbilt has cut down the timing on some of the dances this evening in order to fit all the festivities in, which means we won't be on the floor overly long."

Asher opened his mouth, an argument to the statement about the steps to the quadrille not being difficult on the very tip of his tongue, but before he could get the argument past his lips, Permilia sent him a wry smile, paired with what could only be described as an adorable shrug.

"In all honesty, I've trampled a few feet here and there over the years, but what lady hasn't had that happen to them a time or two or . . . three?"

Having never had his feet trampled by a lady but unwilling to disclose that particular information to her, Asher struggled to compose some type of response and settled for a single "Ah . . ." when nothing appropriate sprang to mind. He was spared a further response, though, when Permilia took to craning her neck and perusing the crowd.

"Ah, wonderful. She's right over there," she said as if he should know exactly who the *she* was and why Permilia was searching for a certain she in the first place.

"I'm afraid you have me at a disadvantage," he said when she quirked a delicate brow his way.

"My stepmother, Ida Griswold."

"I'm familiar with your stepmother, Permilia, but what does she have to do with our current situation?"

"You promised you'd stroll past her with me on your arm before our quadrille."

"Indeed I did, but I fear, given that the orchestra members have now picked up their instruments, we may have missed our opportunity to do any strolling."

Permilia's shoulders sagged another inch before she looked past him, drew herself up, smiled a smile that looked incredibly forced, and tightened her fingers on his arm in what he could only assume was some type of a telling gesture on her part.

"Ida's looking this way," she said out of the corner of her mouth, barely moving her lips. "Turn around as casually as you can, smiling at me in the process, quite as if you're beyond delighted to be in my company."

"Turn . . . around?"

He wasn't certain, but he thought Permilia might have let out a grunt. "How else will she be able to see I've taken her advice and lured you to my side using my feminine wiles?"

"What feminine wiles have you been using on me?"

Waving away his question even as her forced smile seemed to widen, she moved closer to him, her reasoning behind the moving becoming perfectly clear when she stepped on his foot.

"Honestly, Asher, there's no time to explain that business properly, but do know that I'm woefully inadequate when it comes to plying any wiles, so there's no need for you to look as if I've been up to no good. Having settled that, if you would now be so kind as to turn and face my stepmother, I'd be ever so grateful."

A dozen questions rolled through his mind, the most important being why Ida Griswold had seemingly been encouraging Permilia to lure him to her side, but Asher knew he'd get no answers to his questions unless he cooperated with Permilia's request. He turned in what he thought was a casual fashion but was less than amused when, after his turning, she stepped on his foot again.

"You're not smiling—you're scowling," she muttered through

76

lips stretched into the most frightening smile he'd ever seen on a young lady before.

"It's a little difficult to smile when one's foot is throbbing," he muttered, even as he forced *his* lips into a smile that he could only hope wasn't as frightening-looking as Permilia's. When she gave him a quick jerk of her head, he took the gesture to mean he was complying with her rather bossy instructions, so keeping his smile firmly in place, he directed his attention to where he assumed Ida Griswold was standing.

It took every ounce of control he possessed to keep a smile on his face when his gaze settled on Ida and he discovered that she was watching Permilia with wide eyes and with such apprehension that a trickle of unease slithered right down Asher's spine.

Apprehension was not an expression he'd been expecting to see, and . . . it was not a reassuring sight in the least.

"I think she's seen us" was all he could think to say.

"Of course she has, but . . ." She leaned closer to him, giving him another tantalizing whiff of her perfume. "Would it be too much to ask of you to tip your head back and release a hearty laugh, as if I've just said something extremely witty?"

All thoughts of tantalizing scents disappeared in a flash. "Tip . . . my . . . head back?"

"And laugh," she added before she sucked in a sharp breath. "But you'll need to wipe that confused expression off your face immediately. On my word, that particular expression won't benefit me in the least, especially since it's one that numerous gentlemen have sent me in the past, right before they bolt off for destinations far from my vicinity, a circumstance that has distressed Ida no small amount."

Knowing they'd never reach the ballroom floor in time to participate in the quadrille if he continued arguing with her, Asher tipped his head back and released what he thought was a perfectly credible laugh. The remnants of that laugh, however, became stuck in his throat a moment later when Permilia sent him a telling shake of her head before she tugged on his arm and prodded him forward at a rapid rate.

"I said *hearty* laugh, not maniacal, but no time to try again since the quadrille truly is about to begin," she muttered, releasing his arm when they finally managed to join the line of dancers who'd already assembled on the floor. Taking her place opposite him, Permilia lifted her head, smiled a smile that seemed, at least to him, rather determined, and then hurled herself into motion a second later when the sound of music swelled around them.

For the briefest of moments, Asher found himself rooted to the spot.

While the rest of the ladies had begun gliding to the right, with their gentlemen partners stepping ever so smartly to the left, Permilia had taken a very large step . . . backward. That step, regrettably, had her careening smack-dab into another young lady—one who stumbled around for a good few seconds until she finally righted herself. The young lady then sent Permilia a look of admonishment, which Permilia didn't notice because she was veering off in a different direction, causing additional mayhem as she veered, especially since she was once again traveling the wrong way.

Fearing that certain disaster was soon to strike if he didn't intervene, Asher forced feet that preferred to stay rooted to the floor into motion. Reaching Permilia's side, he took hold of her arm, nudging her somewhat forcefully in the direction all of the other dancers were now traveling.

To his utter disbelief, she shrugged out of his hold a moment later. Without so much as a glance to see if he, her partner, was in accord with what she was about to do, Permilia then launched herself into a gap that had opened up between the dancing couples, a gap not meant to be launched into, leaving him with no choice but to follow her.

As he waded through dancers who were trying their very best to avoid Permilia's flailing limbs, he couldn't help but think that the word she'd chosen to describe her dancing abilities— *adequate,* if he wasn't much mistaken—did not do justice to what Permilia was currently perpetuating

He wasn't quite certain what word he'd have used instead, although . . . *earnest, enthusiastic,* or perhaps . . . *unhinged* sprang to mind.

She appeared to have no sense of rhythm as she jolted back and forth, almost as if a song completely different than the one the orchestra was currently playing was running amok in her mind. She was also counting under her breath, but not the normal one, two, three, one, two, three.

No, Permilia, oddly enough, seemed to be counting to ten, and in a convoluted manner—one, two . . . three, four, five, six . . . seven . . . eight, nine . . . ten.

When he realized he was becoming somewhat hypnotized by Permilia's strange counting ritual and the movement of her body as she counted, he reached out and took hold of her arm, drawing her close while the rest of the dancers glided in graceful circles around them.

"I do beg your pardon, Permilia, but I seem to have steered us in the wrong direction," he whispered into her ear before he tightened his grip on her and led her back into the circle of dancers, all of whom immediately gave them a wide berth.

Permilia did not seem to notice as she drew in a deep breath and began counting again, moving directly beside him until she stepped on his foot, sent him a smile of apology, and then, for some unexplainable reason, turned completely around and headed off the way they'd just come.

He couldn't help but wonder if she'd mistaken the quadrille

they were supposed to be dancing for some other quadrille, or
. . . if she thought the Go-As-You-Please title of this particular dance meant that dancers could move any which way they
pleased.

Swallowing a laugh when the thought struck him that, given
her somewhat curious manner of looking at the world, Permilia
most likely believed exactly that, Asher squared his shoulders
and drew in a deep breath. Releasing that breath a second later,
he headed back through the crowd of dancers, determined to
locate Permilia once again and assist her in performing the
proper steps of the quadrille, or at the very least, get her moving
in the right direction once and for all. Dodging one guest after
another, he found himself the recipient of incredibly sympathetic looks being tossed his way.

He couldn't say he was surprised by the looks, but what
he *was* surprised by was the annoyance that began traveling
through his veins *because* of them.

That gentlemen who enjoyed his elevated position within society never partnered ladies other than the most accomplished,
there was no question. However, he, oddly enough, found it
rather refreshing to be paired with a lady who exhibited enthusiasm instead of restraint as she . . . galloped about the room
rather than glided.

Wincing directly out of those thoughts when he finally
reached Permilia's side again and she greeted him by stepping
on his foot, Asher took her by both arms, turned her around,
and prodded her forward in the direction she was supposed to
be moving.

"This is the part in the quadrille when you're supposed to
follow my lead" was all he could think to say, but to his surprise, Permilia didn't bat so much as a single eye. Instead, she
nodded, smiled, and threw herself into the business of trying
to follow his lead.

Guiding her around the room a few more times, he felt she was finally getting the steps down, although she did step on his feet a good ten times before the music began to slow and then fade away, signaling the end of the dance. As the guests surrounding them broke into polite applause, their claps muffled by the gloves they were wearing, Asher looked down and found Permilia beaming back at him, her blue eyes sparkling with clear delight.

"I think that went extraordinarily well, don't you?" she asked, tucking her hand into the crook of his arm even as she gave a satisfied nod, the action sending her tiara listing to the left.

Unable to stop the grin that spread over his face at the amount of satisfaction Permilia had received from a dance that she apparently felt was an unqualified success instead of the disaster he was fairly sure everyone else thought her performance had been, he reached up and set her tiara back into place. Lowering his hand, he discovered Permilia grinning back at him, quite like the cat who'd discovered the cream . . . and just like that, he realized he'd somehow managed to become completely enthralled with the woman standing beside him.

She was unlike any lady he'd ever known, but instead of wanting to distance himself from her and her peculiar ways, he wanted to learn everything about her because . . . she was charming, enchanting, and he was completely intrigued by her.

Before he could fully wrap his thoughts around that startling realization, Permilia leaned toward him, her perfume clouding his thoughts again.

That circumstance turned out to be rather unfortunate, because she began whispering something about seizing the moment while it was still available. That idea, he was fairly certain, was one he should balk at. However, he simply couldn't seem to muster up the proper words to allow her to know he was not in full agreement with whatever plan she'd just concocted.

Propelling him forward before he had the presence of mind to stop her, Permilia squeezed his arm, told him to smile, and began steering him in the direction of Mrs. Ida Griswold, a lady he couldn't help but notice was looking anything but pleased to see them heading her way.

CHAPTER
SEVEN

"I don't mean to spoil what you obviously believe is going to be a marvelous encounter with your stepmother, Permilia, but do you think it may be somewhat rash to approach her at this particular moment?"

Coming to a stop, Permilia caught Asher's eye. "I'm not certain I understand your hesitation, Asher. This is the perfect moment to approach Ida. We just completed what I consider to be my most successful attempt at a quadrille to date."

Asher blinked somewhat owlishly back at her. "You truly *do* consider our quadrille a success?"

"Of course I do. Why do you think I said it went extraordinarily well? I certainly wouldn't have used that particular word if I thought I'd made a muddle of things." She smiled. "Why, if it escaped your notice, I didn't maim a single person while I was on the floor, and . . ." She held up her hand when he opened his mouth, a protest obviously on the tip of his tongue. "That young lady I ran into at the beginning does not count because she recovered rather prettily and wasn't even limping the last time I saw her."

"Am I to understand you maim fellow dancers frequently?"

"*Maim* might be a touch of an exaggeration, although . . ." She bit her lip. "There was this one gentleman—a Mr. McVickar, I believe—who was convinced by Mrs. Frederick Nelson, a friend of my stepmother's, that I adored dancing the Ticklish Water Polka." She shuddered. "I fear I'm less than adequate with the polka steps, and . . . it did not end well for Mr. McVickar."

Asher took to rubbing his temple. "That wasn't a few years back, was it—when Mr. McVickar was traveling around the city sporting a cane that he was forced to use because of an injury he'd suffered?"

"I'm afraid it was, and once word got out that it was somewhat dangerous to take to the floor with me, well . . . my fate as a wallflower was sealed. But that's neither here nor there. I'm not above using my recent success on the floor to improve my relationship with my stepmother, so . . . we need to go speak with her before the announcement is made that dinner is about to be served."

"I believe there's one more dance before dinner," Asher said as she pulled him forward again, having to exert far more effort than she'd expected since he seemed to be dragging his feet.

"If you've promised that dance to another young lady, I assure you, you'll still have plenty of time to honor that dance. We don't need to linger in my stepmother's presence. I simply need to allow her to see that we're in perfect accord with each other, and then you're free to go on your way." She craned her neck, scanned the crowd surrounding them, and then slowed to a stop. "How curious. I swear Ida was standing right there just a moment ago, but . . . you're taller than I am. Do you see her anywhere?"

Asher quickly looked around the room before he patted her arm, an action that, in her opinion, was never a good sign.

"I do hope you won't be overly distressed by this, Permilia,

84

but I'm fairly confident your stepmother slipped away into the crowd while we were trying to make our way over to her."

"Why would she have done that?"

"I'm not certain, but when I caught a glimpse of her after the quadrille ended, I fear she was scowling our way."

"Ida doesn't believe in scowling."

"Which is rather telling," Asher muttered before he summoned up a bright smile and beamed that smile her way.

Having come to the conclusion that Asher used his smiles when he was attempting to avoid a topic he did not want to discuss, Permilia pressed her lips together. "Were you purposely dragging your feet so that Ida would have ample opportunity to get away from us?"

If anything, Asher's smile increased in brightness. "I'm sure I have no idea what you could be suggesting."

A shot of something warm began to travel through her, something that was, surprisingly enough, not temper, but more along the lines of . . . affection.

He'd been trying to spare her from an unpleasant encounter with her stepmother, an idea so foreign to her that all she could do was simply stand in the midst of the crowd, all of whom were dressed as princesses, knights, and woodland creatures, and stare at the man who was, in actuality, her very own knight in shining armor—at least for the moment.

"You really are a very nice gentleman, aren't you—no matter the rumors I've heard regarding your reputation amongst your business associates?" she finally said, earning a dimming of Asher's smile in the process.

"How in the world have you heard about my business reputation?"

"You're constant fodder for articles in all the newspapers around town."

"You read the *articles* in the newspapers?"

Practically every charitable thought she'd begun holding for the man disappeared in a split second. "Surely you're not one of *those* gentlemen, are you—the ones who still find it peculiar that women actually enjoy reading the articles in a newspaper instead of simply browsing through the society columns?"

"I don't suppose it would benefit me in the least to admit that I do still find that idea peculiar, would it?"

"Not in the least."

He inclined his head. "Then I'll simply beg your pardon and promise I'll try diligently to reform my obviously deficient opinion related to women and their reading habits. And . . . I'll also promise to try my utmost to impress your stepmother with how delightful I find your company."

"That's a tall order you've set for yourself, but"—Permilia smiled and gestured across the ballroom—"if you're determined to impress my stepmother, she's over there, heading toward that hallway."

"Then we should probably get it over with sooner rather than later." With that, and after she'd sent him a nod, Asher set off across the floor, whisking her past the guests standing about the room. Guiding her toward the hallway, he brought her to a stop a few feet away from not only Ida but her stepsister, Lucy, as well.

That those two ladies seemed to be in a tizzy, there could be little doubt. Their heads were bent closely together as they whispered furiously behind raised hands, the reasoning behind their whispering becoming perfectly clear when they raised their heads, caught sight of Permilia, and immediately looked guilty.

The look lasted for only the briefest of seconds, because when they turned their attention to Asher, they were suddenly all smiles and fluttering lashes, the speed at which they'd been able to summon up the smiles having Permilia's lips twitching.

It was one of Ida's most stringent rules that no matter the circumstance, or the juiciness of the gossip being discussed, ladies were to abandon any action a gentleman might view as unattractive the very moment said gentleman entered a lady's presence. They were then expected to adopt a most demure and pleasant attitude, an attitude both Ida and Lucy were now displaying to perfection.

Forcing down the bubble of laughter that threatened to escape, Permilia watched as Asher went about the business of charming her step-relatives, stepping forward to kiss their hands.

All sense of amusement disappeared in a flash, though, when Lucy took to holding fast to Asher's hand, fluttering her lashes so rapidly in his direction that it looked as if she might have gotten something in her eye.

Asher, gentleman that he seemed to be, didn't so much as blink over the idea that Lucy was clearly flirting with him. Instead, and much to Permilia's annoyance, he perused Lucy's dance card and added his name to it.

Avoiding Ida's gaze, one that had immediately taken to sharpening on Permilia as if it was somehow her fault Lucy was now going to be taking to the floor with Asher, Permilia cast her attention to the right and found none other than Mr. Eugene Slater standing a few feet away from them, trying to look rather nonchalant even though Permilia had the sneaking suspicion he might have been deliberately following her.

Being quite unused to gentlemen bothering to follow her, but being rather delighted by the notion nevertheless, she found herself moving his way, pleased to discover she was perfectly able to return the smile he was now sending her.

"Mr. Slater, how lovely to meet up with you once again" she heard come out of her mouth, the words having Mr. Slater staring at her for a long moment before he grinned.

"You've found your voice," he said, moving toward Permilia and then surprising her by taking her hand in his and bringing it to his lips.

"Mr. Rutherford kindly informed me of your occupation, Mr. Slater, and learning you are involved with mining, well . . ."

"Permilia apparently speaks your language."

Turning, she found Asher standing directly behind her, Ida holding one of his arms and Lucy holding the other. He was no longer smiling but watching Mr. Slater in what could only be described as a very considering, and somewhat aggressive, fashion.

Mr. Slater didn't appear to be bothered by Asher's less than friendly attitude in the least as he gazed in clear delight back at her.

"You speak mining?" he asked.

Permilia smiled. "I was raised in the mines, Mr. Slater, so yes, I do speak that particular language."

Mr. Slater leaned closer, her hand still grasped in his. "You're not related to Mr. George Griswold, are you?"

"He's my father."

The delight in Mr. Slater's eyes increased tenfold. "On my word, I had no idea, but in my defense, I readily admit that I'm not out and about often in society. That has led me to commit quite a few social faux pas of late—one being that I was unaware of your true identity when I first approached you."

Permilia drew back the hand Mr. Slater had lingered over a little too long and smiled. "There's no need to fret about not knowing who I am, Mr. Slater, but . . . before we continue with our pleasant chat, allow me to present to you my stepmother, Mrs. George Griswold, and my stepsister, Miss Lucy Webster."

Stepping smartly next to them, Mr. Slater took a moment to perform the expected pleasantries, earning a rare sniff of approval from Ida in the process after he'd kissed her hand in a manner that could only be described as impressive. When he turned and did the same to Lucy, though, earning an earnest fluttering of the lashes from Lucy in response, Ida suddenly looked less than approving.

Clearing her throat, Ida sent Permilia a jerk of her head, one that Permilia wasn't certain she understood.

Concluding, and hoping she was correct with her conclusion, that Ida found Mr. Slater even less appropriate than she did Asher for her daughter, Permilia squared her shoulders, drew in a breath, and stepped to Mr. Slater's side.

"Since it's clear I've recovered my voice, Mr. Slater, I do hope you'll still be willing to take to the floor with me," she said, earning a nod of approval from Ida in the process while earning a blinking of clear disbelief from Asher, a blink she steadfastly ignored, until she remembered that he still had possession of her dance card. Smiling at Mr. Slater, who'd immediately taken to assuring her he'd enjoy nothing more than taking the floor with her, she turned to Asher and held out her hand. "If you'd be so kind, Mr. Rutherford, as to return my dance card to me, I'd be ever so grateful."

"While I'm just pleased as punch that you would enjoy dancing with me," Mr. Slater began as Asher started digging through his jacket pocket, "I distinctly recall Mr. Rutherford making the claim that all of your dances were taken."

Asher pulled out Permilia's dance card and handed it to her, although he seemed to do it somewhat reluctantly. "I wasn't comfortable allowing Miss Griswold to promise you a dance, especially since, if you'll recall, she was incapable of responding to anything you asked of her with a verbal reply."

"Don't tell me you were struck mute again," Lucy said, speaking up as she took a step forward and, surprisingly enough, took to smiling Mr. Slater's way. "I'm sure it was quite unnerving to be faced with a lady who was struck dumb in your presence, but do know that the rest of my family does not suffer from that particular oddity."

"Thank you for that, Lucy," Permilia said, drawing her dance card up and perusing it for a second, hoping that the trepidation she felt after perusing the dances still available for her wasn't obvious to everyone around her. Lifting her head, she found Mr. Slater holding his hand out to her. Handing him the card, she held her breath as he took a moment to read over the dances.

"How wonderful. You have the next dance available, a"—he brought the card closer to his face—"Ticklish Water Polka." Lowering the card, he grinned. "What an odd name for a dance, but it sounds as if it'll be delightful."

Before Permilia could respond to that, Ida sucked in a sharp breath and pushed Lucy forward. "Lucy was just bemoaning the fact, Mr. Slater, that with her being so occupied with dancing the Mother Goose Quadrille—a great honor for her, if you were unaware—she was unable to find the time to have all of her dances spoken for, and . . . why, she simply adores the Ticklish Water Polka."

Lucy's face began to darken, a direct result, no doubt, of finding herself being pawned off on a man who was looking more surprised by Ida's suggestion than delighted by it. Drawing herself up, she opened her mouth, but before she could release a single protest, Ida began talking again, nodding to Permilia as she talked.

"You won't mind stepping aside and allowing Lucy this one little favor, will you, dear?"

Temper flared from nowhere. Leveling her gaze on Ida, Permilia frowned. "I'm not that horrible at the Ticklish Water Polka, and honestly, stepmother, given that I completed the Go-As-You-Please Quadrille quite successfully just a short time ago—a daunting feat if there ever was one—I'm not certain

I understand your hesitancy to have me take to the floor to perform the polka with Mr. Slater."

Ida released a sniff. "Your performance was dreadful at best, and is currently the talk of the ball."

"I only ran into one dancer," Permilia pointed out.

"A situation I'm sure stepmothers all around the world would have been proud of, but . . . the reason behind the talk is not because you ran poor Miss Graham over at the very start of the dance. The talk concerns the idea that after stumbling into Miss Graham you proceeded to travel in the wrong direction for almost the entirety of the dance, even when your poor partner"—she nodded to Asher—"tried to put you to rights and get you moving in the proper direction."

Permilia crossed her arms over her chest. "You can't travel in the wrong direction with the Go-As-You-Please Quadrille since everyone is supposed to go where they please."

"You don't truly believe that, do you?"

A trace of unease slithered up Permilia's spine. "Do not tell me I've been mistaken all these years and that the Go-As-You-Please Quadrille has . . . rules."

Ida began fanning her face. "I'm afraid there are definite rules to that particular quadrille."

Permilia shot a glance to Asher. "Apparently the language divide was greater than I knew with my dance instructor, Mr. Vladimir, who was, well . . . Russian. But, be that as it may, language problem or not, I do believe I owe you a most heartfelt apology, Asher. You must have been beyond embarrassed with me as your partner, and here I was going on and on about how accomplished I'd been on the floor. Although . . . that does explain the confusing business about the part of the dance where you told me I was supposed to follow your lead, something I readily admit I believed you were completely wrong about at the time."

Asher stepped right up next to her. "You were a delightful partner, Permilia, and I can honestly say I've never had such an interesting time performing a quadrille before. It was most gracious of you to follow my lead when I suggested you do so."

The sting of tears caught her by surprise, but before she could do more than blink them away, music filled the room, the sound of it having Asher looking back toward the ballroom.

"I'm sorry to have to leave you at such an inopportune moment," Asher began, "but I've promised the Ticklish Water Polka to Miss Lukemeyer. I'm afraid it wouldn't be very gentlemanly of me to renege on my promise to her." He leaned closer and lowered his voice. "Since you admitted to me not long ago that you maimed poor Mr. McVickar while attempting to dance the polka with him, perhaps you really should consider encouraging Mr. Slater to dance this particular dance with your stepsister."

Giving her arm what felt exactly like a reassuring squeeze, Asher made his excuses to Ida and Lucy, sent Mr. Slater a less than friendly look, and turned and walked away.

"I get the uncanny feeling I've done something to annoy that gentleman," Mr. Slater said.

"I'm sure you haven't," Permilia said, shaking her head when he held out his hand to her. "But speaking of annoying, I have the uncanny feeling you'll be most annoyed with me if I take to the floor with you to dance this particular polka, so . . ." She nodded to Lucy. "I would deem it a great favor, Lucy, if you would dance with Mr. Slater in my stead."

To Permilia's relief, Lucy didn't hesitate. When the orchestra began playing in earnest, signaling the start of the dance, she took the arm Mr. Slater offered her and began walking away. But they slowed to a stop a mere second later when Mr. Slater turned and arched a brow Permilia's way.

"You will join me for dinner, though, won't you?"

"I would be honored to join you for dinner, and I assure you,

you'll be much safer sitting down to dine with me than trying to partner me in a polka."

Sending her a smile, Mr. Slater urged a now-unsmiling Lucy into motion again, leaving Permilia standing with only Ida for company.

"That was very wise of you, dear," Ida said.

"Since I was recently speaking with Asher about poor Mr. McVickar and how I'd injured that gentleman while attempting the Ticklish Water Polka, the horror of the dance was relatively fresh in my mind."

Ida immediately took to looking Permilia over in a very considering fashion. "I wasn't aware you and Mr. Rutherford were on such informal terms with each other."

Dredging up a smile, Permilia shrugged. "I've been taking your advice, stepmother, which, if you'll recall, encouraged me to be on friendly terms with Mr. Rutherford."

"Don't be on too friendly of terms with any gentleman, Permilia, at least not until after arrangements have been settled. Gentlemen rarely bother to buy the fine crystal champagne flutes when they can drink from less expensive goblets instead."

"I'm going to pretend you didn't just say that and go back to what I normally do while at a society event: find a nice wall and settle in for the duration."

"Do not forget you promised to dine with Mr. Slater," Ida said with a wag of her finger in Permilia's direction. "Lucy is far too impressionable at her tender age, and a man dressed as a pirate will almost certainly turn her head. One dance shouldn't turn her head too much, but if she spends additional time with the man . . . well, it's not an idea I'm comfortable contemplating."

"If I were to hazard a guess, I'd say Mr. Slater is a very wealthy gentleman."

"He's in mining."

Permilia frowned. "As is your husband."

Without bothering to reply to what Permilia thought was a most profound statement, Ida glided down the hallway, stepping around the young lady dressed as Joan of Arc before she disappeared from view.

The sight of Joan of Arc, who was still brandishing a notebook instead of a sword, banished all thoughts of dances, eligible gentlemen, and annoying stepmothers and stepsisters from Permilia's mind.

Realizing that she'd allowed herself to become completely distracted from the truly important task laid out for her that evening—that being gathering information for the best column she'd ever written in her life—Permilia headed across the room, searching for an out-of-the-way place she could use to get back to work.

Smiling when she found another large fern by the entrance to the ladies' retiring room, she walked as casually as she could toward it, bending down a second later to retrieve an abandoned dance card from the ground. Straightening, she dusted off the card, but before she could take up her position behind the fern, Gertrude dashed up to join her, breathing rather heavily and having a distinct look of panic in her eyes.

"I've lost Mrs. Davenport," Gertrude managed to get out before she bent over and sucked in a large breath of air.

"I'm sure she's not lost."

Gertrude straightened and frowned. "Well, quite, but I've misplaced her for more than an hour. That's far too long to allow Mrs. Davenport to be misplaced. There's no telling what mischief she might have gotten herself into by now."

Although Gertrude had never confided in Permilia regarding exactly what Mrs. Davenport got up to when she disappeared at each and every society event, Permilia had a notion it might not be considered . . . aboveboard. Stepping closer to Gertrude, she gave her friend's arm a squeeze.

"Would you like me to try and find her?"

Relief immediately replaced the panic in Gertrude's eyes. "Would you mind? I've come to believe that Mrs. Davenport is on to me and is now deliberately avoiding me, which means . . . she's definitely become embroiled in something . . . disturbing." She drew in a breath and blew it out. "You may be more successful than I've been in finding her, since she won't be expecting you to try and run her to ground."

"It sounds a little disturbing when you put it like that."

Gertrude lifted her chin. "You have no idea how disturbing this situation could turn if we don't find Mrs. Davenport and run her to ground before someone else discovers her. And if you're fortunate enough to find her, do try and see if there seems to be anything suspicious in her reticule."

"How, pray tell, would I get a glimpse of the contents of her reticule?"

"I'll leave the details of that up to you." With those less than helpful words, Gertrude moved closer to Permilia, whispered something about needing all the luck she could get, and then gave Permilia a push, leaving Permilia with no choice but to proceed forward with her quest, a quest she hoped would not see her landing in a disturbing situation as well.

CHAPTER EIGHT

Twenty minutes later, it was becoming quite apparent that Mrs. Davenport did not want to be found.

Having traveled back up to the third-floor gymnasium and meandered as casually as she could through all the many rooms located up there, and having absolutely no success running her target to ground, Permilia had been forced to return to the second floor. The dilemma with that, though, was that some of the areas of the second floor were no longer open to guests, and those areas had almost all the lights extinguished in them, leaving her meandering around in shadows.

Creeping down yet another dimly lit hallway, Permilia prayed that if she did find Mrs. Davenport, she wouldn't find her in the midst of doing something of a questionable nature. What that something might be, she had not the faintest idea, but since Gertrude had certainly lent the impression Mrs. Davenport was prone to mischief, Permilia knew there was little chance that she'd stumble on the woman behaving herself.

That idea was a little unsettling, even though she was perfectly aware that Mrs. Davenport was known throughout society as an eccentric sort.

She had a propensity for dyeing her hair black, exactly like Mrs. Astor did, and a fondness for wearing rouge and rice powder whenever she stepped out of her house. Because of that, it was next to impossible to gauge the woman's true age, although Permilia thought she might be in her late sixties. For a woman of that age, she'd managed to maintain a trim figure, which certainly made the business of finding her more difficult than if Mrs. Davenport had been a lady prone to plumpness.

Besides the woman's physical attributes, Permilia knew relatively little about her except that she was known to be in possession of a very large fortune, had no family to speak of, at least none in New York, and was apparently delving into a bit of skullduggery. What that skullduggery was, or why a society matron would delve into that nonsense in the first place, was apparently anyone's guess.

Turning left when she reached the end of the hallway, Permilia found herself faced with another shadowy space in front of her. For a second, she debated giving up her quest, until she remembered that Gertrude could very well suffer a loss of employment if Mrs. Davenport was discovered doing something of a questionable nature. Society did not approve of questionable behavior, especially from their society matrons, and could very well banish Mrs. Davenport from their gatherings, those gatherings being one of the main reasons the woman employed Gertrude.

The sound of a grunt drew Permilia out of her thoughts and toward a door only a few feet away from her.

When the grunt was directly followed by the distinct sound of something crashing to the ground, Permilia slipped farther into the shadows, pressing herself against the wall. Hoping that the person responsible for the crash, a person who might very well be the oh-so-elusive Mrs. Davenport, would abandon whatever it was they were doing and return to the festivities, Permilia decided her best option was to remain where she was and wait the person out.

It turned out to be a long wait. After a few minutes had passed and not a single soul exited the room where the crash had occurred, Permilia drew herself up, stepped out of the shadows, and moved toward the room, ignoring the little voice in her head that kept whispering she was being an idiot.

Stepping through the door that had been left open just the tiniest bit, she came to a sudden stop when she got a good look at the room she'd just entered. A single gas lamp was throwing a golden glow over what seemed to be a collection of objects, some of those objects still in brown wrappings.

Statues, paintings, and even a few stuffed birds were scattered about, but there was not another living soul in sight.

Turning, Permilia was just edging through the door again when another sound—this one along the lines of a thud—drifted to her from somewhere on the opposite side of the room.

Squinting in the direction of the sound, she saw another door, one that looked as if it might lead to some type of closet. Tiptoeing across the room, she took hold of the doorknob and, before allowing herself time to rethink the action, twisted it as quietly as she could and opened the door.

What she found after stepping through the door took her by complete surprise. Instead of a closet, she was standing in another room, this one designed as a second art room, the main art room being located on the first floor and accessible to guests. The walls in this room were papered in a deep red, and the furniture looked as if it had been lifted straight from an ancient castle. A fur rug—one that had certainly come from a bear, given the bear's head that seemed to be watching her from the edge of that rug—was placed directly in the center of

98

the room, while a gold cart filled with crystal decanters stood next to crimson drapes.

This room was clearly not intended for anyone but Mr. and Mrs. Vanderbilt to enjoy, which meant if she was found out, there'd be all sorts of trouble to pay. Sweeping the room with her gaze, she stilled when she caught a glimpse of movement to her right. Before she could investigate further, though, voices drifted in from the room she'd just vacated.

Without the slightest hesitation, she dropped to the ground and crawled across the floor, wriggling as fast as she could underneath a drop-leaf table. Lifting her head when she felt she was sufficiently hidden, she found her gaze caught and held by none other than Mrs. Davenport, said lady having tucked herself neatly underneath what appeared to be a Jacobean chair. That Mrs. Davenport was not looking the least little bit disturbed by their current situation was rather telling in and of itself—as if the lady made a habit out of hiding in places she was not supposed to be.

"You do know that if we make it out of here unscathed, you owe me some type of an explanation, don't you?" Permilia whispered.

The only response Mrs. Davenport gave was to place a finger to her lips even as she nodded to the door that was still slightly ajar.

Pressing her lips firmly together even though she had plenty of things left to say to Mrs. Davenport, Permilia turned her attention to the door just as someone began speaking on the other side in a lowered tone of voice, a voice that had the hair on the back of Permilia's neck standing at attention.

"Discretion is imperative" were the first words Permilia could make out clearly, those words doing absolutely nothing to calm the anxiety that had taken to swirling through her veins.

"So you've said," another voice rasped. "Numerous times, but do know that discretion comes with a hefty price."

"As I've mentioned before, money is no object as long as the little problem my partner and I have been dealing with of late comes to a rather expedient . . . end."

Every muscle in Permilia's body stiffened, holding her quite immobile as she realized that the situation she'd landed herself in was quite disturbing, especially since it sounded as if someone was in the midst of hiring on a man to commit—

"How soon did you want your problem taken care of?" the raspy-voiced gentleman asked.

"As soon as you're able to plan it out in the most efficient manner possible. My partner and I are anxious to finish this and would appreciate the deed being completed before the man is able to get that blasted tearoom of his up and running."

A bead of perspiration dribbled down Permilia's face, brought about by the mention of the tearoom. According to articles she'd read in all the papers, Asher Rutherford was in the process of creating a tearoom on the fourth floor of his store.

It was a brilliant idea, and one that the city had embraced wholeheartedly, but surely the gentlemen on the other side of the door, who were sounding more and more like gentlemen prone to criminal activity, could not be speaking about—

"I wouldn't be able to continue my chosen profession if I performed my services in anything other than the most efficient of ways," Raspy-man continued, the rasp in his voice steadily increasing, as if he were taking great pains to disguise his true voice.

That disguising was certainly a prudent decision on the man's part since his conversation was, indeed, being overheard, but it was a frustrating situation for Permilia since she had not the slightest inkling who the voice belonged to, which meant she was going to have to—

"And that right there, my good man, is exactly why I have no qualms paying you the obscene amount of money you're asking for in order to take care of the Asher Rutherford problem I'm experiencing. He, as you and everyone else in town is well aware, is a very prominent gentleman. His demise must be made to look like an unfortunate accident. Otherwise, well, we'll never be able to let down our guard."

Raspy-man released an ominous-sounding chuckle. "Mr. Rutherford has acquired a long list of enemies because of the rather unusual hiring methods he embraces for that store of his. Even if questions arise after his . . . accident, there are far more likely suspects out there to draw the notice of the authorities than you or your partner." Raspy-man cleared his throat. "May I assume you're currently in possession of the money I require before I begin making the proper arrangements?"

"Why else would I have agreed to your demand of meeting you here at this ball, and securing you a ticket to it, if I was not in possession of . . ."

Permilia stayed as still as she could, straining to hear more of the conversation, but the men's voices became next to impossible to understand, possibly because they'd moved farther away from her.

Realizing that the transaction for murder the men had apparently agreed to was rapidly wrapping up, and knowing she needed to get a look at the men in question in order to put an end to their plan, Permilia began inching forward ever so slowly. She was halfway out from beneath the table when she happened to glance up and notice that Mrs. Davenport was in the process of edging out of her hiding place as well. The woman was completely silent as she edged—yet another indication that she spent a significant amount of her time pursuing nefarious agendas.

To Permilia's concern, though, Mrs. Davenport stopped edging, got a horrified expression on her face right before she drew in a wheezy sort of breath, and then . . . sneezed.

It wasn't a delicate sneeze by any stretch of the imagination, but one that practically sent the windows to rattling and one that, unfortunately, had not gone undetected.

"Someone's in that room" were the first words Permilia heard after Mrs. Davenport's sneeze stopped reverberating in her ears.

"I'll see to it," the raspy-voiced man said, clear menace marking his every word, the menace sending Permilia immediately into motion. Scrambling to her feet, she dashed over to the door that separated her and Mrs. Davenport from certain madness and slammed it shut. Muttering a quick prayer of thanks when she discovered a key resting in the lock, she gave it a quick twist, blowing out a breath of relief when she jiggled the knob and found it securely locked.

"I say, dear, good show," Mrs. Davenport exclaimed, drawing Permilia's attention as she rose to her feet, fished a handkerchief out of a reticule that was bulging with heaven knew what, blew her nose, and returned the handkerchief to her reticule. "I thought we were done for."

"While I would truly enjoy discussing why we're currently in a position to be done for in the first place," Permilia began, "we're far from being out of danger."

As if to testify that was exactly the case, the doorknob took that moment to begin rattling.

"Too right you are," Mrs. Davenport said. "May I dare hope that you have some sort of plan to see us safely away from here?"

Looking around the room, Permilia headed for a pair of thick brocade drapes that had been pulled closed, flinging them open a second later. Pressing her nose to the glass, she released a sigh before she turned and caught Mrs. Davenport's eye. "I'm afraid, seeing as how we are on the second floor, that we'd be falling to our certain deaths on those artfully placed boulders right below if we try to make an escape out the window."

"There's no handy tree we can use?"

"I'm fairly sure those handy trees young ladies constantly seem to have handy are only available in the pages of novels, Mrs. Davenport. From here there is not a single tree to be seen, and since there's no bed in this room, we don't even have linens to use to make a rope and climb out of here."

Mrs. Davenport shook her head. "Which is truly unfortunate, as bed linens have aided me more than a few times over the years when I've gotten in a few . . . pickles."

"And while I'm fairly certain those pickles would make for some fascinating stories, I'm afraid now is not the time. Although"—Permilia nodded to the stuffed reticule Mrs. Davenport was clinging to in a most telling way—"perhaps now, as I search for another way out of here, would be the perfect time for you to . . . return to their proper places whatever the contents may be of your bag."

To Permilia's surprise, Mrs. Davenport, instead of looking even the slightest bit guilty, sent a rather knowing smile Permilia's way. "I would be more than happy to do just that as soon as you disclose to me what you have residing in your muff."

A determined rattling of the door saved Permilia any response to that concerning statement. "Maybe the prudent option at this particular moment is to agree to save the sharing of our respective mysteries for a more appropriate time."

"I thought you might say something like that," Mrs. Davenport said a touch smugly before she moved into motion, hustled to the opposite side of the room, and then pulled open another set of drapes, but drapes that were not concealing a window.

Instead, a large rectangular box set into the wall met Permilia's gaze, a sight that had her striding across the room to get a closer look.

"Is that a . . . dumbwaiter?" she asked, glancing to Mrs. Davenport.

"It is."

"How did you know that was here?"

Mrs. Davenport blinked innocent eyes back at her. "Sheer luck, I would imagine."

"I highly doubt that, but . . ." Permilia moved to the dumb-waiter, flipped open the latch, shoved the dumbwaiter's door up, and found herself, thankfully, looking at a remarkably large space, quite larger than she'd been expecting to find.

"I imagine Mr. Vanderbilt had that made overly large in order to accommodate all of the treasures he likes to inspect in the room adjacent to this one," Mrs. Davenport said with yet another blink of innocent eyes. "And isn't it oh-so-fortunate that someone left the dumbwaiter available on this floor because . . . well, that would have been tricky if we'd have had to climb down those ropes instead of hopping into the storage compartment."

"I'm going to simply agree with you that it's a fortunate circumstance indeed to find this dumbwaiter ready and wait-ing for us, because"—Permilia shuddered—"the alternative to that is rather frightening to consider, especially since I have the distinct feeling you had something to do with the dumbwaiter being so readily available. But enough about that. In you go, Mrs. Davenport."

Pretending not to see the additional batting of innocent lashes coming from Mrs. Davenport, Permilia practically shoved the woman into the dumbwaiter, following her a second later.

It was not a comfortable fit, but before she had a chance to rearrange herself, the door burst open and a gentleman fell into the room.

She reached and pulled the door down, barely managing to squeeze her foot into the space she now occupied before the door shut completely, realizing a second later that she'd somehow managed to leave one of her shoes behind.

Knowing it was completely ridiculous to bemoan the loss of a shoe, even if it was a one-of-a-kind piece, Permilia pushed aside the urge to reopen the door and grab up her shoe, knowing her time would be better spent figuring out how to get the dumbwaiter to move.

"I found a lever here," Mrs. Davenport said, and before Permilia could do more than draw in a quick breath, they were falling.

CHAPTER NINE

Having truly never considered that she might breathe her last breath while stuffed into a dumbwaiter, Permilia closed her eyes and saw her entire life pass before her, a life that she certainly hadn't enjoyed as much as she should the past few years.

Whispering a brief prayer, not asking for help but more along the lines of asking for forgiveness for not enjoying the life she'd been given of late, she stopped mid-prayer when she realized the dumbwaiter was not plummeting downward, but was instead inching along inch by creaking inch.

"I think Mr. Vanderbilt might need to consider investing in a good can of oil," Mrs. Davenport said right as they came to a shuddering halt and the door opened with a loud squeak.

Permilia couldn't actually say who was more surprised—the staff member dressed in maroon Vanderbilt livery who was gawking back at her once the door was fully open, or her as she realized they'd been deposited in a far corner of the kitchen—not exactly a place one wanted to be deposited in the midst of a ball, and especially not a place one wanted to be deposited in when one was trying to be . . . discreet.

"Ah, I knew that would be a most thrilling adventure," Mrs. Davenport exclaimed. "Although I'm not certain I should have taken darling Willie's dare to try out his dumbwaiter in such a way." She released a delightful laugh. "Would you be a dear, my good man, and help us out of here? I daresay we weren't expecting to be so cramped on our wild ride in Willie's delightful dumbwaiter."

The man peered back at them with one brow raised. "Mr. Vanderbilt encouraged you to get in the dumbwaiter as if it were a steam elevator?"

"You don't honestly believe that two ladies would have come up with such a harebrained idea on their own, do you?" Mrs. Davenport returned.

The man extended them a short bow. "An excellent point."

Accepting the hand the man extended to her, even though she was longing to set him straight on his obviously archaic views regarding women, Permilia climbed out of the dumbwaiter, shook out her skirts, and pretended not to notice that her white snow-queen costume was looking a little worse for wear, what with all the creases and dust on it.

Stepping out of the way in order to allow Mrs. Davenport room to climb out of the dumbwaiter, Permilia listed to the right, remembering in an instant that she was now in possession of only one of her shoes.

"Are you quite all right, miss?" the Vanderbilt servant asked.

"I'm fine. I simply seem to have misplaced my shoe."

Bending forward, he poked his head in the dumbwaiter. "I'm afraid there's no shoe in here. Would you care for me to send someone to look for it?"

"There's no need for that," Mrs. Davenport said before Permilia could respond. "I'm sure Willie saw the missing shoe and is holding it for us, so . . . if you'll excuse us, we'll simply be on our way."

"Mr. Vanderbilt is currently in the gymnasium with Mrs. Vanderbilt, because dinner began being served thirty minutes ago."

Mrs. Davenport let out an honest-to-goodness giggle. "Of course he is. How silly of me to have forgotten that he told us to join him in the gymnasium after our ride." Taking hold of Permilia's arm, she nodded to the man even as she prodded Permilia into motion. "Thank you so much for your assistance, sir. I'll be certain to mention it to Mr. Vanderbilt, but if you'll excuse us, I'm rather famished."

Permilia soon found herself limping at a rapid rate of speed through the kitchen and then up to the third floor using a servant's staircase that Mrs. Davenport suggested in case the villains were en route to intercept them. She tugged Mrs. Davenport to a stop when they stepped into the hallway.

"We can't show up for dinner looking like this. We're a mess."

Mrs. Davenport looked her over with a remarkably sharp brown eye. "Indeed we are, or at least you are, so . . . to the retiring room."

By the time they'd gotten themselves in order, another five minutes had passed. Two of those minutes had been spent with Permilia forcefully trying to remove her tiara—which Mrs. Davenport had insisted on polishing up with her sleeve—from Mrs. Davenport's rather strong grip. Walking on feet that no longer sported any shoes at all—her one remaining shoe stuffed into the muff—Permilia took hold of the woman's arm and they quit the retiring room.

"You need to stop looking guilty," Mrs. Davenport whispered before she began smiling, looking for all intents and purposes as if they were simply two ladies who were returning from a trip to the retiring room, not a care in the world, and certainly not two ladies who'd just overheard a plot revolving around . . . murder.

"Forgive me, but I'm apparently not as familiar as you are with how to react after experiencing what I believe was a most dastardly situation," Permilia said out of the corner of her mouth, turning them toward the gymnasium, where the dinner was being served.

"Given the manner in which you've been lurking around the edges of ballrooms for what must be going on two years now, dear, I'm not certain you should be throwing such a judgmental attitude my way."

"You've noticed my lurking?"

"And have applauded it," Mrs. Davenport returned. "I readily admit, though, that I have yet to figure out what you're up to, but don't fret because . . . I will."

"It's nothing of an illegal nature."

"That's what we all say, dear, but enough about that. Smile at the ready and again, look innocent." With that piece of less than helpful advice, Mrs. Davenport tightened the grip she had on Permilia's arm and sailed into the gymnasium.

"I do hope we haven't missed too many courses" was all Mrs. Davenport said before she released Permilia's arm and tottered off, dodging Vanderbilt servers who were brandishing silver trays filled with all manner of delicacies.

"How in the world can she eat at a time like this?" Permilia asked no one in particular, earning an arch of a brow from a lady dressed in a delightful gown of gold silk, one cut in the style of a courtier. Sending the lady a nod, Permilia hurried farther into the gymnasium, amazed to discover that while everyone had been dancing in the ballroom on the first floor, an entire meal had been laid out in the room she'd almost been squashed by a pillar in. Hundreds of round tables were placed about the room, those tables now filled with twelve hundred guests, all of whom seemed to be enjoying a most excellent meal. Shaking her head at the money spent to accomplish such a feat, Permilia continued forward, knowing her first order of business was to find Asher and warn him of his impending doom.

Walking as casually as she could around the tables, she finally spotted Asher, along with his dinner companion, Miss Claudia Lukemeyer. Stopping briefly to collect her thoughts, because she certainly couldn't just blurt out the upsetting idea that someone wanted Asher dead, Permilia squared her shoulders. Glancing at the other guests dining at Asher's table, she blinked when she recognized the people who'd chosen to sit with him.

To Asher's left was Miss Lukemeyer, but to Asher's right . . . Well, Permilia had no idea why her stepmother had chosen to sit in that particular seat. Then, sitting directly next to Ida was Lucy, then Mr. Eugene Slater, and then . . . a rather telling empty chair, one that had more than likely been saved for her.

To Permilia's eye, it was obvious that Lucy was not bothered in the least by the idea she'd stolen Permilia's dinner companion, especially since she was smiling quite charmingly at Mr. Slater, batting her lashes in a far too flirtatious way, although that flirtatiousness certainly didn't seem to be bothering the gentleman who'd been claiming only a short time ago that he'd been utterly bewitched by Permilia.

The only conclusion Permilia was capable of making about that unfortunate circumstance was that Mr. Slater was apparently a gentleman who could be bewitched at the drop of a hat—or a flutter of a lash, as the case seemed to be. Oddly enough, a rather unexpected sense of relief flowed through her. That relief was brought about no doubt by the idea that before she'd been placed in a situation where her head might have very well been turned by Mr. Slater's glib tongue, she'd uncovered Mr. Slater's fickle nature.

Fickleness in a gentleman was not becoming in the least. Permilia's gaze flicked to Lucy, who certainly didn't appear as if she took any type of issue with the gentleman who'd joined her for dinner, especially since she was gazing back at the man with clear adoration in her eyes.

Switching her attention to Ida, Permilia discovered that her stepmother, on the other hand, seemed to be taking great issue with the attention Mr. Slater was sending her daughter. However, since that gentleman was keeping his gaze firmly on Lucy, he was not privy to the glares currently being sent his way from Ida. Those glares, if the gentleman had bothered to notice, would have certainly had him leaning away from Lucy instead of moving closer to her, inch by careful inch.

"Permilia, there you are. Everyone was becoming so worried."

Looking around, Permilia found Asher already on his feet and moving toward her.

"Where have you been?" he asked, reaching her side and taking hold of her arm, guiding her toward the empty seat at the table.

"Yes, where have you been?" Mr. Slater asked, rising to his feet as well.

Waving Mr. Slater back into his seat, Permilia summoned up what she hoped would pass for an innocent smile. "I do apologize for being so inexcusably tardy, but I ran into Mrs. Davenport, and she needed a bit of . . . assistance, and I'm afraid that assistance took longer than I anticipated."

"What type of assistance would Mrs. Davenport need from you?" Ida demanded. She looked down. "And where are your shoes?"

Permilia patted the muff. "One of them is safely secure in here, but the other one . . . Well, I'm afraid it might be gone forever."

"I told you wearing shoes made out of glass beads was not a wise decision," Lucy said.

"And once again, you've been proven quite right." Permilia turned to catch Asher's eye as he stood directly behind her, apparently waiting to assist her into her chair. "It's imperative that I speak with you as soon as possible."

"You're speaking to him now, Miss Griswold," Miss Lukemeyer pointed out with a touch of a snip to her tone.

"So I am, but what I need to tell him is a matter of great delicacy, so if all of you would excuse us for just a moment, we'll be back before the next course is served."

"Permilia, a lady does not make off with another lady's dinner companion, nor does one bring up matters of a delicate nature between courses," Ida said.

"I do apologize, Stepmother, but I fear I have no choice but to abandon my manners because this is a matter of life and death."

Silence settled over the table until Asher cleared his throat.

"Whose death?"

"Yours."

CHAPTER
TEN

For a split second, Asher had absolutely no idea how to respond to Permilia's announcement. But then, when he noticed that her eyes were uncommonly wide, quite as if she was in the midst of imparting some type of silent message to him, he finally realized exactly what she was expecting.

Tipping his head back, he let out the heartiest laugh he was capable of, making certain to add a few honest-to-goodness guffaws in for good measure.

His last guffaw ended on an abrupt note, though, when he happened to catch sight of the expression now residing on Permilia's face. She was not looking back at him as if he were the most brilliant gentleman she'd ever met, but instead as if he'd taken complete leave of his senses.

Leaning in toward her, he lowered his voice. "Too hearty of a response?"

Permilia took a telling step away from him. "If you'll recall, I just disclosed news that may very well concern your imminent death. I would have to say that unless you're the type of gentleman who laughs in the face of danger, yes, that was too hearty of a response, not to mention peculiar."

Tilting his head, Asher frowned. "It's hardly fair to call me peculiar, Permilia, when you just made one of the most outlandish claims I've ever heard in order to explain away the true reason behind why you were tardy for dinner. What nonsensical tale will you come up with next when additional questions are posed concerning how you managed to break a shoe?"

A second later, when she moved up to him and kicked his shin, Asher was exceedingly thankful she had broken a shoe.

Taken completely aback by the kick, he narrowed his eyes. "I'm sure I have no idea why you just did that—particularly since I've been trying to assist you."

"How, pray tell, would laughing at me be considered assistance?"

"I thought that's what you wanted me to do, especially after you requested my laughter earlier this evening when you wanted to convince your stepmother that I found you to be quite amusing."

"What was that?" Ida asked, rising to her feet, which had Mr. Slater rising to his feet as well.

Resisting the urge to groan when he realized what had come out of his mouth—although in his defense, he'd only spoken so rashly because he'd been taken by such surprise when she'd kicked him, Asher summoned up his most charming of smiles and directed it at Ida.

"I forgot to mention to you earlier, Mrs. Griswold, how absolutely delightful I find your stepdaughter to be, and . . . she's very well versed when speaking about the weather, something I'm sure you'll be more than pleased to discover."

Permilia threw her hands up in the air, turned smartly around, and practically raced away from the table, muttering something about having had quite enough of this nonsense and that she was going home.

"What an unusual woman your stepsister is, Miss Webster," Miss Claudia Lukemeyer, the lady he was supposed to be enjoying a most excellent meal with, said with a sympathetic shake of her head Lucy's way.

"You have no idea," Lucy said before she blotted her lips with her linen napkin and promptly threw herself back into a conversation with Mr. Slater, who didn't seem at all concerned that the woman he was supposed to dine with had just disappeared, on shoeless feet, no less, intent on traveling home without the benefit of a chaperone or escort.

Glancing to Ida, Asher frowned. "Forgive me, Mrs. Griswold, but should someone go after her?"

Ida waved his concern aside. "My stepdaughter is a remarkably self-sufficient sort, Mr. Rutherford. She'll be fine. Please . . ." She gestured to his seat. "The servers are waiting to serve our next course."

Distaste settled on his tongue. "I'm afraid I'll have to miss the rest of the meal." He moved to stand directly beside Miss Lukemeyer. "I do hope you'll forgive me, Miss Lukemeyer, but I'm not comfortable allowing Miss Griswold to leave the ball unescorted." He nodded to Mr. Slater. "Would you be so kind as to ascertain that Miss Lukemeyer is included in the conversation as all of you enjoy the rest of your meal?"

"But of course," Mr. Slater said, earning a smile from Miss Lukemeyer and a frown he missed from Lucy.

"There's really no need to go after her, Mr. Rutherford," Ida said as she picked up her glass of wine and took a sip.

"There's every need." Extending the table at large a nod, Asher turned and strode away, unable to disregard the discreet glances and rapidly moving lips that a few people were trying to hide behind their hands.

Quite unused to being the subject of titillating gossip, he increased his pace, unable to help but wonder if this was what it felt like for Permilia and her fellow wallflowers on a nightly basis—unaccepted in all the right circles, but fodder for the gossips nevertheless.

Dodging countless tables and servers as he made his way across the gymnasium floor, Asher finally reached the far side of the room but was interrupted from his pursuit of Permilia when Miss Stillwater stepped in his path.

Taking hold of his arm, she tugged him over to a large fern and practically shoved him behind it. Placing her hands on her hips, she looked him over before giving a shake of her head.

"What in the world has gotten into you tonight, Mr. Rutherford? I hate to be the bearer of sorry news, but you, my old friend, are currently the fodder for some rather salacious gossip."

"How odd for you to broach that matter right at this particular moment since I was just pondering the subject of gossip. Although I was thinking more along the lines of titillating gossip over salacious."

Miss Stillwater swatted him with her hand. "There really isn't much of a difference, darling, but I thought you'd want to know that there are rumors spreading like wildfire that *you've* taken an interest in Miss Penelope Griswold."

"It's *Permilia* Griswold."

She gave an airy wave of her hand. "It's of little consequence to me what her name is, but what is of consequence to me is you, my friend. What could you have been thinking, spending a good portion of your time this evening with a wallflower, and . . . why in the world did she kick you?"

"I didn't realize anyone saw that."

"So it's true?" Miss Stillwater demanded. "She really did kick you? I was hoping the gossips had it wrong."

"It was just in jest, Miss Stillwater."

A lift of a brow was Miss Stillwater's only response to that.

116

"It was," he said. "I misunderstood something Miss Griswold said, and she kicked me in a very . . . friendly sort of way."

"You're now claiming a friendship with her?"

Asher frowned. "Is there a reason you believe I shouldn't claim a friendship with Miss Griswold?"

"She's a wallflower."

"And you truly believe that is a sufficient reason to distance myself from her?"

"If you want to remain part of the fashionable set, yes."

For the briefest of seconds, Asher thought about telling her he had no interest in remaining a part of the fashionable set, but sanity returned in the next second.

His business depended on the generosity of the fashionable set, and he had too much at stake to blithely turn his back on people he'd considered friends for years. Dredging up a smile, he patted Miss Stillwater's arm and then took hold of that arm and led her out from the ferns.

"I do thank you for your concern, along with your counsel, of course. And do know that I'll take every word you said into consideration as I move forward."

"Move forward and cease associating with Miss Griswold?" Miss Stillwater pressed.

Asher kept the smile firmly on his face. "I'm a businessman at heart, Miss Stillwater. I don't lightly discontinue my association with anyone, especially since such an action is never viewed in a favorable manner. Now then, if you'll excuse me, I need to be off."

Miss Stillwater sucked in a sharp breath. "On my word, you're fond of the girl."

"Since Miss Griswold is more than likely older than you, I believe *girl* might be a bit condescending, and yes, I am fond of her, as I am of *most* of my friends." Removing Miss Stillwater's arm from his as discreetly as possible, Asher took a step away from her. "I'm sure you and I will speak again soon, but I truly do need to go and find Miss Griswold. As I mentioned, we've suffered a misunderstanding that was entirely my fault—which means I, being a gentleman, need to seek her out and make amends."

Leaving Miss Stillwater looking more than a smidgen confused, Asher turned and headed for the grand staircase. Moving down the steps as quickly as possible, he slowed to a stop on the second-floor landing when his path was blocked yet again. This time he found himself waylaid by the lady dressed as Joan of Arc, a woman he was fairly certain was one of the reporters Mrs. Vanderbilt had allowed into her ball.

"If you're looking for Miss Griswold, she headed down that hallway a few minutes ago," the lady said, pointing a hand that held a pen in the direction of a dimly lit hallway to Asher's right.

"Are you certain about that?"

She smiled. "Indeed, especially since I was, er, keeping a close eye on her after she left the gymnasium."

"Miss Griswold told me you aren't known to her."

"True, but Miss Griswold is now known to me. And I have to say, she's a most interesting woman to watch, if one bothers to notice her, that is."

Asher took a step closer to the lady. "You're not considering putting Miss Griswold in an article, are you?"

Innocent eyes blinked back at him. "I'm sure I have no idea what you're going on about, but . . . if I may make just the tiniest suggestion? I don't believe guests are supposed to be in the part of the house Miss Griswold is probably visiting as we speak, which means unless you want to see her land in a concerning situation with the Vanderbilt butler, a man who, quite honestly, scares me half to death, I'd go and see about fetching her before she finds herself in trouble."

Not allowing Asher an opportunity to ask what she meant

about the *trouble* business, the woman nodded toward the dimly lit hallway right before she dashed off down the stairs, her chainmail clinking as she dashed.

Unable to help but wonder how his evening kept becoming more and more curious as it unfolded, Asher headed down the hallway, unease settling over him the farther he traveled with no sign of Permilia.

Stepping around a corner, he breathed a sigh of relief when he finally caught sight of her heading directly toward him but with her attention focused the other way.

"Imagine running across you in this particular section of the house," he said.

Letting out a yelp, Permilia stopped in her tracks and raised a hand to her throat. "Honestly, Asher, you just took a good ten years off of my life."

"Years you would still have at your disposal if you weren't up to something interesting."

She released a snort and began walking again, staunchly ignoring the arm he held out to her as she drew nearer. "I'm not up to anything—well, except for trying to locate my lost shoe. Unfortunately, it was not where I know I lost it, which might, in all honesty, be a cause for some concern."

"I thought your shoe broke," Asher said, falling into step beside her as she continued walking down the hallway.

"Lucy said my shoe broke. I simply didn't bother to correct her."

"Why didn't you correct her?"

Permilia shrugged. "It would have taken a great deal of effort, and it would have drawn unfortunate questions, questions I didn't believe you'd care to have me address in front of everyone."

"Ah, I see we're back to the whole someone-wants-me-dead business."

119

She blew out a breath. "I've heard that denial is often the first response to unpleasant news, but really, Asher, you're going to have to accept the idea sooner or later. I would recommend sooner since it really did seem as if these men meant business, and business of the murderous type."

Asher reached out, took hold of her arm, and pulled her to a stop. "I'm not certain, since it's just the two of us now, why you're continuing on with this absurd story you've made up."

Permilia's eyes flashed. "Do I strike you as the type of woman who would be prone to making up absurd stories?"

"Well, no, but you also don't strike me as a woman who'd be prone to abusing a poor man's shin, but that didn't seem to stop you from abusing mine earlier."

"As has been duly noted, I'm not wearing any shoes, so it's highly unlikely I hurt you, but—" she bit her lip—"I will apologize for kicking you. I've never been prone to violence before, but . . . something about you just seems to bring it out in me."

The corners of his lips began to twitch. "Should I take that as a compliment?"

"I don't believe so."

"Very well, I'll be on my guard from this point forward, but I do appreciate the apology, and accept it wholeheartedly." He cleared his throat. "And in the spirit of the moment, I would like to extend you an apology as well, since it wasn't well done of me at all to disclose something to your stepmother that you obviously meant to keep strictly between the two of us."

Permilia inclined her head. "Apology accepted, and at least you didn't get around to disclosing what I said about Ida suggesting I try out my feminine wiles on you. That would have no doubt resulted in her swooning right on the spot, after she'd severed the tenuous ties we share as stepmother and stepdaughter, of course." She blew out a breath. "I'm still not certain why you took what I said about your upcoming murder as being another attempt on my part to have you convince Ida you find me amusing."

"How else was I to take it?"

Her lips thinned. "You should have taken it for what it was meant to be—a warning about a conversation I'd overheard about an imminent threat to your life."

Not having the faintest idea how he should respond to that, Asher settled on simply watching her for a long moment, the earnestness he discovered in her eyes doing much to convince him that she truly thought she'd overheard a conversation centered around his murder.

Resisting the great urge he had to laugh, while finding himself charmed in spite of the absurdity of the situation because she did seem very concerned about his well-being, he took hold of her hand, giving it a good squeeze.

"Surely you must realize that you simply misunderstood the conversation you overheard," he began, wincing when Permilia took to looking furious with him again as she tugged her hand back.

"I misunderstood nothing."

Asher leaned toward her. "Come now, Permilia. Don't you find it somewhat difficult to believe that anyone would want me dead?"

"Not at this particular moment."

He pretended he hadn't heard her. "What I'm fairly certain happened is this—you walked in on a conversation that you misunderstood to be one revolving around a murder plot, but was clearly nothing of the sort." He smiled. "If you approach this logically, as I'm sure you're quite capable of doing, you'll agree that it makes absolutely no sense for anyone to plan out a murder while in the midst of a ball. Why, balls are notorious for being filled with people, which . . ."

"I didn't walk in on the men planning your murder, Asher,"

121

she interrupted. "They happened upon me when I was in a very remote part of this house, trying to track down Mrs. Davenport for Gertrude."

"Why would you have needed to track down Mrs. Davenport?"

She crossed her arms over her chest. "Don't think you can distract me, Asher. Mrs. Davenport has absolutely nothing to do with the true conversation at hand, which is, if you've forgotten, a plot that is currently brewing that centers around the desire to see you good and dead."

"Have you always been so dramatic?"

Turning smartly around, she began marching down the hallway. "I'm not being dramatic."

Breaking into a very rapid stride in order to catch up with her, Asher frowned. "Explain, then, how you were able to get away from would-be murderers."

"If I'd had a choice in the matter, I would have simply waited until they'd completed their nasty conversation, but . . . Mrs. Davenport and her untimely sneeze put a rapid end to that plan."

The corners of his lips began to twitch again. "Of course there would be an untimely sneeze."

She stopped in her tracks. "I don't appreciate you mocking me."

"I wasn't mocking you," he argued. "It was more along the lines of appreciating your apparent proficiency with weaving a thrilling story."

She stuck her nose straight in the air and began marching down the hallway again, not stopping or even looking at him until she reached the end of the hallway. Moving over to the grand staircase, she peered over the banister, perusing the surroundings below her.

"May I dare hope the men wanting to murder me are lingering about?" he couldn't resist asking.

"I didn't *see* the men," she said, not bothering to look his way. "As I mentioned before you began making fun of me, Mrs. Davenport sneezed, which alerted the criminals to our location. In order to make our escape, we had to jump into a dumbwaiter and plummet our way to the kitchen, which is exactly how I ended up losing my shoe."

Asher found he was incapable of forming so much as a single word of response to that statement, but luckily, Permilia didn't seem to expect a response, as she continued on with her wild tale.

"It fell off my foot, you see, as I was stuffing myself into the dumbwaiter, but when I went back to that room just now, it was gone." She bit her lip. "I do hope those men didn't abscond with it, but"—her eyes grew wide—"it would be a definite clue for them to use to track me down."

"Why would they want to track you down?"

"Because they obviously believe I can identify them, of course." She froze in the act of bending over the banister. "Oh dear, it's the Vanderbilt servant who saw Mrs. Davenport and me jump out of the dumbwaiter once it reached the kitchen. I'm afraid he didn't seem to believe the story Mrs. Davenport made up to explain what we were doing in the dumbwaiter."

Trying as hard as he could to swallow the laugh currently bubbling up in his throat, Asher found himself looking directly into Permilia's eyes when she straightened and turned, apparently done with her perusing.

"What?" she demanded, and that was all it took for him to lose the slight bit of control he'd had over his amusement.

Laughter burst out of his mouth and continued for a long moment as everything she'd told him played again and again in his mind, especially the part about stuffing herself into a dumbwaiter, along with Mrs. Davenport, a society matron he couldn't actually imagine participating in something so . . . ridiculous.

Clutching his stomach when he began to get a stitch, he drew in a breath of much-needed air and wiped eyes that had begun to water. His last hiccup of amusement turned into something of a yelp, though, when Permilia drew back her leg and kicked him again, this time as if she truly meant it.

Sobering as best he could, he found her shaking out the folds of her skirt right before she leveled a glare on him.

"You're an idiot. But even though you are an idiot, I do hope you'll consider what I've said and proceed forward with at least a modicum of caution. I would so hate to read in those articles you apparently believe are not for ladies that you've met with a nasty demise."

Spinning around, she dashed straightaway, vanishing down the steps before he had the presence of mind to stop her.

CHAPTER
ELEVEN

"I've never been one to frequently share my opinions with others, Asher, finding that most people truly don't appreciate those opinions in the end. However, since you are one of my very closest friends, I fear it is my duty to tell you where you went horribly, horribly wrong two nights ago at the Vanderbilt ball."

Asher pulled back on the reins and brought his horse, Vagabond, out of his canter and into a walk. Turning in the saddle, he directed his attention toward a man he truly did consider a good friend, Mr. Harrison Sinclair.

As was the case more often than not, it took a great deal of effort on Asher's part to refrain from wincing as his gaze traveled over the man riding beside him.

That Harrison was not a gentleman who embraced an enthusiasm for fashion was immediately evident to anyone who took the time to look closely at the man.

Today Harrison was sporting a tweed riding coat that was frayed at the cuffs, although it did afford the man the proper amount of warmth on what had turned out to be a remarkably chilly end-of-March day. His buff-colored trousers were splattered with mud and had an interesting insert of purple fabric—that did not match any of the colors in his tweed jacket—running down the seams. Granted, given that the trousers were tucked into knee-high boots that hadn't seen a good polishing in what looked like forever, a person was highly unlikely to notice the lack of matching.

Harrison's dark hair, worn far longer than fashion dictated, was tied back with a piece of fabric at the nape of the man's neck, that fabric having been procured from the very hem of the jacket the man was currently wearing.

After Harrison had complained about the wind whipping his hair into his eyes, Asher had just been in the process of pulling out a spare neckcloth he had in his pocket, when he'd heard the sound of ripping. Looking up, he'd discovered Harrison going about the business of tying back his hair, completely unperturbed that he'd just ripped the hem from his coat.

Considering Harrison lacked even the most cursory interest in anything fashionable, and Asher lacked an interest in matters of a nautical nature—which was what consumed Harrison most of the time, since he and his family operated a lucrative shipping business—it was rather surprising they'd even become friends.

"Honestly, Asher, if I'd known you'd descend into a stupor over me voicing my opinion, I would certainly have refrained from broaching the subject of the Vanderbilt ball."

Blinking directly out of his thoughts, Asher smiled. "Forgive me, Harrison. I fear I got distracted by thoughts of your abysmal sense of style and why you're wearing trousers with purple attached to them. Nevertheless, even though your interesting choice of attire today has clearly caused me to forget all semblance of good manners, I now promise to give you my undivided attention. Although . . . now that I think about it . . ." He glanced at the purple again and quickly averted his gaze. "It might be best if I looked at the lovely scenery Central Park has to offer instead of looking at you."

"Won't that make it next to impossible to give me that undivided attention you just promised?"

"Well, indeed, but at least I'll be able to focus on your words, not focus on . . ." Asher gestured to the horror sitting atop a fine horse by the name of Rupert and grinned.

Harrison returned the grin, that action causing the two young ladies who were passing them on the opposite side of the gravel path, along with their chaperone, to practically fall off their horses as they immediately took to giggling and blatantly gawking Harrison's way.

Harrison, as was frequently the case, didn't appear to notice the ladies, completely oblivious to the idea they found his dark hair, formidable build, pale blue eyes, and hawkish features worthy of gawking and giggles.

"If you must know, I thought the purple in my trousers added a dash of style."

Asher rolled his eyes. "How is it even possible that you and I are friends?"

"I don't bore you like most of your society friends, and you don't bore me since you—even with having grown up with that proverbial silver spoon in your mouth—have an incredibly innovative nature."

"I suppose we do rub along quite nicely at that, and I must admit that there's always been something different about you, Harrison—a moral compass, so to speak, that I've always admired. That right there is why you're one of the few people who know about that silver spoon of mine being practically wrenched out of my mouth years ago."

Harrison gave a nod. "I'm certain you know that I'm honored you've trusted me with that information, although I've always wondered why you chose to tell me about your troubles and not one of your other friends."

"You've never been a man to put on airs, Harrison. Because

of that, I knew you wouldn't judge me harshly because of my fall from financial grace."

"You were little more than a boy when your family lost the majority of their money," Harrison pointed out.

"Quite, but . . . society being what it is, I would have been ostracized from my circle of friends if word had gotten around about the loss of most of our fortune. I would have also been judged over that loss as well, and don't even get me started on what would have happened if society had learned we were meeting our bills by hocking our most valuable possessions."

"Which is exactly why I've never had an interest in joining your illustrious circles, although I'm not opposed to joining you for a meal here and there at a few of your clubs." Harrison smiled. "They do seem to serve only the finest dishes at those clubs of yours. But getting back to the conversation at hand, I now find myself curious as to who else knows about what happened to your family or, better yet, what it took for you to rebuild the fortune that was lost."

Asher shrugged. "You know the three men I approached to invest in Rutherford & Company, since you're an investor as well, and"—he tilted his head—"I suppose the only other person to know besides direct family members would be Reverend Orville Drew of Trinity Church."

"Why would you have told Reverend Drew?"

Asher shrugged. "I didn't have much choice in the matter. Trinity Church sent out notices quite a few years back that they were going to be collecting additional fees in order to maintain all the family-owned pews. Because my family didn't have enough money to cover those fees, I had to ask Reverend Drew to allow me to pay a little every month until we were able to get a decent price for some of my mother's jewelry."

Frowning, Harrison slowed his horse to a crawl. "Am I to understand that a person can actually buy a pew?"

"Churches have been putting up pews for auction for years. The more advantageous the position of the pew, the dearer it costs. But if it makes you feel any better, the funds raised from those pews do go toward operating expenses."

Harrison's frown deepened. "Are certain promises ever alluded to with the purchase of these pews, such as a special place in heaven for those with enough funds to support a church in such a way?"

"My grandfather Rutherford is the one who originally bought our family pew, so I can't speak with any authority on what might or might not have been promised. But in defense of the practice, the church has managed to make attendance more regular. Owning a pew is a rather expensive endeavor, and one does enjoy getting one's worth out of such an expense."

"I suppose that would encourage attendance."

"Indeed," Asher said as another group of ladies rode past them, smiling and fluttering their lashes before they galloped off ahead, turning every now and again to smile back at Asher and Harrison. "But getting back to our original conversation, weren't you about to disclose one of your less than frequent opinions to me before we got distracted by your nonexistent fashion sense, buying pews, and the somewhat tarnished silver spoon I once had in my mouth?"

Harrison blinked. "I'd forgotten all about sharing my opinion with you." He clicked his tongue and urged his horse off the gravel path and onto a dirt path, gesturing with a hand for Asher to follow him.

Winding through the trees, Harrison brought his horse to a stop underneath a tree that had yet to bud and climbed down from the saddle.

Doing the same a moment later, Asher joined his friend by the trunk of the tree and arched a brow.

Harrison smiled. "I didn't want to be overheard by any of the young ladies who keep passing by us."

"You've noticed them?"

"They'd be difficult to miss. However, since I believe it does both of us good to vacate our respected businesses every now and again, I'm not willing to give up our rides, even with the annoying attention you draw." Harrison folded his arms over his chest and looked rather disgusted. "You could at least try being less charming, though. That might encourage the ladies to give us a wider berth, and perhaps if you stopped grooming yourself so well, and letting your hair get a bit mussed, well . . . that might make you less noticeable."

"I don't believe *I'm* the one responsible for drawing the attention."

"Because *so* many society ladies hold an interest in a man who grew up on the docks," Harrison muttered before he waved away Asher's protest. "I'm not ashamed of my upbringing, Asher, so there's no need to look so concerned. But getting back to that opinion of mine. I—"

"I think I'd rather discuss the delusion you seem to be clinging to—the one where you're not the gentleman drawing all of the lady interest, and . . ."

"The opinion I've been trying to share with you," Harrison began in an overly loud voice, drowning out whatever else Asher might have been about to say, "is this. . . ." He paused, nodded in clear approval when Asher stopped trying to talk, and continued. "I've been considering what you disclosed to me regarding what transpired at the Vanderbilt ball, and I've decided that where you made the gravest mistake in regard to Miss Permilia Griswold was when you laughed."

"In my defense, Harrison, I thought she was simply perpetuating a bit of a lark."

"Forgive me, Asher, for you know I'm not always knowledgeable concerning the rules of gentlemanly behavior, but I'm somewhat certain that laughing at a lady, especially when said lady is not laughing with you, might be at the top of a what-not-to-do list."

Asher leaned back against the trunk of the tree. "You're quite right, Harrison, and I do realize that I shouldn't have laughed. But it never crossed my mind that she was serious. If you'll recall, she stumbled up to our table—shoeless, at that—and announced, in an overly dramatic tone, that she'd been made privy to a plot that concerned the murder of . . . me."

Harrison cocked a dark brow Asher's way. "I've never known plots of murder to be a source of amusement."

Cocking a brow of his own right back, Asher tilted his head. "You don't honestly believe she was telling the truth about that, do you?"

"You've never led me to believe in the conversations we've had regarding Miss Permilia Griswold that she's a woman prone to exaggeration, so . . . yes, I do believe she was telling the truth."

"There is absolutely no reason for anyone to want to murder me. I'm a simple merchant."

"There's nothing simple about you, Asher," Harrison returned. "And far be it from me to point out the obvious, but I can think of a long list of people who might want to do you in."

"I can't think of a single one. Well, except perhaps for Permilia, since she is incredibly put out with me at the moment. But other than her, I can think of no one who would want to kill me."

"You've made a habit out of luring the very best salesladies away from the leading stores in this city. That right there has earned you at least a dozen enemies."

"The owners of those other stores are more than welcome to lure their old employees right back. They simply need to offer them a competitive wage."

"It is well known that you're paying your employees a higher wage than anyone else out there."

"Which is simply good business."

"Others don't see it that way. They see it as your setting far too high a standard for *all* workers in the city, and that, my friend, is exactly why you may very well have been marked for death."

"I think Permilia's sense of the dramatic is rubbing off on you, because—"

The rest of what Asher had been about to say got lost when an honest-to-goodness arrow whizzed past his ear and firmly lodged in the trunk of the tree he was leaning against.

For a second he simply stared at the arrow, before he turned and looked at Harrison.

"On my word, I didn't realize we'd traveled close to the archery range, but . . . someone is certainly a bad shot since—"

Another arrow struck the tree, a mere foot above his head.

Both he and Harrison dropped to the ground as arrow number three came hurtling out of a grove of trees, this time missing the tree and whizzing right on by.

Rolling to the right to avoid Vagabond's hooves—the arrows seemingly having spooked not only his but Harrison's horse as well—Asher crawled his way to the back side of the tree, finding Harrison already there, wiping blood from his cheek with the sleeve of his tweed coat.

"Were you hit?" Asher asked, peering around the trunk to make certain they weren't about to get ambushed.

"Piece of flying bark," Harrison muttered before he dug into his jacket pocket, producing a small pistol a second later. Cocking it, he sent Asher a smile. "You might want to begin composing a suitable apology since it does seem as if Miss Griswold was not being at all overly dramatic about your impending demise."

"We have no proof as of yet that someone is currently trying to do me in. As I mentioned, we might simply be too close to the archery range."

"It's on the other side of Central Park, past the pond."

"Oh yes, quite right, but Central Park is also known to be a prime spot for robbers to lurk. Perhaps someone took notice of your unusual trousers and has decided they simply had to part you from them."

"Now you're just being obstinate." Harrison peered around the trunk before he blew out a breath. "The horses just bolted through those trees."

"So much for making a fast getaway." Asher dug a hand into his jacket pocket, hoping to find something that could be used as a weapon. Pulling out a bag of sweets he'd been sent to sample for the confectionery shop he'd recently added to his first floor, he set it on the ground and tried again. A moment later he shook his head in disgust as he looked over the contents he'd pulled out—a gentleman's cufflink he'd found on the floor of the men's jewelry department, a necktie, a bottle of cologne he'd been meaning to sample, and a powder puff one of his salesladies had handed him, trying to convince him that offering beauty products in a visible part of the store would be an enormous profit maker.

He couldn't help but think it was a sad state of affairs that he had not a single item that could be used as a weapon, unless he could get close enough to the arrow-shooting criminal to blind him by dousing him with the cologne.

"Is that a . . . powder puff?"

Asher stuffed the puff, along with the candy and the necktie, back into his pocket. "I was hoping I'd have something more useful stashed away."

"If that was a bag of candy you just stuck in your pocket, it could be useful."

Fishing the bag back out again, he handed it over to Harrison. "Useful how?"

Harrison pulled open the string, dumped a handful of the sweets into his hand, and promptly began munching on them. Swallowing, he caught Asher's eye. "I'm starving, and I can't concentrate when I'm starving."

"Which I can certainly understand, but I don't actually believe this is the proper time for a snack," Asher returned. "If you've forgotten, someone is still out there, leveling arrows at us."

"Well, yes, that is true, but if they were going to continue attacking us, they'd have already made their move. I'd say they are lying in wait." Harrison returned his attention to the bag of sweets. "I must say, these are beyond delicious. Just the right amount of orange and cream flavoring, but I do wonder how the maker achieved that?"

Asher ignored the question. "How do you know they have switched to lying in wait?"

"I grew up on the streets. I know things." Harrison popped another sweet into his mouth and let out a moan. "Oh, these are divine."

"I'll keep that in mind when I meet with the producer of the sweets next week, but getting back to the dilemma at hand, should we make a run for it?"

"Not unless you want a backside filled with arrows. I would bet good money the person shooting at us is still out there, just biding his time."

"So we're to just sit here and . . ." Asher stopped speaking, frowning when he heard the clear sound of wheels rumbling over the ground. Peering around the tree, he saw what looked to be a milk wagon approaching, and approaching fast. Pulling back, he held out his hand. "May I borrow the pistol?"

"If memory serves me correctly, you're not a very good shot."

"The only time you've ever seen me shoot is when we participated in that fox hunt over on Long Island, but I happen to like foxes, so I missed on purpose."

"You almost shot Mr. Beaumont instead."

"That's a risk gentlemen must take when they foolishly decide to set hounds and men after helpless foxes."

"Is that why you don't offer furs in your store?"

"While this is a fascinating discussion, Harrison, we are being approached by what I would consider a threat, so . . . may I have your pistol?"

"If you can't shoot a fox, you're certainly not going to be able to shoot a person, so . . ."

The next second, Asher was left with only Harrison's backside for company as his friend crawled around the tree, apparently in order to aim the pistol at the wagon still trundling their way.

"I shall be quite cross if you shoot me, sir, especially since Miss Cadwalader and I have gone to the very great bother of coming to rescue you," a voice rang out, a voice that sounded, interestingly enough, as if it might just belong to Permilia.

CHAPTER
TWELVE

Aiming the delivery wagon she'd borrowed from Mrs. Davenport toward the spot where Asher and another gentleman were pinned down, Permilia pulled back on the reins, slowing their speed but not bringing the wagon to a complete stop. Hoping the height of the milk compartment that made up the body of the wagon would be high enough to provide the gentlemen with much-needed cover, she gestured in what she thought was a fairly self-explanatory way for them to run and join her.

To her extreme annoyance, the gentlemen remained on the ground . . . until the sound of gunfire rang through the air. Before she could do more than jump in her seat, the two men were on their feet and bolting directly her way.

"Gertrude, open the door," she yelled as her horse, a temperamental beast by the name of Mr. Merriweather, suddenly bucked and jerked forward, almost causing her to lose her seat.

Just as Mr. Merriweather's front hooves hit the ground again, the side door of the milk compartment flew open and one of the men jumped in as the other man, one who turned out to be Asher, flung himself onto the seat beside her, and . . . they were off.

"Where are the reins?" Asher yelled.

She nodded toward where the reins were flapping out of reach, having been torn out of her hands when the gunshots had sent her horse into a frenzy.

Asher leaned forward, stopping when Permilia flung out a hand in front of him. "Don't, you could lose your seat," she yelled. "Besides, Mr. Merriweather will calm down soon enough, and he's quite used to being given his head. Just hold on. And if you're the praying type, I'd think about praying for a clear path ahead."

Asher looked at her as if she'd lost her mind, as Mr. Merriweather bolted to the right, a direct result of another bullet being fired their way, this one nicking the side of the delivery wagon.

The bolting, unfortunately, had them trundling straight off the groomed path and directly into a wooded area, the denseness of the trees a clear sign that wagons were not actually supposed to be driven through this particular part of Central Park.

With every bump, rock, and bush they ran over, grunts erupted from the interior of the wagon, but except for closing her eyes and whispering a rather frantic prayer of her own for protection, Permilia was helpless to do anything other than hold on. Her only solace was that with every gallop forward, Mr. Merriweather was delivering them farther and farther away from the person who'd been trying to kill not only Asher, but apparently anyone else who happened to stand in the way of that killing.

Quite honestly, if she'd been the one to hire the man, she'd be a bit concerned over his lack of discretion, especially since the man she'd overheard the night of the Vanderbilt ball—a murderer-for-hire, no less—had demanded additional pay in order to maintain that discretion.

Any other thoughts on the matter were pushed firmly aside when Mr. Merriweather reached the end of the trees and burst back onto one of the groomed trails that circled Central Park. To her relief, he immediately slowed to a canter, and then a walk, tossing his head as if to say he was quite proud of himself for getting everyone to safety.

Leaning forward when she decided it was safe to fetch the reins, she grabbed hold of them and sat back on the seat, turning to find Asher watching her with an unusual expression on his face.

"Is something the matter?" she asked.

"What are you wearing?"

"We've just barely made an escape with our very lives and the first thing you have to ask is what I'm wearing?"

Asher leaned to the right and looked behind them, then turned back to her as he resettled himself on the hard seat of the wagon. "I don't see anyone chasing after us, and I've always been of the belief that ladies enjoy being distracted when they're plunged into a disturbing incident."

Wrinkling her nose, Permilia tightened her grip on the reins. "Do you know many ladies who've been plunged into disturbing incidents?"

"None that spring to mind at this moment, but again, my thoughts are going every which way right now, probably due to all the excitement I've just experienced."

"Then perhaps I should be trying to distract you, instead of the other way around."

He smiled and inclined his head. "Perhaps you should. So . . . explain your outfit."

Finding herself unable to resist his smile, Permilia flipped back one of the braids of the wig Mrs. Davenport had insisted completed her disguise. "I'm a milkmaid, of course, complete with braids for my hairstyle, a lovely apron that apparently all milkmaids are supposed to wear, and . . ." She held out a foot. "Serviceable boots that Mrs. Davenport insisted I needed to complete the look."

"Mrs. Davenport provided you with your costume?"

"You don't really believe I keep a milkmaid disguise at the ready, do you?"

"Excellent point, but . . . she didn't have this milk wagon simply lying around for you to use as well, did she?"

"Curiously enough, she did, as well as an entire building filled with other conveyances, one of which I do believe was a wagon decked out for a grand funeral, complete with glass in the windows and polished to a high shine."

"Any idea as to why Mrs. Davenport has such a collection of peculiar items?"

"I'm not certain, although I'm coming to the conclusion that Mrs. Davenport is one of those unusual ladies who seems to enjoy collecting all manner of objects, such as . . ."

"Figurines of cats," Gertrude suddenly said as she slid open the conversation panel that separated her from Permilia. "She has all sorts of glass cats, although, oddly enough, she has no interest in obtaining a real cat."

"That is odd, Miss Cadwalader," Asher said, swiveling around on the seat right as Permilia did the same.

Gertrude's eyes, practically the only part of her that could be seen through the conversation panel, crinkled at the corners. "Please call me Gertrude, Mr. Rutherford. It seems appropriate considering the less than formal atmosphere we currently find ourselves in."

"I would be honored to forgo the usual formalities, Gertrude, and please feel free to call me Asher."

"Thank you," Gertrude returned. "And now that we've gotten that out of the way, as well as agreeing, I'm sure, that Mrs. Davenport does seem to embrace a highly interesting attitude when it comes to her wide variety of possessions . . . allow me to broach the subject of the gentleman back here with me."

Asher blinked. "Is something the matter with Harrison?"

"Harrison is the gentleman who jumped in here with me?"

"Oh, forgive me, Gertrude," Asher said. "That's Mr. Harrison Sinclair, but did he not bother to introduce himself?"

"I'm afraid he's incapable of that at the moment. He was knocked in the head with one, or perhaps more than one, of the milk bottles that came crashing off the shelves when we launched into that wild ride in order to escape. I fear the gentleman's been rendered somewhat . . . woozy."

"Is he bleeding?" Permilia asked.

"Hard to say since the battery lights Mrs. Davenport installed back here don't afford the best light, and the milk bottles have only recently stopped rumbling around the back."

"I'm fine, barely bleeding at all," a voice yelled from somewhere behind Gertrude.

"What do you think you're doing, sir?" Gertrude demanded, turning from the panel. "Sit back down right this minute."

"It's Harrison, not sir, and . . . you're a pretty little thing, aren't you? I must say, those trousers are simply delightful. Although . . . why do you look as if you've been dipped directly into a sunset?"

Asher turned to Permilia. "Harrison has obviously taken quite the blow to his head, because he's not one to wax poetic or call a lady a *pretty little thing*. He's evidently hallucinating as well, since he seems to believe Gertrude is orange."

Gertrude stuck her face back up to the window and let out a snort. "I really am orange, but I'll leave Permilia to explain the reason for that." Gertrude switched her attention to Permilia. "Perhaps we should consider swinging by a hospital and having a physician take a gander at . . . Mr. Sinclair, did you say?"

"Mr. Sinclair is my father. I'm just Harrison."

"Fine, Just Harrison," Gertrude returned. "I'm Miss Cadwalader, but you may call me Gertrude."

"Gertrude is my favorite name."

Gertrude released a sigh and caught Permilia's eye again. "May I suggest you urge Mr. Merriweather into a bit of a trot? Mr. Sinclair . . ."

"Just Harrison," Harrison corrected.

"Just Harrison," Gertrude continued, "must have sustained a far greater injury to his head than I first thought, so I'll keep an eye on him while you drive us to the hospital. The one off Broadway is probably the closest, and it's not too far from Asher's store." With that, Gertrude slid the panel shut again and disappeared from sight.

Setting Mr. Merriweather into a trot, Permilia directed him out of Central Park and onto Fifth Avenue a short time later. Relief slid down her spine as she maneuvered the wagon through the busy street, knowing that it would be next to impossible, not to mention exceedingly foolish, for any would-be assassin to make another attempt on Asher's life in full view of so many people.

"So . . . how'd Gertrude get orange skin?" Asher asked after she'd gotten Mr. Merriweather headed in the right direction.

"Mrs. Davenport, of course." Permilia shook her head. "She became a little obsessive and decided that Gertrude, what with her pale skin and all, looked less than authentic as a milk wagon driver. The next thing you know, before either Gertrude or I had the presence of mind to protest, she'd whipped up a concoction that we believe she made out of tea, sugar, and some type of beechwood stain she happened to have on hand, which she then proceeded to slather over Gertrude's face, neck, and arms. Unfortunately, instead of giving her skin a weathered tint, it turned her orange."

"Do you suppose it'll wash off?"

"Hard to tell at this point, but it didn't even fade when Gertrude washed her hands before we left Mrs. Davenport's house, which is why she's not currently driving the wagon." Permilia smiled. "At least Gertrude can take a little solace in the fact that the social season has wrapped up and society is leaving town in droves."

"I suppose if there's any solace to be found in being orange, that would be a leading one, but—tell me this—how is it that you and Gertrude were on hand to rescue me and Harrison from that assailant?"

"I've been following you for two days."

Asher blinked. "Why would you do that? Because, forgive me, but after we parted ways at the Vanderbilt ball, I was of the belief you were beyond annoyed with me."

"I'm *still* annoyed with you, but that's no reason to stand idly by and allow someone to kill you."

"I realize that you're a most unusual lady, but it's hardly a lady's place to intercede on a gentleman's behalf simply because she's of the belief someone is determined to kill that gentleman."

Permilia's lips thinned. "And here I was hoping that you might have a more progressive attitude toward women, what with the number of them you employ in your store."

"That has nothing to do with anything," Asher argued. "I employ those women in positions that are acceptable for women to hold—positions that only demand they present merchandise to customers in a pleasing manner, which certainly doesn't see them placed directly in harm's way."

"What about the women who are not fortunate enough to obtain employment in environments such as your store provides, who are forced to labor in the shirtwaist factories and laundries?"

"I'm not sure where you're going with this conversation."

"No one bothers to concern themselves with those women or the dangers they face every time they go to work."

Asher's brows drew together. "Have we moved on to a discussion of the suffrage movement now, because I must caution you to have a care with that type of talk, Permilia. It will not endear you to society in the least if it becomes known you're a supporter of that particular movement."

Drawing herself up, Permilia narrowed her eyes at him. "I am a staunch supporter of the suffrage movement, and I've never been one to hide that, especially since that type of clandestine behavior would do a disservice to our cause."

"You don't actually believe it's a serious cause, do you?"

"Why is it that men always believe that any cause a woman may support is anything but serious, as if the abuse we've suffered while petitioning for basic rights could ever be considered a frivolous matter?" She lifted her chin. "You have a workforce made up of a great deal of women. I truly cannot believe that deep down—very deep down, apparently—you don't feel that those women are just as capable of doing their respective jobs as the men you employ."

"Of course they're just as capable in some capacities, especially since my sales would certainly suffer in the unmentionables department if I tried to hire men to sell the goods there."

Her hands tightened on the reins. "Would you ever consider hiring on a lady in a managerial capacity?"

"I've already attracted unpleasant attention for paying my workers higher wages, Permilia. I'd be run out of the city if I took to hiring women in positions that are always reserved for men."

"I really should have let at least one arrow hit you, directly in the head." When his eyes widened, she hurried to clarify. "Not to kill you—just to knock some sense into that unprogressive mind of yours."

"My mind is fine, thank you very much. But how is it that we got caught up in such a ridiculous conversation to begin with?"

"You're only finding it ridiculous because you're not winning any points. Although, given that you found my conversation to be ridiculous the night of the ball, when I was trying to deliver to you what turned out to be a most prudent warning, one has to now wonder if you find most conversations you have with women to be ridiculous."

Asher simply looked at her for a long moment before he completely changed the subject again. "I tried to call on you, twice in fact, over the past two days to apologize for upsetting you the night of the ball. I was told by your butler on both occasions that you were not receiving callers."

"I couldn't very well receive you, or any callers for that matter, since I was trailing behind you both times you stopped at my home."

"You were . . . behind me?"

"I told you I'd decided to watch over you. And watching over a person who more than likely isn't going to like that watching over requires a great deal of stealth—stealth I was obviously successful in achieving since you never noticed me." She smiled. "Yesterday I was garbed as a widow, all in black and driving a small pony cart—one that Mr. Merriweather absolutely loathes to pull, finding it, I believe, much too small and simple for his tastes."

"Your understanding of your horse is somewhat disturbing, although I'm certain Mr. Merriweather will be absolutely delighted to learn that you'll no longer be taking him out on stealthy endeavors, which instead should see him only attached to stately carriages or . . . ridden sidesaddle."

"Mr. Merriweather prefers for me to ride him astride, which is why I never ride him in Central Park, but travel up the Hudson when I want to allow him to really stretch his legs."

"I'm going to pretend you didn't just divulge that to me, since the idea of you riding at what must amount to breakneck speed chills me to my toes, as does the thought of you trailing after me, something you're now going to promise you'll cease doing."

"As soon as I have your promise that you'll take the proper precautions in order to stay alive—such as hiring on a few guards and notifying the appropriate authorities about the attempt on your life—I'll do just that."

"I'm a man."

She reached over and patted his leg. "How very good of you to realize that, Asher, but being a man does not guarantee you'll be able to keep yourself alive. Men are killed on a daily basis, and I will not allow you to go that way simply because you've decided to be a bit of an idiot."

"I'm not an idiot."

"You may continue telling yourself that, but since you didn't even bother to disrupt your very rigid schedule, after I disclosed a murder plot against you, I'm not going to agree with your declaration."

"I don't keep a rigid schedule."

"From what I've been able to learn through following you as well as doing some sleuthing around your store—asking some innocent questions while I've been pretending to shop—you maintain an exceptionally rigid schedule. You arrive at your store at precisely eight in the morning every day—except for Sunday, when you're closed. You then spend the next four hours doing whatever business you need to attend to inside your store, before leaving at exactly twelve noon to travel to either the Astor Hotel or the Union Club in order to get a bite to eat. You then travel to Central Park and ride around for forty minutes, returning to your store precisely at two, staying there until six in the evening. You then ride home, usually on your horse, unless it's raining, which means you'll take one of the store carriages, and then depart two hours later to attend the opera, dinner, or a ball."

"You found all of that out through . . . your sleuthing?"

"That and following you around for the past two days."

"Weren't you bored?"

Since she certainly couldn't tell him that she'd spent a good portion of her first day while he was attending to business writing her column about the Vanderbilt ball, she settled for sending him a smile and a shrug. "Why do you think Gertrude's with me?"

"She's hardly much of a companion, being stuck in the compartment because she's turned orange and all."

"True, which is why you're going to promise me here and now that you'll seek out proper protection by alerting the authorities and hiring on men to watch out for you. If you'll promise me that, I'll promise that Gertrude and I will abandon further surveillance missions, which will allow us to discontinue whiling away our days in boredom."

"You're very annoying." Asher shifted on the wagon seat, his shifting coming to an abrupt end when he leaned forward, his gaze sharpening on something in the street.

"Is that . . . the Huxley sisters?"

Craning her neck, Permilia saw an old-fashioned buggy weaving a bit dangerously in and out of traffic, as was often the case when one of the Huxley sisters was driving it. "That is their buggy, but it's not unusual to see them driving toward Broadway, especially since they live just past your store."

"True, but do you see what they have trailing behind their buggy?"

Lifting up on the seat in order to get a better view, Permilia searched through the crowded street again, glancing past other carriages, delivery wagons, and . . .

She abruptly retook her seat. "They have your horse—and

Harrison Sinclair's horse as well, I have to imagine—attached to the back of their buggy."

"Indeed, which begs the question . . . where did they find the horses and where are they taking them?"

"I would think they're heading to your store, since everyone on Broadway is familiar with Vagabond. He's a most splendid animal with very distinctive markings on his head and forelegs."

"You've noticed Vagabond's markings?"

"I'm a wallflower, Asher. We spend most of our time noticing things."

"What an interesting thought, and one I'd never considered before. But getting back to the spinster sisters, it seems a little out of character for them to be returning my horse. They're not known to be overly helpful types."

Permilia frowned. "Why is it that when people remark on women who have not married by a certain age, they always describe them as spinsters in exactly the condescending tone of voice you just used? Unmarried men of advanced ages are always referred to as gentlemen bachelors instead of something equally insulting such as . . . crusty curmudgeons or—"

"Forgive me for interrupting what I'm certain is going to be a blistering lecture in which more of my many deficiencies will be brought to light, but . . . the hospital is just up ahead, which means you need to pull the wagon over. And while you see Harrison settled, I'm going to go see about getting our horses back."

"But I don't even know Harrison Sinclair, nor does Gertrude."

"Gertrude's had plenty of time to become acquainted with him, and you saw him that once in Central Park when you were ice-skating. Besides, even though you don't know him well—"

"Or at all," Permilia interrupted.

"It's a proven fact that we gentlemen prefer to be seen after by feminine sorts when we're suffering from an injury or malady.

147

That means Harrison is more likely to enjoy you and Gertrude seeing after him than having me do the deed." He smiled. "Besides, Harrison will want his horse after he's finished at the hospital, and this way, we'll not waste time if you see after him and I see after his horse."

"But you can't go charging up Broadway on your own. If you've forgotten, you just escaped from a mad assassin, one who may even now be lying in wait for you."

"I highly doubt the person who failed to kill me earlier has had the proper amount of time to enact *another* plan to kill me, so . . . I'll meet you back at Rutherford & Company after you've seen Harrison properly attended to, or if you don't show up there in a timely fashion, I'll come back to the hospital."

Edging Mr. Merriweather to the side of the street and bringing him to a stop directly beside the hospital, Permilia blew out a breath. "What if the Huxley sisters don't see fit to return the horses to your store but take them back to their home?"

"Then I suppose I'll be forced to pay them a call."

"They're not ladies you should be visiting on your own. It is well known throughout society that they're beyond peculiar."

Asher sat forward on the seat. "While there's no arguing with that, I certainly don't believe the Misses Huxley were behind the plot to kill me."

Opening her mouth with an argument on the tip of her tongue, Permilia found herself swallowing that argument when Asher jumped off the wagon seat, sent her one of his annoyingly charming smiles, and began to stride down the street without allowing her the opportunity of directing even a single additional word of warning his way.

CHAPTER
THIRTEEN

Striding down the sidewalk next to Broadway, Asher exchanged nods with a gentleman who managed the bank a few buildings down from Rutherford & Company. Reaching up to tip his hat to a group of ladies strolling his way, he lowered his hand when he discovered he seemed to be missing his hat and settled for sending the ladies an inclination of his head instead.

Exactly when his hat had gone missing, he couldn't say with any certainty, but if he were to hazard a guess, he thought it might have fallen off while he'd been in the midst of the wild ride Permilia had taken through Central Park.

That she'd had the audacity to follow him about the city for two days was a rather disconcerting idea, and one that certainly deserved further contemplation now that he had the time to consider the matter.

She had, without his consent, placed herself smack-dab into a situation that could have very well seen her dead, or at the very least, grievously injured.

Even though she'd made the claim to him that she was not well suited for society life, she was still, unquestionably, a lady.

As such, she had no business trying to assume a role that gentlemen throughout the ages had assumed—that being the role of rescuer.

While he'd certainly appreciated her timely intervention, he was a man—and as a man, he was perfectly capable of saving himself.

Having to admit that he'd allowed a woman to race to his rescue was embarrassing to say the least, and . . .

His feet simply stopped moving as a rather unexpected thought flung to mind, his lack of movement causing the poor gentleman who'd been walking behind him to take a hasty step to the left in order to avoid a collision.

Extending the gentleman his deepest apologies, Asher found himself incapable of moving forward as unpleasant notions took that very moment to begin storming through his mind.

The reason Permilia had taken to following him about town was not simply because she was a woman who enjoyed insinuating herself in other people's business. Instead, she'd obviously come to the conclusion that he hadn't believed her about the murder plot and decided to take matters into her own hands.

She'd evidently done that because she believed he would soon find himself dead if she didn't intervene, because . . . she'd recognized him for what he truly was—a man sheltered from the realities of the world.

Asher sucked in a much-needed breath of air and pressed a hand to his temple, as if that would be enough to stop the unwanted thoughts whirling around in his head, but unfortunately, the whirling continued.

He was a gentleman who'd been raised in an affluent and civilized setting. As such, he'd not been exposed to the nastiness of the world at large—the greatest hardship he'd ever faced being that of learning the family fortune had diminished considerably and knowing it was left to him to replenish that fortune and save them all from financial ruin.

At the time, that had seemed like an insurmountable obstacle, but now—looking at it from afar, and from the perspective of a man who'd apparently incurred the hatred of someone to such an extent that they wanted him dead—it didn't seem worthy to be called a hardship.

It was little wonder, living in the sheltered world he'd apparently been living in for far too long, that he'd blithely dismissed Permilia's story, waving aside her concern for his safety as if it had been a trifling matter.

In his defense, he did live in a world where people were not usually marked for murder . . . nor did assassins lurk their way through an evening of frivolity, accepting payment for their dirty deeds while an orchestra played and the guests danced their way through the Ticklish Water Polka, but . . .

Permilia, while currently living in the world he lived in, had the common sense to realize there was a very real threat to his life, and . . . she'd acted accordingly.

Instead of being annoyed with her for taking it upon herself to assume a role she shouldn't have had to assume in the first place, he should have been grateful that she'd had the bravery needed to keep him alive.

That right there was exactly what was truly bothering him.

When Permilia had been confronted with what likely was an assassin the night of the Vanderbilt ball, she'd not panicked as one would have expected a lady to do. Instead, she'd stuffed herself, along with Mrs. Davenport, into a dumbwaiter and escaped from a most dastardly situation without the assistance of a gentleman.

Asher was not certain he would have been able to claim that same success, nor could he even be certain he'd still be alive at this very moment if she hadn't come riding in her milk wagon and saved the day.

What was truly telling and certainly didn't speak well of his character was how he'd gone about repaying her for her bravery.

Instead of professing his fervent appreciation over her timely appearance in Central Park, he'd acted like a complete idiot by inquiring about what she was wearing.

That inquiry had been beyond ludicrous, and that he'd actually admitted he'd done so in order to distract her, the poor, wilting flower she obviously was not, was hardly a mark in his favor.

He had a reputation for being considered a charming gentleman about town, and . . . one of the most eligible gentlemen in the city at the moment.

Those titles needed to be stripped straightaway, especially since, when faced with an honest-to-goodness emergency, he had not acted as a gentleman was expected to act and taken charge of the situation, but had turned to talk of . . . clothing.

He was a disgrace to the title of *gentleman*.

Resolving right there and then, in the midst of the foot traffic on Broadway, that he would strive to change that unfortunate situation, Asher moved into motion again.

That he truly had no idea how to accomplish the daunting task of becoming more, well, manly, was a cause for concern. But a small step in moving toward that goal might very well be retrieving his horse, along with Harrison's horse, from the Huxley sisters, if they had, indeed, kept the horses instead of returning them to Rutherford & Company.

The Misses Huxley were known to be curious ladies, possessed of sharp tongues and peculiar behavior. And while he by no means thought them to be dangerous, it would take a certain amount of manliness on his part to approach the sisters, especially since he employed numerous men who would normally have been sent to accomplish such an unpleasant task.

His shoulders sagged as he realized that doing an unpleasant task on his own instead of pawning it off on one of his employees, who would have no say in accepting or declining the task, was scarcely a positive point in his favor.

Telling himself that he was going to have to do better than that if he truly wanted to improve himself, he squared his shoulders and strode forward again but was forced to stop a few steps later when one of his regular customers, Mrs. Strong, stepped into his path.

Since he couldn't doff a hat that was no longer on his head, he extended her a bow and smiled. "Good afternoon, Mrs. Strong."

Mrs. Strong smiled back at him. "Good afternoon to you, Mr. Rutherford, and may I say that it's lovely to find you looking so well." She glanced at the watch pinned to the underside of her coat. "It's almost past three and I must tell you that members of your staff are growing quite frantic, having expected you back at two." She leaned closer to him. "The salesladies in the glove department are very concerned about your whereabouts, Mr. Rutherford, and are having a most difficult time performing their jobs in what I'd consider a satisfactory manner. You really must seek those salesladies out straightaway, otherwise, I'm afraid your sales in the glove department may very well suffer today."

"How interesting to learn you're so familiar with my schedule, Mrs. Strong" was all Asher could think of to respond to that.

Frowning, Mrs. Strong looked up from her watch. "It's not as if your schedule is a mystery, Mr. Rutherford. Everyone knows you're a gentleman who appreciates a strict schedule. Why, ladies have been known to reset their watches because of your schedule. Although . . ." She shook her head. "If anyone thought to do that today, they'd be sorely disappointed since you've strayed from what has become expected of you. May I dare hope that there's not a troubling reason behind that straying?"

"Everything is perfectly fine."

"You're missing your hat," she pointed out, as if that proved he was anything but fine.

"Indeed I am."

Peering up into his face, Mrs. Strong actually reached out a hand and gave him a rather motherly pat. "You're looking a bit peaked, Mr. Rutherford. I suggest a nice cup of tea, which should help you feel more the thing."

Wagging a gloved finger his way, she turned and marched down the sidewalk, quickly disappearing into the crowd.

Wondering again how it could have possibly happened that he'd turned into such a predictable sort, which certainly wasn't a dashing or exciting title to hold, and certainly wouldn't impress someone like Permilia, since she was . . .

Shaking himself straight from those thoughts, since this was certainly not the time to be dwelling on Permilia, he forced his feet into motion again and moved down the sidewalk.

He'd gotten all of ten feet before he noticed Mr. Cushing, a man he employed as a doorman at Rutherford & Company, charging down the sidewalk toward him, a large smile of what could only be described as relief spreading over the man's face.

"Thank goodness you're back, Mr. Rutherford. The sales-ladies are beside themselves, having concocted all sorts of outlandish stories to explain your absence from the store this afternoon, some of those tales concerning your demise."

"Which isn't as farfetched as you may think," Asher muttered before he forced a smile and fell into step beside Mr. Cushing. "But surely everyone wasn't concerned for me? I'm not that late returning from my afternoon ride."

"You're never late, Mr. Rutherford."

"Surely I am, at least occasionally."

"No. The few times you haven't returned precisely at two, you've left notice with Mrs. Banks. She then adds a note on your schedule and no one takes to worrying." He shook his head. "Mrs. Banks has been pacing the floor outside your office for the past hour, telling anyone who will listen that something dastardly has happened to you. She's even composed a letter she intends to send off to the authorities, telling them you've gone missing."

"I'm only a little over an hour late."

"Which is quite unlike you, sir."

Asher blew out a breath. "Apparently you're right, but if I may ask a favor of you, Mr. Cushing, would you be so kind as to seek out Mrs. Banks and tell her I'm fine?"

"Begging your pardon, sir, but don't you believe that's something your secretary will want to hear from you?"

"I would be quite willing to speak with her, Mr. Cushing, but I must first travel to the Rutherford & Company stable to discover if the Misses Huxley returned my horse, along with Mr. Sinclair's horse, before I can attend to any other business."

Mr. Cushing frowned. "Right before I spotted you walking down the sidewalk, I was speaking with the head groom, Mr. Slavic, and he did not mention Vagabond having been returned."

"And that right there proves I was exactly right to part ways with Miss Griswold, no matter that she thought I'd taken leave of my senses."

"Sir?"

Asher swallowed a sigh when he took note of the clear confusion now stamped on Mr. Cushing's face. "Don't mind me, Mr. Cushing. I'm afraid I've had a very trying day so far, and learning Vagabond has not been returned means my day is certainly not going to improve any time soon."

"Surely you're not suggesting that the spinster sisters have stolen your horse?"

"I don't believe they've *stolen* my horse. I would say more along the lines of retrieving it, at least that's what I'm hoping—a realistic hope, I would have to imagine, since everyone knows the Huxley sisters are two of the wealthiest ladies in the city. Since we're on the subject of the sisters, Mr. Cushing, whatever you do, do not allow Miss Permilia Griswold to hear you say the word *spinster* in her presence. You'll only be opening yourself up for a good lecture if you do."

Mr. Cushing's brow furrowed. "I'll try to refrain from that, then, sir, if I ever happen to find myself having an actual conversation with . . . Miss Griswold, you said?"

"You may find yourself having a conversation with that lady sooner than you'd expect. I asked her to join me at the store after she gets Mr. Sinclair seen to by a physician at the hospital."

"Mr. Sinclair has been taken to the hospital?"

"He has, but I'm sure he'll be fixed up in a trice. He suffered a blow to his head, which is why I need to retrieve his horse. I'd hate to tax that head of his further by not providing him with the return of Rupert."

"Should I assume you, along with Mr. Sinclair, suffered from some manner of an accident today?"

"I believe a more apt term to describe what we suffered, Mr. Cushing, would be an ambush."

Mr. Cushing, oddly enough, took to nodding his head in a very knowing fashion. "I'm not surprised. Given the company Mr. Sinclair's been known to keep, it was only a matter of time until someone went after him."

"Would you be surprised to learn I was the target of the ambush?"

Mr. Cushing, instead of looking suitably impressed by the danger Asher had drawn his way, let out a chuckle. "Very amusing, Mr. Rutherford, and exceedingly thoughtful of you to try and detract attention from your friend's dangerous reputation." He gave a last chuckle and moved toward the front door of Rutherford & Company. "I'll go tell Mrs. Banks that you're fine, as well as inform the rest of the staff you have not met an unfortunate demise." With that, Mr. Cushing vanished into the store, mumbling something about Asher's excellent sense of humor under his breath.

As he watched his doorman disappear, Asher couldn't help but shake his head.

Clearly, it was the conception throughout the city that he was punctual, safe, and . . . unworthy of attracting the interest of an assassin—conceptions that were less than pleasurable to swallow.

Realizing that this was not exactly the moment to contemplate unproductive notions, he again headed down the sidewalk.

Passing by a bank, a jewelry store, and then a tobacco shop, he stepped off the curb and into the street. Dodging a delivery wagon filled with newspapers, he slipped around a buggy carrying ladies dressed in the latest fashions, and finally made it to the sidewalk on the other side of Broadway.

Smoothing hair that had taken to falling over his forehead back into place, he continued forward, not stopping until he arrived in front of the Huxley house.

Three stories of marble, topped with a mansard roof, built in a style similar to A. T. Stewart's mansion on Fifth Avenue, looked slightly out of place, set as it was between two empty overgrown lots, lots Asher knew to belong to the Huxley sisters. That the lots had never been developed was one of the mysteries of Broadway, especially since real estate on this particular street kept increasing in value. Demand was at an all-time high, especially for high-end shops.

Walking up to the wrought-iron gate that separated the house from the crowds traveling to and fro on the sidewalk, Asher pulled up the latch and moved through the gate, making certain it was firmly latched behind him before he proceeded up the sidewalk.

He'd just made it to the steps that led to the front door when that door opened and Mr. Barclay, the Huxley family butler, stepped out.

Asher wasn't well acquainted with Mr. Barclay, but because the Huxley butler spent a great deal of time standing on the stoop of the Huxley house, perusing the traffic traveling down Broadway, they had exchanged the expected nods and occasional comments about the weather every once in a while.

"Mr. Rutherford, how kind of you to call," Mr. Barclay began, inclining his head Asher's way. "May I assume you're here about a horse?"

"Of course he's here about a horse, Mr. Barclay. Why else would he pay us a call, seeing as how he's never bothered to pay us a proper call before?"

Looking past Mr. Barclay, Asher discovered Miss Mabel Huxley strolling through the front door.

That she was a handsome woman, there was no question, although she'd have been downright lovely if not for the pinched look she always seemed to adopt. Her brown hair, streaked with only a touch of gray, was twisted into an elaborate knot on top of her head, while the well-cut and stylish gown she was wearing displayed her trim figure to advantage. A fine bone structure and relatively few wrinkles made it exceedingly difficult to place her age, but the clear annoyance that rested in her green eyes did little to encourage Asher's expectations for a pleasant visit.

Presenting her with a bow, and then taking her hand when she stopped directly in front of him, he pressed a kiss to her bare knuckles and summoned up the charm he was known for, grateful he at least had that at his disposal at the moment, if nothing else.

"You are looking very well today, Miss Huxley."

"You may reserve the charm, Mr. Rutherford, for someone who may be impressed by it. I've already taken the liberty of having your horse returned to the Rutherford & Company stables, along with Mr. Sinclair's horse as well, which means there's absolutely no reason for you to be overly pleasant."

Given the manner in which the rest of his day had gone, Asher wasn't taken the slightest bit aback by Miss Huxley's disagreeable response.

Keeping his smile firmly in place, because he was not about to relinquish the one thing he did have going for him—his charm— Asher nodded as pleasantly as he could in Miss Huxley's direction. "Mr. Sinclair will be delighted to learn his horse is safe and sound, Miss Huxley, but tell me, how were you aware that horse belonged to Mr. Sinclair?"

"My sister and I enjoy watching the comings and goings on Broadway from our third-floor windows. We have quite the vantage point from up there, and, truth be told, we've invested in all manner of telescopes and even opera glasses to aid us in our observations. I have taken a special interest in watching Mr. Sinclair as he comes and goes from your store." She actually took to fanning her face with her hand. "He's a most impressive gentleman, and one not many women would fail to notice."

Having absolutely no idea how Miss Huxley could possibly expect him to respond to that, Asher was spared any remark at all when Miss Huxley stopped fanning her face and narrowed her eyes at him. "Why was your horse wandering around Central Park unattended?"

"Embarrassing as this is to admit, my horse, and Mr. Sinclair's horse, managed to get away from us when they were startled by a loud noise and bolted away before we could secure them."

"You would have me believe that Mr. Sinclair was thrown from his horse?"

"While I find it somewhat concerning that you apparently find it remarkably easy to believe that I could be thrown from my horse, Mr. Sinclair and I were not riding the horses when the loud noise rang out."

"How did you manage to get back to the store without your horse?" she fired at him next.

"It was not without difficulty, Miss Huxley, but tell me this, how did you manage to secure our horses? I did not notice a groom when I saw you traveling toward Broadway a short time ago."

"One does not need a gentleman, Mr. Rutherford, to go about the business of life. But since you've acknowledged that you saw me driving toward Broadway, do allow me to explain the reasoning behind not stopping at your store to return your horse, but continuing on to my home instead."

Crickets seemed to descend over the front stoop as Miss Huxley simply stopped talking, almost as if she'd neglected to remember she was in the midst of a story. Turning around when he realized she'd become distracted by something on the street, Asher glanced up Broadway and then down, finding absolutely nothing worthy of a distraction.

"Mrs. Astor," Miss Huxley said, as if that explained everything.

"Yes, well, how exciting," Asher began. "Although since you've admitted to observing Broadway on a regular basis, I would be surprised if you didn't frequently see Mrs. Astor's carriage traveling up and down the street."

Miss Huxley's face looked more pinched than usual. "She drives down this street deliberately, taunting me and my sister with her superiority."

"Surely you don't really believe that."

"Mrs. Astor saw Henrietta and I excluded from most society events after we, unfortunately, didn't enjoy much success with our social debut. She was also largely responsible for seeing us banished to the wallflower section during the few events to which Father managed to secure us invitations." Miss Huxley took a second to release a sniff. "She's a rude, spiteful woman, and she still seems to derive pleasure from our failure to take within society."

"How very unfair that must seem to you." Asher began edging as casually as he could backward. "And while I'd love to delve further into the disappointments society has been known to dish out to people, I really should be on my way. My absence has apparently been noted at the store and I mustn't allow the staff to continue worrying about me."

"Ah, yes, that's where I was going with my conversation—your horse." Before Asher could attain his goal of making a hasty departure, Miss Huxley stepped closer to him and took a remarkably firm hold of his arm. "I did not return your horse to the Rutherford & Company stable because securing your horse, along with Mr. Sinclair's, put my sister and myself off our usual schedule. I am not bothered by nonsense such as that, but my sister, Miss Henrietta, is a stickler for punctuality, and she was becoming distressed over the idea we would be late sitting down for tea."

Miss Huxley suddenly took to smiling at him in a rather disturbing way. "That punctuality is a characteristic I'm sure you're delighted to discover you share with my sister."

"Quite . . . delighted."

She nodded. "As you should be, and you'll also be delighted to learn that you'll join us for tea today."

Of anything he'd been expecting of Miss Huxley, an invitation to tea had certainly never crossed his mind.

"I wouldn't want to impose."

"And I wouldn't want you to insult me by refusing my invitation, so . . ." She turned and inclined her head to the butler who'd continued to lurk on the stoop. "Mr. Barclay, would you get the door for us?"

Before Asher could summon up even the flimsiest of excuses, he found himself ushered through the door and into a hallway that seemed to be made entirely of marble.

"What a lovely home you have, Miss Huxley."

"You may call me Miss Mabel since we'll soon be in the company of my sister, and trying to decipher which Miss Huxley a person is speaking about becomes tedious after only a few minutes. And, as for my home, it's thoughtful of you to say that, Mr. Rutherford, but I'm perfectly aware that the entranceway and hall appear more along the lines of a mausoleum than a home, what with all the marble Father insisted on using." She lifted her chin. "He was always trying so diligently to impress people belonging to that illustrious Knickerbocker set, such as the Astors, but I fear the more he tried, the more disdainful they became of us."

"I'm sure that's not true."

Miss Mabel pulled him down the hallway and stopped directly underneath a portrait of a man who looked rather rough around the edges. Nodding to the portrait, Miss Mabel caught his eye. "That is my father, a most unpleasant man who was never happy with his life, no matter the great amount of money he made while he was alive. He built this monstrosity of a house simply to impress the elite of society, never realizing that he was building it on a street that was destined to become a desirable retail destination over a residential one."

"It's still a very handsome home."

"I much prefer the smaller house we used to live in years and years ago. It was located on the back side of Gramercy Park."

"Perhaps you should consider having an agent inquire about the status of that house. It might be a property that someone is willing to sell for the right price."

"My sister and I still own the property, Mr. Rutherford, but felt compelled quite a few years back to allow our nephew to

162

move into it. We can hardly demand he remove himself now, especially since he's mentioned time and time again over the years how grateful he is to us for allowing him such a lovely home to live in."

Asher frowned. "I never knew you and your sister had another sibling, and a nephew."

"It's not a topic we care to discuss." Tightening her grip on his arm, she prodded him into motion again, pulling him past a line of paintings that all seemed to be of her father.

Stepping out of the hallway a moment later, Asher found himself pleasantly surprised to discover the room they'd entered, a library from the looks of it, was decorated in a remarkably cheerful manner.

Delicate furniture upholstered in different shades of blue was scattered about the room, while a fire crackled merrily in a fireplace crafted out of what seemed to be white stones, quite like the ones found in riverbeds. Wispy curtains hung from each of the floor-to-ceiling windows that made up an entire wall, pulled closed as so many families preferred in order to keep the people bustling back and forth on the sidewalks from gawking into their lives.

Bookshelves lined the other walls, while a silver tea service sat on a low table positioned directly in the center of the room.

Miss Mabel's sister, Miss Henrietta Huxley, a lady who looked remarkably like Miss Mabel except for the fact that she had white hair with not so much as a trace of the original color left in it, was sitting on a fainting couch to the left of the fireplace. She was reading a newspaper, but it was apparent she was taking issue with one of the articles since she kept grimacing every other second as her eyes traveled down the page.

Flinging aside the paper a second later, she took off the spectacles she'd been using to read, set them on a side table, blinked a time or two, turned her attention his way, blinked again, and then rose to her feet.

"Ah, Mr. Rutherford, this is a surprise. I certainly never expected you to come in person to inquire about your horse. But do know that my sister has already sent it back to your stable, although if she's already informed you of that . . . well, I'm sure I have no idea why you're still lingering about Huxley House."

Finding himself somewhat thankful now that he hadn't sent someone else to inquire about the horse, almost as if by coming himself he'd managed to dispel a small amount of what sounded like disdain on Miss Henrietta's part, he moved across the library and stopped right in front of her. Taking hold of her hand, he pretended not to notice that she immediately tried to tug it back from him, and placed a kiss on the very tips of fingers that appeared to be smudged with ink from the paper she'd just been reading. "You're looking delightful today, Miss Huxley."

Miss Henrietta Huxley pursed her lips. "As I just mentioned, your horse has already been returned to you so there's little need to waste your renowned charm on me, Mr. Rutherford. And do stop with the Miss Huxley business. It gets so confusing when my sister and I are both in the room. You will call me Miss Henrietta from this point forward."

"Has anyone ever told you, Miss Henrietta, that you and your sister think almost exactly the same?"

"I'm sure you're mistaken about that," Miss Henrietta said with a sniff.

"Henrietta, behave," her sister cautioned, walking up to join them. "You're being uncommonly surly at the moment, and I've already told Mr. Rutherford we have no need of his charm, which is probably why he just remarked about our similarities."

"And you have the audacity to bring up *my* surliness in the conversation," Miss Henrietta countered before she drew herself up and caught Asher's eye. "To make amends for that surliness, Mr. Rutherford, I must insist you join us for tea."

"I've already extended him that offer," Miss Mabel said.

"Then why, pray tell, are we standing around? If we wait much longer, the tea will grow cold, and . . . I'll be completely off my schedule if I'm made to wait for another pot to brew."

Pressing his lips together to keep from smiling, Asher moved to the chair Miss Henrietta gestured him toward, waiting until she, along with her sister, took their seats on the blue-and-white-striped fainting couch Miss Henrietta had only recently vacated before he sat down.

"Have you told him about how difficult it was for us to obtain this special brew?" Miss Henrietta demanded as Mr. Barclay walked into the room and moved to the tea service.

"I was waiting until the poor man got comfortable before launching into a conversation that revolves around our most treasured hobby," Miss Mabel began before she turned her attention to Asher. "That hobby, I'm sure you'll be pleased to learn, given the interest we've learned you share with us, is searching out and collecting new blends of tea."

Feeling a little fonder of the sisters than he'd been feeling only a moment before, Asher sat forward. "Have you heard that I'm in the process of creating a tearoom on the fourth floor of Rutherford & Company?"

Miss Henrietta folded her hands in her lap and smiled. "But of course we have, Mr. Rutherford. In all honesty, we're quite anxious to try out the tea you intend to serve there, see if it measures up to our standards."

"One would hope, now that you've been made aware of our appreciation for tea, that we'll be given an invitation to visit the shop before it opens to the public," Miss Mabel added.

"I would be honored to have you visit the shop, and I will

have Mrs. Banks make arrangements for your visit just as soon as construction on the shop is completed."

Miss Mabel exchanged a look with her sister. "Perhaps those charming manners of his shouldn't be considered overrated after all."

"Indeed they should not," Miss Henrietta said, lapsing into silence when Mr. Barclay began making quite the production of pouring out the new blend of tea the sisters had been exclaiming about, straightening after he'd set aside the pot. He then went about the business of handing cups made of delicate bone china all around.

Accepting the cup Mr. Barclay handed him, Asher was just in the process of bringing it to his lips when the sound of someone running down the hallway drifted to his ears. Seconds later, the door to the library burst all the way open and a whirlwind entered the room, a whirlwind who just happened to go by the name of . . . Permilia.

CHAPTER
FOURTEEN

It took every ounce of restraint Permilia had to resist the temptation to rush across the library and knock the cup Asher had raised almost to his lips straight out of his hand. That temptation, she was quite certain, was a direct result of all the plots she'd been imagining ever since he'd left her company, some of those plots involving the all-too-peculiar Huxley sisters.

She knew full well she might be imagining the whole plot business in regard to the sisters, but given the way the day had gone, it could turn out to be more than coincidence that the Huxley sisters had come into possession of Asher's and Harrison's horses.

For all anyone knew, these sisters could be in on the sinister plan to do away with Asher. And when the assailant in Central Park had not met with any success, they might have taken it upon themselves to lure Asher into their house by absconding with his horse.

The idea that the man had placed himself smack-dab into a situation that could very well see him dead had temper boiling through her veins, temper she tried to control by drawing in a deep breath and slowly releasing it.

She was less than successful controlling that temper when she noticed the Huxley sisters watching her from their positions by the fireplace, calmly sipping their tea as if they weren't concerned at all that a woman who was a complete stranger to them had burst into their home so unexpectedly.

Their calmness, in Permilia's opinion, all but proved the rumors she'd heard about these particular sisters—rumors that centered around their curious natures and the fact that they rarely socialized with anyone but each other.

Because of those rumors, and because Asher, one would think, should be aware of the Huxley sisters' unusual reputation, he should have known better than to blithely pay a call on them, let alone sit down to join them for a cup of tea in their library.

Given the daunting circumstances he was currently facing, everyone had to be considered a suspect, which meant the Huxley sisters could be the ones responsible for the hiring of the assassin in the first place.

Clearly, Asher had yet to fully comprehend that very real danger was nipping at his heels.

Lifting her chin, she marched across the room, coming to a stop, though, when a distinguished-looking gentleman, one who could only be the butler, stepped in front of her, blocking her path.

"I'm afraid I'm going to have to insist you leave, miss . . . immediately. You should be thankful I'm not going to call in the authorities, since you snuck in here without permission."

"I knocked on the front door, and when no one answered, I turned the doorknob and found the door unlocked." She nodded. "That, to me, was an indication that anyone was welcome to enter, so that is exactly what I did. And I'll be happy to depart from the house just as soon as I fetch Mr. Rutherford."

"I think not," the butler returned in a voice that was low, smooth, and could have certainly found a home on any stage.

"Oh, do let her stay, Mr. Barclay," one of the Huxley sisters purred. "It's a rare occasion indeed for us to have even one guest for tea, let alone two."

The butler, a Mr. Barclay from the sound of it, stiffened and turned, presenting Permilia with his back. "Forgive me, Miss Henrietta, but given the manner in which this woman is dressed, she's evidently not a lady, which means I really must discourage you from amusing yourself with her."

An honest-to-goodness chill swept down Permilia's spine as she wondered what type of amusement the Huxley sisters could possibly derive from having her sit down to tea with them. It was highly doubtful that *she'd* get any amusement out of it, although . . . perhaps that was exactly what the sisters would find amusing, which was a rather troubling notion in and of itself.

Before she had an opportunity to ponder it further, Asher got to his feet. Thankfully, he abandoned the cup he'd been holding before he began walking her way, a cup that Permilia couldn't help but think might contain something other than strictly tea in it, something that might be along the lines of . . . poison . . . if her assumption about the sisters was on target.

She forced herself to stand her ground when Asher sent her a look that seemed to hold a touch of temper and blew out a breath of relief when he directed his attention away from her and to the Huxley sisters.

"I do beg your pardon for this, ladies, but I feel it might be for the best if I were to escort this fine young lady out of your home and directly to the nearest asylum."

One of the sisters let out a laugh, the sound ringing through the room, although to Permilia's ear, it sounded somewhat mad, exactly what one would hear if they were to visit that asylum Asher had just mentioned.

"I so enjoy visiting asylums, as does my sister, but . . . before you cart the woman away, Mr. Rutherford, I simply must insist you perform the expected introductions."

Asher, curiously enough, took that particular moment to abandon the proper manners he was well known for and shook his head. "I don't believe that's necessary, Miss Henrietta."

"Oh, but it is," Miss Henrietta countered.

"I assure you, it's not," Asher countered right back.

Realizing that she was dealing with two people who seemed to possess somewhat stubborn natures, and not wanting to stay at the Huxley house any longer than necessary, especially after just discovering the ladies enjoyed visiting asylums, Permilia stepped forward.

"I'm Miss Permilia Griswold."

One of the sisters set aside her tea before she oh-so-slowly rose to her feet. "Are you really?" She tilted her head. "You don't look like Permilia Griswold."

"Since I know for a fact that you and I, Miss Huxley, have never been introduced, nor have I ever attended an event where you or your sister have been present, I must now inquire how you would even know what I look like."

Instead of answering her, the woman stepped forward, tapping her finger against her chin as she set about the troubling business of perusing Permilia. "Ah, you're cheeky, I'll give you that, but I'm not surprised, given that mother of yours. But . . . are you wearing a wig?"

Permilia managed a nod, more interested in the remark about her mother than any remark about a wig. "You knew my mother?"

"Not well, mind you, but we were acquainted," the woman said as she began walking around Permilia. "Take off the wig."

"I don't do well with demands, Miss Huxley."

"Please, call me Miss Mabel, and my sister, Miss Henrietta,

and do know that not doing well with demands is a trait I believe you've received from your father."

"You know my father?"

"Of course she knows your father, dear," Miss Henrietta said. "She was quite fond of him at one time, but then . . . well . . . life intervened and he went his way and we went ours."

Darting a glance to Miss Mabel, who'd stopped walking around her and was looking completely unconcerned that her sister had just divulged incredibly personal information, Permilia reached up and pulled the wig straight off her head, hoping her compliance might afford her some answers from the sisters, answers she had a feeling they were going to dole out in a slow and painful way.

Anyone who freely admitted that they enjoyed visiting asylums was evidently possessed of a Machiavellian nature, which meant they would enjoy toying with her if only to see how long they could.

"Ah, there's the lovely girl I've watched mature over the past few years, although from afar," Miss Mabel exclaimed, going so far as to clap her hands in delight right before she took to clucking. "But lovely though you are, dear, you're also a bit of a mess at the moment."

"It's been a trying day."

Miss Mabel threw a glance Asher's way, then returned her gaze to Permilia. "That does seem to be the general consensus of this particular day, but tell me, does your father know you're out and about dressed like . . . What are you supposed to be, dear?"

"My father is currently not in town, but it's been years since he's concerned himself with what I wear, given that I am a lady of a certain age, no longer a green girl fresh out of the schoolroom."

"She makes an excellent point," Miss Henrietta said as she pulled a pair of spectacles from a nearby table, shoved them on her nose, and then took to clucking as well. "Good heavens, you are a mess, dear, which is rather surprising since I've never observed you to be anything but very well put together."

"Forgive me, but it almost sounds as if the two of you have been observing me rather closely over the years."

"They have a room . . . on the third floor," Asher said, speaking up. "It's special and used for the sole purpose of observation."

"And you agreed to take tea with them knowing this?" she whispered under her breath, evidently not whispering low enough because Miss Mabel laughed.

"We didn't invite Mr. Rutherford into our home to harm him," Miss Mabel said as she let out another peal of laughter. "Why, one would almost think you were afraid we'd poisoned his tea or something quite as dastardly."

Not wanting to admit that was exactly what she'd thought, Permilia summoned up a smile. "Of course I didn't think that."

Miss Mabel waved that aside with a flick of her wrist before she moved closer and took hold of Permilia's arm, giving it a rather hearty pat. "How *is* your father these days, dear?"

"He's well, but . . ." Permilia wrinkled her nose. "If you were at one time fond of him, why is it that I've never heard him speak of you before?"

"Oh, that hurts." Miss Mabel raised a hand to her chest. "While we were fond of each other, dear, we were never romantically involved—although not for a lack of wishing on my part, and perhaps his at one time." She let out a touch of a sigh. "George was a frequent guest at our table, which is how I first became acquainted with him, brought home by my father because he enjoyed mentoring George, who was just entering the mining industry at that time."

"My father was *mentored* by your father?"

"Oh my, yes," Miss Mabel said. "Father owned an ironwork

factory, among many other ventures, so he was quite capable of steering George in the right direction as pertained to what type of mining George should pursue."

"But you were never romantically involved with him?"

"I'm afraid not, but . . ." Miss Mabel stopped talking, sighed ever so softly again, and then smiled. "You must join us for tea."

Permilia's eyes widened. "Oh, there's no need for that, and I truly don't want to impose."

"I think that ship has sailed, dear, considering you imposed yourself on us in a most dramatic way when you took it upon yourself to burst into our home."

When put that way, and because her stepmother had tried her very best to instill at least a semblance of manners in Permilia, she decided to agree. "I'd love to join you for tea."

"Wonderful." Miss Mabel turned to Mr. Barclay, who was looking less than pleased. "Would you be so kind as to pour Miss Griswold a cup, Mr. Barclay?"

"Forgive me, Miss Mabel, but I must protest. Asking the daughter of a man you were quite fond of to sit down to tea with you will not bode well for you in the end."

"Don't be ridiculous. Again, George and I were never romantically involved."

"Only because you heeded your father's advice and never allowed Mr. Griswold to know you would have been agreeable to his showing you affections of the romantic sort."

Dead silence settled over the room until Asher cleared his throat, stepped over to the tea service, and smiled his most charming of smiles. "Would you allow me the honor of freshening up everyone's tea, while pouring a full cup for Permilia?"

"That would be kind of you," Miss Henrietta said, rising to her feet and moving to her sister's side right as Mr. Barclay turned smartly around and left the library without another word.

"You know he's just being protective of you," Permilia heard Miss Henrietta whisper to her sister before she took Miss Mabel by the arm and pulled her back to the fainting couch. Sitting down beside her, Miss Henrietta took up her sister's hand.

Walking over to a chair Asher had nodded to before he'd set about pouring the tea, Permilia sat down, rearranging the folds of her costume. Lifting her head, she found the sisters watching her every movement.

"Why are you in disguise, dear?" Miss Mabel asked, accepting the cup of tea Asher had refilled for her before she returned her attention to Permilia.

"That's a little difficult to explain," Permilia said, breathing a sigh of relief when Asher walked over to her and handed her a cup of tea, the relief turning to a smidgen of temper a second later when he leaned close to her ear and began whispering.

"You would have been spared thinking up an explanation in the first place if you would have abandoned the role of rescuer you've apparently decided to adopt on my behalf—a role, I assure you, I don't need you to adopt."

"So says the man who willingly walked directly into the spider's web," she whispered back, earning a narrowing of the eyes from Asher in the process as he straightened and moved back to his own chair, taking a seat.

"It seems as if the two of you are in the midst of some type of spat," Miss Mabel said cheerfully.

"Mr. Rutherford and I are frequently at odds, Miss Mabel," Permilia began. "But I assure you, it's nothing for you to worry about."

Miss Henrietta sat forward, set the cup Asher had only recently given her aside, leaned down, snatched up a pile of newspapers that had been placed on the floor next to the fainting couch, and immediately took to burying her nose behind one. A second later, she peered at Permilia over the top of the paper.

"I read something about you in the paper today, Permilia. Well, more than just *some*thing, actually, but . . . it was noted that you and Mr. Rutherford spent a questionable amount of time together at the Vanderbilt ball." She nodded in a rather knowing fashion. "Should I expect to read an announcement soon, perhaps after your father returns to town and Mr. Rutherford has an opportunity to handle the matter properly?"

Permilia blinked. "I'm sure I have no idea what you're talking about."

Miss Henrietta disappeared behind the paper again. "It says right here that Miss Griswold participated in the Go-As-You-Please Quadrille with Mr. Rutherford, although given that she was less than adept with the steps, it was a clear sign Mr. Rutherford holds her in deepest affection since he was seen speaking with her after their disaster on the ballroom floor."

"It does not say that." Permilia set her cup aside on a delicate table right next to her chair before she stood up and moved to stand in front of Miss Henrietta.

"You may read it for yourself," Miss Henrietta said, handing over the newspaper before she dove back into her pile, not putting Permilia's mind to rest when she added, "I know there's more written about you. Give me a moment."

Not bothering to retake her seat, Permilia bent her head and began reading the article. By the time she was done, she was feeling a little queasy. Turning, she handed the paper to Asher and immediately retook her seat, as if her legs no longer wanted to support her.

"They printed my name . . . Miss Griswold," she whispered.

"As well as mine." Asher lowered the paper. "They never do that."

Miss Mabel took a sip of her tea and nodded her head in a knowing fashion. "I knew when I first learned that Alva Vanderbilt—who used to be Alva Smith, if you didn't know—

an upstart woman if there ever was one, born and raised in the South, and . . ." She took another sip of tea. "Her family owned slaves."

"You're getting distracted, Mabel, from whatever point you were wanting to make," Miss Henrietta said from behind her paper.

"Goodness, you're quite right." Miss Mabel pursed her lips for a second, then nodded. "What I was going to say, before I became distracted with thoughts of Alva and how she deliberately went after that nice William K., with no true love in her heart, only fortunes that could be had in her mind, well . . ."

Miss Henrietta rattled the paper. "Mabel, you're doing it again."

Releasing what sounded like a long-suffering sigh, Miss Mabel took another sip of tea and then lifted her chin. "We were not invited to the Vanderbilt ball, although we were acquainted with the Commodore. He was the Vanderbilt who earned the family fortune to begin with, leaving the majority of that fortune to his son, William H. Vanderbilt, even though there were plenty of other children the Commodore had with his first wife, God rest her soul, who deserved a bigger piece of the pie, so to speak."

"You should do a God rest *his* soul, since the Commodore is dead as well," Miss Henrietta remarked, her head still hidden behind the newspaper.

"God rest Commodore Vanderbilt's soul," Miss Mabel said, although she looked less than thrilled to do so. "You know, Henrietta, he wasn't a very nice man," she said, going completely off topic again.

"Father wasn't a very nice man either, but we still appreciate when people say 'God rest his soul.'"

Miss Henrietta lowered the paper, and then she and Miss Mabel took to looking Permilia and Asher's way, their well-defined brows quirked in exactly the same position.

"God rest Mr. Huxley's soul?" Permilia said, right as Asher did the same.

"Ah, how lovely," Miss Henrietta said. "Even if he was a horrible, horrible man." With that, she disappeared behind the paper again.

"He really was," Miss Mabel agreed. "But to continue with my thought before I completely forget what that thought is— Alva has, all by herself, dealt society a blow that they haven't even realized they've been given yet."

Permilia sat back in her seat. "She invited the press into her home."

Miss Mabel beamed at Permilia as if she'd just stated something brilliant. "Too right she did, and . . . I believe she encouraged them to branch out from the tried-and-true society columns the New York Four Hundred approves of, using real names instead of initials, even though it's always been known whom those initials belong to."

"Ah, here it is. I found another mention of the two of you," Miss Henrietta said, peering over the paper again. "This article, penned by an author who now seems downright respectable though two years ago she caused an uproar within society by describing gowns that had been worn to a Patriarch Ball—gives an explanation, if you will, for the disaster you made of the Go-As-You-Please Quadrille."

Permilia, knowing full well that Miss Henrietta had now come across her Miss Quill column, batted what she could only hope were innocent eyes Miss Henrietta's way. "An explanation?"

"Miss Quill writes that she overheard information that concerns you mistakenly believing the 'Go As You Please' truly meant you could go anywhere you please during the dance instead of not having to be dressed in a particular costume to participate in the dance."

"Did you truly believe that?" Miss Mabel asked.

"What everyone always seems to forget," Permilia began, "is that I was not raised in society, but in the midst of miners who aren't exactly up to date on the latest quadrille steps."

"That's why George married Ida, to take you in hand," Miss Mabel said, a comment that had Permilia's breath lodging in her throat.

"What do you mean?" she finally managed to ask.

"The George I knew was not concerned about society or their ways at all, which was one of the reasons Father didn't want me developing any great affection for the man. George would have been perfectly fine walking completely away from society forever, even with the fortune he eventually made, if he'd had a son. He didn't, though, he had you, and . . . he must have eventually come to the conclusion he was doing you a grave disservice."

"He's done me a graver disservice by forcing me into society instead of allowing me to take over the running of his mines."

The moment the words left her mouth, Permilia felt ashamed of herself. Until her father had married Ida, she'd shared a bond with him that she'd never expected to lose. Even though she was furious with her father at the moment, had been furious with him for years, she'd never thought she'd turn into the type of woman to say such disparaging things about him, and to people she barely knew. "Forgive me. I shouldn't have said that."

"Perhaps we should enjoy our tea before it grows cold," Miss Mabel suggested.

Needing a distraction, and not quite as hesitant to drink tea that had come from the same pot as that of Miss Mabel, who'd already taken a few sips, Permilia picked up her cup.

Raising it to her lips, she took the smallest of sips, blinking in surprise a second later. "Good heavens. That's delicious." She took another sip, having to resist the great urge she felt to smack her lips.

Watching Asher lift his cup, she smiled when he took a sip, his eyes widened, and he sat forward in his seat, pinning Miss Mabel with a rather determined eye.

"I do believe I'm going to have to insist you divulge where you've gotten this because . . . this is a tea I simply must acquire for my shop."

To Permilia's relief, all talk of disappointments, inappropriate newspaper articles, and the reason Permilia was dressed as a milkmaid were pushed aside as everyone enjoyed their tea. An easy atmosphere settled over the library, until the door opened and Mr. Barclay stepped in.

"I've received word that Mr. Tooker will be arriving soon, apparently having decided to join you, Miss Mabel and Miss Henrietta, for dinner," the butler said. "His note said he will be arriving at four thirty, and it's nearly that now."

Permilia set aside her cup. "Who is Mr. Tooker?"

Miss Mabel rose to her feet and smiled a smile that was a little too bright. "He's our nephew, dear, and as sorry as I am to have to say this, you and Mr. Rutherford are going to have to leave . . . immediately."

Chapter
Fifteen

"While I must admit that I've always wondered what the Knickerbocker Club looked like on the inside," Harrison said, "and I *am* suitably impressed by our opulent surroundings at the moment . . . I find I can't fully appreciate this experience, given the oddness of finding myself here instead of at Astor House. If you've neglected to realize, this is the day of the week I always join you at Astor House for lunch—and at noon, not eleven."

Pulling his attention away from the window and the view he'd been enjoying of 28th Street, Asher found Harrison contemplating him from the high-backed leather chair he was lounging in.

There was little question that Harrison suffered no ill-effects from his accident of the day before, His eyes were clear, he'd complained of no pain in his head, and his mind seemed to have returned to its original razor-sharp state, making him far too observant at the moment.

"Would you believe I recently came to the realization, what with my father currently escorting my mother through the designer salons of Europe, that no one was making use of our membership here? And, as I'm sure you've been able to deduce, because of the exclusive nature of this particular club, dues are rather dear to maintain. That right there explains why I became uncomfortable being neglectful of our attendance, especially since I've never been a gentleman to embrace a wasteful nature."

"I could almost believe that if not for the unusual situations we've found ourselves in of late, not the least of those being ambushed in the middle of Central Park and shot at with arrows. We were then rescued by two charming, albeit curiously dressed, young ladies, who went about whisking us to safety in a questionable milk wagon that certainly did not have its milk bottles properly secured. If that weren't enough, you and Permilia then sat down to tea with the Huxley sisters, women known throughout the city for their unquestionably disturbing attitudes. Because of all that, I'm fairly sure there's a completely different reason to explain why we're *really* at the Knickerbocker Club."

"Did you know that they hold their membership here to only seven hundred?"

"Fascinating to learn, while at the same time dashing any hope I may have held that a future application I *might* have considered making here will *ever* be approved, but . . . you're avoiding my question."

When Harrison took to crossing his arms over his chest and staring at Asher without even bothering to blink—a tactic he'd developed when negotiating important business deals over the years—Asher blew out a breath, knowing it would be easier to just admit defeat.

Besides, considering Asher had decided to become a more formidable type of gentleman, he'd hardly be successful in building that type of reputation if he were witnessed fidgeting in his chair simply because he was pinned under his friend's unnerving stare.

Leaning forward, he looked around, ascertained no was

listening in on them, and then lowered his voice, just in case. "I've decided I need to make some changes in my life."

"Ah, finally listening to Permilia, are you—choosing to make yourself a more difficult target by switching up your schedule?"

Asher sat back in his chair. "So you find me to be a predictable man as well?"

Harrison picked up his glass of Apollinaris water and took a drink. "You say that as if there's something lacking with being a predictable man."

"I've never known anyone to strive to be predictable, Harrison. It's boring and lacks any semblance of danger."

"Where in the world is that coming from?"

Asher began to drum his fingers on the arm of the chair. "Do you know that my doorman, Mr. Cushing, found it amusing to even contemplate the idea that an assassin had been hired to kill me?" Asher waved a hand Harrison's way. "But he had no difficulty whatsoever believing you'd attract the notice of a killer, and . . . he was also of the opinion that the killer would have no chance of success in completing his mission with you as the target since everyone seems to believe that *you're* a dangerous man."

"Mr. Cushing actually said that I'm a dangerous man?"

"Well, no, not out loud, but it was definitely implied."

Harrison's brows drew together. "I'm not certain where you expect me to go with this conversation."

Leaning forward, Asher caught Harrison's eye. "I want you to teach me how to become a dangerous gentleman, one who looks as if he eats nails for breakfast and bullets for lunch."

Harrison choked on the Apollinaris water he'd been in the process of drinking and spent the next minute wheezing and gasping as he tried to catch his breath. Waving away a Knickerbocker server who'd appeared to offer him assistance, Harrison drew in a rasping breath. Clearing his throat a second later, he nodded to the server who'd not bothered to move so much as a single step, having more than likely been taught that allowing a gentleman to die while he was visiting the Knickerbocker Club was to be avoided at all costs.

"I'm fine—really I am," Harrison finally managed to say.

"Was the water not to your liking, sir? Was it perhaps too strong for you?"

Harrison pulled out a ratty-looking handkerchief and wiped eyes that had taken to streaming. "It's water, my good man, not brandy, but perhaps it was the lemon—put in per my request, of course—that did me in."

"Lemons can be tricky, sir."

"Indeed."

The server put his hands behind his back. "Would you prefer something more soothing, perhaps . . . tea . . . or maybe a nice lemonade?"

"Tea will be fine, since as was just mentioned I seem to be having difficulties with lemons today."

"Very good sir." The server inclined his head, did the same to Asher, then turned and moved on silent feet out of the reading room they were sitting in.

Shoving his handkerchief back in his pocket, Harrison stretched his legs out in front of him and folded his hands over his stomach.

"Now that I can breathe again," he began, "allow me to set the record straight. I do not eat, nor have I ever eaten, nails for breakfast, preferring instead a nice dish of eggs, the fluffier the better, along with toast if there's jam to spread on it, and . . ." He grinned. "I know most dangerous men are assumed to drink coffee, and black coffee at that, but"—he shuddered—"I can't abide the stuff and normally enjoy a large glass of milk with my meal. As for bullets for lunch, well, I daresay you can't name a lunch we've enjoyed together where I've ordered bullets."

Asher stretched out his legs as well. "The fact that you don't actually eat nails or bullets is completely beside the point. You *look* like you could, and that right there is what I need you to teach me."

"Are you certain you didn't suffer a head injury as well yesterday, one that rattled that interesting brain of yours and has you so out of sorts today?"

"I'm not suffering from a brain malady, Harrison. Far from it. If you must know, I've finally realized that I've settled into a rather predictable life—become complacent, some might say. I need to make some changes before I turn into one of those stodgy old men who find disappointment around every corner."

"Ah, so this is about Permilia."

"How did you arrive at that conclusion?"

"When a gentleman longs to make significant changes in his life, it's always due to a woman."

Asher simply stared at his friend for a second before he shook his head. "Or it might very well be a direct result of that gentleman—when he was under attack by a bow-wielding assassin—watching as his friend pulled the expected pistol out of his pocket, but when *he* stuck his hand into his *own* pocket . . . the only weapon he had at his disposal was a powder puff."

"And candy, which staved off the hunger pangs of that friend with the pistol," Harrison added as his lips twitched at the corners.

Asher narrowed his eyes. "A dangerous man would not be caught dead with a powder puff in his pocket, which means I've become a dandy."

"There's a word you don't often hear these days."

"Which further proves my point."

Sitting upright when the server returned with his tea, Harrison accepted the cup, thanked the man, and busied himself stirring his drink before he caught Asher's eye.

"You're not a dandy. You simply have an appreciation for fashion, one that has allowed you to build up quite the fortune."

"You've built up a fortune as well, but your building up of a fortune has entailed using the sweat of your own brow while battling the forces of nature as you travel the high seas, testing out your ships."

"I've seen you sweat numerous times."

"When?"

"Well, ah, I distinctly remember a time when you were delivered a note, while you were at Delmonico's, notifying you that a large shipment of silk something or others had been delivered to the store earlier than expected. Since the only man at the store at that particular time was a guard with a touch of rheumatism, you took it upon yourself to leave Delmonico's and unpack the wagons with your own two hands."

"You weren't even there, so how do you know for certain I broke a sweat?"

"Because I saw you afterward, and . . . your hair was disheveled."

"Name another."

Harrison shook his head. "I think not, because my point has been sufficiently made."

"You can't think of another time, can you, when I might have taken to sweating?"

"I'm not a man who has ever been overly observant about such matters, Asher. And while I'm sure you're enjoying being so obstinate, in my opinion, you're being overly hard on yourself."

"I'm not being hard enough, Harrison. I've willingly chosen to live within the relatively small community of the socially elite, and because of that decision, I'm woefully ill-equipped to deal with the real world."

"You're one of my closest friends, Asher, and as you and I both know, I'm not a member of the socially elite, which means your world is not as small as you think." Harrison lifted his teacup and took a sip. "However, having said that, I think, if you were being honest with yourself, you'd admit that all of this angst is a direct result of the affection you feel for Permilia."

"I never said I hold Permilia in affection."

Harrison waved that aside. "You didn't need to, but if I may continue sharing my opinion with you, I believe you're concerned that she won't return that affection, which has made you doubt yourself as a man."

"Are you quite certain the physician who looked at your head yesterday found it to be in fine form?"

"You know perfectly well that the physician found me to be quite well. You were standing right beside me when he pronounced me almost as fit as a fiddle."

"Did you consider the idea that he might have found you so fit because he was simply anxious to get back to studying Gertrude's unusual condition?"

Harrison smiled. "Her skin did seem to continue turning a brighter shade of orange as the minutes ticked by."

"Which is why you may not have been properly seen to, given the attention Gertrude was commanding."

"You sat with me for two hours as we waited for the hospital staff to complete their experiments on Gertrude, so you know full well I was not concussed, just a bit rattled because I'd been clobbered over the head with milk bottles." He smiled. "I must say I was thankful the one physician made a point of telling Gertrude that I shouldn't be held responsible for anything I might have said directly after suffering that clobbering."

"So she's forgiven you for calling her a *pretty little thing*?" Asher asked, having no qualms whatsoever in embracing the idea of changing the subject.

"I can only hope that my three sisters are never privy to the fact that those particular words slipped out of my mouth, brain injury or not, because they'd certainly waste no time in taking me to task on Gertrude's behalf."

Asher frowned. "That almost sounds as if your sisters have become progressive sorts."

Harrison returned the frown. "Of course they're progressive, Asher, as I would expect them to be. They're included in every aspect of our shipping business. And since I've grown up with a mother who knows just as much about shipping as my father does, I'm definitely of the opinion that women have been soundly insulted over the years, given that their abilities have been misunderstood to such a great degree."

"One really does have to wonder why we're friends when we hold such different opinions on almost everything."

"Being anything but supportive of the suffrage movement is an opinion you should reconsider, my friend, but . . . since we are friends and I'm of the belief that, as such, it's perfectly fine for us to agree to disagree, let us return to what we were speaking about before."

"Miss Gertrude Cadwalader," Asher said with a nod.

Sending him a far too knowing look, Harrison took another sip of his tea. "Miss Gertrude Cadwalader is a fascinating woman, kind as well, since she did not take offense at me calling her a pretty little thing. Although, come to think of it, that lack of offense might have been more because she mentioned how poor the lighting was in the milk compartment and didn't believe I'd been able to see her properly enough to make a sound judgment about her looks."

"You don't find her to be attractive?"

"I didn't say that. She's delightful, orange skin and all, even while wearing ratty trousers and sporting a hairstyle that she claimed Mrs. Davenport, her companion, had been responsible for." Harrison's look turned a little distant. "I think there's much more to Gertrude than meets the eye, which is why I'm pleased to announce that she promised to go sailing with me once the weather turns warmer, and when the skin the doctors were unable to turn back to its original color fades just a touch."

The distant look vanished in the blink of an eye as Harrison returned his attention to Asher. "But enough about Miss Cadwalader. To refresh that deliberately faulty memory of yours, we were actually discussing Permilia what seems like eons ago, so we'll return the conversation to her."

"Must we?"

"I fear we must. And since you seem reluctant to move the conversation forward, allow me to point out that, while you claim to not hold her in affection, I believe that affection was sparked between the two of you over two months ago, when you haggled with her at Central Park—when she took you to task over what you were charging for those ice skates, if memory serves me correctly."

"Why would you think I'd develop affection for a woman who was so proficient with haggling that I wanted to wring that lovely neck of hers?"

"You were fascinated with the very idea that a woman was familiar enough with the price of skates that she could haggle with you about that price."

"It turned out to be an unsuccessful haggling session on my end, since Permilia ended up paying exactly what she wanted for the skates. If anything, I was beyond annoyed with her."

"I'm certain you were annoyed with her, but underneath that annoyance, you appreciated her spirit, and . . ." Harrison drew in a breath. "Before you make the claim that allowing her to win the day reinforces the idea that you're a dandy, or makes you anything less than a gentleman, it doesn't. If anything, it reinforces the idea that you're a true gentleman in every sense of the word."

"I didn't deliberately allow her to win the day."

Harrison rolled his eyes. "You're being obstinate again, and you know you did because she fascinates you and you didn't want to disappoint her. But . . . I hope that you also understand that she's fascinated with you as well."

"She's not fascinated with me," Asher argued. "She grew up in the midst of miners, which means she's more likely to be fascinated with a man like Mr. Slater, a man deeply involved in the mining industry, over a man like me."

Harrison set aside his tea. "But she agreed to dance with you, not Mr. Slater, and if you ask me, that right there is telling."

The corners of Asher's lips began to curve. "Did I mention to you that she misunderstood what the Go-As-You-Please Quadrille was all about, so spent almost the entire dance moving in the wrong direction, leaving mayhem in her wake?"

"I *like* this woman." Harrison grinned. "And you like her as well, but speaking of that quadrille has recalled me to those articles in the paper yesterday." He turned rather somber. "I was concerned about Permilia's distracted air once you and she returned to the hospital to collect me and Gertrude. At first, I thought she was distracted because of the unlikely invitation to tea the two of you enjoyed at the hands of the Huxley sisters, but then . . . when she made such an abrupt departure from the hospital, after having maintained her distracted air for quite some time, I got to wondering." He blew out a breath. "Do you think that those articles you and Permilia learned about while having tea with the Huxley sisters bothered her more than she was letting on?"

Asher nodded. "I think they may have done just that. Permilia does not seem to be a lady to forget an appointment, but when she looked at her watch while we were waiting for Gertrude, and realized she'd almost missed an engagement she'd promised to attend, the clear worry in her eyes lent credence to the idea that she was certainly in a distracted frame of mind."

"I wonder if she was able to meet her obligations for that engagement in the end, or if she missed it entirely? She would have clearly needed to change out of the disguise she was wearing, and growing up with three sisters, I'm well aware of how long it can take for a lady to make herself presentable."

Asher smiled. "I don't envy you your sisters, Harrison, even though all three of them are charming sorts—mischievous sorts as well, of course, but charming. However, getting back to Permilia, because I was concerned about her behavior, I did take it upon myself to call at the Griswold house after I'd seen you and Gertrude home. Permilia was not there, so I concluded she'd left to attend whatever engagement she'd forgotten about."

"You don't know what that engagement was, though?"

"No, she never mentioned where she was expected, and when I was ushered into the Griswold household in order to speak with Permilia's stepmother, Ida, well, she had not the least idea where her stepdaughter had been heading for the evening."

"Didn't that seem a bit curious to you, that Mrs. Griswold would not know the location of her own stepdaughter?"

"It's not as if Ida Griswold raised Permilia, Harrison. And since Permilia is hardly a green girl out of the schoolroom, I have the impression that she does exactly what she pleases when her presence is not required at a society event."

"I imagine Mrs. Griswold does not afford her daughter, Miss Lucy Webster, that same freedom," Harrison said.

"I imagine she doesn't, especially since Lucy was at home last night and seemed quite eager for me to join them for tea." Asher smiled. "She spent a good thirty minutes chatting about the ball and how I thought her Little Bo Peep costume had been received, and then"—his smile faded—"she began questioning me about Mr. Eugene Slater, a gentleman I know relatively little about, and one I wasn't that keen to discuss."

"Because he's shown an interest in Permilia."

Asher pretended he hadn't heard that remark. "I felt it was not well done of Lucy to inquire about a man who'd shown such interest in her stepsister. It struck me as a fairly unsisterly thing to do."

"And you didn't want to discuss Mr. Slater because he *did* have an interest in Permilia."

"I have no cause to believe he *doesn't* still hold an interest in Permilia."

Sitting forward, Harrison shook his head. "Because I have three sisters, Asher, and because my family has amassed a rather substantial fortune, I have to broach a subject that's not exactly pleasant—that subject being the real reason Mr. Slater is showing an interest in both Permilia and her stepsister."

Asher sat forward as well. "You believe Mr. Slater may be more interested in the Griswold mining ventures than either Permilia or Lucy?"

"I've seen it happen in my family—more than once, unfortunately."

"But Permilia is a delightful lady in her own right, no matter the large fortune behind her name, and . . ." Asher stopped speaking when he noticed the knowing look now residing in Harrison's eyes. Edging back into his seat, he folded his arms across his chest. "Did I tell you that I've secured the services of the Pinkerton Detective Agency?"

"It's about time, what with someone seemingly being incredibly keen to kill you."

"Indeed, and I willingly admit I do feel better having them watching my back. I've been assured that their best men will be put on my case and that if all goes according to plan, I'll live a long and prosperous life."

"Do they have any ideas regarding who might be behind the threats against you?"

"They seem to think it's one of my competitors, disgruntled

over my hiring practices, which is why those competitors are being interviewed as we speak."

"That'll be certain to earn you additional friends."

"Quite, but . . . at the very least, Permilia should receive a touch of satisfaction that I've now taken the risk to my life seriously and have acted accordingly."

"That's probably the only satisfaction she'll receive today, given the distress she's certain to have been experiencing over the damage those newspaper articles have done to her reputation."

"You don't truly believe that Permilia has suffered real damage to her reputation because of a few ridiculous articles printed in the papers, do you?"

"Have you bothered to read everything that's been written about the two of you?"

"I thought it was just one or two articles, and the one Miss Quill wrote wasn't even damaging."

"You and Permilia were mentioned in every single paper printed in the city, almost as if the reporters were being paid from more than one source and spread their rather limited articles around, embellishing those articles in the process."

Harrison leaned forward until he was on the very edge of his seat. "And, while I'm sure that what I'm about to suggest will come as something of a shock, I'm not hesitant to broach the subject since I'm now firmly convinced you hold Permilia in high regard. Because of that, and because of the insinuations that have been leveled against the two of you, I really do believe the only option you have moving forward is to offer her your name."

CHAPTER
SIXTEEN

"Are you quite certain you don't want to talk about the reasoning behind your abrupt plans to depart for Paris tomorrow morning?"

Turning away from the steamer trunk, where she'd just placed a delicate chemise she'd purchased from an out-of-the-way shop located by Battery Park, Permilia smiled at Gertrude, who was sitting on the floor of Permilia's room, sorting through stockings.

"While I find it incredibly kind of you to be concerned on my behalf, Gertrude, I think you have quite enough going on at the moment, what with being Mrs. Davenport's paid companion and all."

"My days with Mrs. Davenport aren't always a trial. And when she does happen to step over a few lines here and there, she's always willing to make it up to me, hence my full day off today with pay and a promise to never turn me orange again."

Permilia grinned. "I must say it was amusing when we found ourselves arguing with the staff over the idea that Harrison was the one who needed immediate medical attention, not you."

"As soon as they discovered that lump on the back of his head, they were much keener to believe us, but"—Gertrude grinned—"they certainly didn't abandon their interest in me, what with all the poking and prodding they subjected me to." Gertrude's grin widened. "However, since they did get my skin to lighten up just a bit with that alcohol solution and assured me that I'll be completely orange-free in a week or two, I no longer take issue with their fussing. Besides . . . I did get to spend additional time with the charming Mr. Harrison Sinclair. I was just tickled to death when he and Asher insisted on staying with me at the hospital after you left for your appointment. I told both gentlemen I was perfectly capable of hiring a hansom cab to see myself home, but neither of them would hear a single word about that."

"I do hope you didn't come to regret encouraging me to take the delivery wagon."

Gertrude took to looking rather smug. "As I just mentioned, being stuck at the hospital with two delightful gentlemen, especially Mr. Harrison Sinclair, was not exactly a hardship for me—because again . . . he's delightful. And I certainly wasn't put out with you that you needed to get on your way. You were obviously distracted, and it wasn't as if you left me on my deathbed. I was simply an unusual color, not injured."

"I am sorry for leaving you, even with delightful gentlemen." Permilia tilted her head. "May I presume that you now hold a bit of affection for Harrison?"

Gertrude waved a still slightly orange hand in the air. "I may find him to be unusually delightful, but I am, at heart, a realist. Gentlemen like Harrison rarely, if ever, become interested in someone like me, which is why I would never allow myself to become romantically interested in someone like him."

Moving away from the steamer trunk and walking across the room, Permilia took a seat on the floor directly beside Gertrude. "He seemed rather interested in you yesterday."

194

"Because I was orange. You have to admit that not many people have an opportunity to encounter an orange woman these days."

"He called you a pretty little thing."

"Which was not well-done of him at all. But . . . in his defense, he had suffered a few blows to the head when he uttered that unfortunate phrase."

"I've found that people usually utter the truth when their defenses are down, or . . . in Harrison's case, battered."

Setting the stocking she'd been folding aside, Gertrude lifted her head. "An interesting notion, to be sure, but now is hardly the time to discuss such trivial matters. In case you've forgotten, you're being carted off to Paris tomorrow. And forgive me if I'm much mistaken, but I do believe that might have been a spur-of-the-moment decision, and not a decision you were responsible for." She caught Permilia's eye. "I've been considering all sorts of dire scenarios ever since I received your note two hours ago, disclosing your intention to sail on tomorrow's tide. The only reasonable scenario I've come up with is that you've brought on the wrath of your stepmother and this is your punishment for incurring that wrath."

Permilia blew out a breath. "Ida's embarrassed over the articles that have been published in the newspapers of late. Because of that, she's decided that in order to avoid the shame I've apparently brought on my family by doing . . . well, nothing untoward, we're going to repair to Paris. We may even take a tour of the continents, depending on how long it takes for the gossip to die down."

"That sounds as if it will be a grand adventure," Gertrude said somewhat weakly.

"It won't be, especially since Lucy is in high dudgeon over the very idea of being whisked out of the country right when she's in the midst of becoming further acquainted with Mr. Eugene

Slater. *He's* taken to courting her, and *she's* apparently decided she's head over heels in love with him, even though she barely knows the man."

Gertrude's lips thinned. "I thought Mr. Slater was keen on courting you."

"I'm not put out about his change of courting targets. I've now come to the conclusion that he purposefully sought me out at the ball because he was interested in becoming better acquainted with my father and his mining ventures. That meant he was never interested in me, only the advantage an alliance with me would bring to him."

"Surely you're wrong about that."

"I'm afraid I'm probably not. And while I did try to broach this disturbing speculation with Lucy, she flatly refused to listen to me, claiming instead that I was simply jealous of her and her standing within society, and didn't care to see her happy because of that jealousy."

"Lucy is such a charming girl."

Permilia smiled. "Indeed, although in her defense, it really wasn't her fault that she was remarkably spoiled growing up, what with her father being so much older than Ida and never imagining he'd be blessed to have a child. Then, after Lucy suffered the loss of her indulgent father, Ida tried to overcompensate to make up for that loss, showering dear Lucy with whatever Lucy wanted. It did not do her any favors, nor did it help develop any sense of compassion for anyone other than herself, but . . . perhaps Mr. Slater will be good for her in the end, since he doesn't strike me as the type of man to be taken advantage of."

"Why would you say that?"

"I grew up amongst miners, Gertrude. They're a difficult breed, and it takes a man of strength to manage them. It appears Mr. Slater manages his mines quite well, and that suggests

196

he's not a man to be trifled with, nor will he be a man moved by pretty tears or prone to give in to the demands Lucy will inevitably start making."

"Hopefully she'll figure that out before any vows are spoken."

"My father, being a man remarkably similar to Mr. Slater, will insist, if nothing else, on a long courtship, although . . . he might surprise me and embrace the idea of Lucy and Mr. Slater wholeheartedly, especially since I'm not getting any younger, and I apparently lost the interest of the only man who'd be capable of taking over my father's ventures to my stepsister."

Gertrude tilted her head. "You don't sound overly upset about that."

"I'm hardly likely to be upset over losing the affections of a man I barely know."

"There is that, and there is the idea that your affections may have already been placed squarely on someone else."

Heat settled in Permilia's cheeks. "I'm sure I have no idea what you're suggesting."

"I'm sure you do, but tell me this, while you said Lucy is disappointed to be whisked away because of Mr. Slater, are you suffering a disappointment as well, since you're being whisked away from Asher, delaying the proposal I'm certain he's contemplating making?"

Permilia's mouth dropped open. "What?"

"Surely you've considered the possibility—what with the ruckus those articles have caused around the city—that Asher would do the proper thing and ask you to marry him."

"Are you quite certain those treatments they gave you yesterday haven't done something to your mind?"

"My mind is fine, thank you very much, but I have to wonder about the state of yours. You've been out in society for quite a few seasons. You have to be remarkably familiar with how innuendos and sly suggestions are handled—and if you've forgotten, they're handled with a walk down the aisle."

"Asher and I did nothing untoward at the Vanderbilt ball, which means there was, and is, no reason for me to even contemplate something of that nature."

"But you were written about at length in the papers."

"Unfortunately, that is true, and that right there was exactly what was behind my distraction at the hospital, that distraction almost having me miss a most important appointment last night. However, I willingly admit that I was more distracted by the idea that someone had the audacity to print an exaggeration of the true circumstances that occurred between Asher and me at the ball over any harm my reputation might have suffered. Although . . ." She caught Gertrude's eye. "Good heavens, I do hope this hasn't harmed Asher's reputation. He clearly prizes his standing within society and needs that standing in order to increase sales at his store."

"I thought you believed Asher makes more than his fair share of profits at his store, since you've claimed more than a few times that he overcharges for his merchandise."

"And he does, but I've since come to understand that the reasoning behind his high prices has more to do with his paying his employees a higher wage than any greed on Asher's part. And, because he's been able to secure the employment of the best salesladies and sales gentlemen in the city, his customers receive uncommonly fine service, that service paid for by the cost of his goods."

"It sounds to me as if you've had a distinct change of attitude toward Mr. Asher Rutherford, which means . . ." Gertrude nodded rather knowingly. "You wouldn't be opposed if he did ask you for your hand, would you?"

The very idea of Asher Rutherford asking for her hand had Permilia's stomach churning ever so slightly, but not in a queasy way, more in an . . . anticipatory fashion, which . . . She pushed herself up from the floor and moved back to her steamer trunk, busying herself with packing the essential clothing she would need in Paris, more as a way to avoid Gertrude's sharp eyes than any great desire to pack for a trip she had no wish to make.

"You're well suited for him," Gertrude said, her words having Permilia turning around to face her again.

"I'm afraid I can't agree with that, Gertrude. Asher grew up in the very midst of society, learning and apparently enjoying all the rules that go along with belonging to that society. I grew up in the midst of nowhere, attending not the finest schools but learning through tutors my father hired who weren't exactly proficient in teaching me the expected feminine graces."

"Which was a blessing for you, as I'm sure you're very well aware."

"My unusual education, while providing me with knowledge that's normally reserved for men, did not prepare me for the world I'm now forced to live in, making me an outsider instead."

"Being a member of the fashionable set, Permilia, is highly overrated. I, for one, am thankful you've never fit in— otherwise you and I would have never been given the opportunity to become friends."

"Which has been lovely, to be sure, but I would never fit into Asher's world."

"You have more in common with him than you know. You may make the claim that you're a frugal shopper, but you've got one of the best eyes for fashion and design I've ever seen, which means you speak Asher's language. Quite honestly, I think the two of you would make a formidable team if you joined forces."

"As appealing as that may sound, Asher has disclosed to me his unfortunate opinions on women and where they belong in the scheme of life. Joining forces with a woman in order to work together is not something I believe Asher would ever consider doing."

"I can't see Asher remaining stuck in such opinions as he becomes better acquainted with you."

"Since I'm off for Europe tomorrow, Gertrude, Asher's views on women will most likely not change anytime in the . . ."

A knock on Permilia's bedchamber door had the rest of her words trailing to an end. Turning, she found one of the Griswold maids, Maude, poking her head in the door.

"Pardon me for interrupting, Miss Permilia, but a note just arrived for you, one that states right on the front of the parchment that it's a matter of great urgency."

Gesturing Maude into the room, Permilia met her halfway, taking the note. Frowning when she recognized the writing scrawled across the front as belonging to none other than her editor, she moved to the window under the pretense of needing better light to read the note.

Slipping her finger under the fold, she broke the seal and opened up the page, scanning the contents. Lifting her head, she summoned up a smile.

"Nothing to worry about, but I'm afraid we're going to have to cut our visit a bit short, Gertrude."

Gertrude's gaze darted to the note in Permilia's hand. "May I assume that note has something to do with the oh-so-mysterious appointment you had last night, the one you almost forgot about?"

Permilia's smile widened. "In all truthfulness, no, this note has nothing to do with that meeting, but if you would be so kind as to stay, Maude, and to close that door so we won't be overheard, I'd appreciate your assistance in this matter."

With Gertrude looking more confused than ever, and Maude moving to shut the door, Permilia walked over to where a settee was placed by the side of the window, making short work of clearing off the clothing she'd considered packing for Paris. Pulling up a spare chair once she'd cleared off the settee, she waved Gertrude and Maude forward.

As everyone took their seats, Permilia leaned forward and lowered her voice. "This is not common knowledge, Gertrude, but it suddenly struck me, especially since I'm going to be out of the country for an extended period of time, that perhaps you, being one of my very good friends, would be interested in assisting me with a dilemma I just realized I face."

Maude raised a hand to her chest. "Goodness, Miss Permilia, I only just now realized that your leaving is indeed a dilemma, what with the support you give Miss Snook and all."

"Who is . . . Miss Snook?" Gertrude asked.

"She's the owner of Miss Snook's School for the Improvement of Feminine Minds," Permilia said. "A school I became involved with not long after my father married Ida and moved me permanently to New York."

Gertrude sat back against the settee. "Does Ida know that you're involved with what sounds to me as if it might be a controversial school?"

"Of course not," Permilia began. "Miss Snook's school is for young women who have not been given any advantages in their lives, and—"

"Like me," Maude interrupted. "Along with a lot of other women who work as domestics simply because we lack the education needed to do anything else." She smiled at Gertrude. "I've been improving my speech for the past four years, along with my reading abilities, because I'm hopeful that someday I may very well be fortunate enough to become a companion, like you are for Mrs. Davenport." Maude's eyes grew wide. "I didn't mean to suggest, though, that I would be on an equal footing with you, Miss Cadwalader, seeing as how you are related to some of the most well-regarded families in New York."

Gertrude waved away Maude's words. "I was raised in genteel poverty, Maude. And while my being related to well-regarded families did make it possible for me to obtain a well-rounded education, I was only able to attend the schools I did because of the generosity of others." She smiled. "I think it's wonderful that you're striving to improve yourself with education, although I'm not certain how I could possibly help."

"How's your math?" Permilia asked.

Gertrude bit her lip. "The basics . . . Or are you inquiring how I do with the more advanced subjects? I'm not much good for anything more than multiplication and division."

Maude cleared her throat. "If Miss Cadwalader is not comfortable taking on the science and math classes you teach, Miss Griswold, she could always teach deportment and perhaps carry on with the lessons you were giving on dressing to impress future employers. Although . . ." Maude glanced Gertrude's way and winced, probably because Gertrude, while looking almost normal today, did have a few more bows in her hair than most ladies would choose to wear, and her gown, interestingly enough, was littered with an overabundance of buttons—compliments, no doubt, of Mrs. Davenport's artistic nature.

"I'm very good with deportment," Gertrude said with a grin. "And while I would be more than willing to help here and there with teaching, was there anything besides teaching you needed assistance with while you're off in Paris?"

Taking a moment to consider the matter, Permilia frowned. "Well, Miss Snook does occasionally ask me to step in to find positions for some of the young women who get let go when their participation in the school becomes known to irate employers. If you feel comfortable broaching the subject, you could enlist Mrs. Davenport's aid in that regard since I won't be available to get those women hired on here."

"That's how I got my current position," Maude said with a nod Permilia's way.

Permilia rose to her feet. "And since I've been called away on another matter, I might not have the time needed to seek Miss Snook out and explain why I'm off to Paris, so . . ." She moved to the small desk where she wrote the majority of her articles for the *New York Sun* and pulled out a fresh sheet of paper. Taking a moment to write down her message, she straightened and walked back over to Gertrude, handing her the note. "I've written down the address of the school for you, as well as a message to deliver to Miss Snook—that message being that I will see to it that the funds I provide her with on a monthly basis will still be delivered to her on schedule."

Gertrude got up from the settee and put the note in the pocket of her gown, a pocket that had not one but two buttons to see it securely closed. "I'm surprised Ida hasn't discovered your secret about the school over the years, especially if you're its benefactor."

"I'm sure you'll now understand more fully why I've become such a frugal shopper. That frugality has been one of the ways I've been able to divert most of my pin money to the school while still being able to maintain a fashionable wardrobe that doesn't embarrass my stepmother." Permilia blew out a sigh. "I was quite unused to being restricted to such limited funds after my father married Ida, but in all honesty, it has made me become rather creative with my spending, and has given me a greater appreciation for the value of a dollar."

The clock on the wall began to chime, recalling Permilia to the idea she needed to be getting on her way to the paper.

"But now, I do fear I'm going to have to say good-bye, because I need to address some business that was disclosed in that note I just received. Although . . . now that I've just told you one of my secrets, it seems somewhat silly to not confess all."

Gertrude shook her head. "One confession is fine for now, Permilia, but when you return from Paris, I'll be more than happy to hear all about your other secrets, ones I'm sure will explain all of that lurking and scribbling on dance cards you do at each and every society event."

With that, and after she'd given Permilia a rather delightful hug, Gertrude stepped back, pulled gloves over her slightly orange hands, and pulled down a bit of netting from her hat that sufficiently obscured her face, or more specifically, her orange cheeks. Wishing Permilia the best of luck, she took hold of Maude's arm and together they walked from the room, their heads together as they launched into a discussion about Miss Snook's unusual school.

Feeling a great sense of relief that she wasn't leaving Miss Snook in a complete lurch, what with Gertrude's enthusiasm to help, Permilia walked to her wardrobe and fetched a coat.

Letting herself out of the house a short time later, while doing her utmost best to avoid Ida and Lucy—which wasn't as difficult as she'd expected since they'd apparently gone out—Permilia slung the satchel she always took with her when she visited the *New York Sun* over her shoulder, her handy disguise nestled in the confines of the bag.

Squinting against the bright sun beaming from a cloudless sky, Permilia headed up the street, intent on hitching a ride on an omnibus, a source of transportation she used often when visiting her editor.

She had gotten all of three houses down the sidewalk when an unexpected chill swept down her spine, that chill bringing her feet slowly to a stop. Glancing up and down the sidewalk, she didn't notice anything out of sorts, but when she lifted her hand against the uncommonly bright sun, her gaze traveled over and then back to a gentleman standing on the opposite side of Park Avenue.

There was something about him, something . . . disturbing, and something that kept her frozen to the spot. Why she felt that way, she couldn't actually say, since he appeared to simply be a man perusing a newspaper, although . . . She squinted and regarded him further.

It almost seemed as if he was now deliberately hiding his face behind that paper, having hitched it up a good few inches after she'd caught sight of him.

When he turned and headed off down the sidewalk, she got a brief glimpse of his profile, a profile that looked curiously familiar, although she couldn't place where she'd seen the man before.

Tightening her grip on her satchel, she set off down the sidewalk after the man, keeping an eye on him as she walked, a rather daunting feat considering they were separated by the traffic traveling along Park Avenue.

When a large wagon sporting the name of *Henry Siede Furs* rumbled past, the height of the wagon obscuring her view, Permilia craned her neck to make certain the mysterious man was still on the other side of the sidewalk . . . and stopped in her tracks a moment later when she realized he'd disappeared from sight.

Debating whether or not she had the time to locate the man, she glanced one last time over the length of the sidewalk, a small smile tugging the corners of her lips when she spotted a man, and then another, both of whom were perusing a newspaper.

Her smile turned into a grin as the thought sprang to mind that she was beginning to see murder plots and skullduggery around every corner, when in actuality, it was simply normal scenes of life playing out before her eyes. Setting off down the sidewalk again, she flagged down a hansom cab, realizing she was now running behind schedule and did not have the time to catch a ride on an omnibus.

205

Settling back into the seat, she turned her thoughts from dastardly plots and settled them on the reasons her editor might have summoned her into the *New York Sun*.

Anticipation coiled through her as the idea struck that perhaps her editor had been so impressed with the column she'd written about the Vanderbilt ball that he was finally going to give her a much-deserved raise.

CHAPTER
SEVENTEEN

"What do you mean, I need to switch up my articles?" Permilia demanded, flipping up the veil attached to the hat she'd exchanged with her traveling hat right before she'd exited the hansom cab and entered the *New York Sun* building. Narrowing her gaze on her editor, Mr. Charles Dana, a man she normally enjoyed speaking with but certainly wasn't enjoying today, her temper edged up a notch when he sent her what seemed to be a rolling of his eyes.

"Honestly, Miss Griswold, why is it that reporters have to be such a dramatic lot? I'm not questioning your ability to pen a credible column. I'm simply telling you that you're going to have to spice up that column in order to be competitive with the other society columns that are springing up in all the other papers in town."

"Spice it up? I'm afraid you're going to have to be more specific than that since I truly have no idea what *spicing* could possibly entail."

"I need you to be more diligent from this point forward in making certain your articles have those titillating tidbits about individual society members that readers are most assuredly going to demand. Those tidbits need to pertain to not what is being worn or what dances are being danced, but what happens when the music stops and the gossip begins."

Permilia crossed her arms over her chest. "I'm sorry, but I thought I was writing for the *New York Sun,* not the *New York Herald.*"

"The *New York Herald* sold every copy of its paper when it came out with its Vanderbilt edition. We were not that fortunate."

"I'm sure that their scintillating articles *were* found to be riveting by the masses, but I find it hard to believe that articles penned with salacious content will find favor for long. This is simply a peculiar circumstance, driven by the frenzy the Vanderbilt ball caused throughout the city. I highly doubt it will settle into a trend."

Mr. Dana leaned back in his roller chair, placing his hands behind his head. "I'm afraid the times are changing, Miss Griswold. Now that readers have gotten a taste of the scandalous, they're not going to be content to return to the vanilla articles of the past."

"I don't believe you're giving our readers enough credit. A little bit of gossip and scandal is all well and good, just like ice cream, but one cannot exist on ice cream for long. You mark my words, readers will grow tired of the nasty feeling they'll get after consuming rubbish for more than a week or two."

Mr. Dana dropped a hand and patted his rather thick stomach. "I've been known to exist on substances sweeter than ice cream for extended periods of time, Miss Griswold. And while you may think I'm not giving the readers enough credit, I believe you're simply reluctant to accept the true nature of people. Rubbish can be addicting, and because readers have now been given a taste of what has been forbidden in the past, they're not going to relinquish that taste willingly. Because of that, and because publishing a paper is business, not a charity endeavor, we need to give our readers what they're now salivating for."

"What about the integrity of the paper?"

"We'll certainly continue to offer responsible reporting when it comes to matters of actual news, but you write one of our society columns. It's not held to the same standards as the rest of the paper. And forgive me for what I'm about to say, because I'm fairly certain it will hurt your delicate writerly feelings, but"—he leaned forward, placing both of his hands on his desk—"your coverage of the Vanderbilt ball was severely lacking when compared to the coverage other reporters made of that exact same ball. Why, you didn't even mention the name of the young lady who went to the ball with a stuffed cat perched on her head."

"I never mention names, only initials, which to a certain extent protects the identity of the person I'm writing about, especially outside our rather small social circle."

"And that type of thinking is exactly what allowed the *New York Herald* to best us. They printed the cat lady's full name— which was Miss Kate Strong, if you weren't aware. They even described everything about Miss Strong's unusual costume, including the numerous cat tails she'd had sewn into the skirt of her costume, along with a choker she wore around her neck. That choker had a pendant hanging from it, one that had the word *Puss* engraved into it." He leveled a stern look on Permilia. "Did you not take notice of that interesting little detail?"

"Considering it was a rather large pendant, of course I did. But since everyone knows that Miss Strong's nickname is Puss, it would have been irresponsible of me to include that detail, just as unseemly as providing her full name. If you've forgotten, society does not care to be specifically named in any of our newspapers."

Mr. Dana continued on as if she hadn't spoken. "The *New York Herald* also had five inches of text dedicated to the subject of you and Mr. Rutherford—as in Mr. Asher Rutherford, who happens to be a gentleman worthy of an entire column dedicated strictly to him. Imagine my distress when I read that five inches and realized that you had barely mentioned Mr. Rutherford at all in your column."

Lifting her chin, Permilia sat forward. "If you will recall, I wrote that Miss G. and Mr. R. participated in the Go-As-You-Please Quadrille. I even wrote what I thought was a clever little bit about Miss G. becoming confused about the actual rules of that particular quadrille. For me, that was being downright bold."

Mr. Dana leaned halfway across his desk as his face turned an interesting shade of red. "The other papers told a different story about you and Mr. Rutherford. They told a remarkably riveting tale centered around the notion that the two of you spent an uncommon amount of time with each other."

"See, that's the problem right there, sir. We as reporters have a responsibility to report the truth, not to construct some fiction piece written solely to stir up trouble."

"You're not going to make the claim that you spent little to no time with Mr. Rutherford, are you?"

"I suppose I spent more time with him than I did any other gentleman at the ball, but . . . that's not exactly newsworthy."

"It'll be newsworthy once the two of you post an announcement, which is what all the papers are now holding their breaths for, wanting to be the first to publish that news."

"An . . . announcement?"

Mr. Dana slammed one of his hands down on the desk. "Yes, Miss Griswold, an announcement, and one of the intended matrimonial type." He shook a thick finger her way. "I want your promise here and now that the *Sun* will get an exclusive on that announcement. That means you cannot allow the information to become public until I have the presses up and running with details that include the way he proposed, your reaction to that proposal, when the wedding will be held, along with what church . . . and the names you have chosen for your first three children."

"Forgive me, but have you perhaps taken to having a few nips from a bottle in the afternoon? And not from a bottle of milk, if that was in question."

Ignoring what Permilia thought was a perfectly reasonable question, and one that would have explained much, Mr. Dana leveled a rather intense gaze on her. "Your promise, Miss Griswold, and now, if you please."

Permilia crossed her arms over her chest. "I hate to disappoint you, Mr. Dana, but . . . Mr. Rutherford and I have no intention of making any type of announcement. Why, we barely know each other, danced only one dance together, and didn't even join each other to dine."

Mr. Dana let out a grunt right before he dropped his head and began rummaging through a stack of papers on his desk, pulling out a sheet of rather rumpled newsprint a second later. Smoothing it out over his desk, he ran his finger down one of the columns, stopping when he found whatever it was he was searching for and lifting his head again. The look he settled on Permilia was hardly reassuring.

"According to our friends at the *New York Times*, you were noticed arguing with Mr. Rutherford while dinner was being served. Because of that, you may want to revise your statement about not dining with the man, unless what you truly meant to say is that you missed dining with the man because you became involved in an argument with him—thus putting you off your food."

Permilia wrinkled her nose. "Mr. Rutherford was partnered

with Miss Lukemeyer for dinner at the ball, which means I have absolutely no reason to revise my claim of not dining with him."

Mr. Dana nodded in a far too knowing fashion. "Ah, well, that explains why the article went on to claim that Miss Lukemeyer was observed to be looking quite put out for some unknown reason."

"And that right there is what's known as shoddy reporting, Mr. Dana, since anyone with eyes in their head could have deduced that Miss Lukemeyer was distressed because I interrupted her meal with Mr. Rutherford because of some unfortunate news I . . ."

Snapping her mouth shut the second she realized what her temper had almost allowed her to disclose, Permilia took to inspecting the cut of her sleeve, pulling absently at a thread that was coming loose.

Mr. Dana stood up and, curiously enough, looked rather excited. "I didn't read anything that could be construed as unfortunate news at the Vanderbilt ball in a single paper, which means this could be the exclusive we need to prove we're still the best paper in the city."

Permilia blinked. "Oh, I don't think we need to prove anything of the kind, sir."

Moving around the desk in a surprisingly agile fashion, given his somewhat bulky frame, Mr. Dana snagged a spare chair as he moved, pulling it right up beside Permilia, ignoring what she'd just said as he sat down.

"Tell me all the details regarding the unfortunate news that had you interrupting Mr. Rutherford when he was supposed to be dining with Miss Lukemeyer."

Permilia lifted her chin. "Did I mention that my stepmother, stepsister, and even Mr. Eugene Slater were sitting down to dine at that table with Mr. Rutherford and Miss Lukemeyer?"

Mr. Dana lifted his chin right back at her. "Unless that has something pertinent to do with the story of the unfortunate news, I really don't have an interest in the other guests sitting at that table."

"I was supposed to dine with Mr. Slater, but I was delayed, and he sat down to dine with my sister instead."

"You're beginning to annoy me, but traveling back to this delay, what was the reason behind it?"

Permilia began to drum her fingers on the arm of the uncomfortable chair she was sitting in. "Did you ever consider that I'd simply lost track of the time doing what I was supposed to be doing for you, searching out information for my article?"

Mr. Dana sent her another roll of his eyes. "Since everyone knows that gossip is always served as a side dish at any society meal, if you'd really been doing your job, you'd have been sitting at a table, listening in on the tales that were surely being bandied about." He shifted on his chair. "However, since it's clear you've not yet been convinced that disclosing to me, your employer, information that could benefit the paper is the proper thing to do, tell me more about your stepsister and how it came to be that she sat down to dine with a man you said was supposed to partner you."

Realizing that she'd made a grave error in using her stepsister as a distraction, especially since she was rapidly coming to the conclusion that Mr. Dana would not hesitate to print anything of a salacious nature if he felt it would sell more copies of his paper, Permilia summoned up a smile and abruptly changed the topic. "Did I mention that I'm off to Paris tomorrow, going there to do a bit of shopping at all the couture salons, which will allow me to provide you with some delightful fashion articles?"

Mr. Dana glared at her for all of five seconds before his eyes suddenly widened. "Your stepsister stole your dinner partner straight from you, didn't she?"

213

"I'm not certain how you expect me to respond to that."

"I would have expected you to include that little tidbit in with the nonsense you wrote about yourself and Mr. Rutherford, perhaps insinuating in the process that there's strife between you and Miss Webster."

"That would have made for an interesting breakfast conversation between me and Lucy, not to mention the indigestion it would have given my stepmother."

"It might have been a bonding experience for everyone involved," Mr. Dana countered. "You and your stepsister against the dastardly Miss Quill, star reporter for the *New York Sun*."

"I am Miss Quill."

"Well, of course you are, but your stepsister doesn't know that, nor does anyone else save me." Mr. Dana blew out a breath. "Considering I employ reporters who are supposed to be the best of the best, it's rather disheartening that none of them have uncovered your identity, but there you have it." He waved a hand her way. "As far as they seem to be concerned, you, as you're dressed now, are simply one of many informants I have around the city, an informant with a preference for hiding her identity behind widow weeds and veils."

"You have informants all around the city?"

Mr. Dana's gaze sharpened on Permilia's face. "Would they come in handy in helping you with that *unfortunate* news?"

The truth of the matter was yes, they would. But since Permilia got the distinct impression Mr. Dana would only allow her to use his informants if she agreed to some type of exclusive article, centered around what amounted to a scandalous murder plot . . . She pushed the temptation of his implied offer aside.

Squaring her shoulders, she forced a smile. "Do you know that when I received your note earlier, asking me to come speak with you, I believed it was going to be a pleasant meeting, one I hoped would end with you offering me a much-deserved increase in pay?"

Rising to his feet, Mr. Dana stomped his way back behind his desk, took his seat again in his well-worn and somewhat squeaky chair, and then caused Permilia to jump when he banged his fist on his desk.

It took significant effort on her part not to remark about his earlier statement that reporters were a dramatic lot—when in reality, it seemed as if editors were more prone to that particular condition.

"I have no words to reply to that increase-in-pay nonsense, Miss Griswold. You are the daughter of one of the wealthiest men in the country, and as such I never understood why you insisted on being paid a salary when I first offered you your position."

Permilia's temper began to simmer. "Forgive me for pointing this out, Mr. Dana, but it seems to me as if you have more than enough words to speak on the subject. And . . . I find it truly insulting that you would question why I insisted on a salary for a position you approached me about, not the other way around, even with me being the daughter of a wealthy man."

Mr. Dana let out a snort. "It's a known fact that wallflowers spend their time in sheer boredom at all the society events they're expected to attend. I gave you an opportunity to stave off that boredom."

Permilia rose to her feet. "Only because you needed someone who could travel with ease behind the scenes, observing society without anyone noticing. Because of me and my Miss Quill column, you had an advantage over all the other papers that did not have a wallflower at their disposal."

Mr. Dana rose to his feet as well. "We'll only continue having an advantage if you agree to put your nonsense aside and report on what our readers want to read."

"I will not set aside my principles simply to sell more papers."

"I'll give you a fifty-cent-a-week raise."

Permilia tapped her toe against the hard floor underneath her feet. "How generous of you, Mr. Dana, especially since it's just been made clear you don't feel as if I deserve *any* money for the work I do, but . . . I think not."

Mr. Dana narrowed his eyes as his jaw turned stubborn. "Then I'm afraid, if you won't agree to write what I need written, this is where you and I, Miss Griswold, part ways."

Her toe stopped mid-tap. "Are you letting me go?"

"I do believe I am."

CHAPTER
EIGHTEEN

Marching out of the *New York Sun* with her head held high, her vision obscured because she'd not bothered to take the time to adjust her veil properly, Permilia stumbled her way down the sidewalk, finally forced to stop when she barely missed toppling over an elderly gentleman.

Shoving aside one of the layers of netting that made up the veil, and annoyed with herself that she'd almost caused someone an injury simply because she was in a temper, she reached out a hand and steadied the man now wobbling on his feet.

Professing her deepest apologies to him—even though he immediately reassured her that it was his fault, not hers, marking him as a true gentleman—she watched as he hobbled off, his kindness a distinct help in dissipating the temper that had been flowing through her.

That dissipation did not last as long as expected, though, especially when a *New York Sun* reporter, a man she'd seen around the building often over the two years she'd worked for the paper, hurried past her. He was clutching a sheaf of papers in his hand, obviously returning from his latest assignment.

The sight of him brought into stark relief the pesky little notion that she would never be sent out on assignment again because . . .

She'd been dismissed from her position, stripped of her responsibilities with barely a blink of an eye, rather as if she hadn't been very essential in the first place. Quite honestly, now that she thought about it, she evidently hadn't been essential, given that Mr. Dana seemed to believe he could easily replace her with people who apparently wouldn't think twice about setting their scruples aside in order to give the public what it wanted—scandal, titillation, and . . . gossip.

As if her being dismissed hadn't been bad enough, Mr. Dana had refused to give her the wages owed to her, stating in a matter-of-fact sort of manner that since she'd done such an abysmal job reporting on the Vanderbilt ball, she deserved . . . nothing.

The very idea that she'd been released from her position, especially when she'd been anticipating an increase in salary, was humiliating, irritating, and downright concerning now that she considered the matter fully.

Realizing that lingering in the middle of the sidewalk was certainly not going to allow her to puzzle matters out to satisfaction, she stiffened her spine and started forward. Dodging other walkers on the sidewalk, she blew out what she thought was a well-deserved sigh as she contemplated the troubling situation her dismissal had caused.

She was the sole benefactor of Miss Snook's School for the Improvement of Feminine Minds. Without the funds she earned from the paper, it was going to be difficult for Miss Snook to pay the rent on the building used for the school, keep the lights on and the coal furnace burning, or even provide her students with paper and writing utensils.

The only saving grace Permilia could see at the moment was

that she did receive a rather substantial amount of pin money from her father. But while she certainly wouldn't balk at turning over all that money to Miss Snook to keep the school up and running, Ida would certainly take notice if Permilia suddenly became even more frugal than she already was—especially since they were traveling to Paris, and Permilia always splurged every time she traveled to Paris . . . on pastries.

If there was one item on the face of the earth for which she wouldn't haggle over the price, it was pastries. And Paris, unfortunately, had the best pastries she'd ever eaten, a fact Ida was fully aware of. She would certainly notice if Permilia abstained from purchasing the treats.

Slowing her pace, she glanced down, wondering if perhaps she could make the claim that she was watching her figure as a way to explain why she'd need to go pastry-free until she found other means to earn some much-needed funds, but unfortunately, she was as willowy as normal.

She blew out a breath and picked up her pace when she saw that an omnibus was just now trundling down the street. Having no desire to linger any longer than necessary in an area where she'd just suffered one of the greatest humiliations of her life, she stepped briskly around a lady strolling down the street, raising a hand to flag down the omnibus.

"Miss, excuse me, miss?"

Turning, even though she was fairly certain she wasn't the miss in question, Permilia discovered a young man racing her way, waving one hand at her while swinging a small box tied with twine in the other.

Stopping in her tracks when she realized that she *was* the lady he was trying to catch, she peered through the netting of her veil, watching the man close the distance that separated them. Stopping beside her a few seconds later, he drew in a wheezing sort of breath, then lifted up the box and held it out to her.

"I've been asked to give this to you, Miss . . . ah . . . well, I wasn't told your name, just told to run down the woman wearing the veil, but I'm supposed to tell you that this is yours."

Taking the package, she frowned. "Do you know who this is from?"

"The man who asked me to run after you simply said that you would appreciate it since it was yours, or . . ." The man tilted his head. "Perhaps he said you'd earned it. I'm afraid I wasn't listening as well as I should have been."

"Is this man an employee of the *Sun?*"

"He might be, especially since he caught me right as I was walking past the building."

Permilia smiled. "It's nice to see my faith in humanity hasn't been completely misplaced, since this is surely from Mr. Dana, who would not be capable of running me to ground, given the problems with his back and all. But that has nothing to do with this lovely gesture, a gesture that means Mr. Dana has apparently come to his senses."

The young man's brow wrinkled. "Which I'm sure is lovely for you to realize, although I'm not certain who Mr. Dana is, but since I've now completed my task of running you down, I'll bid you farewell and hope your faith in humanity continues to improve."

Slipping her satchel off her shoulder, Permilia opened it and tucked the package inside, pulling out a few coins she kept in a side pocket. Holding the coins out to the man, she frowned when he shook his head.

"I've already been compensated for my troubles, miss, but thank you for the offer." Tipping his hat to her, he turned and hurried away in the direction he'd just come.

Feeling even more charitable toward her former editor since he'd apparently shelled out his own money in order to ascertain she'd leave the *Sun* with what she thought had to be the wages she'd been owed, Permilia slipped the strap of the satchel over her shoulder and continued forward.

Reaching the omnibus, which had, surprisingly enough, waited for her, she climbed onboard and took a seat, setting her satchel on the floor before she straightened and looked out the window.

All the breath seemed to get stuck in her throat when she discovered a man standing on the sidewalk and staring directly at her, a man she swore was the same one she'd seen earlier right outside her house, and a man who looked, now that she saw his face more clearly, distinctly familiar.

When he lifted a hand and tipped his hat to her, she felt the hair stand up on the nape of her neck. Wanting to get a better look at the man, she took hold of the veil, but before she could lift it, the omnibus surged into motion, causing her to list to one side. By the time she pushed herself upright, the man had disappeared from view.

Having absolutely no idea why anyone would be watching her, she crossed her arms over her chest, and then froze as the only reasonable explanation as to why anyone would take to following her reluctantly sprang to mind.

She'd heard a plot centered around murder, which made her a distinct threat to the two men who'd been discussing that murder, but . . .

She'd not seen the men in question, nor had they seen her, which made what she'd just reasoned out to be anything but a reasonable conclusion. Unless . . .

Worrying her lip, Permilia forced herself to think.

The only way anyone would know she was the person who overheard them was if they'd heard her warn Asher about the murder plot in the midst of dinner. That possibility seemed somewhat unlikely, although she certainly hadn't been mindful of keeping her voice down when she'd blurted out the startling

221

business about someone wanting him dead. But a more logical explanation might be that . . .

Someone had found her shoe—and learned it belonged to her.

The absurdity of that had her releasing a small laugh, that laugh fading straight to nothing when her foot bumped into her satchel and a feeling of dread spread from the tips of her toes all the way up her body.

Telling herself she was being a complete ninny but knowing she needed to put the absurd idea to rest, Permilia leaned over and opened the satchel, pulling out the box she'd assumed had been from her editor.

Placing it on her lap, she considered it for a long moment, then flipped up the veil that was still obscuring her view, knowing there was little point in hiding her identity since she was no longer Miss Quill and could no longer bring about the wrath of society due to her articles.

Reaching for the box, she untied the twine and then found herself hesitating as she considered the package.

"What do you have there in the box?"

Lifting her head, Permilia found that the woman sitting in the seat in front of her had twisted around and was now leaning over the back of her seat, her gaze fixated on the box in Permilia's lap.

Not certain she cared for the interest the woman was sending her way, Permilia settled for a shrug. "I'm not certain."

The woman's eyes widened. "I once had a friend who had a box she wasn't certain about. When she opened it, she found a nasty surprise."

"What type of nasty surprise?"

"A dead mouse, or perhaps it was a dead bird, but it was definitely something dead."

Glancing at the box again, Permilia frowned. "Perhaps it might be for the best if I wait until I get home to discover what's in here."

"Maybe it's not something dead."

Knowing she was being ridiculous, because in all probability the box really had come from her editor, Permilia forced fingers that didn't seem to want to work properly into motion, lifting the top off of the box a moment later. Bracing herself, she looked down, finding a folded note and a box stuffed with cotton.

Plucking out the note, she felt a sense of relief when she noticed what was scrawled across the front of it—*For Miss Quill.*

It *was* from her editor, although what he was thinking using her pen name, she had no idea. Setting the note aside, since she was more curious about what Mr. Dana had put in the box than reading whatever he could have written to her, she dug through the cotton, her fingers closing around something remarkably solid. Pulling it out of the cotton, she immediately lost the sense of relief she'd been feeling, because what she held in her hand was the last thing she wanted to see.

Her shoe, the one-of-a-kind beaded-glass slipper she'd purchased from Miss Betsy Miller, the same woman who'd designed her snow-queen costume, had apparently found its way home to her.

"Ohh . . . now that is a far better present than finding something dead, and . . . it looks just like the slipper a princess would wear, the ones you hear about in old folk tales."

Forcing a smile even though she definitely wasn't feeling cheerful, Permilia looked up and found the woman gazing intently at the slipper. "It is somewhat like a princess slipper, quite like the one I well remember in the Brothers Grimm tale, although . . . I'm afraid there won't be a Prince Charming rushing onboard this omnibus to slip this particular slipper on my foot."

"Perhaps your Prince Charming is waiting for you to get off the omnibus, dear. But I suppose that would only happen if you have a Prince Charming in your life."

Permilia's first instinct was to vehemently deny that she even knew a Prince Charming type, but then, to her very great surprise, an image of Asher flashed to mind.

It wasn't an image of him dressed as he'd been at the ball, in an outfit that could very easily be considered princely, but instead, it was an image of him dressed in a smart coat and carefully pressed trousers, a suitable hat on his head as he went about the business of looking rather, well, businesslike.

That her image of him also had him on bended knee, slipping her slipper over her stockinged foot, was somewhat . . . disturbing, as was the notion that he, of all people, would even flash to mind in the midst of what could only be considered a disaster.

The very idea that he was floating about her thoughts in such a romantic fashion was a different matter altogether, although it wasn't a matter that disturbed her as much as she would have thought, because . . .

Somehow, during the few months she'd come to know Asher, starting from the time she'd haggled with him about the price he was charging for skates, to when she'd spent time with him at the ball, and then rescued him from the clutches of a killer in Central Park, she'd begun to think of him a little . . . differently.

No longer was he simply fodder for her Miss Quill column because he was a notable gentleman of the city. Instead, with his charming smile and habit of keeping to a most rigid schedule, he'd somehow managed to secure her interest. She recognized he was not an industrialist, seemed to have no interest in mining, and had grown up a snob, but . . . he had not seemed to mind a whit about her embarrassing them both on the ballroom floor at the Vanderbilt ball.

That right there had been a true measure of the man's character, and that might have very well been what secured her interest in the man.

It was unfortunate that she was sailing off to Paris on the next—

"If you don't want the shoe, I'd be more than happy to take it off your hands."

Shaking herself out of thoughts that she couldn't even believe she was thinking, especially since she'd just been delivered a disturbing message, Permilia stuffed the shoe back into the box. "That's very kind of you, but I do believe I should probably keep this particular shoe."

"It seems a shame you weren't sent a matched pair, but I imagine, if you truly wanted a pair, it wouldn't be too difficult to find where that one came from, if it's from somewhere in the city, that is. I can't imagine there are too many shops that sell sparkly shoes."

"You're right. There aren't."

Nodding more to herself than the woman still watching her so closely, Permilia knew exactly what she needed to do. Picking up the note that had come with the shoe, she noticed the name scrawled across the front of it again and felt her stomach roil as a truth she'd not understood until just that moment settled in.

Someone had discovered her true identity, but besides that, someone had discovered she was Miss Quill, which meant . . . the return of the shoe could either be seen as a warning or as an indication that a blackmail attempt would soon be made.

"You're looking a little green, dearie, would you like me to hold the box for you?"

When Permilia realized that the woman in front of her was rising from her seat and reaching over that seat in what could only be described as a somewhat threatening manner, she tucked the letter, along with the box, into her satchel and pulled the cord that ran along the floor of the omnibus, signaling the driver that she wanted to get off.

As the omnibus slowed to a stop, she hurried out of her seat, hustled straight down the aisle, and stepped to the sidewalk before the woman she'd been speaking with had a chance to follow her. To her relief, the omnibus moved back into motion, leaving Permilia behind.

Taking a second to get her bearings, she started forward, not stopping until she reached a hansom cab parked on the side of the road, the driver immediately stepping down from his seat in order to get the door for her.

"Where would you like to go, miss?" he asked.

For a second, she debated having him take her down to Miss Betsy Miller's shop, until she took note of the time on the watch pinned to the underside of her sleeve. Knowing that Betsy had probably already closed down for the day, she opened her mouth to tell the driver to take her home, closing it again a second later.

With her thoughts going every which way and her emotions in a certain jumble, what she needed at the moment was a place she could find peace. That peace would not be found at her home if Ida and Lucy were there.

Nodding to herself, she gave the driver directions to Grace Church off of Broadway and got into the cab, settling back against the seat as the driver returned to his and took up the reins.

With a lurch, the cab started forward, traveling at a sound clip, and before Permilia knew it, they were in front of Grace Church, the Gothic-style architecture not failing to impress Permilia even given her preoccupied state of mind.

After paying the fare, she walked across the street and eased her way inside the church. Moving quietly down the aisle of the chapel, she reached a pew she knew quite well, one she sat in every Sunday—sometimes twice, depending on how many sermons Ida felt they needed to hear—and scooted to the very middle of it, taking her seat.

A small plaque with her family name on it met her gaze, making her smile, even as the odd thought struck that her father had never had any intentions of owning his own pew, the purchase of it only done to appease Ida, whose husband had owned the pew previously but had left it in a precarious state when he'd died.

Taking a moment to close her eyes, Permilia tried to find the sense of peace that she usually felt whenever she sat in the chapel, but today, no matter how she tried to settle her mind, that peace simply wouldn't come.

The only consolation she could find was that her mind was not quite as jumbled as it had been. Because of that, she decided there was no sense wasting the quiet that surrounded her.

She was in the midst of a mystery, and there was no time like the present to try and solve it.

Reaching into the satchel, she drew out the shoe and then the letter.

Unfolding the piece of paper, she squinted at the words on the page, taken completely aback over what had been written. Drawing the paper closer, she read the words again, mouthing them as she read silently.

Dear Miss Quill, or should I say, Miss G.?

I'm returning your shoe to you as a warning. Your identity has been compromised—your eavesdropping on a conversation you should not have overheard is now known to me—and you'd be well served to get out of the city as soon as possible.

Sincerely,
A dangerous gentleman

For what felt like forever, she simply stared at the words written on the page. She'd been expecting blackmail or, at the very least, a threat, but . . . she hadn't been expecting a warning.

Lifting her head, she stared vacantly toward the front of the chapel, for once not capable of truly appreciating the beauty that rested behind the pulpit, or even noticing that the late-afternoon sun was casting myriad colors through the stained-glass windows.

It wasn't until she noticed someone stepping out of the sun-cast colors that she realized she was not alone.

Her pulse began to race through her veins until she realized that the someone was none other than Reverend Benjamin Perry.

He was an associate minister at Grace Church, a mild-mannered man with an easy smile and peaceful nature, and was exactly the man Permilia needed to see at the moment.

Walking toward her with his measured stride, he reached her pew and inclined his head.

"Miss Griswold. This is a pleasant surprise. May I join you?"

"Please," Permilia said, gesturing to the space beside her.

Reverend Perry sat down and inquired about her family, and that was all it took for everything she'd been storing inside for what felt like forever to pour out.

Time ceased to exist as she released all the matters that had been lying heavy on her heart, moving from the disappointment of not being given the opportunity to run the family mining business, to her absolute failure within society, and ending with her dismissal from a position she'd been forced to keep secret from everyone, and the very real threat she was facing because of the murder plot she'd overheard.

When she was finished, Reverend Perry considered her for a long moment, and then he smiled.

"You really ought to think about coming to speak with me more often, Miss Griswold," he began, his smile growing wider.

"However, while I'm certain your life seems as if it's at its very lowest point, I'd like you to consider a few things."

He reached out and laid his hand over hers. "One of the first times we spoke, you brought up the dissatisfaction you were experiencing having to enter a society that clearly didn't accept you."

"Which has certainly been proven to be true over the years."

He nodded. "Indeed, but do you recall what advice I gave you when we spoke of your dissatisfaction?"

Permilia tilted her head. "You told me to give my concerns over to God, but then to not simply sit idly by and wait for Him to fix my life for me, but to look for opportunities that He might send my way if only I was observant enough to recognize those opportunities."

"And did you find an opportunity to stave off the dissatisfaction you were feeling with your life at that time?"

Permilia's gaze glanced back to the pulpit again, lingering on the beautiful cross that was the focal point of the chapel. "I met Miss Snook not long after you and I had that conversation, and . . ." She smiled and caught Reverend Perry's eye. "I met her here, after a Sunday service."

"And you became involved with that school, which helped to give you a sense of purpose. You were able to make a difference in the lives of numerous young women, those women now being given more opportunities due to the education you were instrumental in helping them receive."

"I never really thought about my involvement with Miss Snook's school in quite that way before." She blew out a breath. "I must admit that I might not have seen my involvement as an opportunity orchestrated by God just for me."

"We rarely see those opportunities for what they are, Miss Griswold, but . . . if I may, allow me to point out yet another instance where I believe God stepped in to assist you."

"When Lucy came of age, which made my stepmother lose some of the focus she'd been sending my way?"

Reverend Perry laughed. "No, that's not what I was going to point out at all. I was going to mention the time, soon after your stepmother cut your allowance almost in half, when Miss Snook ran incredibly short on funds, but then . . . you were offered an extraordinary position with the *New York Sun*. That position not only allowed you to save Miss Snook and her school, it also helped alleviate the boredom of attending society event after society event, while honing your skills as a writer in the process."

"I don't know if I'd go so far as to claim I'm a true writer, Reverend Perry. I mostly just wrote about the fashions everyone was wearing, along with descriptions of the houses I found myself in, or the foods being served at the dinners I attended."

Reverend Perry patted Permilia's arm. "You're not giving yourself enough credit, Miss Griswold. I've read your articles and have heartily enjoyed them. Your writing has given me a lovely picture of what happens behind all those closed doors that society will never open to me. It's also allowed me to sit right beside you at a formal dinner, almost tasting the terrapin or lemon ices society is so fond of, while not adding inches to my waistline. That, my dear, is a gift and proves that you have a certain skill with the written word—one not many people are granted."

A hint of heat settled on Permilia's cheeks. "That is very kind of you, Reverend Perry, and I do appreciate your words. But if you've forgotten, I've been dismissed from the paper so my writing skills are no longer going to be put to any use."

Reverend Perry gazed at Permilia from eyes filled with wisdom—and a touch of amusement, if she wasn't much mistaken.

"Have you ever considered the idea that some of our life

230

experiences should be looked upon as stepping stones, needed in order to cross the stream at large, but not meant to be lingered on forever?"

"I suppose I've never considered my life experiences in quite that light."

"Then I recommend you begin considering them that way, which will open you up even further to the unexpected."

"But what should I do about the men who may want to kill me, or Mr. Rutherford, and the affection I'm just now realizing I hold for him, or the disappointment that affection will surely cause my father since he does seem keen on my bringing a gentleman into the family who'll want to take over the mining business, and . . ." She sucked in a much-needed breath of air and continued. "Should I go to Paris with my stepmother and stepsister, or would it be awful of me to finally put my foot down and say enough to all the nonsense I've been accepting in order to keep the peace?"

Reverend Perry's eyes began to twinkle. "I'm just a simple man of the cloth, Miss Griswold. I don't have the answers you seek, but what I would suggest you do is this—turn your troubles over to God, and then . . . keep an open mind and willingness to accept what He may have in store for you. As we've just discussed, you've been pleasantly surprised in the past, which means there's hope you'll be pleasantly surprised in the future. I'm also, being a rather pragmatic sort, going to suggest you pay a visit to the police. You're clearly in some type of danger, and while I'm sure God is watching over you, we really should use the common sense He gave us, which means you should alert the authorities to the danger you're in."

Returning the smile the reverend was sending her way, Permilia finally felt a touch of the peace she'd been searching for when she'd walked into Grace Church. Knowing the man sitting

231

next to her had made some very valid points, and realizing that her best option at the moment was to turn everything over to God and then pray for the best, and perhaps pay a visit to the local police, she drew in a deep breath, lowered her head, and settled into prayer.

CHAPTER NINETEEN

The moment Asher was ushered into the Griswold house and heard what sounded like objects of a breakable nature being shattered somewhere off in the distance, he fought a distinct urge to bolt straight back out the door.

When shrieks of obvious rage joined the shattering, he abandoned the fight, turned smartly around, and headed for the exit. His path, however, became suddenly blocked by another gentleman who'd chosen that exact moment to walk into the house through the very door Asher needed to use to make an escape. That gentleman, Asher immediately recognized as none other than George Griswold, Permilia's father.

He was a handsome man, large and incredibly broad through the shoulders, lending the immediate impression he was a man of action. He also sported a chin that spoke of a stubborn nature, something his daughter had apparently inherited from him.

Taking off his hat and handing it to the butler, Mr. Griswold ran a hand through hair a lighter shade of red than Permilia's before he stepped farther into the hallway, clutching a leather traveling satchel in his other hand. That satchel was telling in that it indicated the man was evidently just now returning from a trip, that assumption proven a second later when the butler took the satchel from Mr. Griswold, inquiring how the business had gone.

"It was a productive trip, Mr. Dankin. Thank you for asking. And I suppose there's no need for me to ask how matters were here at home while I was gone," he said right as the shrieking escalated to what Asher thought was a concerning level, even though Mr. Griswold barely batted an eye over the ruckus being made in his home.

"Business as usual," Mr. Dankin said before he moved to hand the satchel to a footman who'd appeared silently in the entranceway, or perhaps he hadn't approached on truly silent feet, but had the sounds of his approach masked by the intensifying noise coming from somewhere in the house.

Shaking his head ever so slowly at that news, Mr. Griswold began unbuttoning his overcoat, pausing halfway through that task when he seemed to notice Asher standing in front of him.

"Ah, we have guests," Mr. Griswold exclaimed, raising his voice to be heard over what sounded like an entire collection of dishes being thrown at a wall. "George Griswold. And you would be"—Mr. Griswold studied Asher for only the briefest of seconds—"Mr. Asher Rutherford, if I'm not mistaken." With that, and not seeming to expect a response just yet, since the shrieking had escalated once again, Mr. Griswold finished unbuttoning his coat and shrugged out of it, handing it to the butler, who'd returned to his side.

Stepping forward, he extended his hand to Asher, pitching his voice to be heard over the continued noise. "I was hoping you'd see fit to pay me a call, which saves me the bother of hunting you down."

Taken slightly aback over that less than encouraging greeting, Asher grasped the extended hand and gave it a shake, giving the door that the butler was now in the process of securely locking a bit of a longing look before he returned his attention to Mr. Griswold, who was watching him expectantly.

Clearing his throat, Asher released his hold on Mr. Griswold's hand and tried his best to summon up a smile. "One might almost believe, given the use of the phrase 'hunting you down,' that you're put out with me for some reason, sir."

"That would be a reasonable assumption," Mr. Griswold said right before another bout of shrieks began. "May I suggest we repair to my study in order to avoid whatever drama is currently transpiring in my house?"

"Don't you think it might be prudent to discover what's behind the drama before we repair to your study? It sounds as if someone's in remarkable distress."

"It's just Lucy, and she's dramatic at least twice a week."

The matter-of-fact way in which Mr. Griswold tossed out those particular words had Asher setting aside any true concern he had about the drama unfolding out of his sight. Falling into step beside Permilia's father, he soon found himself climbing up a curving set of stairs. Reaching the second level, he followed Mr. Griswold down a long hallway, stepping into what could only be described as a shabbily appointed but incredibly masculine study a moment later.

The walls were done up in a dark wood, while brown drapes were drawn firmly shut at the windows, not lending the room even the slightest touch of light from the evening sky—the light in the room dependent instead on the gas sconces on the walls. The furniture was heavy and dark as well, with the chairs upholstered in weathered leather.

A roaring fire was already blazing in the fireplace, as if the butler, Mr. Dankin, had been expecting Mr. Griswold. And a pile of newspapers—freshly pressed, from the looks of it—were stacked on the floor.

Gesturing Asher toward one of the leather chairs, Mr. Griswold proceeded across the room, stopping in front of a well-stocked cart filled with numerous crystal decanters. "May I interest you in a brandy?" he asked.

"That would be most kind."

As Mr. Griswold poured the brandy, Asher settled into a worn chair that turned out to be remarkably comfortable. "May I assume you were responsible for the décor we're now enjoying?"

Looking up, Mr. Griswold smiled. "Ida was put out with me for a solid month after I insisted on moving furnishings I've had forever into this fancy house we purchased after we got married, but . . . a man's got to have somewhere to go that has his own mark on it." He gestured around the room. "Because this room is not what anyone in the social set would find attractive, I'm normally left alone in here, unless Permilia's home and decides to join me—which isn't as often as I'd like." He turned back to the brandy. "Ida and Lucy can't abide the atmosphere in here, so this is where I spend a good deal of time when Lucy takes to being . . . theatrical."

Asher shifted in the chair. "Forgive me for being forward, sir, since you and I have never spoken—although we have exchanged nods a few times at some of our mutual clubs—but has it ever occurred to you, if Lucy is prone to dramatics so frequently, that you might want to think about purchasing items that aren't quite so easy to break? I would have to imagine her temper costs you more than a pretty penny at times."

"I've stocked the library—that's where I'm sure Lucy can be found at the moment—with inexpensive pieces of pottery and glassware, which has defrayed the expense of Lucy and her horrendous temper."

"Have you ever thought about putting an end to her outbursts altogether, sir?"

Mr. Griswold walked across the room and handed Asher a

glass of brandy. "I would be lying if I said I haven't, but . . . being a stepfather is precarious business, Mr. Rutherford. It's fraught with pretty tears from a stepdaughter and her mother, my wife, which has made my life less than peaceful over the past six years."

He took the chair right next to Asher's. "Permilia was never one to cry, you see, so after I married Ida and discovered both she and Lucy were prone to that troubling business, well, I've been quite like a fish out of water ever since."

"I imagine Permilia was a very precocious child."

All sense of affability disappeared in a flash as Mr. Griswold's eyes hardened before he sat forward. "You seem to be on rather familiar terms with my daughter, Mr. Rutherford, which brings us back to the reason behind my mentioning that I would have been forced to hunt you down if you hadn't shown up here in a timely manner."

"I'm still not certain I understand why you would need to hunt me down, sir."

"I don't know a father alive who wouldn't hunt down the scoundrel responsible for besmirching his daughter's reputation."

The small sip of brandy Asher had taken right before Mr. Griswold's unexpected response went down the wrong way. The next minute, one of the longest in Asher's life, or so it seemed, was spent gasping for breath while Mr. Griswold calmly regarded him with what might have been a small smile on his face.

Sucking in a breath of much-needed air, Asher set his brandy aside on a scarred oak table.

"I can assure you, Mr. Griswold, that I have done nothing to besmirch Permilia's reputation. And forgive me, but if you truly understood your daughter, you'd know that she'd never allow a gentleman to even think about doing any besmirching without causing that man serious harm, or . . . shooting him."

"So she's still carrying her pistol, is she?"

Asher's eyes widened. "I don't know about that. I was simply trying to make a point, but . . . do you really suppose she carries a pistol with her at all times?"

"She used to, when we traveled the country, visiting the mines, but Ida might have made her give up that habit, once she decided to take Permilia in hand and make a lady out of her."

"I would think Permilia has always been a lady, sir. Perhaps a little rough around the edges, but a lady all the same. I also think that your daughter doesn't appreciate Ida trying to take her in hand, or appreciate the idea that you're apparently holding out hope that she'll attract the attention of a gentleman who will be able to take over your mining ventures one day."

Mr. Griswold blinked. "You obviously think far too much, Mr. Rutherford. Although I would like to know where you got the idea that Permilia believes I'm still holding out hope of her finding a suitable marriage prospect."

"Permilia told me, of course."

Leaning back into the leather chair, Mr. Griswold considered Asher over the rim of his glass. "Did she, now?"

"Indeed, at the Vanderbilt ball—and right around the time she'd begun to notice she was drawing unexpected attention from guests."

"Gentlemen guests?"

Asher smiled. "One could hardly blame them for noticing Permilia that night, sir. She was looking very lovely indeed— although I don't believe she understands her appeal."

"And you find her appealing, do you?"

Seeing little point in denying what he'd come to accept as truth, Asher nodded. "She's very appealing—when she's not annoying me, that is."

"It was implied in all the papers that the two of you spent an unacceptable amount of time together at the ball."

"We danced one dance together, although we did speak with each other quite a few times."

Mr. Griswold nodded to the pile of papers on the floor. "I don't need to pull those out in order to refresh what I read from papers on the train, but according to three papers, you were seen arguing in the midst of dinner, the implication there being that you were experiencing a couple's spat."

"Our arguing had more to do with my not believing your daughter had overheard a murder plot with me as the intended victim rather than any romantic troubles between us."

"Ah, so you do admit there is something of a romantic nature between the two of you."

Asher's brows drew together. "How did you get that from my disclosing a murder plot?"

Smiling, Mr. Griswold raised his glass. "There was something about your tone of voice when you said the word *romantic*, but since you have broached the subject of the murder plot, I imagine that explains why you have Pinkerton detectives following you."

"You know I hired detectives?"

"That was mentioned to me by the Pinkerton detectives *I* hired to investigate *you*—although, you may rest assured that they didn't disclose why you'd hired them, stating some non-sense about client confidentiality."

Asher's lips twitched when he noticed the clear disgruntle-ment on Mr. Griswold's face. "May I assume you were most put out when you weren't given the information you requested?"

"A bit, but don't think for a second that I wasn't given in-formation about you that the Pinkerton Agency *didn't* find to be confidential."

Even though Asher had a fairly good idea what the Pinkerton Agency had disclosed about him, he asked anyway. "And what did you learn?"

Setting his glass aside, Mr. Griswold looked at him for a long moment. "You're practically a self-made man, something I have no idea why you keep from becoming public. And you're rumored to be an outstanding man of business, with innovative ideas that have taken your store to the head of the pack, so to speak." He tilted his head. "You were able, at a relatively young age, to convince bankers to loan you the capital needed to build your store with only a small amount of collateral, which I believe you obtained from selling off family possessions. You were then able to fill that store with the finest goods, which makes me believe you're not nearly the dandy you present to society, but more of a shark simply attired in fashionable clothing."

Feeling surprisingly comfortable with the man sitting across from him, Asher smiled. "It's always been about the image, Mr. Griswold, but I do thank you for the shark analogy. I was recently questioning the whole dandy business with a friend of mine, Mr. Harrison Sinclair. However, since he wasn't exactly keen to help me achieve the whole looking-as-if-I-eat-nails-for-breakfast image, I think I'll now hold fast to the shark image your words brought to mind."

"Ah, you're worried about impressing Permilia, aren't you?"

Asher frowned. "I don't recall mentioning a word about impressing Permilia just now."

"You didn't have to. When a man starts contemplating changing himself, or questioning how others perceive him, it's always about a woman."

"That's almost exactly what my friend Mr. Harrison Sinclair said to me recently."

"He must be a very astute man, this Mr. Sinclair. But a word of advice from a man who has seen much of life—you won't find happiness by being anything other than who you're really meant to be."

"Which is why *you* should have considered the whole marrying-Ida business a little more diligently, Father, before you jumped into a world neither you nor I enjoy."

Looking toward the door, Asher found Permilia standing there. She was looking incredibly delightful, even though she had what looked to be a widow's hat complete with a pushed-up veil on her head. The only reason he could think she'd sport such a hat was because . . .

Rising to his feet right as Mr. Griswold did the same, he opened his mouth, but found himself pausing with his response when Permilia moved directly to her father. She immediately gave him a most affectionate kiss on his cheek, the action speaking volumes about her true relationship with the man, even if she'd just practically shouted to the world that she was annoyed with her father for the life he'd thrust them into.

Turning away from her father, she smiled at Asher right before she narrowed her eyes at him. "Why didn't you tell me you were a self-made man?"

Asher blinked, moved right up next to her, took her hand, and brushed her fingertips with his lips. "How long have you been standing in the doorway?"

"I wasn't standing in the doorway, I was lurking behind the scenes—something we wallflowers are known to do."

Smiling, he squeezed her hand. "One would have thought, given what happened the last time you were lurking about—when you uncovered a murder plot—you'd be less keen to continue your lurking."

"Old habits are hard to break," she said, drawing back her hand before she gestured to the chairs. "But don't mind me. I'll be more than content to just sit aside and enjoy what seems to be quite the chat." With that, Permilia turned around and plopped into the first available chair, wincing for just a second before she twisted to the right, stuck her hand in what turned out to be a pocket of her gown, and pulled out a pistol a mere second later.

"I thought something was jabbing me" was all she said as she laid the pistol on the table next to her, leaving little doubt that she still carried a weapon on her person more often than not.

Feeling distinctly outgunned because he had no doubt Mr. Griswold was not a man to ever be without his weapon, Asher cleared his throat, retook his seat, and vowed then and there that, in order to truly warrant the whole shark in dandy's clothing title, he would get himself a flashy pistol and make sure he remembered to take it with him whenever he left his house.

"I was relieved to hear those men outside are from the Pinkerton Agency," Permilia said, drawing his attention. "I'm also relieved that I didn't shoot them when I thought they may be up to something dastardly."

Asher frowned. "I'm sure they'll be relieved as well that you're no longer considering doing them in. But speaking of something dastardly . . . why are you wearing a hat with a veil attached to it? And don't tell me it's soon to be a new fashion, since I am remarkably up-to-date on what fashion trends we'll soon see."

"It's too bad you can't influence those trends more, though, Asher," she returned, completely ignoring his question. "I've been noticing that the fashion plates for next season are showing even larger bustled designs. And far be it from little old me, a woman, to point this out, but we don't actually like wearing birdcages on our behinds. It's rather uncomfortable, not to mention nearly impossible to sit down."

"Perhaps if the Parisian designers would cease with their outlandish designs, we in the fashion industry over here in America wouldn't be forced to torture women and stuff them into clothing that truly does need birdcage-sized bustles to allow it to hang properly."

"Perhaps *you* should try to find American designers who

242

have more sense than their Parisian counterparts, quite like the designer I used to create my snow-queen costume for the Vanderbilt ball."

Finding himself, curiously enough, enjoying their argument immensely, Asher leaned forward and was just about to retort, but before he could get a single point past his lips, he realized that what she'd just suggested was an intriguing idea and demanded further contemplation.

Her costume at the Vanderbilt ball had been exquisitely designed and tailored to perfection. And now that he thought on it, Permilia was always incredibly well-dressed, although always in fashions that he knew she hadn't purchased in any of the leading stores in New York, or spent much money on, given the frugal manner in which she seemed to enjoy living.

If he could secure the talents of the designer who'd created Permilia's costume, he'd be uniquely positioned to offer true couture-like designs, quite like what all the ladies flocked to Paris to find every spring. That would set him apart in yet another way from the tried-and-true stores that lined Broadway, while—

The door to Mr. Griswold's study suddenly flew open, banging against the wall a second later, the surprise of it having Asher jumping from his chair as Permilia did the same. Right after that, his mouth gaped open because Permilia, after she'd jumped from her chair, had snatched up her pistol and was already pointing it—with a steady hand, no less—directly at the person entering the room.

"You might as well shoot me, Permilia, and get it over with, seeing as how you've finally managed to figure out a way to ruin this family once and for all, getting us banned from society in the process, no less." With that declaration, Lucy stomped dramatically into the room.

Lowering the pistol, Permilia frowned. "What in the world are you going on about now, Lucy?"

Ida took that moment to march into the room, waving a newspaper, her face mottled with temper.

"We've found you out, Permilia, and . . ." Ida flung herself into the nearest chair and took to fanning her face with the newspaper before she directed her attention to Mr. Griswold, who'd risen to his feet and was watching the scene unfold with what could only be described as resignation on his face—as if he'd heard these very complaints time and time again.

"She's ruined us for good this time, George," Ida proclaimed, her fanning picking up in intensity.

"It's lovely to see you as well, dear," Mr. Griswold replied, moving across the room to stop beside the chair Ida was sitting in. Frowning, he looked down at her. "While I realize you are the authority in this household on all things proper, have *you* neglected to realize that I'm entertaining a guest at the moment?" He turned and nodded Asher's way. "Mr. Rutherford and I were just enjoying a nice chat, but . . . I don't believe you've greeted him properly."

Ida's eyes flashed for all of a second before she rose gracefully to her feet and glided across the room, stopping in front of him. "Mr. Rutherford. How unexpected to find you here in my husband's study. One would have thought you'd have the butler announce you when you first arrived."

Taking her hand in his, he raised it to his lips. "I'm afraid I may have arrived at an inopportune time, Mrs. Griswold, which is why the butler did not announce me, and your husband encouraged me to join him up here."

Ida retrieved her hand and pursed her lips before she rounded on Permilia, who seemed to be in the midst of some type of silent standoff with Lucy, both young ladies glaring at each other—although at least only one of them was currently armed, that lady being Permilia.

Asher had a feeling if Lucy had been in possession of a pistol, given the temper he'd come to understand she had, she might have taken to firing it off, which, given the clear annoyance on Permilia's face, wouldn't have boded well for Lucy.

"Would you care for us to send Mr. Rutherford on his way before we disclose the shame you've brought upon the family?" Ida demanded.

Permilia looked away from Lucy and frowned at her step-mother. "Asher's more than welcome to hear whatever you have to say, Ida," Permilia began, not bothering to so much as blink when Ida started muttering under her breath about the disrespect Permilia was extending her by forgoing the whole stepmother title. "I've done relatively little of late that could bring shame on the family, so by all means . . . disclose away."

With that, Permilia moved back to her chair, took a seat, and placed the pistol directly across her lap.

"I highly expect you'll be regretting the decision to have Mr. Rutherford stay while your shame is exposed," Lucy said, her voice practically dripping venom and her eyes narrowed in rage as she advanced farther into the room, her focus settled on Permilia. "Quite frankly, I have to imagine you never expected me, of all people, to discover your secret."

"What secret?"

Lucy lifted her chin. "That secret that will finally allow you to ruin us all."

Arching a brow, Permilia crossed her arms over her chest. "Well, go on. . . . Since you're obviously dying to let the cat out of the bag, here's your chance. What's the secret?"

Looking more than a little smug, Lucy crossed her arms as well. "That you're Miss Quill, of course."

CHAPTER
TWENTY

For some curious reason, of any secret Permilia had thought Lucy was about to disclose, her being Miss Quill had not even crossed her mind.

She'd assumed that Lucy was going to embellish some obscure detail that one of the many reporters had implied in their articles about her, but disclosing her secret identity . . . That was low, even for Lucy.

Clearly, even though they'd lived together for over six years, Lucy had never achieved even a small measure of sisterly love for Permilia. If anything, given the sheer spitefulness of the disclosure, Permilia was now convinced that her stepsister absolutely loathed her.

Glancing at Asher and her father, Permilia was hardly encouraged to discover those two gentlemen staring back at her with their mouths slightly agape. Realizing that she would get no support from them just yet, if ever, she blew out a breath and rose to her feet. She slipped her pistol as casually as she could into the pocket of her walking gown—since she didn't particularly want to leave it out in the open, what with Lucy's questionable temperament—lifted her chin, and forced her attention back to her stepsister.

It was clear that Lucy was not suffering from an inability to react, like everyone else in the room. Instead, she was practically humming with anticipation as she watched Permilia, eyes brimming with malice. In all honesty, Permilia could only conclude that her stepsister had been waiting for years to deliver Permilia her comeuppance and was now undeniably pleased that the comeuppance day had finally arrived.

Swallowing the scathing reprimand that had been on the very tip of her tongue, Permilia drew in yet another steadying breath, reminding herself that Lucy—willful, spoiled, and possessing an unpleasant sense of entitlement—was, in actuality, a victim of her upbringing.

She'd been pampered, coddled, and catered to throughout her entire life, and because of that, she was almost incapable of understanding how concerning her self-centered attitude truly was. But Permilia knew that, while Lucy was a most unlikable sort, she needed kindness over hostility, peace instead of war, and a slightly loving stepsister over one filled with animosity.

"I'm sure it was very unsettling to learn about my secret identity, Lucy," Permilia began. "And I certainly am sorry to have distressed you. However, there are relatively few people who know I'm Miss Quill, those people being all of you in this room, my editor, of course, one of my friends, and . . . maybe one other person. That being said, I'm not exactly certain why you're so distressed. Your life has not been disrupted at all, nor will it be unless you happen to allow society to learn what you've uncovered."

"How can you not understand why I'm distressed? You've been fraternizing with the enemy—which is the press, if you don't realize—and that, stepsister dear, makes you a traitor to me and everyone else in society."

"While I certainly don't agree with that conclusion, allow me to point out that it would have been prudent on your part to wait until it was just the two of us before you broached this topic. I assure you, there's a perfectly reasonable explanation for why I assumed the role of Miss Quill, but now you've involved people other than just the two of us, including Asher, which complicates the matter."

Lucy uncrossed her arms and plunked her hands on her hips. "If I need remind you, Permilia, you encouraged me to divulge all in front of Mr. Rutherford, which I have now obliged you by doing."

Permilia lifted her chin. "You surely have obliged me in that regard, Lucy, although I'm sure you realized I had no idea that you were about to disclose my greatest secret. Having said that, I can't help but wonder if, had I encouraged you not to divulge my secret, you would have held your tongue, or if you'd simply have gone ahead and blurted out what you have to believe is information that will lead to my downfall."

Lucy began to advance Permilia's way. "If you think for one minute that I was going to allow you to bamboozle poor Mr. Rutherford into believing you're simply a misunderstood wallflower, you're sadly mistaken. You allowed him to become fodder for the gossips, even going so far as to draw additional attention to the man in your very own column and, by so doing, paved the way for me to discover the true identity of Miss Quill."

"I'm not sure I understand exactly how you puzzled it out."

"You told us that you'd misunderstood the Go-As-You-Please directions. There were relatively few people in our direct vicinity when you made that admission, and since I knew full well that Mr. Rutherford was not Miss Quill, nor was Mr. Slater, for that matter, I realized that left only you."

Permilia blinked, impressed that Lucy had been able to make

such a deduction, especially since she'd never been a lady who embraced a great love of thinking.

"That was well done of you, Lucy, but in my defense—not that you'll believe me, of course—I only included the bit about the Go-As-You-Please in my column in order to diffuse the embarrassment I knew Asher had suffered because of my negligence in understanding the steps."

She shot Asher a glance, surprised to discover that he didn't appear to be furious, although he certainly wasn't looking overly pleased with her either. "I know all of this must seem most disconcerting to you, Asher, but I do hope you know that I was not trying to deliberately bring more attention your way by including mention of the two of us in my Miss Quill column."

Asher frowned. "You really are Miss Quill?"

"I am, or rather, I was up until today." She gave a shudder. "But that's an unfortunate story for another time."

Ida drew herself up and marched Permilia's way, coming to a stop mere inches away from her. "You mentioned that there may be another person who has learned your identity as Miss Quill. May we count on that person's discretion in this matter?"

Permilia refused another shudder. "Since I don't know the identity of that person, I can't vouch for his or her discretion. But I do take comfort in the idea I haven't yet received a blackmail notice, which is, in my humble opinion, a positive sign."

Ida seemed to swell on the spot. "You might have now drawn the notice of a blackmailer?"

"It's either that or a murderer, or it might simply be a person wanting to warn me that there is someone out there *wanting* to murder me . . . and a person who might just happen to be aware of my other identity as well."

"Forgive me, Permilia"—her father moved into motion and quickly reached her side—"but it seems there might be far more people than you've admitted to who know you're Miss Quill."

Permilia bit her lip. "I'm sure it appears that way, Father, but besides the people I already mentioned, along with my friend Miss Snook, there's just that man who had a note delivered to me today with *Miss Quill* written on it." She thought about that for a moment, then shrugged. "Although . . . that man also sent me the shoe I lost at the ball so he obviously knows I'm Miss Griswold as well. And because my lost shoe has reemerged, I'm going to have to assume the other man who was present when Asher's murder was discussed might also be aware of who I really am. I can't say with any certainty *that* man knows I'm Miss Quill. He may simply want to see Miss Griswold taken care of, completely unconcerned that I'm a society columnist. But that means you might have a valid point about there being more people than I owned up to at first."

Her father cleared his throat. "It appears this situation is far more complicated than I imagined it to be. It might be for the best if all of us were to take a seat."

Thinking that was a most excellent idea, especially since it would allow her a moment to collect her thoughts, which had gotten in a bit of a jumble after she started trying to figure out how many people knew her identity, or might want her dead, Permilia moved to a leather chair and sat down.

Lucy did the same, taking a seat in a chair beside her mother, although both mother and daughter were sitting rather gingerly on the very edge of their chairs, quite as if they believed they'd be permanently sullied by sitting on anything other than the best. Permilia turned her attention to her father and Asher, who'd waited for the ladies to be seated before they sat down.

For a very long moment, silence settled over the room, until George cleared his throat again and set his sights on Permilia.

"I think we deserve an explanation as to what could have compelled you to take on a position at a newspaper and then write a column that even I know society took issue with when it first came out." He shook his head. "Did you not realize that in so doing you were jeopardizing any chance you might have had of finally taking firmly within society?"

Permilia blinked. "Forgive me, Father, but that almost sounds as if you believe I've been successful in being accepted loosely within society."

George blinked right back at her. "Of course you have. Ida's been telling me you've made great strides over the past few seasons."

"Compared to what?"

Turning his gaze on his wife, George quirked a brow. "Did you not mention a time or two over the last few years that my girl was making progress?"

Ida nodded to Asher. "If you've not noticed, George, you currently have Mr. Asher Rutherford sitting in the midst of your study. If that's not progress on Permilia's part, I don't know what would be."

"He's not here to court me," Permilia argued before she frowned and looked at Asher. "You're not, are you?"

Asher, to her very great surprise, smiled. "In all honesty, Permilia, with all the madness of the past hour, I've quite forgotten my original reason for traveling here. I do clearly remember wanting to discuss your reputation and the blow it has suffered due to the articles that were written about us. Although just so we're clear, I don't believe your Miss Quill column hurt either of our reputations in the least. I also find it incredibly charming that you would go through the bother to write an article that cast you in a somewhat clumsy light in order to spare my reputation additional censure. Not many ladies would have gone through that bother, or purposefully drawn more attention, and not of the enviable type, to themselves so willingly. That right there shows that—no matter that society has yet to fully embrace you and your quirky nature—you're a true lady in every sense of the word, and I, for one, am pleased to know you."

Since what he'd just said were some of the nicest words anyone had spoken to her for a very long time, Permilia found herself unable to speak, but she was spared a response when Asher rose to his feet and moved her way.

"Since we do find ourselves the topic of some unpleasant speculation, and since I do feel a strong sense of affection for you, I believe the only option at the moment, and one that will save your reputation forever, is to allow me to court you for a suitable period of time and then have you accept the protection of my name."

Permilia briefly found herself, annoyingly enough, still incapable of speech, and Asher had now taken to beaming back at her, indicating he was evidently taking her speechlessness as a sign she was overjoyed by his offer, but . . .

She was nothing of the sort.

Even though she'd accepted her lot as a wallflower and had reconciled herself to the idea that she would more than likely remain a spinster, she did allow herself to dream upon occasion.

In her dreams, she'd conjured up her own very special gentleman, but not once had that gentleman proposed the idea of courtship and then marriage in such a matter-of-fact, almost businesslike, fashion.

While she freely embraced the idea that she was a most progressive sort, that did not mean she was unwilling to experience a touch of romance that included slightly sentimental words paired with a lingering over her hand and . . . perhaps a kiss or two.

Being told her only option to save her reputation was to accept Asher's less than romantic offer had her hackles up.

Straightening shoulders that had taken to sagging, Permilia lifted her chin. "While I certainly appreciate an offer that sounds exactly like it might have been reluctantly made after all other options had been considered by you—with the assistance of Mr. Harrison Sinclair, if I'm not much mistaken—I'm going to respectfully decline your proposal."

"Don't be an idiot," Ida hissed before Asher had an opportunity to say a single thing. "You won't get another offer, Permilia, and this is your chance to finally be accepted, at least somewhat, within society. Besides, if you were to marry Mr. Rutherford, your elevated status within society would improve Lucy's chances of making a most desirable match." She narrowed her eyes at Permilia. "After all of the trouble you've caused me over the years, I don't believe I'm asking too much of you to accept Mr. Rutherford's more than generous offer."

"Mother," Lucy practically shouted as she jumped to her feet, her face beginning to mottle, "I don't want Permilia to be rewarded for her bad behavior by finding herself a husband who is considered one of the most eligible gentlemen in society. That's not a suitable punishment. If anything . . ." She turned to Asher and began batting her lashes. "It would also save my family from ruin if you were to offer for me, because it would detract from Permilia's shame, if word ever gets out about her secret identity, and"—she fluttered her lashes again—"I would make a far more appropriate wife for an established New York society gentleman than Permilia ever would."

"Sit down, Lucy, and mind your tongue. You're embarrassing not only yourself and Mr. Rutherford, but your mother and me as well."

Time ceased to exist as everyone, Permilia included, turned, almost in slow motion it seemed, toward George, who'd taken to standing. That he was a formidable man, there could be no question. His eyes were hard, his jaw clenched, and it was evident he was a man capable of building a fortune with his own two hands in an uninviting environment.

He'd never, as far as Permilia knew, shown this side of himself in Ida and Lucy's presence, but showing it he most certainly was at the moment, and he made quite the impressive figure.

"Don't speak to my daughter that way, George," Ida practically spat, advancing on her husband and breaking the curious atmosphere that had descended over the room. "When I agreed to marry you, I told you that Lucy was my responsibility and that you were to have no say in how she was going to be raised." She nodded to Asher. "While Mr. Rutherford is not exactly what I had in mind for Lucy as a husband, he is from an old family, possesses the required family fortune, and his dabbling in trade can be forgiven because of that family fortune behind him."

"Not that I want to enter into this particular argument," Asher began. "But I do believe, Mrs. Griswold, since this does seem to be the moment to divulge secrets, although your husband already knows this about me, that I should disclose here and now the pesky truth that the majority of my family fortune was lost years ago due to some disastrous investment opportunities. Because I wanted to spare my parents the pain of losing almost everything they held dear, I decided to try my hand at starting my own business. Seeing a need for a new type of store, one where customer service would rule the day, Rutherford & Company was born, after a bit of begging on my part to get the required backers."

Ida raised a hand to her throat. "Your mother never mentioned so much as a whisper to me about her financial difficulties, and we've sat down to tea on numerous occasions through the years."

"It's not as if that's a subject most society members are comfortable talking about, Ida," George said, drawing his wife's attention. "As you yourself know far too well."

Ida blinked, blinked again, and then turned an interesting

shade of red. "That is not a topic I'm willing to delve into at the moment, or ever."

George arched a brow. "But you're willing to discuss every other titillating subject matter that's come up in the last hour. Far be it from me to point out the obvious, Ida, but you seem rather judgmental and sanctimonious for a woman who admits, at least to yourself and to me, of course, that you married beneath yourself in order to escape the poverty your late husband left you in."

Drawing herself up to her full height, Ida shot a look to Lucy, who was frozen in her chair, her eyes wide and disbelieving, then returned her gaze to George. "I did marry beneath me, but it's not as if you had lily-white reasons for marrying me either. You've said yourself on more than one occasion that you only married me because of your precious daughter, and yet not once have you spoken a word of appreciation for the amount of trouble she's caused me, especially since she never excelled at the feminine arts you tasked me with teaching her."

Permilia rose slowly to her feet. "Do not tell me, Father, that you truly did marry Ida because of . . . me."

George's eyes softened ever so slightly. "Of course I did."

"But . . . why?"

"You were left without a mother from far too early an age. And while I enjoyed every minute you and I spent together while you were growing up, I didn't want you to miss out on the pleasure of being a young lady." He blew out a breath. "You were always drawn to feminine bits of lace and whatnot whenever we'd visit country stores. And while I knew that I was being selfish by not sending you away to a finishing school, I just couldn't abandon your upbringing to anyone other than myself."

"But you abandoned me to Ida's care."

"That wasn't an easy choice on my part," George argued.

"But after you and I came to this city on a matter of business, and we went to Delmonico's, well, I knew I'd been severely negligent in your education, especially in regard to the feminine arts."

Permilia frowned. "Because I didn't know how to maneuver around the silver?"

"And I didn't know how to teach you, since I couldn't maneuver around the silver either." George ran a hand through his hair. "Not long after that, I ran across Ida while I was enjoying lunch with Mr. Morgan, one of my bankers, and . . . she seemed to be the answer to my prayers." He nodded Ida's way. "You were well known throughout society, possessed all the right connections, along with remarkable manners and knowledge of everything proper. And when I discovered you were in a rather precarious state, it seemed only logical that you and I would wed."

"But I never wanted to enter New York society," Permilia said in almost a whisper.

"I thought that would change."

"One would have thought, given that you were present when my father did the same thing to me, George, that you would have known that trying to foist your daughter into New York society was only going to push her away from you in the end."

Turning to the new voice that had just sounded around the room, Permilia discovered none other than Miss Mabel Huxley strolling ever so casually into the room, followed by her sister, Miss Henrietta, and a man Permilia had never seen before.

Before anyone had an opportunity to greet them properly, Miss Mabel—seemingly unconcerned that she'd thrown herself into a situation she hadn't been asked to enter—came to a stop, settled her gaze on George, and continued her speech.

"And far be it from me to point out the obvious, but tying yourself to a shrew like Ida did not do your poor daughter any favors. Ida has always been known to be an incredibly self-serving soul, so she would have put little to no effort into seeing your darling Permilia accepted into society. She holds anyone who didn't grow up in the very midst of society in great disdain, which means one can only conclude that the only reason she married you was for your money."

George took a single step toward Miss Mabel, but before he had an opportunity to speak, Ida bolted across the room, picked up one of the crystal decanters that Permilia's father always had accessible on a beverage cart in his study, and hurled it, not at George but at Miss Mabel, leaving little doubt about where her daughter had gotten her vitriolic temper.

Chapter
Twenty-One

As Ida picked up one decanter after another, switching her aim to George Griswold after he'd rushed across the room to block Miss Mabel from harm, Asher finally managed to get feet that had seemed glued to the ground into motion. Dodging one flying object after another, he winced when a decanter holding what smelled like bourbon glanced off his shoulder, leaving a large wet spot on his fine woolen jacket in the process.

Not allowing the hit to distract him from his goal, he finally reached Ida's side. Wrestling a cut-glass decanter that certainly could be considered a weapon out of her hands, he set it down out of her reach. Grabbing hold of her when it seemed as if she was trying to slip around him, he took hold of her arms, restraining her when she began to struggle.

The part of him that had been raised to never use any type of force against a lady regretted his actions, but the part of him that was dripping in bourbon, and had seen the rage resting in Ida's eyes as she'd gone about the business of trying to harm Miss Mabel and Mr. Griswold, was applauding his efforts, even if he regretted the need to take them.

Leaning in toward her and hoping she was not a woman prone to biting, he lowered his voice. "You need to get a hold of yourself, Mrs. Griswold. If you've forgotten, the Huxley sisters are not ladies to trifle with. And since you seem so concerned about Lucy and her future prospects, well, I would suggest you abandon your attack and perhaps try to summon up a few apologies."

Instead of heeding what Asher had thought was stellar advice, Ida turned purple in the face—that particular color lending her a completely deranged appearance. The purple, paired with the troubling fact that her hair had escaped most of its pins, what with all the exertion that had been needed to fling bottles around the room, had her looking anything but the respectable lady society was used to seeing.

"How dare you presume to lecture me, Mr. Rutherford. From what you just disclosed, you really are nothing more than a common merchant, perpetuating a fraud on society by presenting yourself as a man of inherited wealth instead of one of those repulsive self-made men."

Asher frowned. "While this is not going to come across as very gentlemanly of me—and I will apologize in advance for that—you are quite like the pot calling the kettle black, aren't you?"

"I've never sullied my hand peddling wares."

"Perhaps not, but you did marry a self-made man—and not out of any love, from what I've been able to gather. You married Mr. Griswold because you were left in genteel poverty when your husband died, and while there are many women who have done the exact same thing, they normally extend their husbands a bit of appreciation. You, on the other hand, can barely conceal the loathing you hold for Mr. Griswold and his daughter, and that, Mrs. Griswold, does not reflect well on your character."

Ida shook herself out of his hold. "You would loathe Permilia as well if you'd spent as much time as I've spent over the past few years trying to get her accepted into society without experiencing a smidgen of success. I was charged with arranging dancing lessons, deportment lessons, and every other lesson you can think of that a young lady needs to become refined, but she never embraced or appreciated the lessons I arranged for her. She certainly didn't throw her heart and soul into trying to get society to adore her."

Asher tilted his head. "While I'm sure you expect your little speech to garner some sympathy from me, Mrs. Griswold, I find it garners more questions instead. Tell me this—since you've been involved with society your entire life, even moved in the very highest of circles, how was it possible that you didn't find any success with Permilia? Your status should have guaranteed that every door would be open to her, and suitors should have flocked to win her hand."

"My status will only take a young lady so far, Mr. Rutherford, and given that Permilia's looks are not what anyone would consider fashionable—what with all that red hair she flatly refused to allow me to have dyed—I can hardly be blamed for her lack of success."

Asher blinked and shot a look to Permilia, who was standing stock-still directly in front of the chair she'd risen from, her mouth hanging just the slightest touch open, as if she couldn't quite reconcile herself to everything being disclosed in such a short period of time.

"I, for one, am certainly glad that you never agreed to change the color of your hair, Permilia," he said. "I think the red is a most delightful color, and it suits you to perfection."

Turning her head toward him, Permilia pressed her lips together, glanced at Ida, who'd begun muttering something undecipherable under her breath, and then took Asher completely by surprise when she sent him a rather cheeky wink.

Unfortunately, Ida seemed to notice the wink, and before Asher could stop her, she'd slipped around him and headed off across the room, not toward Permilia, but rather toward George, who was still standing in front of Miss Mabel and Miss Henrietta, arms crossed over his broad chest and his stance protective.

"Do give it a rest, George," Ida spat. "I'm not going to hurt the Misses Huxley, but I must say here and now that I find it most distressing how you'd throw yourself in front of them, which lends clear credence to the idea that you're not being a proper husband to me at the moment."

George seemed to grow even larger. "And you believe that abusing our guests is being a proper wife to me?"

Completely ignoring his statement, Ida turned on her heel and sent a nod Permilia's way. "I suppose you're happy with yourself now, causing this discord between me and your father. I wouldn't be at all surprised to learn that this was the outcome you wanted all along, what with how incompetent you seem to be with anything revolving around proper behavior, and blaming that incompetency on me and some poor Russian dance instructor."

Permilia narrowed her eyes. "That Russian dance instructor did not speak English. I told you that the day he showed up in our house, but you wouldn't listen, so you're just as at fault as I am for my misunderstanding of the proper rules to the Go-As-You-Please Quadrille."

Ida turned purple again right before she began marching Permilia's way. "If you would have had even a semblance of grace, I wouldn't have had to resort to hiring a Russian to teach you to dance in the first place. However, since you are not graceful, and I was told time and time again that you lacked the patience to practice the steps as diligently as the other dance instructors I hired for you expected, you have no one to blame but yourself for being taught by someone who didn't speak the language."

George strode across the room, his expression anything but pleasant as he scowled at his wife. "Permilia may not have excelled with her dancing classes, Ida, but she sits a horse better than any man I know, can scramble through a mine shaft without missing a step, and wields a sword with so much grace that she's been known to cause people to descend into a hypnotic state just from watching her."

"Stellar qualities indeed, especially since sword wielding is in such demand at all the society events," Ida returned. "But if you've forgotten, she has also infiltrated society while masquerading as a true lady, then abused that very society by writing about our balls and dinners under the pseudonym of Miss Quill, which . . ." Ida's eyes widened, she shot a look to the Huxley sisters, and then she pressed her lips firmly together and didn't say another word.

"Goodness, but we really have landed ourselves into the midst of something interesting," Miss Mabel said, drawing everyone's attention. Then, instead of taking her leave, which Asher would have expected her to do since the atmosphere in the study was definitely not of a warm-and-fuzzy nature, Miss Mabel grabbed hold of her sister's hand. With a smile spreading over her face, she then pulled Miss Henrietta across the room, not stopping until she reached a settee so shabby Asher was surprised Ida even allowed it to stay in the house.

Plopping down on the settee, Miss Mabel took to giving the cushions a good thump, grinning a second later as an unexpected cloud of dust erupted from her thumping.

Miss Mabel turned the grin on George, her face looking a good ten years younger. "How delightful to discover that you still have this old settee, George. Why, if you'll recall, I was with you when you purchased this."

"Oh dear . . . I had a feeling coming here was going to open up an entire can of worms," Miss Henrietta began, looking grim as she dropped down next to her sister.

Miss Mabel pursed her lips for the briefest of seconds. "Occasionally, sister dear, worms need to be let out of their cans, especially worms that are clearly abusing my dear George, taking advantage of his generous nature." She turned her head and pinned Ida under a steely gaze. "It truly is unfortunate that ladies of your ilk have been left in charge of society for so long, but I do find a small hope in the idea that leadership will soon see a great change in our city, especially if women like Alva Vanderbilt have any say in the matter, which I do believe they will."

"Alva Vanderbilt is an upstart who just happened to marry into one of the wealthiest families in the country," Ida snapped.

Miss Mabel nodded before she began smiling pleasantly at Ida, as if they weren't in the midst of exchanging barbed words. "It is so fascinating to watch you criticize a woman who was able to force her way into society by the sheer amount of wealth she married into—especially since you were only able to stay in that very society by marrying George, who, rumor has it, is also one of the wealthiest men in America."

Ida's eyes flashed. "I have no idea why you believe I care what you—a spinster, if you've forgotten, Miss Huxley—have to say, and . . . now that I think about it, what are you even doing here?"

Miss Mabel shrugged. "After Henrietta and I had a lovely chat with your stepdaughter the other day, I thought it was past time I came and paid George a visit." She smiled pleasantly again. "We were quite good friends back in the day, and since I am now on friendly terms with Permilia, I didn't want her to feel I was being neglectful of our new friendship."

"Forgive me, Aunt Mabel, but since when have you become friends with Miss Permilia Griswold? And forgive me again, but I was under the impression we were off to Delmonico's this evening for a nice meal and a glass or two of claret, not traveling here to insert ourselves into what is certainly none of our business."

Turning, Asher narrowed his eyes on a man who, in the midst of the drama swirling around the study, had been all but forgotten—and a man who was just now stepping farther into the room.

He was not known to Asher, but upon closer observation, Asher recognized him as a man who occasionally rode his horse down Broadway—probably in order to visit Huxley House, since the man had just called Miss Mabel, aunt. With his receding brown hair, average height, and slim build, he was a rather unremarkable-looking gentleman.

When Miss Mabel ignored the man's question and instead turned and launched into a whispered conversation with her sister, Asher stepped forward. "I do beg your pardon, sir. What with the curious atmosphere of the room at the moment, I fear all of us quite neglected the expected pleasantries. I'm Mr. Asher Rutherford."

"I'm well aware of who you are, Mr. Rutherford, being you are such an innovator when it comes to that exceptional department store of yours," the man returned in a surprisingly high voice, tinged with a slight nasal quality. He stepped smartly up to Asher and took the hand Asher was now extending him in a less than firm grip. Giving it the expected shake, he stepped back, breaking their contact. "I'm Mr. Jasper Tooker."

"He's our nephew," Miss Mabel called from her position on the settee, her words having George clearing his throat and looking rather confused.

"I don't recall you having another sibling, Mabel," he said.

"Well, we do, a half sibling, if you will." Mabel's lips pursed. "She's not exactly a topic for polite conversation."

Mr. Tooker caught Asher's eye. "I fear my aunts are in rare

form this afternoon, Mr. Rutherford. They're a handful at the best of times, and I'm afraid to say, this isn't one of those times."

He walked around Asher and headed off across the room, stopping in front of his aunt. "You should have a care with what you say about my mother, Aunt Mabel. It wasn't her fault that your father, my grandfather, kept . . ." His voice trailed off to nothing, and he summoned a weak smile that he sent all around, right before he began taking a pointed interest in the ceiling.

An uncomfortable silence settled over the room until Miss Mabel cleared her throat and turned her gaze on Permilia. "Did I hear correctly that you are responsible for that charming Miss Quill column?"

Permilia briefly caught Asher's eye before returning her attention to Miss Mabel. "How kind of you to call it a charming column, Miss Mabel, and I do fear I must own up to being the person behind the pen—although . . . I would appreciate if you would keep that information to yourself. As you might have noticed, my family has not been pleased with some of my antics of late."

Miss Mabel patted the spot on the settee, waiting until Permilia sat down beside her before she drew Permilia's hand into her own. "Your secret is safe with us, dear, although given how well written your column has always been, you should be proud of what you've accomplished, not embarrassed about it."

"Don't encourage her," Ida snapped. "It was not well done of me to allow my temper to get the better of me and disclose that information to you, but if word gets out about her true identity . . . well, we'll be ruined for certain, I'll be banned from my most beloved society, and Lucy will become a confirmed spinster."

"Since Mr. Slater is already courting her," Permilia said, "I don't believe that's going to be an issue."

Asher was hardly surprised when yet another silence descended over the study, but this silence didn't linger long because

Mr. Tooker abandoned his perusal of the ceiling and nodded to his aunts. "I believe it might be for the best for us to take our leave and let these good people sort out their madness without having uninvited onlookers interfering."

"But it's just getting good," Miss Mabel protested.

"Which is exactly why we need to leave." Mr. Tooker held out his hand to his aunt, which she staunchly ignored.

"I'm afraid he's quite right," Miss Henrietta said, getting to her feet. Pulling Miss Mabel up beside her a second later, even though her sister was more than vocal with her protests and kept sending Ida unfriendly looks, Miss Henrietta caught Asher's eye. "Be certain to stop by our house in the next week or two, Mr. Rutherford. Mabel and I have found yet another tea we're quite enjoying, and it might be a good tea for you to offer when your tearoom opens."

Asher inclined his head. "I will certainly do that, as well as bring a formal invitation for you and your sister to join me for the grand celebration to honor the opening of the tearoom. That opening, I'm delighted to announce, is going to be much sooner than expected, given that construction is ahead of schedule." He nodded to Mr. Tooker. "You're welcome to join your aunts as well."

Mr. Tooker inclined his head. "I will certainly plan on doing just that, especially since it was always a dream of my aunts to open up their own tea shop, which they never did, but at least they can be there to watch you enjoy the experience of opening up a shop."

With that, Mr. Tooker took hold of Miss Henrietta's arm, then did the same with Miss Mabel, and with a brief nod, he escorted them out of the room.

"What a strange family," Ida said, not bothering to lower her voice even though it was likely the Huxley sisters and their nephew could still hear her.

JEN TURANO

George moved to the door, shut it, then walked back across the room, sitting down in a well-worn chair. "The Huxley sisters can hardly be blamed for being considered a little strange, Ida, what with the father they had." He ran a hand through hair that was decidedly untidy. "Mr. Huxley was not a pleasant man, and quite honestly, I always found him to be somewhat intimidating. If I'm recalling correctly, there was a rumor that he was a bit of a philanderer, which might explain why I never heard of the Huxley sisters' half-sibling."

"That certainly explains why Mabel and Henrietta remained spinsters," Ida said, throwing herself into the nearest chair. "Bad blood will out in the end, and they obviously have bad blood."

"Mabel didn't have to remain a spinster," George said, his eyes narrowing at his wife. "She had quite a few admirers back in the day, but her father had great aspirations to become a member of high society. Since none of those admirers possessed the proper social connections, I'm afraid Mr. Huxley discouraged them from pursuing Mabel."

Ida made a sound like an angry cat. "Should I assume you were to be counted as one of those admirers, George?"

"While I was very fond of Mabel, any affection that may have blossomed between us came to a swift end when I met Permilia's mother." He switched his attention to Permilia. "She was a wonderful woman, and even though we weren't given long to be together before she was called home, we enjoyed a delightful marriage, and I've always been thankful she gave me you."

"Which is oh-so-touching," Ida drawled, "but has nothing to do with the disaster we're facing now that even more people have found out about Permilia's secret life."

"People you were responsible for telling," George returned.

Ida waved that straight aside before leveling a glare Permilia's way. "I, for one, believe it's past time explanations were given, and then . . . we'll need to decide what to do with you."

267

"There's nothing to be done with me, Ida," Permilia began. "It's not as if I'm some criminal on the loose. I simply wrote a society column, and while that may seem untoward in the social circles we travel in, it would not have even been necessary if you didn't restrict my access to my trust fund, or cut my pin money allowance in half. Because you did that, I really had no choice but to accept the offer I was extended from the *New York Sun*, which means you're just as much to blame as I am."

"What obligations could you have possibly had?" Ida asked.

Before Permilia could answer, George sat forward, a tic beginning to develop on the side of his jaw. Turning a hard eye on Ida, he then turned his attention to Permilia. "What do you mean, Ida restricted your access to your trust fund, and . . . did you say your pin money was cut in half?"

Permilia's shoulders took to sagging, a circumstance she did nothing to correct, even when Ida started *tsk*ing under her breath.

"If you hadn't allowed yourself to become so distant from me over the past few years, Father, you would have known what Ida was doing. And while the argument has been made that you only married her because you wanted me to gain a feminine influence in my life, I don't believe that's the whole truth. I think you were lonely and had been for a very long time, which, paired with your desire to see me adopt a more ladylike demeanor, had you actively searching for someone to spend the rest of your life with."

She held up a hand when George started to protest, cutting him off before she turned to Ida. "As for your question regarding what obligations I had . . . while I know this will distress you even more, I'm heavily involved with Miss Snook's School for the Improvement of Feminine Minds. Since I'm the sole benefactor of that school, when my funds were limited, I really had no choice but to accept employment when it was offered to me."

268

Releasing a breath, she turned her attention to Lucy, who was being remarkably quiet, as if she was doing her utmost not to attract attention to herself.

"As for you, Lucy, I'm going to say that I am sorry you're so distressed by the information you discovered about me. However, I highly doubt that information will harm you in the end, especially since it does seem as if Mr. Eugene Slater is keen on courting you."

"He's agreed to lend us the use of his yacht tomorrow to sail us over to Paris," Lucy said, then immediately retreated into silence when George rose to his feet and settled his attention on his stepdaughter.

"Mr. Eugene Slater, as in the man who has been trying to get me to consolidate my mining ventures with his?"

Lucy's only response was to sink farther into the depths of the large chair, her eyes now as wide as saucers.

"Lucy is unfamiliar with you in a temper, Father," Permilia began, "so do try to mind your blustering. But getting back to Mr. Slater, yes, I do believe we're speaking of the same man, and learning you're familiar with him is truly concerning."

She nodded to Lucy. "I know you and I do not share an affable relationship, Lucy, but I am older than you, and as such, I have seen more of the world. While Mr. Slater is indeed a rather dashing gentleman and is, from all accounts, incredibly wealthy, don't sell yourself short and settle for him, especially if it does become clear he's more interested in Father's mines than he is in you." She smiled. "You're incredibly annoying, willful, and spoiled, but I don't want to have to add *miserable* to that unpleasant list."

Turning from Lucy, she settled her sights on Asher, a circumstance he did not find encouraging, given what she'd said so far.

Lifting her chin, she caught his eye. "It was very charming of you to show up at my home and extend me an offer of courtship and perhaps more, simply because we became the subject of unexpected gossip. But as I believe has become quite clear, I'm not meant to spend my life in society, which seems to me to be quite the opposite of where you're meant to spend your life. You're a fine gentleman, every bit as dashing as Mr. Slater, and you've accomplished something most men in your position would not have been able to do—build a first-rate business when the world as you'd always known it was pulled out from underneath your feet."

She rose from the chair and sent him a rather sad smile. "You'll be a great success, I know it, but I'm releasing you from any obligation you may feel toward me . . . and bidding you adieu."

She nodded to her father. "I'm bidding you adieu for now as well, Father, because while it is clear that you brought me to the city out of love, you should have consulted with me before you threw me into the lion's den. You certainly should have consulted with me before deciding to not allow me to run your business, a circumstance that hurt me deeply and still hurts to this day."

George took a step toward his daughter. "If I believed you truly loved mining, Permilia, I would have never brought you to New York, but . . . you don't love it. You never have. In your heart, you're a lady through and through, enjoying fine fabrics, perfumes, and everything else associated with being feminine—except, perhaps, dancing. Yes, you're every bit as capable as a man to run my business, but I would have been doing you a grave disservice if I had turned my business over to you. You don't belong in that world, Permilia. It's far too coarse for you. That isn't to say that you're not meant for another business, just not mine."

A single tear trailed down Permilia's cheek, but when Asher moved to join her, she held up a hand, stopping him in his tracks before she returned her attention to her father.

"You may very well be right, Father, but before I came home today, I stopped by Grace Church and had a most interesting conversation with Reverend Perry. He recommended I turn over my troubles to the only One capable of leading me in the right direction. Now that I consider everything, and now that we've gotten so much out into the open—matters I never even considered before—I have the strangest feeling this is a turning point in my life. In order for me to be able to understand where God may be steering me, I need to distance myself from all of you and try to find a place where I can just be me for a bit. Hopefully, if I can take some time by myself, I'll be able to decide what path I'm supposed to take next."

"You're leaving the city?" Asher asked.

"Probably not, or at least not for long, since I do have obligations here and will need to seek out employment at some point."

"You have no need to seek out employment, Permilia," George argued. "Especially since I intend to make certain you have full access to your trust fund from this point forward."

"And while I do appreciate that, Father, and certainly am not going to refuse that access, I still need to find my purpose in this life."

She dipped into a curtsy that was sheer perfection, one even Ida couldn't fault. "Now then, if you'll excuse me, I'm off to fetch the trunk I packed for Paris, because . . . my future awaits."

CHAPTER
TWENTY-TWO

TWO WEEKS LATER

At the sound of voices, Permilia lifted her head from the journal she'd begun keeping and settled her attention on the door of her suite of rooms at the Fifth Avenue Hotel. When the voices became more distinct, she smiled as she realized Gertrude had come to call.

Marking her spot in the journal with the dance card Asher had signed at the Vanderbilt ball, Permilia scooted the chair she was sitting in away from a charming writing desk fashioned in a Georgian style.

Walking across the well-appointed sitting room, one that included an Aubusson carpet to add the proper touch of elegance, she opened the door. Standing a few feet from her in the hallway, Gertrude—now almost completely back to her normal color—was in the midst of an earnest discussion with Agent McParland, one of the Pinkerton agents Asher had hired to guard Permilia every second of the day.

She knew full well Pinkerton agents were quite dear to employ—since she'd badgered Agent McParland the week before to tell her how much he was paid. He hadn't exactly been keen on doing that, but when she told him she wouldn't be comfortable allowing the Pinkerton Agency to continue guarding her if she wasn't told the cost of their services, he'd relented.

When she'd brought up what she felt was a grave extravagance to Asher, one of the many times he'd stopped by the hotel in order to bring her up-to-date on *their case* as he'd taken to calling it, he'd brushed her concerns straight aside. And when she'd persisted, trying to convince him to at least allow her to take care of half the bill, he'd resorted to claiming it was his fault her life was in danger, even though she wasn't exactly certain that was the truth.

It had hardly been Asher's fault that she'd been off snooping around the Vanderbilt ball when she'd overheard the men discussing Asher's murder. But since Asher seemed determined to play the part of an overprotective friend, and she found the thought of that overprotectiveness to be somewhat delightful, she'd relented and allowed him to have his way in the end.

"Ah, Permilia," Gertrude exclaimed, stepping away from Agent McParland, who was looking rather abashed that he apparently hadn't noticed the door being opened. "You're looking very springlike today. What an interesting shade of green, and I have to say that embroidery around the cuffs of your sleeves is simply exquisite."

Permilia smiled. "Thank you, Gertrude. The woman who designed my costume for the Vanderbilt ball, Miss Miller, also whipped up this charming walking dress. I asked for something to combat the dreariness that frequently comes with our rainy springs here in the city, and this is what she designed for me."

"Forgive me, Miss Griswold," Agent McParland said, stepping forward. "But you normally don't trouble yourself with dressing in the first state of fashion unless you're planning on leaving the hotel. May I assume that you've once again forgotten to alert us to a trip you intend to take today?"

Permilia's eyes widened. "Good heavens, but I do believe you may be right. Miss Cadwalader and I have made plans to travel to Miss Snook's School for the Improvement of Feminine Minds. I left a note at the front desk this morning, asking them to ready Mr. Merriweather for me." She grimaced. "He's probably already been taken out of the stables, and I would hate to disappoint him and have him returned to the stables, especially since he's been rather surly of late."

"I believe the entire Pinkerton Agency is familiar with how surly your horse has been of late, Miss Griswold. If you'll recall, he led us on quite the merry chase a few days ago, apparently wanting to show you and everyone tasked with following you that day who was in charge, and it certainly wasn't any of us."

Permilia smiled. "He is a somewhat quirky creature, but at least we were able to have a nice afternoon drive, one that took us up the Hudson River and almost to Sleepy Hollow."

"It was pouring down rain, you were driving an open buggy, and all of the agents, myself included, were riding our horses," Agent McParland pointed out.

Her shoulders sagged. "Would you prefer Miss Cadwalader and I *not* go to Miss Snook's School for the Improvement of Feminine Minds today?"

"Of course you and Miss Cadwalader will go to Miss Snook's School for the Improvement of Feminine Minds, but honestly, could you not ask Miss Snook if she could shorten the name of her school? That's far too much of a mouthful for me. Because you enjoy visiting the school a few times per week, we agents are forced to say it over and over again in order to arrange proper protection for you, and . . . the name gets stuck in a person's mind after a while."

Permilia inclined her head. "I'll see what I can do."

JEN TURANO

"Thank you," Agent McParland said, gesturing her and Gertrude into the room and taking hold of the doorknob after they'd crossed the threshold. "Now then, since I need to alert the agency about why we've left the hotel, the two of you will need to find something to occupy yourselves with until I come back to fetch you." With that, he pulled the door shut, leaving a guilty Permilia in his wake.

"I wish I could say I don't forget to tell them my plans often, but I'm afraid I'm just so used to going out whenever I please that it's not something I've grown accustomed to as of yet."

Gertrude smiled. "At least, since you're no longer employed as Miss Quill, you don't have to think up credible excuses as to why you're going to the *New York Sun*. I'm fairly certain since you're being guarded by the best, they'd have figured out your secret in about a minute."

Permilia returned the smile. "I imagine you're right." She tilted her head. "Since you brought it up, you haven't said much about my disclosure regarding my secret identity. Were you not bothered by the idea that I'm the lady behind the quill?"

Gertrude waved that right away as they walked across the sitting room. "In all honesty, I was rather relieved to learn there was a perfectly reasonable explanation as to why you were always in possession of so many dance cards, and why you were always watching people so intently and then scribbling down tidbits on those cards."

"I'm sure that did appear rather curious."

Walking through the door that led to the bedchamber, Gertrude slowed to a stop and shrugged. "We wallflowers are expected to be a curious lot, Permilia. Most of us harbor many secrets, but at least yours turned out to be a fun one. I have to think that seeing your words in print, even while not using your real name, must have been thrilling."

"It was certainly a blessing to have been given that opportunity.

It staved off the boredom that had been plaguing me while I languished at all those society events. It also afforded Miss Snook the funds she so desperately needed. I'm afraid my stepmother will never agree that the risk I took with my reputation and with the family reputation was worth it, even though I highly doubt my true identity will ever come to light—especially since I have a sneaking suspicion my editor is in the process of hiring someone to take over the Miss Quill column."

Walking into the bedchamber, Permilia nodded Gertrude toward a well-sprung chair situated by the window. After Gertrude got herself settled, Permilia headed for the freestanding wardrobe that took up a good section of the far wall, passing the four-poster bed, marble fireplace, and assorted pieces of comfortable furniture scattered about the room. Reaching her destination, she tugged open the heavy wooden door and pulled out a traveling coat that would fend off the chill of the dreary April day.

"It's quite troubling that you've been forced to live so roughly of late," Gertrude said.

With her lips curving at that bit of nonsense, Permilia picked up the hat that matched the traveling coat, closing the wardrobe door before she turned and caught Gertrude's eye.

"It is troubling indeed, and if you would really like to feel sorry for how roughly I've been forced to live the past two weeks"—she nodded toward a door just past the wardrobe—"you should take a gander at the bathing chamber. The marble bathtub can fit at least three people, and the maids deliver fresh, fluffy towels every day, along with a fresh basket of delicious-smelling soap that encourages me to take more than one bath a day."

"Oh, that is a shame to hear." Gertrude blew out a sigh. "Especially since I've been given the formidable task of convincing you to accept Mrs. Davenport's offer of a room in her house, but I don't think her offer can compete with the amenities you're enjoying here."

Walking over to the small vanity table that held her hairbrush, hatpins, and a variety of other personal items she'd brought with her, Permilia sat down on the velvet-covered stool. "While it was incredibly sweet of Mrs. Davenport to offer me the use of her home, I'm really enjoying my time here, embracing my newfound freedom, so to speak."

"Mrs. Davenport is concerned that freedom is going to come with a heavy price—that price being you found murdered in your cozy, fit-for-a-queen bed."

"She's a very dramatic sort, especially since she knows full well that Asher has employed the Pinkerton Agency to guard me. Because of that, I'm not certain I understand why she believes a murderer would be able to sneak through the Fifth Avenue Hotel, especially on the top floor, which you can only reach with a special key, and then get past the Pinkerton men, break down my door, and murder me." Permilia frowned. "Do you think she'd feel better if she knew I always sleep with a pistol under my pillow and that I have my favorite sword stashed underneath my bed?"

"She might feel better knowing that, although I find that information somewhat disturbing—but that's neither here nor there. She's not a lady who puts things easily out of her mind once they're in there, so be prepared for her to continue inviting you. Also know that when she does not get her way, she can turn ornery."

"Perhaps if we can come up with a reasonable explanation as to why I want to stay, it'll make her feel better."

"I already tried telling her that the Pinkerton agents feel that they can protect you better here since your hotel suite is inaccessible to strangers, but Mrs. Davenport doesn't trust the Pinkerton men."

"Whyever not?"

Gertrude shuddered. "I haven't been brave enough to ask her that question."

Permilia felt her lips twitch. "I can't say that I blame you for your hesitancy, especially since Mrs. Davenport is a woman who didn't balk in the least when I stuffed her into a dumbwaiter with the threat of us plummeting to our deaths hanging over our heads. Most women wouldn't have reacted nearly as calmly."

"She does seem to thrive when she's in the midst of skullduggery, which probably explains her distrust of the Pinkerton men. Truth be told, I was just attempting a bit of skullduggery of my own by subtly questioning that agent outside, trying to see if he had any information about Mrs. Davenport that I may be unaware of."

"Did he?"

"He's apparently one of those annoying goes-by-the-book types. I think he may have known something about her, but he wasn't disclosing even a hint of what that something might be."

"And that right there is exactly why I'll be staying at the oh-so-charming Fifth Avenue Hotel for the foreseeable future, but do tell Mrs. Davenport that I sincerely appreciate the offer. I haven't met many society members who've been willing to offer me such a kindness, and I don't take that kindness lightly. However, given everything else that's been happening in my life of late, I don't think I'm quite willing to place myself in another situation where skullduggery may happen on a frequent basis."

Gertrude nodded, even though she looked somewhat glum. "Perfectly understandable, but I have no idea how to break the news to Mrs. Davenport. She was so certain you'd agree to come stay, especially since everyone knows how expensive it is to stay here, and everyone also knows how frugal you are."

Swiveling around on the vanity stool, Permilia regarded her

reflection for a moment before she reached for the tin that held her pins. Digging out a few of them, she set about the business of getting her hat on her head.

"That right there is what you can use to explain my reluctance to leave the Fifth Avenue Hotel. I'm pleased to report that I was able to negotiate a much more acceptable rate, one that suits my frugal nature and allows me to sleep with ease at night. Since that negotiation was no easy task, I'm sure Mrs. Davenport will understand exactly why I don't want my hard-fought victory to go to waste."

"Is it a normal occurrence for the Fifth Avenue Hotel to negotiate their rates?"

Permilia stuck a hatpin into the side of the hat, turning her head once she was certain it would hold. "I would think not. Management appeared rather taken aback when I broached the subject of an adjustment." She grinned. "I believe the only reason they accommodated my request was because they didn't quite know how to go about haggling with a woman who happened to be one of their cherished guests. But just so you're not worried that I took advantage of them, given my history of haggling, I didn't ask for that much of a discount, just enough to where I feel as if I've been given a fair price."

"You're a little unusual—you know that, right?"

"This from a woman who agreed to wear chicken feathers to the fanciest ball of the season, but . . ." Permilia frowned and turned on the stool, looking Gertrude over. "Why do you look relatively normal today?"

Gertrude smiled and raised a hand to the tidy chignon securing her hair to the back of her head, the small hat she'd attached to that head sporting only a single flower. "Mrs. Davenport had to leave early for a visit with friends, and because of that, and because she did not want my company, I was spared one of her artistic moments."

"With her proclivity for skullduggery, doesn't it make you nervous when she goes off without you?"

"It does, but since I'm her companion, not her governess or caretaker, it's not my place to insist I tag along with her. God willing, she'll be fine. If she gets caught doing whatever it is she does when I'm not around, I'll take that as a sign that God is suggesting to her in a less than subtle fashion that she should consider changing her ways."

"That's a very sensible take on the situation."

"I'm nothing if not sensible, but speaking of God and His ways, have you come to any conclusions about that new path you think God may have in store for you?"

"I'm afraid not, even though I've set aside a few hours every day to pray and jot down notes in a journal, seeing if anything will jump out at me that will guide me in a new direction." She blew out a breath. "I was considering going back to see if Reverend Perry had any additional suggestions, but I would have to imagine that he'll tell me it's all in God's time or something like that. I simply need to be patient, that patience helped along with all the other matters I've been dealing with of late."

"What other matters?"

"Did I mention that, besides hiring on an entire battalion of agents to guard me, Asher has made it a point to visit me at least once a day?"

"No . . . you neglected to mention that."

"Oh, well, now it's mentioned."

Gertrude narrowed her eyes. "Why, pray tell, does he visit you so often?" She got up from her chair and moved toward Permilia. "Have you considered that . . ." Her voice trailed off as she bit her lip.

"Considered what?"

"It's odd Asher would visit you in a hotel room, since you are an unmarried lady and he's an unmarried gentleman. This *is*, after all, the man who proposed a courtship with you simply because he felt your reputation was ruined due to a few articles." She stopped at Permilia's side. "Perhaps his coming here is a way to encourage you to accept his offer of courtship since if he's discovered with you, your reputation will certainly be ruined forever."

"He brings his secretary, Mrs. Banks, to act as our chaperone, and besides that, he knows full well that I have no interest in entering into a courtship with him. We hardly know each other."

"That's why people enter into courtships, Permilia, to get to know each other."

"You may have a point, but I'm not interested in having him court me."

Gertrude rolled her eyes. "Please. You and Asher are made for each other. You're just being stubborn. Far be it from me to point out the obvious, but I believe your feelings were hurt when he made a muddle out of proposing the courtship business in the first place, and that right there is what's holding you back from allowing him to know you hold him in great affection."

"I never said I hold him in great affection. I barely know him." She lifted her chin. "And before you argue with that, know that he simply visits me because of the mutual threat against us, and because of some interesting business opportunities I've been able to direct his way."

"What type of business opportunities?"

"Well, a week or so ago, Asher and I met with some of the Pinkerton agents to go over what they'd uncovered so far. In that meeting, we learned that the agents are quite certain that the threat to Asher does not originate from other shop owners. The agents were quite diligent in their interviewing of staff members, customers, and even relations of the shop owners, and with that diligence came absolutely no evidence that a shop owner wanted to have Asher murdered—put out of business, perhaps, but not put under the ground."

"What an eloquent way you have with words."

Permilia grinned. "Indeed, but . . . after having those leads turn up nothing, the agents then turned their attention to my missing shoe—or rather, the shoe that was returned to me."

"Because . . . ?"

"I told them it was a one-of-a-kind design, which led them to believe—quite as I was believing—that the man who returned it to me might have discovered my identity through the woman I purchased it from, Miss Betsy Miller."

"And . . . ?"

"The agents paid Miss Miller a visit, and sure enough, a man had come into her store with my shoe in his hand, telling her that the shoe had been found at the Vanderbilt ball." Permilia's lips curved just a touch. "That scoundrel of a man then led poor Miss Miller to believe that it was a situation straight out of a fairy tale, one that painted him as a gentleman desperate to find the woman he knew would be his true love—if only he could find the woman who'd lost that particular shoe. That right there is exactly why Miss Miller divulged my name to him."

"She did not," Gertrude breathed.

"She did. And then, after the man—whom Miss Miller described as large, well-groomed, and a bit of a treat for the eyes—discovered where I lived, he apparently traveled to my house, waited for me to exit, and followed me to the *New York Sun*. He then puzzled out my secret identity, although I haven't figured out exactly how he did that, unless he's an uncommonly astute man and noticed that I entered the hansom cab as myself and exited it as a veiled lady, which, you must admit, would raise a few questions."

"It would, but . . . I think it was more a lucky hunch on his part than being uncommonly astute."

"You're probably right about that, unless he was like Lucy and thought it was rather odd that Miss Quill would take to delving into writing more personal tidbits than she normally does about me and Asher." Permilia tilted her head. "Or, he could have followed me into the *Sun*, eavesdropped on my conversation with my editor, and then . . . while I was getting dismissed from my position, decided to pen me what I've now come to believe is a warning."

Gertrude frowned. "So Miss Miller's description of this man—large and a treat for the eyes—is accurate as to what the man you thought was following you looked like?"

"It was, and again, he seems familiar to me, but no matter how hard I rack my mind, I simply cannot place him."

"I would imagine, given the large guest list at the Vanderbilt ball, that you saw him there. And if that does turn out to be the case, you might have actually written something down about him on one of those cards you were using that night, something that will jolt your memory."

Permilia rose from the stool, moved directly up to Gertrude, and gave her a quick hug. "That's brilliant, Gertrude, and as luck would have it, I have those cards here at the hotel. They're stashed away in the muff—where I hid them in case Ida or Lucy came snooping around—and that muff is in the bottom of the traveling trunk I brought with me."

A knock on the door interrupted Gertrude's squeal. Permilia sent her friend a grin and hurried through the bedchamber and then through the sitting room, reaching the door a moment later. Pulling it open, she found Agent McParland, exactly whom she'd been expecting to see, although he was looking less than pleased with her, a circumstance that occurred far too often of late.

"How many times must we go over the protocol regarding how you should open the door, Miss Griswold?" he asked.

She wrinkled her nose. "Did I forget to ask who was knocking at the door?"

He arched a brow and didn't bother to reply. Instead, he handed her a folded note. "You've been invited for tea at the Misses Huxley's."

"How do you know that?"

"I read the note, of course."

"Don't you believe that might be taking matters of safety a dash too far?"

"Not if it had turned out to be a note penned by a nefarious sort, eager to lure you out of your hidey-hole with some clever fiction."

"It wasn't penned by a nefarious sort, although I suppose the Huxley sisters could be described as slightly peculiar."

"Exactly, which is why I'm going to suggest that you pen one of those charming I-regret-that-I-won't-be-able-to-attend-tea notes back to the Huxley sisters, which I will then see delivered to them."

"I can't refuse tea with the Huxley sisters. Miss Mabel is an old friend of my father's."

"An old friend does not necessarily mean she's a current one," Agent McParland pointed out.

"True, but . . . she'll be ever so hurt if Miss Cadwalader and I don't stop in for tea." She smiled. "If it makes you feel more at ease, though, we can then use the excuse of being expected at Miss Snook's School for the Improvement of Feminine Minds as a reason to not linger long."

"I'm afraid that doesn't exactly put me at ease. However, if you're determined to accept the invitation, you'll need to hurry. The Huxley sisters want you to arrive at their house promptly at one."

Permilia blinked. "But it's twelve thirty now."

"Since you just admitted you find the Huxley sisters to be

slightly peculiar, surely you're not taken by complete surprise that they'd expect you for tea with little notice, do you?"

"Which is an excellent point, sir, but since time is certainly a'wasting, allow me to go fetch Gertrude and we'll get right on our way."

Hurrying back to the bedchamber, Permilia found Gertrude headfirst in the trunk, straightening a mere moment later with the fur muff in her hand. "I found it, and reading the cards will be a perfect way to pass the time it'll take to get to Miss Snook's School for the Improvement of Feminine Minds."

"Indeed, if we were actually still traveling there first," Permilia began. "We've been invited for tea at Huxley House."

Gertrude shook her head. "I don't know if I'm quite ready to be introduced to the Huxley sisters, Permilia, no matter that you seem to find them harmless." She blew out a breath. "Mrs. Davenport told me that she finds the sisters to be most unnerving, and given Mrs. Davenport's curious ways, well, that right there is saying something."

"Miss Mabel and Miss Henrietta are not that bad, Gertrude. Quite honestly, I think they're simply misunderstood."

"Misunderstood or escapees from the asylum," Gertrude argued even as she tucked the fur muff under her arm and lifted her chin. "But since we will be accompanied by a Pinkerton agent or two, and you do seem determined to go to tea with scary ladies, I'll agree to accompany you."

"Thank you."

"As payment for my agreement, while I sort through the dance cards on the drive to Huxley House, you will explain to me—in detail, if you please—exactly what type of business opportunities you've been discussing with Asher, and how those opportunities may be connected in some way to that new path in life you believe God's putting you on."

Permilia frowned. "I never said anything about the business

opportunities having anything to do with my future path or God."

Giving Permilia a look that seemed to hold some type of significance—although what that significance was, Permilia really couldn't say—Gertrude took to *tsk*ing under her breath in a rather telling way before she sailed out of the room, leaving Permilia with the distinct feeling she was missing something of grave importance.

CHAPTER
TWENTY-THREE

"Is it my imagination or are we traveling in a somewhat round-about way to get to Broadway and the Huxley residence?" Gertrude asked ten minutes later as they traveled down Lexington Avenue.

"Mr. Merriweather was pulling at the reins so much that I've been allowing him his head, but no need to fret, we're just a few blocks away from our destination. Since he's now under the impression he's in charge, he'll be keener to allow me to steer him onto Twenty-Second Street, and from there, it's just a hop, skip, and a jump to Broadway."

"Has it ever occurred to you that Mr. Merriweather might be happier if you were to find him a nice out-of-the-way farm, one where he could be put out to pasture and be in charge all day long?"

Wincing, Permilia chanced a glance at her horse, relieved to discover he hadn't picked up on the phrase *out to pasture*. "Good heavens, Gertrude, have a care with what you say. If Mr. Merriweather had heard you, well . . ." She gave a shudder. "Now that the weather is breaking, I'll be able to take him for rides in the country, without a buggy attached to him, and that, I'm certain, will soothe his testy nature, at least until winter rolls around again. But for now, we need to get back to those dance cards." She nodded to the dance card Gertrude had just pulled out of the muff. "Anything on that one that might be a match for the man Miss Miller described as inquiring about my shoe?"

"I don't think so, although, forgive me for pointing this out, but your handwriting leaves much to be desired."

"Which is probably why I had to invest in a typewriter because my editor could never figure out what I was trying to write. Because I had to purchase a typewriter, though, I soon discovered how difficult typing can be, which is why Miss Snook is now offering typing lessons on the typewriters I managed to find for her school at a great price." She smiled. "I have high hopes that the young women interested in learning that skill will soon be able to find proper employment in offices around the city."

Setting the card aside, Gertrude pulled out another, scanned it, brought it closer to her eyes, then blew out a breath. "I think this one is simply describing Mr. Ward McAllister. He did attend as the Count de la Mole, didn't he?"

"He did indeed. And while I did make note of the idea that he was getting many admiring looks directed toward his well-turned-out legs, displayed in a pair of heavy silk stockings relevant to the time period of his costume, I purposely did not include that in my Miss Quill article, finding it a little too gossipy for me. That exclusion, I'm afraid, gave my editor an excuse to take me to task, as well as justify my dismissal, especially since the *New-York Tribune* had not a single qualm about the gossipy nature of Mr. McAllister's well-displayed legs and wrote about them at length."

Gertrude gave a sad shake of her head. "It's a troubling world we live in these days, Permilia. And because Mrs. Vanderbilt opened her home to the press, although in a somewhat covert manner, I believe the assumptions regarding what is fit for print are changing. Because of that, perhaps it was a blessing you got dismissed from your position. Your dismissal will now allow you to turn your efforts in a new direction." She leaned forward and began waving a hand at something up ahead. "But enough about that for the moment. I think you might need to take Mr. Merriweather in hand. We're almost to the turn that will take us to Broadway."

"Good heavens, you're quite right." Permilia took the reins in a firmer hand, and even though Mr. Merriweather tossed his mane and let out a few snorts, he did make the turn, although at a somewhat faster clip than Permilia would have made if she'd been in complete control. With a nicker of what sounded exactly like amusement, he set off, moving at a fast clip down the street that would lead them to Broadway.

Once she was certain Mr. Merriweather was not going to do anything of a questionable nature, such as take another turn to get them off course, Permilia turned back to Gertrude, who was once again perusing old dance cards. "Did you find something?"

"If I'm deciphering this correctly, you've written a description of a dashing pirate, then something about flirting and dinner."

Permilia shook her head. "Those were notes about Mr. Eugene Slater, and since I know for a fact that he was sitting down to dine with Lucy when I overheard the murder plot, he's not our man."

"I wonder how his courtship of Lucy is going, now that he, your stepsister, stepmother, and father went off to Paris together."

"Because Lucy truly does seem attracted to Mr. Slater, even with the notion that Mr. Slater might be more interested in my father's business than in her, I'm going to say the trip is going better than expected. Lucy, for all her willfulness, can be a charming young lady when she sets her mind to it, and Mr. Slater might be exactly what she needs, since I do believe he approaches life in a no-nonsense manner. And if he happens to impress my father on this journey, even though my father told Mr. Slater to his face that he was skeptical of the man's motives, he may find himself in an enviable position someday, especially since I don't see my father staying in the mining business forever."

"And your father and Ida?"

"I'm hopeful they're being civil to each other, and also hopeful they'll take this time in Paris to put aside the hurtful words they said to each other and figure out a way to move forward as husband and wife."

"You believe they'll stay together?"

"Ida would never allow her position within society to suffer from a divorce, and my father would never abandon her, no matter that he married her for all the wrong reasons." She smiled. "But enough about that. We're almost to our destination, so we'll have to put the dance cards away until after we finish our tea and get on the road again."

Nodding, Gertrude gave the dance card she was holding one last glance, then grinned. "Which is just as well since I really can't decipher most of the notes you made. This one has champagne, lion, and it might be a Richmond, or Richard, or . . . Well, perhaps you can have a go at them later, since—"

"Good heavens. May I see that?" Permilia held out her hand.

Handing it over, Gertrude frowned. "What is it?"

Reading her notes, which were a little difficult to decipher even though she had written them, Permilia raised her head. "He was dressed as Richard Coeur de Lion." She closed her eyes, summoning up an image of the man she'd noticed at the ball. "He smiled at me and then began walking my way just

290

a short time later, holding two glasses of champagne, one of those glasses seemingly meant for me."

She opened her eyes and found Gertrude staring back at her with her brow furrowed.

"Was he the man you fled from?"

"He was. Although I suppose that right there is exactly why I couldn't place the man until now. I was so taken aback that a gentleman was bringing me champagne that I didn't linger in his presence long, and . . . I wonder if he deliberately sought me out because of Asher?"

"That doesn't make any sense, since you didn't go to the ball with Asher, nor had you spent much time with him up until the ball."

"True. Although isn't it odd, now that I think about it, that Asher and I really were rather comfortable with each other the night of the ball, given that we truly were not that well acquainted with each other?"

"It's not odd at all, if you consider that perhaps—and this is just a perhaps—he has something to do with the new path that's being arranged for you to travel on, a path that Reverend Perry suggested you explore."

Permilia wrinkled her nose. "Hmm . . . I suppose there might be something to that, although I haven't allowed myself to consider that particular matter much since I find the whole idea of Asher to be a little disconcerting. Now, however, is hardly the moment to dwell on that since we still have to puzzle out who the man in the Richard Coeur de Lion costume actually is."

"How would you suggest we do that? I didn't notice the man at the ball, and you'd apparently never seen him until the night of the ball."

Taking a second to slow Mr. Merriweather's pace when they reached the intersection leading into Broadway, Permilia got him heading in the right direction and then turned back to Gertrude.

"The only solution I can think of is to pay Mrs. Vanderbilt a call later on today, after we have tea with the Huxley sisters. Since she created the guest list, she should know what our mystery man's name is." Permilia smiled. "She may even have a picture of him since she had Mr. Jose Maria Mora take individual photographs of her guests."

"I didn't sit for a photograph."

"Well, neither did I, but that could have been because I left the ball early, and you were busy tracking Mrs. Davenport down every other minute."

"Excellent point, although we can't simply pay a call on Mrs. Vanderbilt. Granted, she's far more approachable than Mrs. Astor, but by the time we finish with our tea, calling hours will be long over. Besides, Mrs. Davenport mentioned something about Mrs. Vanderbilt having left for Europe to visit all the salons so that her fall wardrobe will be delivered in plenty of time for the next season."

Permilia bit her lip. "That's unfortunate. But speaking of this mystery man, if he truly is an assassin, why wouldn't he have done away with me after he learned my identity, and why, pray tell, would he have returned my shoe?"

"Perhaps we should run those questions past your Pinkerton agents since they are highly trained professionals who are used to this type of intrigue. I'm just a companion."

Permilia sent her friend a smile. "You're not *just* an anything, Gertrude, which I do hope you'll take to remembering." She nodded to the Huxley house, which was just ahead. "You'd best prepare yourself for the most interesting cup of tea you've ever had, although if you can put the curious nature of the Huxley sisters aside, you'll find that they do serve a most excellent cup of tea."

Guiding Mr. Merriweather to the side of the street, Permilia put on the brake and then waited for Agent McParland and the agent he was paired with most often, Agent Scobell, to get down from their horses and take up their proper positions on either side of Permilia's buggy.

"Rather unusual way to get from Fifth Avenue to Broadway," Agent McParland remarked.

Before Permilia could answer, Mr. Merriweather gave a telling toss of his mane, which seemed to explain the detour far more sufficiently than Permilia would have been able to have done.

"You're a menace," Agent McParland said to Mr. Merriweather before scanning the surroundings, and then, evidently feeling there was no danger lurking about, he stepped up to the buggy and assisted Permilia down to the sidewalk.

"Before you take so much as a single step toward the Huxley residence, we need to go over a few rules," Agent McParland said in what Permilia was beginning to recognize as his no-nonsense tone of voice.

"Surely there's no need for that."

He responded with a quirk of his brow, but then he blew out what almost sounded like a breath of relief and raised a hand in clear greeting.

"Mr. Rutherford, thank goodness you're here. Miss Griswold was just about to turn difficult."

Opening her mouth to argue with that assessment, Permilia suddenly found herself completely forgetting what she was going to argue when she turned her head and found Asher striding her way.

He was smiling a smile that had her toes curling, but since she found her toes curling all too often of late when she was in his presence, she didn't find that circumstance to be as disturbing as it had seemed only a week before.

Sending him a smile in return when he stopped right in front of her, she took a second to look him up and down, her smile widening when he took hold of her hand and brought her gloved fingertips to his lips.

"You're looking very dapper today, Asher," she said as her pulse began to rachet up a notch when he lingered over her hand.

"You say that as if you truly do appreciate a dapper gentleman," he returned, lowering her hand even as his smile faded ever so slightly.

"And you say that as if you think there's something wrong with a gentleman being dapper, but"—she grinned—"while I know it's an accepted thought of the day that women prefer those rugged, disheveled types, probably because of all those popular dime-store novels, I, for one, prefer a well-dressed, well-groomed gentleman, and . . ." Her eyes widened, and her lips pressed shut when she realized what she'd just almost disclosed—a disclosure she hadn't truly thought about, and one that was hardly proper to blurt out in proper company.

She, Miss Permilia Griswold, found Mr. Asher Rutherford to be a more than attractive type, and . . . more to the point, she was . . . attracted to him.

Everything about him appealed to her, from his expertly tailored suits, to the way his eyes crinkled when he smiled, and even his ability to haggle and argue with her over the cost of goods.

He was a respectable man, an enterprising one as well, since he'd built his store not with a great deal of family money but through his own hard work and business savvy—and . . . she'd ruined any chance they had of a romantic relationship by tossing aside his offer to court her, which meant . . .

"Ah, Permilia, this is a delightful surprise, and one I wasn't expecting to find at the Huxley residence."

Blinking directly out of her thoughts, Permilia looked past Asher and discovered Harrison standing there, smiling back at her with his charming smile, one that did absolutely nothing to her pulse. Stepping up to greet him properly, she blinked again as her gaze traveled over him.

"Harrison, do forgive me, I didn't notice you there, but it's lovely to see you, and I'm surprised to find you at the Huxley residence as well." She found herself unable to pull her gaze from the plaid trousers he was wearing—a plaid that was unusual in that it was different shades of purple, not matching the purple in his jacket.

"I've come to the conclusion he doesn't see colors like we do," Asher said.

"Well, thank goodness for that," she said with a grin, giving Harrison her hand, which he kissed before returning the grin.

"Asher's already informed me that I'm a fashion disaster today. Perhaps if you and he were to join forces and take me in hand, I wouldn't be left to stumble around the city looking so interesting."

"I'm sure Asher's capable of taking you in hand all by himself" was all she could think to respond.

"I'm sure he is if I'd only cooperate. Although, while we're on the subject of fashion, tell me this—do you find gentlemen who look as if they eat nails for breakfast and bullets for lunch to be fashionable and attractive?"

She tilted her head. "While it is true that I did grow up in the very midst of gentlemen like that, not that they truly ate nails or bullets, I've recently come to the decision that I prefer refinement in a gentleman and appreciate a man who can wear a tailored suit with ease, and . . ." She stopped talking again when Harrison beamed a bright smile at her, patted her on the shoulder as if she were a clever girl, and strode away without another word, raising a hand to wave to Gertrude a second later.

Turning back to Asher, she found him watching her rather oddly, but before she could contemplate the look, she was distracted by the sight of Miss Mabel strolling out of the house, her strolling coming to a halt when she reached the wrought-iron gate that separated them.

"This is an interesting surprise," Mabel said as she glanced from Permilia to Asher and then took to studying the Pinkerton agents, who were studying her right back.

"I'm not certain why you're surprised to see me, Miss Mabel. You sent a note around to the Fifth Avenue Hotel less than an hour ago, asking me to come around for tea," Permilia said.

"I received a note at the store, inviting me for tea as well," Asher added.

Miss Mabel pulled her attention away from the Pinkerton agents. "How curious, although I imagine it must have been Miss Henrietta who sent the note." She smiled. "She's been worried about me since I've been rather maudlin of late, what with the regrets of my life plaguing me at the oddest of times." Her smiled widened as she gestured toward the house. "Since all of you were kind enough to accept her spur-of-the-moment invitation, we mustn't keep her waiting, so let us go and enjoy some tea."

As Asher took hold of her arm, and Gertrude and Harrison fell into step behind them, Permilia set her attention on Miss Mabel, who'd gone ahead of them and was now gesturing them into her home.

For some odd reason, the gesturing sent a shiver of foreboding straight down Permilia's spine. Slowing her pace, she glanced to the right and found Agent Scobell and Agent McParland taking up their defensive positions, while the two agents who'd apparently been guarding Asher darted around the Huxley house, evidently on their way to take up positions at the back of the house.

Curiously enough, even the knowledge that the Pinkerton

agents were diligently on the case did little to dispel the sense of foreboding.

Stepping through the door, and then discovering the Huxley butler shutting that door and making a great show of locking it, Permilia found herself unsurprised to discover the sense of foreboding turning into a feeling of downright alarm.

Chapter
Twenty-Four

The pleasant warmth Asher had been feeling ever since Permilia had proclaimed him dapper while not even taking notice of Harrison, who never went unnoticed by the ladies, diminished ever so slightly when he heard the distinct click of what almost sounded like a lock being set into place.

Slowing his steps, he turned and felt every vestige of warmth disappear when he saw the Huxley butler, Mr. Barclay, stuff an old-fashioned key in the inner pocket of his tailored jacket.

"I say, Mr. Barclay," Asher began, withdrawing his arm from Permilia's even though he'd been enjoying the feel of her arm in his. "Is it truly necessary to lock the door since you're available to man it?"

Mr. Barclay patted the spot where the key had just been safely stored away. "One can't be too careful these days, Mr. Rutherford. And ever since Miss Griswold burst right into this very house the other day—uninvited, if you'll recall—I've taken to making certain the front door is now locked at all times."

"Why is everyone dawdling?" Miss Mabel called from somewhere down the hallway, having already vanished from view.

"We'd better catch her," Permilia said, taking hold not of his arm but of his hand, a more intimate gesture, in Asher's point of view, and one that had the sense of warmth returning. Pulled into motion a second later, he headed down the hallway, coming to a stop right beside Gertrude and Harrison, who were perusing a few of the portraits hanging on the walls.

"And here I thought some of Mrs. Davenport's ancestors were eerie," Gertrude began, jumping on the spot right after those words left her mouth when Miss Mabel marched up to them, looking exactly like she might be losing patience with their dawdling.

"If you've forgotten, tea is rarely served in the hallway," she said, stopping right beside Gertrude, who was looking rather guilty.

"Do forgive us, Miss Huxley," Gertrude began. "I'm to blame for the continued dawdling, but I was just admiring the portraits of your ancestors, although I have to say I've never seen ancestors who were so similar in appearance."

"All the portraits hanging in this house are of my father," Miss Mabel returned.

Gertrude blinked. "How . . . unusual, but . . . surely there must be a portrait of your mother somewhere in the house, and I would hope there's one of you and your sister as well."

"I'm afraid not." Miss Mabel's brow furrowed. "I don't believe you and I have ever been introduced. I know that you're Miss Gertrude Cadwalader, though, companion of Mrs. Davenport, a lady who wasn't always as peculiar as she is these days, but I'm sure you're well aware of that."

Gertrude blinked right back at her. "I'm sure I'm not aware of anything of the sort. However, since I'm not one to discuss my employer or her business, let us return to our proper introduction. I am Miss Gertrude Cadwalader, and I'm very pleased to meet you, Miss Huxley."

"You may call me Miss Mabel." She turned her attention to Harrison, looked him up and down with a very considering eye, and then nodded. "You are, of course, Mr. Harrison Sinclair, a gentleman who distinctly reminds me of Permilia's father."

Permilia tilted her head and considered Harrison for a moment. "I suppose he does resemble Father, although I don't think Father is prone to wearing the color purple."

Miss Mabel nodded as she walked around Harrison, again looking him up and down. "True, this is true, but this young man is built along remarkably similar lines as your father, however . . ." She lifted her head and smiled rather coyly at Harrison. "I'm sure I should beg your pardon for ogling you, Mr. Sinclair, but at my age, I've gotten quite used to ogling whomever I please."

Harrison, instead of appearing to take even the least bit of offense, grinned. "How charming it is to learn you know my name, Miss Huxley, but if you'll allow me to do the proper?" He stepped closer to her before she could reply. Taking her hand, he placed a kiss on it and then stepped back. "I am Mr. Harrison Sinclair, and it's a true pleasure to meet you, Miss Mabel Huxley."

"The pleasure is all mine, dear," Miss Mabel all but purred. "Do tell me, how is that schooner progressing, the one that's rumored to be one of the fastest ever built, and the one that's taken you three years to assemble?"

"You've heard about my schooner?" Harrison asked.

"As I mentioned before, I'm a lady of a certain age, and since I reached that certain age as a confirmed spinster, I've gotten incredibly adept at observing my surroundings and the antics that transpire within those surroundings."

"Forgive me for pointing this out, Miss Mabel, but we're currently nowhere near the docks, where my schooner is being assembled."

"No, we're not" was all Miss Mabel said to that before she headed off down the hall again. "Come along," she called over her shoulder.

"Is it just me or do any of the rest of you feel as if we shouldn't be here?" Harrison asked, taking Gertrude's arm while Asher took Permilia's hand and tucked it firmly into the crook of his arm.

"I think we should make a pact right now to drink the tea as quickly as we can and get out of here as quickly as possible," Asher said, eliciting immediate nods all around.

"Gertrude and I already have plans to visit Miss Snook's School for the Improvement of Feminine Minds," Permilia began. "We can use that as an excuse to leave within the hour." She smiled. "You're more than welcome to join us."

For some curious reason, Asher did not feel the need to balk at that idea at all. "That sounds like a delightful place to visit," he said right as Miss Mabel marched back up to them, planting her hands on her hips.

"We'll never get around to having tea at this rate," Miss Mabel said.

Before Asher could do what he was rumored to do so well, soothe away the temper of an annoyed lady, Harrison stepped forward. Smiling one of his most charming smiles, he took hold of Miss Mabel's arm. "Allow me to escort you into the . . . library?"

"That is where my sister is at the moment."

"Wonderful," Harrison exclaimed before he headed down the hallway, his charm having Miss Mabel smiling by the time they reached the library door.

"I should probably allow Henrietta to know you're here before we walk in on her," Miss Mabel said. "I'll be back in a moment." She released Harrison's arm and disappeared through the library door.

"Since Miss Henrietta is the one Miss Mabel believes issued us the invitation, wouldn't you imagine she's currently anticipating our arrival?" Permilia asked.

"One would think that would be the case," Harrison returned right as Miss Mabel edged out of the library and frowned.

"This is going to seem rather curious, but Henrietta's sleeping."

Gertrude nodded. "That happens with Mrs. Davenport all the time, and if Miss Henrietta is anything like Mrs. Davenport, she won't appreciate being awakened, so perhaps we should just come back another time."

"But what about my maudlin feelings and how the tea was going to improve those feelings?" Miss Mabel asked.

Summoning up a smile, one that proved she was quite adept at dealing with women in possession of maudlin feelings on a frequent basis, Gertrude inclined her head. "If you're of the belief your sister truly wants to soothe your maudlin feelings away, we'll be more than happy to wait right here while you wake your sister up and inform her that her guests have arrived."

"Excellent," Miss Mabel said. "I'll return directly." With a swish of her skirt, she edged through the partially open door to the library and vanished from sight again.

"Even if Miss Henrietta is prone to napping, I find it incredibly peculiar that she'd fall asleep when she only sent out those invitations to tea a short time ago. She must have remembered that she'd requested our presence at one," Permilia whispered.

"It is peculiar, and does nothing to reassure me that all is right in the Huxley house," Asher said quietly. "Which means we might . . ."

Whatever else he'd been about to say was forgotten when what could only be described as screeching suddenly rang out, the screeches clearly coming from an irate Miss Henrietta.

"Why in the world would you wake me, Mabel? I told you

302

I didn't sleep well last night, and I'd just dropped off into a pleasant dream, one where you were not present, which rarely happens, as you very well know, and now . . . Well, here you are, standing in front of me and looking far too cheerful about it."

"Stop hollering at me," Miss Mabel yelled back. "I wouldn't have felt compelled to wake you if you hadn't felt compelled to invite guests over to tea, guests you apparently forgot about, but guests who are right outside this door right this very minute."

"There are not guests at the door."

"I assure you, there are."

When the sisters launched into a rather heated bickering exchange, Asher decided to take matters into his own hands, proving to Miss Henrietta without a shadow of a doubt that guests had, indeed, come to call—although . . . it was becoming downright concerning that neither sister seemed to have remembered they'd invited guests over in the first place.

"Good afternoon, Miss Henrietta," he said, pushing open the library door and stepping just over the threshold, his gaze settling on Miss Henrietta, who was sprawled on a fainting couch located directly beside the fireplace.

Pushing herself upright, Miss Henrietta blinked, rubbed her eyes, then scowled at her sister. "Why didn't you tell me you'd invited Mr. Rutherford over, or"—she craned her neck—"Miss Griswold, and another young lady who might be Miss Cadwalader, and"—her eyes widened as she took to smoothing down her hair—"Mr. Harrison Sinclair."

Miss Mabel, who'd been in the process of moving over to a chair situated in front of the fireplace, stopped midstep and turned. "I didn't invite them. You did."

"Why would I go to the bother of inviting anyone for tea? You know I've never been the social one of the two of us."

Miss Mabel immediately stuck her nose in the air. "I thought you'd done so in order to cheer me up, given the despair I've been feeling of late over never pursuing the affection I once felt for George, and then missing another opportunity of doing just that when he returned to town. If only I had sought him out when he first traveled to the city on business, he might not now be tied to that shrew of a woman, the former Ida Webster."

To Asher's concern, Miss Henrietta narrowed her eyes and released a distinct scoff. "Honestly, Mabel, since when have you taken to embracing that fantasy you spread about years ago, the one where you held George Griswold in high esteem but were kept apart from him because of Father?"

Miss Mabel turned a rather sickly shade of white. "I have no idea what you're talking about, Henrietta. You know I held great affection for George, as well as a few other gentlemen who wanted to court me, and I have mourned the lack of anyone returning my affections for decades."

"You loved the idea of George and the other gentlemen because it annoyed Father, a man who wanted you to marry well to elevate his social status in life. And considering Father suffered a very convenient yet unfortunate death not long after he forbade you to see George again—along with quite a few other men, if my memory serves me correctly—it's always been my belief that you used the loss of those gentlemen as an excuse to finally justify taking care of Father once and for all."

As the library fell completely silent, Asher chanced a glance at Miss Mabel, finding that the whiteness of her face was rapidly being replaced with red. Realizing that an intervention was going to be necessary before someone got hurt, he took one step forward, but before he could reach Miss Mabel's side, she let out a shriek that sounded exactly as if it had come from a banshee before she bolted into motion and launched herself in the direction of her sister.

CHAPTER
TWENTY-FIVE

Because Asher and Harrison both seemed reluctant to intervene with what could only be described as a brawl between the two sisters, Permilia realized it was going to be up to her to stop the nonsense occurring right in front of her eyes. However, because Ida had never bothered to explain what was expected of a society lady when faced with this particular situation, Permilia found herself hesitating for just a second as she debated which of the two options that sprang to mind would be most acceptable.

Deciding the sisters would be less than pleased if she were to fire the pistol she'd tucked into her walking dress at the ceiling—especially because the ceiling was painted with a lovely scene of what seemed to be some type of cherubs—Permilia went for option number two, that involving a vase of fresh flowers.

Dashing across the room, she plucked the vase from the table, plucked the flowers straight out of it, dropping them on the floor, and then tossing the remaining water, of which there was a great deal, directly over top of the sisters, who were kicking, biting, and pulling hair.

In the blink of an eye, the kicking stopped, as did the hair pulling, and the screeches they'd been making took to sounding more along the lines of sputters.

Taking a step away from the fainting couch, Permilia handed the vase to Asher, who'd moved up to join her. Crossing her arms over her chest, she tilted her head and regarded the ladies, who were dripping water all over the floor as they struggled to get to their feet.

"What in the world possessed you, Permilia, to douse my sister and me with water? I assure you, we squabble with each other frequently, so your interference was not needed, nor wanted." Miss Mabel shoved a hank of sodden hair out of her face before she settled a glare on Permilia.

"I couldn't simply stand by and watch the two of you pummel each other, which I do hope is *not* a frequent happenstance, since it's barbaric," Permilia returned. "If you've neglected to remember, you currently have a library filled with guests you invited for tea, and forgive me, but forcing us to witness your appalling behavior is not making any of us thankful we accepted your invitation."

"As I do believe I mentioned before, Permilia, I didn't invite you to tea," Miss Mabel said. "Henrietta did, so if you feel compelled to take someone to task, take her, not me."

Miss Henrietta released a bit of a snort. "I have no idea what nonsense you've taken to spouting now, Mabel, because I assure you, I did not invite anyone to tea. And, if I had, I certainly wouldn't have taken to snoozing right before those guests were expected to arrive because, even for me, that would have been beyond the pale."

The sense of foreboding Permilia had been feeling when she'd first entered the house returned with a vengeance, especially when Miss Mabel and Miss Henrietta exchanged significant looks right before Miss Mabel squared her shoulders and lifted her chin. "Well, right then, everyone has to leave . . . immediately."

Before Permilia could ask a single question, she found her hand taken firmly in Asher's while Harrison did the same with Gertrude, and mumbling what must have been the expected pleasantries, Asher pulled her toward the door at a fast clip.

Before they could make it through that door, however, they found their path blocked by the man Permilia only knew as Richard Coeur de Lion and . . . Mr. Jasper Tooker, nephew of the Huxley sisters.

"Ah, Miss Griswold," Mr. Tooker exclaimed right as Asher stepped in front of her, a protective gesture that distracted her from everything else that Mr. Tooker said as she simply seemed to melt right there in the midst of the Huxley library, melt because Asher really was a very upstanding sort of gentleman, willing to defend her, which she found quite intriguing, especially since . . .

" . . . truly unfortunate that both of you saw fit to bring uninvited guests, and do know that I will be most distressed about having to do away with them."

Shaking herself directly back into the conversation, Permilia peered around Asher and found that while she'd been lost in a lovely daydream, Mr. Tooker had pulled out a pistol and was even now pointing it directly Asher's way.

"What do you think you're about, Mr. Tooker?" she demanded, trying to edge around Asher but finding he didn't seem very keen to allow her to do that, what with the way he kept weaving back and forth, blocking her forward momentum.

"You seem to be a bright sort, Miss Griswold," Mr. Tooker returned, looking around Asher to catch her eye. "I'm sure you'll be able to puzzle out that I'm tying up a few loose ends, ones that I certainly don't want haunting me for the rest of my days." He smiled a smile that did little to reassure her. "However, since I'm also certain everyone has numerous questions they're dying to ask me, and I'm not an unreasonable man, if all of you will kindly take a seat in the library, I've asked Mr. Barclay to fix us some tea. Doesn't that sound delightful?"

"Surely you realize that offering us tea while holding us hostage before you then attempt to do away with us is an offer we're hardly going to be eager to accept," Permilia began. "And given that there are any number of Pinkerton agents right outside this very house, I'm sure I have no idea how you believe you'll be able to get away with what clearly sounds like murder."

"Come now, Miss Griswold, you don't truly believe that I waltzed into the house using the front door, do you? That would have drawn unwanted notice, and I can assure you, notice is not something I care to attract. That's why I won't be exiting the house through the front door, nor the back door, for that matter."

"How will you leave, then?" she pressed.

"He must know about the tunnels," Miss Mabel whispered.

"Tunnels?"

"The ones our father built that can be accessed from the two lots on either side of the house," Miss Mabel explained. "They were supposed to give him access to his other wives, but . . . well . . . that didn't quite work out as he'd planned."

"Did you say *wives*?" Gertrude asked.

"He had two of them, and was pursuing a third when he died," Mr. Tooker said quite cheerfully before he gestured to the room behind them. "But we'll get into that after all of you get resettled in the library."

"And to think I've been shocked over Mrs. Davenport's intrigues," Permilia heard Gertrude mutter before they turned as one and were marched back across the room by a pistol-wielding Mr. Tooker and the other man, whose identity and how he fit into their current drama was unknown.

Taking her hand in his, Asher leaned closer and lowered his voice. "Don't worry. We'll be fine. I'm armed, and with a real weapon this time."

Having no idea what Asher meant by that, or what he meant when he muttered something about a powder puff, Permilia settled for giving his hand a squeeze as she lowered her voice as well. "I'm armed too, and if Harrison isn't, well, I have a spare pistol he can borrow."

Asher's brows drew together. "You have more than one weapon on you?"

"Of course."

"No chitchat—keep moving," Mr. Tooker called from behind them.

Walking across the room, Permilia took a seat on a small settee, scooting over to make room for Asher, who sat down directly beside her. Taking hold of her hand again, he turned to Harrison, who was already sitting in a chair right beside Gertrude and had taken to narrowing his eyes at Mr. Tooker.

"Any ideas?" Asher whispered.

"I say we wait for him and the other man to get distracted, and then we take them out," Harrison returned before he settled back in his chair, folded his arms over his chest, and returned his attention to Mr. Tooker.

Mr. Tooker evidently didn't care to be on the receiving end of Harrison's attention because he turned to the man he'd brought with him and waved him forward, directly toward Harrison.

"Tie him up, if you please, Mr. Sprague, and then lock him in that storage closet over there. I find that having too many people gathered in one place elicits too many questions." Mr. Tooker then nodded to Gertrude. "You might as well tie her up too. Ladies do tend to chat incessantly when they're nervous, and chatting grates on my nerves."

"I have never been accused of incessant chatting," Gertrude said, her words earning a frown from Mr. Tooker right before he strode across the room, whipped a pristine handkerchief out of his pocket, and stuffed it directly into Gertrude's mouth.

That had Harrison letting out a growl as he began rising from the chair, his growl coming to a rapid end when Mr. Tooker, as calmly as you please, brought the pistol down on Harrison's head, the blow sending Harrison to the floor, rendered unconscious.

"Jasper, how could you?" Miss Mabel demanded in a horrified voice as the entire atmosphere in the room changed, as if the very real threat they were actually facing had just become crystal clear.

"Stop harping, Aunt Mabel. I care even less for harping than I do for chatting." Mr. Tooker gestured to Mr. Sprague. "Tie him up and drag him to the closet. I don't want to have to look at him any longer."

While Mr. Sprague tied up Harrison—who thankfully was already beginning to stir, although he'd yet to open his eyes—Mr. Tooker removed his necktie, pulled Gertrude to her feet, demanded she put her hands behind her back, then tied them together with the necktie in a very efficient manner. Pulling her over to the storage room when he was done, he shoved her through the door, warned her to stay quiet, then strode to the center of the room and smiled a charming smile.

"Now then, while we wait for Mr. Barclay and our tea—and don't get your hopes up that he'll alert anyone to the situation, since I threatened to kill his precious Huxley employees if anyone but him returns to this room with the tea—I suppose I should set about doing some explaining."

Pulling her gaze from Harrison, who was now being dragged by his feet across the library, Permilia jumped ever so slightly when the storage room door slammed shut, then braced herself

310

when Mr. Tooker's smile slid straight off his face right before he glared at Mr. Sprague.

"While I understand that you clearly are not the best assassin in the country, Mr. Sprague—no matter that the advertisement you placed in all the local papers stated something quite contrary to that idea—you should know, even as incompetent as you are, that this particular moment demands quiet. Slamming doors will not assure us the privacy we need, especially since it might alert those pesky Pinkerton agents roaming around the outside of this very house that something is amiss."

"Sorry," Mr. Sprague muttered before he pulled up a chair and sat down right beside Permilia.

Blinking back at the man when he, curiously enough, took to smiling at her, even as he took to staring, Permilia frowned. "You placed an advertisement in the newspapers advertising that you're an assassin?"

If anything, Mr. Sprague's smile increased. Leaning toward her, he lowered his voice. "I did indeed, although I was very careful with how I worded it, never using the word *assassin* but simply alluding to what my true occupation is by suggestive phrases."

"Such as?"

"*Problems dispatched with discretion* springs to mind."

"Which was false advertising, if you ask me," Mr. Tooker said. "It was hardly discreet of you to fire off arrows at Mr. Rutherford in the midst of Central Park. And you have yet to explain to satisfaction why you chose arrows in the first place."

Mr. Sprague lifted his head. "You told me to make it appear like an accident."

"A nice gunshot resulting from what the authorities would have believed was a robbery attempt would have worked nicely," Mr. Tooker pointed out.

Mr. Sprague nodded. "Indeed, and if you'll recall, I told you

I began shooting at them when a delivery wagon appeared out of nowhere, but . . . that was rotten luck since the appearance of the wagon rattled my concentration and I fear the rattling affected my aim."

When two bright spots of red appeared on Mr. Tooker's pale cheeks, Permilia decided a redirection of the conversation was in order before Miss Mabel and Miss Henrietta's nephew did something impulsive like shoot the very assassin he'd hired to kill everyone.

"Why hire an assassin to go after Asher in the first place?" she asked, earning a nod of approval from Mr. Tooker in the process, although his nodding came to an abrupt halt when Miss Henrietta cleared her throat, drawing everyone's attention.

"It's because of the tearoom Asher's set to open."

Asher sat forward. "That's ridiculous. Why would anyone solicit an assassin to kill me simply because I'm opening up a tearoom?"

Before Miss Henrietta could respond, Mr. Sprague spoke up. "Mr. Tooker wanted to impress his aunts, you see, by doing away with the competition." He smiled. "It turns out that those two over there . . ." He nodded to Miss Mabel and Miss Henrietta. "Well, they evidently always dreamed of opening up their own tea shop, and had even looked into having that fancy architect, Mr. Hunt—the one who did up the Vanderbilt house, which I must add is a most remarkable house, and I'm so grateful I was able to see it, since that's where I met up with Mr. Tooker for my initial payment, and . . ."

"You do recall we're on a limited time schedule, Mr. Sprague, don't you?" Mr. Tooker interrupted through what appeared to be gritted teeth.

"Ah yes, forgive me, I tend to wax on." Mr. Sprague smiled. "In short, Mr. Tooker's aunts apparently suffered a rather large disappointment when they learned about Mr. Rutherford's plans to open a tearoom on the fourth floor of his store. That's when Mr. Tooker decided to earn his aunts' undying gratitude by doing away with Mr. Rutherford and sequentially paving the way for their own tea shop plans to recommence."

Miss Mabel rose to her feet and placed a hand to her chest. "You were willing to murder someone in order to win our gratitude?"

Mr. Tooker sent Miss Mabel a smile of what almost seemed to be affection. "Indeed, especially because you and Aunt Henrietta have always tolerated me, Aunt Mabel, but I've always known you did so simply because your father was my grandfather and you felt obligated to provide for me, at least in some small way."

Narrowing her eyes, Miss Mabel lifted her chin. "We gave you a house, Jasper, along with a trust fund, which means we've provided you with more than most people have to get along with, and I certainly don't appreciate you suggesting we've not done enough."

"You gave me your old house, one that had remained vacant for years, and I'm limited to how much money I can access from my trust fund."

Miss Henrietta rose to her feet. "Because you would have squandered it, being your father's son, a man I have no idea why our sister married, God rest his soul. You also possess a questionable temperament, something I'm quite sure you inherited from that mother of yours, and given those two marks against you, you're fortunate we've had anything to do with you at all."

Mr. Tooker's smile vanished as his eyes began to spew heat. "Don't you dare have a go at my mother."

"It really isn't acceptable, Miss Mabel, to speak ill of the dead," Permilia began, hoping to take just a touch of the heat out of Mr. Tooker's eyes, especially since he'd taken to looking somewhat insane.

Miss Mabel, to Permilia's complete astonishment, let out a snort. "His mother isn't dead. Cybil is alive and well and set up quite nicely in a house Henrietta and I provided for her down in Boston after her husband died when Jasper was still a child."

The sense of foreboding that Permilia had been trying to hold at bay returned in a split second. "When I overheard that conversation, Mr. Tooker, one I now know was between you and Mr. Sprague here, you mentioned something about a partner. While I readily admit I was just wondering if that partner might have been one of your aunts, I'm quickly coming to the belief that it's your mother."

Mr. Tooker, instead of agreeing or disagreeing, suddenly swung the pistol in Permilia's direction, cocking it as he did so. "You're beginning to annoy me, Miss Griswold, and before I kill you, allow me to say that you caused me no small amount of aggravation, what with your snooping and all. I want you to know that you, and you alone, are solely responsible for the impending departure of the oh-so-incompetent Mr. Sprague from the face of this earth."

"You're going to kill *me*?" Mr. Sprague asked, jumping out of his seat and searching his pockets, quite as if searching for a weapon.

"Sit down, Mr. Sprague, or *I'll* kill you myself right here and now."

Looking to the door, Permilia found Mr. Barclay entering the library, carrying a tray with a silver tea service on it, but he was certainly not the person who'd been responsible for the latest threat.

That threat had come from the tall woman dressed in the first state of fashion, her pale hair perfectly coiffed beneath a hat that had cost more than a pretty penny. That she was holding a gun in one hand with remarkable ease gave clear testimony to the idea that hers was not an idle threat. And given that she was holding a cane in her other hand, one that probably held some type of weapon, since the woman didn't possess even a hint of a limp, had Permilia realizing their chances of leaving the library unscathed had just dimmed significantly.

Sauntering across the room, the woman moved directly up to Miss Mabel and Miss Henrietta. Tilting her head, she smiled. "Hello . . . sisters."

"I keep thinking we're nearing the end of this dramatic event, but more and more pieces keep getting thrown into the puzzle," Asher said quietly.

"Wait until you hear the truth about me," Mr. Sprague said as he edged his chair a few inches closer to where Asher was sitting, as if he'd decided to align himself with Asher instead of the man who'd apparently hired him.

Before Mr. Sprague had an opportunity to expand on that, though, the woman Permilia was now beginning to believe was Mr. Tooker's mother turned around and nodded Permilia's way.

"Is *she* the reason your plan was put into jeopardy, dear?"

Before Permilia could respond, Asher rose to his feet and stepped in front of her. "Since the plan you're speaking about revolves around my demise, I believe we should leave Miss Griswold out of the matter."

"Ah, Mr. Rutherford," the woman began, advancing Asher's way. "It's so unfortunate that you and I have to meet under these trying conditions. I do so enjoy shopping at your delightful store, and do know that your death is truly nothing personal. But I'm afraid my son went and incurred a great deal of debt in order to surprise his dear aunties by procuring a location for that dratted tea shop they've been longing to open for years. He incurred additional debt by pushing building plans along, having to grease quite a few palms in the process. After all of that, the poor dear then discovered that you, Mr. Rutherford, have spoiled everything by planning to open up a tea shop of your own, which, I'm sad to say, wasn't a very friendly thing for you to have done."

She released a laugh that sent shivers down Permilia's spine. "We knew our little tea shop wouldn't stand the slightest chance of enjoying any success being in competition with yours. So the only plan darling Jasper could come up with to salvage the day was to bring about your demise, a plan that should have gone off without a hitch, until . . ." She shot a look of pure animosity Permilia's way.

"You really should know by now, Miss Griswold, that snooping is not an acceptable pastime for a young lady. But you decided to snoop, Mr. Sprague turned out to be an enormous disappointment in the assassin department, and well, I'm afraid matters have simply gotten away from us, which means . . . all of you must die."

"You would kill your own sisters, Cybil?" Miss Henrietta demanded, plunking her hands on her hips as she advanced on the woman named Cybil.

Cybil raised the walking stick, the action having Miss Henrietta's advance coming to a rapid end. "You've never thought of me as your true sister, Henrietta. I've always been a second-class citizen in your eyes, simply because you and Mabel felt I wasn't legitimate. But since my mother, God rest her soul, had no idea Father was already married to your mother when he married her, I've always believed that I'm every bit as legitimate as you two are, no matter that society, along with the courts, believes differently."

"Ah, so this is about Father's will," Miss Henrietta said after she retook her seat and grabbed the hand of Miss Mabel, who'd retaken her seat on the fainting couch as well.

"He left me with practically nothing, and that was after he'd murdered my mother and tried to murder me as well."

"This is not going to be beneficial to our situation," Asher said under his breath, and to Permilia's surprise, he eased his hand ever so casually into his jacket pocket, his action undetected by Mr. Tooker or his mother, both of whom were in the midst of an argument with the Huxley sisters, an argument getting louder by the second.

When Permilia chanced a glance at Mr. Sprague, the man hired to assassinate Asher, he was watching Asher with a very considering look in his eyes before he turned his attention to Permilia and actually sent her . . . a wink.

"Don't worry, Miss Griswold. Since it would seem I'm just as doomed as everyone else, I'm throwing my lot in with you and Mr. Rutherford, knowing that doing so will greatly increase my chances of getting out of this house alive."

"Aren't you paid to kill people?" Permilia whispered, having to lean forward to be heard over Miss Mabel's and Cybil's shouting.

"I'm not actually an assassin. I'm an aspiring writer who used to work for the *New York Sun*, but after getting dismissed from my position for embellishing my stories so much they came across as fiction, I decided I'd try my hand at a novel." He blew out a breath. "Mysteries and murder stories are always a safe bet, so wanting to write an authentic story of a killer-for-hire, I paid for an advertisement hawking my fictitious skills, never imagining anyone would respond, and . . ." His eyes grew wide. "Mr. Tooker wasn't the only person in the city looking to hire an assassin."

Permilia let out a grunt. "Which certainly explains how you were able to secure my secret identity. You're used to sniffing out stories as a reporter."

"Truth be told, my learning you're Miss Quill was more luck than stellar reporting, Miss Griswold. Everyone at the *Sun* knows the veiled lady writes the Miss Quill column, even if Mr. Dana pretends they don't, and when you stepped out of the hansom cab I'd taken the time to follow, well, you could have knocked me over with a feather."

Permilia frowned. "How'd you get the invitation to the Vanderbilt ball? And how'd you get the funds to pay for that costume, one that I know full well cost you more than a pretty penny?"

"I do beg your pardon," Cybil drawled, appearing directly in front of Permilia and tapping her walking stick on the floor. "I hope we haven't been boring you with talk of murder, poisoning, polygamy, and other scandalous tidbits, but since it appears that whatever you and Mr. Sprague were discussing is evidently far more riveting than our conversation, do share it with the room."

When Mr. Sprague let out what sounded exactly like a whimper, Permilia resisted the urge to roll her eyes and squared her shoulders instead.

"I was asking him how it came to be that he was able to receive an invitation to the Vanderbilt ball."

"I procured him an invitation," Mr. Tooker said, speaking up as he walked across the library to join his mother.

Permilia's brows drew together, but before she could ask another question, Miss Henrietta came stomping after him, taking hold of his arm—which Permilia felt was a risky move—and then giving that arm a shake.

"Why would Alva Vanderbilt send you an invitation to her ball? It was your aunt and I who had a connection to Commodore Vanderbilt back in the day, and yet we didn't get an invitation sent to us."

Mr. Tooker shook himself out of Miss Henrietta's hold. "Oh, but you did, Aunt Henrietta. I just happened to be visiting when the invitation was hand-delivered. Since Mr. Sprague had made it a condition of his taking on the job that I get him an invitation to the ball, I helped myself to your invitations, taking

318

them to a man I know on the Lower East Side who changed the names on them."

"You made an invitation to the Vanderbilt ball a condition of taking on the job to murder Asher?" Permilia asked, turning back to Mr. Sprague, who gave her a shrug before he blew out a breath.

"It was the Vanderbilt ball. Everyone wanted to go, and since Mr. Tooker seemed incredibly keen to hire me on, I figured it wouldn't hurt to ask." He winced when Mr. Tooker took a step toward him. "Who could have known he'd find a way to manage that practically impossible feat, or agree to pay me such a large sum that I felt comfortable incurring the debt to dress myself in style?"

"You're not really an assassin, are you, dear?" Cybil asked, turning her walking stick in Mr. Sprague's direction, which had Permilia casting around her thoughts for a suitable distraction topic.

"How do you know that Mr. Huxley killed your mother?" was the first distraction idea to pop to mind, an idea she immediately regretted when Cybil let out a hiss, twisted the handle of her walking stick, then placed the sharp point of the blade that had been revealed on the bottom of that stick directly over Permilia's heart.

"You're very annoying, Miss Griswold, but somewhat clever as well. Because of that, I'll tell you all about our sordid family history, and then . . . because that's information we Huxley women don't care to have bandied about, I'll have to kill you."

Not allowing herself to so much as blink over what she knew was not an empty threat, Permilia waited as Cybil stared her down, until the woman finally removed the blade and stepped back, moving to take the chair Gertrude had once been sitting in.

"My father, Mr. Frank Huxley, was not a pleasant man, nor was he a moral one," Cybil began. "He married Mabel and

Henrietta's mother but then became annoyed with her when she wasn't able to produce a son, only daughters. Instead of simply killing her off, as a normal man would have done, he sought out the affections of another woman, my mother, and married her without allowing her to know he had another wife and two daughters on the other side of town. When my mother gave birth to me, he was disappointed, of course, but his business was really beginning to grow, and not having any disposable time to search out another new wife, he contented himself for a while with increasing his fortune and knowing he would eventually produce a son."

"That never happened, though," Miss Mabel said from her position on the fainting couch. "My mother suffered numerous miscarriages and even had a few stillborn children, two of whom were boys."

"My mother as well," Cybil said.

Miss Henrietta blew out a loud breath. "Father finally decided that he'd have to use his daughters to obtain a proper son, and wanting to attract just the right sort of son-in-law, he built this house and had my mother try to get us accepted into proper society."

Miss Mabel crossed her arms over her chest. "Society loathed us from the very beginning, some in that society even going so far as to remark on the way Father ate his peas with his knife whenever he was invited to dine at someone's house. Of course he was only invited if that particular society gentleman had need of Father's money."

"That's why he wouldn't allow my father, or any of the other gentlemen who desired your attention, to pay you proper court, wasn't it?" Permilia asked, turning to Miss Mabel, who nodded.

"Your father was ambitious but couldn't provide the entrance into society Father had decided he wanted, so when Henrietta and I were unsuccessful getting accepted into society, he introduced us to"—Miss Mabel jerked her head toward Cybil—"Cybil."

"And that's when he decided to build two more houses on either side of this one," Cybil said, her eyes dark with temper. "One of them for me and my mother, and the other for the new wife he'd decided he was going to have to take if he stood any chance at all of having a son." She shook her head. "He'd apparently grown tired of having to travel across the city to visit one wife or the other."

"His decision to corral his different families was the beginning of everything going bad," Miss Henrietta whispered. "Mother died first, of a broken heart I've always thought."

Cybil let out a snort. "She didn't die of a broken heart. My mother poisoned her."

"What?" Miss Henrietta and Miss Mabel demanded together.

Lifting a shoulder in a dismissive manner, Cybil studied the carvings on the handle of her walking stick. "Mother had had no inkling about Frank's other family, so when she saw this house—especially since it was far nicer than the small house across town that Frank had provided for her—and then learned that her so-called husband was finally willing to build her a mansion of her own, but one that would place her directly next to his legal wife, and a house away from what he hoped to be his third wife, well . . ." Cybil looked up. "I do believe it caused poor Mother to lose any little bit of sanity she'd retained after having her world turned upside down. She paid a visit to Frank's first wife, taking her a gift of special tea, and when she left this house, the first wife was dead, clearing the way for my mother to take her rightful place."

"Until Grandfather killed her, having decided she was behind the murder of his first wife and not wanting to take a wait-and-see attitude to determine if he'd be the next person poisoned," Mr. Tooker said.

"This is going to make a fascinating book if I live to write it," Mr. Sprague said, drawing everyone's attention.

Cybil stared at Mr. Sprague for a long moment, wrinkled her nose, and . . . laughed. "What a very interesting assassin you make, Mr. Sprague, but I do fear you won't be writing any books." She turned to her son. "After we leave here today, you and I will be having a chat about how you managed to bungle everything. If you would have simply listened to me from the very beginning, we would have done away with your aunts, and that would have been the end of it."

"He wouldn't have done away with us, not after he had a peek at our will," Miss Henrietta said.

"You knew I saw your will?" Mr. Tooker asked.

"We keep an eye on you whenever you come to visit," Miss Henrietta said. "And a few months back, when you excused yourself to use the washroom, we followed you and watched through a hidey-hole in the wall as you went not to the washroom but to my office." She smiled. "I left the will on top of the desk on purpose." Her smile faded. "But I never imagined that having you read it would put these events into motion. I simply believed that if you learned you and your mother were cut off without a dime if anything of a suspicious nature happened to us, that you'd do your utmost to keep us alive."

"Is that true, Jasper?" Cybil demanded.

"Why do you think I was trying to win my way into their good graces by taking on such debt in order to provide them with their own tea shop?" Mr. Tooker spat. "Even if they didn't die a suspicious death, they weren't leaving us the bulk of their fortune, so I had to do something to convince them otherwise, and paving the way for them to finally be able to realize their dream of a tea shop was the best I could come up with."

"That was a ridiculous idea," Asher said, speaking up. "You

don't plan to murder a complete stranger simply to win your way into someone's good graces."

When Mr. Tooker raised the hand he was still holding the pistol in and aimed it directly at Asher, Permilia decided she'd had quite enough. Rising to her feet, she stuck her hand in her pocket, but before she could retrieve her pistol, Cybil was on her feet, her walking stick at the ready. Tossing her pistol to her son, she advanced Permilia's way.

"How sweet, Miss Griswold, to discover you're willing to take a bullet for your love, but . . . are you willing to take a blade to your throat?"

Not hesitating for a single second, Permilia whirled around, jumped over the settee, and grabbed what turned out to be an umbrella from an old milk canister that was home to a variety of different objects.

"Ah, a fight to the death, then, is it?" Cybil said before she let out a laugh that had chills running up Permilia's spine before she rushed Permilia's way right as her son charged at Asher.

Being quite used to dueling, given her rather unusual youth, Permilia soon found herself battling a crazed woman wielding what was certainly a very sharp blade. The sharpness of that blade was proven without a shadow of a doubt when Permilia slipped and ended up getting her arm sliced open before she could recover.

Fending off Cybil with an umbrella that wasn't meant to withstand such abuse, she soon found herself being backed into a corner and could only pray in that moment that the end would either be swift or God would hear her prayers and send her some much-needed help.

The sound of a pistol blasting on the other side of the room gave her immediate hope, and when Cybil turned and let out an enraged shriek, evidently taking note of her son falling ever so slowly to the ground, Permilia saw her chance and raised her umbrella one last time. Bringing it down on Cybil's head, she saw the umbrella split in two and feared the worst when Cybil spun around to face her again.

But then, as Cybil's eyes rolled back in her head and the woman plummeted to the floor, Permilia breathed a silent prayer of thanks right before she saw Asher rushing across the room, a smoking pistol in his hands and something indescribable in his eyes.

Catching her up in his arms, he buried his head into the crook of her neck and held her tight. He pulled back a moment later, looked in her eyes, and smiled. "You, Miss Permilia Griswold, are quite the extraordinary woman, and—"

She drew in a breath. "You're not going to propose courtship again, are you, not with me in such a sorry state and bleeding all over you?" She blew out the breath. "It's hardly a romantic setting."

Asher blinked, dug out a spare necktie he just happened to have in his pocket, and bound it around her arm, which had begun to bleed rather profusely as well as sting.

"For your information, I was not going to propose court-ship, but something I believe you'll find even more appealing."

Lifting her head, she caught his eye. "What could you propose that would be more appealing than courting me?"

He smiled. "Since again, this is apparently not the time to talk of courtship, although I do find it encouraging that you seemingly find that idea rather more appealing than you once did, what I was going to propose is this."

He put a finger under her chin and leaned in toward her. "Miss Permilia Griswold, I have never in my life been more frightened than when I thought I was going to watch you die, but since we're not dead, I've decided to do something I never thought I would."

He drew in a deep breath. "I've been beyond impressed with

all the suggestions you've given me of late, ones that have seen me hire on innovative stylists and procure goods for a better price than even I'd be able to manage. Because of your incredible instincts, and your heart and mind of a true merchant, I'd like to offer you a position with Rutherford & Company, a position that comes with its very own title."

Even though she'd been expecting something of a romantic nature, his offer was more romantic than anything she'd ever imagined being given.

Staunchly refusing to give in to the urge to declare herself falling a bit in love with the man she'd just been bleeding all over, because in her heart she knew this was not exactly the right moment for that, she permitted herself the luxury of a grin instead.

When he grinned in return, she reached for him, standing on tiptoe in order to be able to whisper into his ear.

"I would love nothing more than to accept your offer of a position in your store, but do know that I'll not go easy on you while negotiating my salary just because we almost died together."

"I would expect nothing less."

And then, as Pinkerton agents swarmed into the library and Harrison, with Gertrude in tow, burst out of the storage room, Asher took Permilia's face between his hands, lowered his head, and . . . kissed her.

CHAPTER
TWENTY-SIX

ONE MONTH LATER

Jostling her way through the early-morning crowd that was bustling down the sidewalk adjacent to Broadway, Permilia clutched to her chest the large box filled with a variety of samples she'd procured at numerous out-of-the-way shops.

Glancing to her left, she smiled at Mr. Samuel Sprague, who was hurrying right beside her, clutching another box filled with samples and looking rather grumpy since he was not a gentleman well suited to morning excursions.

"I don't understand why we had to travel to the Lower East Side at such a ridiculous hour," he said, proving her grumpy theory since there was a definite surly tone to his protest. "That cobbler would have still been there after lunch, which means I could still be sleeping right now."

Biting back a smile as she watched Mr. Sprague stomp his way down the sidewalk, Permilia couldn't help but think for what felt like the millionth time that it was still curious to her that Asher had hired Mr. Sprague, of all people—as her personal assistant, no less.

She hadn't exactly thought she needed an assistant. However, when Asher had realized that she sought out new talent in designers, cobblers, and seamstresses in some of the seedier parts of the city, as in Five Points—his awareness brought to him directly from Mrs. Davenport—he'd gotten a little . . . testy.

What Mrs. Davenport had been doing in Five Points was anyone's guess, but Asher had not been keen on pondering that particular matter, preferring to dwell instead on exactly what had possessed Permilia to travel to Five Points on her own, and what could be done to make certain she didn't travel there on her own ever again.

Since she'd not been willing to put her quest to seek out fresh and different talent aside, or limit that quest to only the safest parts of the city, especially since she knew full well that sometimes the best talent was created out of necessity to put food on a table, Asher had decided a compromise was in order.

He had not, to her delight, tried to coddle her or treat her like a fragile creature, choosing instead to provide her with an assistant who could travel with her, allowing her to continue doing her job while guarding her back as she did that job.

When Mr. Sprague had turned up the very next day, knocking on the office door Asher had provided her, Permilia had been somewhat surprised to learn he was going to be her assistant, until he'd explained exactly what that position was going to entail.

While it had certainly been proven that Mr. Sprague had been an abject failure as a pretend assassin-for-hire, he had turned out to be rather accurate with a pistol, proving that accuracy that horrible day at the Huxley house when Cybil had regained consciousness right as the Pinkerton agents had been ready to cart her away.

Not expecting a woman who'd been rendered senseless to suddenly spring to her feet, Agent McParland had found his firearm grabbed away from him. Cybil had then aimed the firearm directly at Permilia but had been thwarted in her attempt to murder Permilia when Mr. Sprague stepped forward and shot the firearm right out of Cybil's hand.

That impressive bit of marksmanship, aided by Mr. Sprague's disclosure that he'd missed shooting Asher on purpose that day in Central Park, was exactly why Asher had chosen him to accompany Permilia around the city as her assistant. Mr. Sprague was in desperate need of funds, since he had given the Huxley sisters what remained of the money Mr. Tooker had given him to kill Asher, and he found that his new position afforded him the funds he needed while giving him a flexible schedule. That flexibility allowed him time to polish up his first novel, which Permilia had the sneaking suspicion was going to be a riveting read.

"We really should abandon excursions that are so early, Miss Griswold, because I do believe getting out of bed before the sun is fully risen is certainly a sad, sad circumstance."

Permilia sent a shake of her head Mr. Sprague's way. "We couldn't have done that, because Miss Betsy Miller needed the shoes we just picked up from her cobbler friend. She needs these shoes to take to a sales meeting later this morning in order to convince Mr. Rutherford that this particular cobbler would be a great addition to the store."

Mr. Sprague cheered up immediately. "You have a meeting with Miss Miller, you say?"

"Indeed, and I might very well need the two of you, after the meeting is over, to put all the samples together so that the presentation I am making later on this week to the other buyers will go well."

"I'll go get started on some of that organizing straightaway, and . . . I'll take that box for you."

Marveling just a bit at how interesting life could turn, Permilia placed her box on top of Mr. Sprague's and allowed her lips to curve just a touch as he bustled through the door that Mr. Cushing, the Rutherford & Company doorman, was holding open.

The very idea that Mr. Sprague had first become acquainted with Miss Miller while he'd been searching out Permilia's identity and was now romantically drawn to Miss Miller, and Miss Miller to him, lent credence to the idea that Reverend Perry had been right all along. God did open new paths for His children to take, and He often opened those paths in the most unusual of ways.

Her path, she was beginning to realize, had seen God sending her to Miss Snook's School for the Improvement of Feminine Minds, then off to the *New York Sun* in order to secure the funds needed to keep the school up and running, and then . . . using what she'd learned at the *New York Sun* to further help Asher grow his business.

She'd been thrilled when Asher had suggested she put her talent for spotting new fashions to use in his advertising department creating copy for ads. But he hadn't stopped there, encouraging her to learn all aspects of his store, and using her contacts within the city to bring his store the best talent around, even if that talent was found in unexpected places.

"Good morning, Miss Griswold," Mr. Cushing said, doffing his hat as he held open the door for her, his greeting pulling her from her thoughts.

"Good morning to you as well, Mr. Cushing." She walked through the open doorway and found herself all alone in the grand entranceway to Rutherford & Company.

Since it was far too early for any customers to be mingling throughout the store, and it was still too early for most of the employees to arrive, Permilia allowed herself to simply wander around the first floor, enjoying the quiet as she wandered.

Trailing through the accessory department, she moved into the haberdashery, taking her time as she looked through the new styles Asher had personally selected to offer their gentlemen guests.

"Does any of it meet with your approval?"

Returning a silk handkerchief to a wooden box displaying all the colors available, Permilia looked up, smiling when she saw Asher walking her way.

He was looking exceptionally stylish this morning, wearing a navy suit paired with a plaid waistcoat, starched white collar, and expertly tied tie. His hair was combed exactly as it was always combed, not a single strand out of place, and as he drew closer she got a distinct whiff of his cologne, a blend created specifically for him—sandalwood, a touch of lime, and something she hadn't been able to decipher but thought might simply be Asher.

"You're looking quite fashionable today, Permilia." He stopped next to her and, taking her hand in his, placed the now-expected kiss on it—even as she found herself wishing he would kiss her properly again, something he'd not done since they'd almost died at the Huxley house.

She was fairly certain he'd not kissed her because he'd realized that since she'd accepted his offer of employment, that made her an employee, and everyone knew it was hardly appropriate for an employer to take to kissing his employee, but . . . still. If she'd known he'd abandon all romantic interest in her, she might have very well chosen to reject his offer of employment in the hopes he'd turn the offer into a more personal one, one that would have her name changing—

"Is something the matter?" he asked, lowering her hand but only to tuck it firmly into the crook of his arm.

"Just thinking about the meeting I'm soon to have with Miss Miller" was all she was comfortable saying.

"Ah, Miss Miller. What a delightful addition she's made to the staff. Shall we move up to the third floor and see how the department that is soon to highlight her designs is coming along?"

"I would love to."

Walking with Asher through the first floor and to the steam elevator, Permilia stepped inside it, then blinked when Asher gestured to the lever.

"Do try to keep yourself in check, Permilia. In all honesty, last week when you insisted on operating this elevator for the first time, I was in fear for my life."

"My hand slipped on the lever," she said before she pulled the grate closed, and then, as if she'd been running a steam elevator her entire life, she brought them to the third floor without a single jolt.

Opening the door after the elevator had come to a complete stop, she smiled. "Third floor—ladies' fashions, including suits, shawls, and the designs of Miss Betsy Miller." She flung out her hand, stopping Asher from getting out. "I almost forget to include carpeting, which is something I've been meaning to speak with you about, because I think carpets belong in the basement."

"They're one of our biggest profit makers," Asher argued, stepping out of the elevator with her.

"And if a customer wants a carpet, they'll travel to the basement to find them."

"I thought you wanted me to consider using part of the basement for a new venture in the store, one that would allow us to sell items of a less expensive nature."

Permilia frowned. "I didn't know you were considering my idea."

Asher frowned right back at her. "Why wouldn't I consider your idea? You've proven in a remarkably short period of time that you were born to be a merchant."

And just like that, Permilia realized that she'd lost her heart to this charming, subtly driven gentleman, who didn't seem to have the slightest inkling these days that she'd changed her mind about the whole holding him in highest affection business, and . . .

"Did you know that Miss Mabel has already shown up for work today?"

Shaking herself straight from the feelings that had threatened to overwhelm her, Permilia tilted her head. "Why would she have gotten here so early?"

"I'm not actually certain, except she did mutter something about Miss Henrietta wanting to check on Miss Snook and the progress she's making turning their house into a new school." Asher smiled. "I think she just enjoys having something she's solely in charge of, that something being the tearoom."

"She's quite good at running it for you."

"And she's quite good at mingling with the customers," Asher added, his tone a mix of amusement and surprise.

"It's been healthy for her to get some distance from Miss Henrietta, as it has also been healthy for Miss Henrietta to get some distance from Miss Mabel." Permilia smiled. "And it has certainly been healthy for them to learn that Cybil is the one responsible for their father's death, although I find it sad to think that Miss Mabel spent all those years believing Miss Henrietta killed their father, while Miss Henrietta was thinking Miss Mabel had."

"I am thankful you had the foresight to bring in Reverend Perry to counsel them over everything they'd experienced in their lives, what with the polygamy, the murders, the unrequited love, the lies, and a nephew who'd decided to poison you and me that day we'd been invited to Huxley House for tea. Then, if I'm understanding what the Pinkerton detectives concluded, he was going to force his aunts to change their will, promising them he wouldn't kill them if they complied with his demands."

"Which they would have never believed."

Asher nodded. "Indeed, but I don't think either Jasper Tooker or his mother are what anyone would consider sane. I think he truly believed he could convince his aunts to change their will, which would have then allowed him to poison them and frame the poor butler for the murder of everyone in the end."

"Which wouldn't have worked since Mr. Barclay would have simply had to tell the Pinkerton detectives the truth."

"Again, I don't think there's any way of understanding the workings of a less than sane mind."

"True, and while I know that, I almost feel sorry for Jasper Tooker and his mother. It must be horrible to live a life with hearts filled with so much evil."

"I'm afraid I'm not that magnanimous since they were determined to kill you, but enough about that madness. They will stay firmly behind bars for a very, very long time, while you and I will now be free to improve this store without the threat of someone trying to murder us."

With that, Asher steered her around a counter displaying a variety of shawls and into the area where construction was being done on a special space for Miss Miller's creations. Pushing aside the floor-to-ceiling drapes set up to shield customers from that construction, Asher drew her to a stop.

"I don't think I've thanked you properly for introducing me to Miss Betsy Miller, or for convincing her to come work for Rutherford & Company," he began with a warm smile that had Permilia smiling in return. "I have a feeling that her designs will someday give Mr. Worth a run for his money, and I do believe those same creations will allow New York City to finally claim a couture fashion title of our own."

"I'll be sure to tell her that. And since Miss Miller has offered to teach a few design classes at Miss Snook's school, I have a feeling New York will soon find itself in possession of more couture-capable designers than it's ever seen."

Asher inclined his head. "And paired with the fashion classes you've decided to teach at the school, I do believe we're soon to become direct rivals with Paris in regard to claiming the title of the most fashionable city in the world."

Permilia's smile turned into a grin. "Miss Snook's school has certainly benefited from becoming known to Miss Mabel and Miss Henrietta, what with the sisters deciding to aid Miss Snook's cause by giving her the house on Broadway to use for her classes. That has allowed them to return to the house Mr. Tooker no longer occupies, the one by Gramercy Park they've been missing for years."

Releasing her hand, but only to take hold of her arm, Asher started to walk across the floor with her. "It is interesting how events have played out, but speaking of interesting, do you have a few minutes to spare so that I can show you something?"

"Of course."

Leading her over to a curved staircase, Asher walked with her up to the fourth floor. Turning right when they reached the landing, they then moved down the hallway that led to her small office, along with the offices of most of the other managers, buyers, and members of the financial staff. Opening the door to her office for her, Asher ushered her inside and then followed her.

She moved across the small space, wishing she'd taken just a little more care to tidy up her office the evening before when she noticed the mounds of sample merchandise she'd gathered over the past few weeks stacked higgledy-piggledy about. Her desk was well and truly buried beneath advertisement copy she'd been working on. Stopping beside one of two chairs the office held, she picked up a stack of scarves and placed them on top of her cluttered desk.

"There," she said, dusting her hands together. "You have a chair now if you'd like to take a seat."

"Our final destination isn't your office."

"Then why did we come in here?"

"To make the moment more dramatic, of course."

With that, and without saying another word, Asher took hold of her hand and pulled her out of her office and down the hallway again. Walking past the entrance to the tearoom, Permilia sent a nod to Miss Mabel, who poked her head out of the tearoom and sent them a cheery good morning, her cheerfulness still something that took Permilia aback at times.

Calling a good morning of her own over her shoulder when Asher picked up his pace, Permilia then found herself moving at a remarkably fast clip down the long hallway that led to Asher's office.

Stopping before he reached his door, though, and in front of a door that had *Vice President* painted on the beveled glass of the door, he opened it up and pulled her inside. Letting go of her hand, he gestured to the cherrywood desk that was the focal point of the room. "What do you think?"

She frowned. "About . . . the desk?"

"Do you find it too masculine?"

"Is it not supposed to be masculine?"

For some reason, Asher didn't answer right away but drew in a deep breath, released it, then drew in another.

"It's meant for you, so I don't want you to find it too masculine."

For a split second, Permilia forgot to breathe. Tilting her head, she looked at the desk, then looked at Asher, then looked around the office—which was at least five times larger than the office she had now—and looked back at the door.

Striding over to it, she considered the words that looked as if they'd been freshly painted.

335

"I don't understand," she began slowly.

Asher strode over to join her, took her hand, and then looked at the letters painted on the glass for a long second or two. Nodding his head as if he approved of what he was seeing, he then shut the door before he pulled her across the room and over to a small settee done up in a lovely green-and-yellow-striped upholstery. Helping her take a seat, he waited until she got settled and then joined her.

Taking her hand back in his, he cleared his throat and looked rather determined. "Do you recall me walking outside with Reverend Perry after he was finished counseling the Huxley sisters a few weeks back?"

"I do."

Asher ran a hand through his hair. "Well, while I was walking with him, he started talking, as he seems to like to do, and what he said was not what I'd been expecting him to say."

"Because?"

"He didn't talk about the Huxley sisters or how God would be certain to fix their lives, or how Jasper Tooker or his mother would be judged by God's hand."

"Ah, you were expecting him to speak as if he were delivering a sermon, not speak as if he was simply a man talking to another man."

"Exactly."

"Reverend Perry enjoys being just a man, Asher."

"Indeed, and he seems to be a somewhat intuitive man, because he brought up things that I needed to hear."

"He does enjoy doing that as well."

Asher smiled. "Quite, but when I got to thinking about what he'd said—about how he believes that God has us experience different situations, some pleasant, some not, all to get us turned on a certain path, if we so choose to take that path, I realized that you and I might have very well been meandering on a variety of different paths, all of which eventually led to the two of our paths crossing."

Permilia found she'd lost the ability to speak again and only seemed capable of nodding her head, which fortunately, Asher took as a sign to continue.

"I always assumed I'd marry a young lady who held a proper position in society, and a young lady who'd want to spend the money I labored to make but not concern herself with my business, and certainly not concern herself with making my business better." He smiled. "But that was before I met you, and . . ."

Before Permilia could regain the use of her voice, Asher was off the settee and kneeling on bended knee before her.

"You will have the position of Vice President of Rutherford & Company no matter what your answer to my next question will be because you deserve that position. However . . ."

To Permilia's confusion, he got to his feet, pulled her up beside him, and then tugged her over to the cherrywood desk, where he opened up the top drawer. Pulling out two sheets of paper, he took a deep breath and then laid the first piece of paper on top of the desk.

On it was a name—*Miss Griswold*.

"I had the art department make up a sample of what your name would look like painted on the door, and since I do want this to be your choice, I wanted you to know that Miss Griswold is a fine choice."

Permilia smiled—she couldn't help herself. "But . . . ?"

He returned the smile before he laid the other piece of paper over top of the first one.

Tears blinded her, but since she'd already seen what was painted on the page, it didn't matter, especially since what she'd seen had been—

Mrs. Asher Rutherford.

Managing a nod, and what might have passed for the word

yes, Permilia felt her heart swell to near bursting when Asher let out a *yes* of his own before he pulled her into his arms, where he immediately took to kissing her—and soundly kissing her at that.

When the sound of Rutherford & Company employees arriving for a normal day at the store drifted into Permilia's new office, she stepped back and smiled, happier than she'd ever thought she'd be.

"I believe I forgot to express my everlasting love for you, and . . . everlasting affection, and . . . well, everything else a gentleman is supposed to profess when he asks a lady to marry him," Asher said, although given the distinct twinkle in his eyes, he didn't look all that concerned about his forgetfulness.

"Since you've just expressed all those things, in a rather curious way, I'll make it a point to not bring up your neglectfulness for the next fifty years or so, but . . ." She smiled and took his hand, placing a kiss on it. "I also was a bit neglectful. In order to correct that, allow me to simply say that I love you, more than I would have ever thought, and more than you'll probably ever know."

Pulling her in for one last kiss, Asher pressed his lips to hers, and then stepped back and caught her eye. "Shall we go tell the staff?"

The door to Permilia's new office took that moment to open, right before Gertrude poked her head in.

"Sorry for the interruption, and for eavesdropping on a door that was definitely closed, but there is a glass insert in this door, and while it's beveled and distorts one's view, you can still make out figures." Gertrude grinned. "And given the closeness of the figures, I and everyone else who came in for that surprise congratulatory tea that Miss Mabel arranged—since she got what was on those pieces of paper out of the art department—might very well know that there's to be a future partnership, and not one strictly of the business type."

338

"Miss Mabel's throwing us a surprise tea?"

Gertrude nodded as she pulled Permilia right out of her new office. "She is."

"But she wanted us to reassure you that it really is a celebratory affair and no one will be poisoned," Harrison added, stepping up to Permilia and giving her a hug before he moved to Asher and hugged him as well.

As she walked down the hallway and then into the tearoom, Permilia's entire being warmed as she found her entrance greeted with smiles, laughter, and even a bit of applause.

Realizing that she'd finally found the place she was meant to be—a place that wasn't her father's mining business, or surrounded by society ladies, or even writing a society column under an assumed name—Permilia stepped farther into the room with Asher now at her side, and knew she was home.

Bowing her head before she joined the crowd of people waiting for her, she felt tears sting her eyes as words she'd heard often in church sprang to mind.

"Every good gift and every perfect gift is from above, and cometh down from the Father of lights, with whom is no variableness, neither shadow of turning."

Feeling quite as if the book of James had said exactly what was in her heart, she lifted her head, smiled, and whispered, "Amen."

339

EPILOGUE

Pulling away from one of the most riveting first drafts he had ever read in his life—one that had been written by Mr. Samuel Sprague, a man he had dismissed—Mr. Charles Dana, editor of the *New York Sun*, settled his attention on the young editor knocking on the side of the doorframe.

"This had better be good," Mr. Dana all but growled.

Holding up a package, the young man smiled. "It's a present for you, so yes, I do believe it might be good."

"We'll see about that."

Placing the package on the desk, the man seemed about to linger, but an actual growl from Mr. Dana had him fleeing the office.

As the door slammed behind the fleeing man, Mr. Dana pulled the gaily wrapped box to him and considered it for a long moment.

"Who would be sending me a present?" he asked the empty room.

Certainly not expecting an answer, he untied the bow and

341

lifted the lid, finding a horribly scribbled note lying on top of what appeared to be thin pieces of crumpled paper.

Pulling the note out of the box, he smiled when he recognized the horrible handwriting.

It was from Miss Permilia Griswold, the former Miss Quill and one of only a handful of people he actually regretted dismissing.

Shoving his glasses to the bridge of his nose, he scanned the note.

Dear Mr. Dana,

Enclosed please find the exclusive you once demanded of me—an exclusive I'm giving you, not because I feel you're owed it, but because I always felt you were a nice gentleman, no matter your grave error in judgment when you fired me.

Consider us squared away, and hopefully I'll be seeing you soon.

With deepest regards,
Miss Quill

Smiling as he dug through the box, he pulled out a single sheet of heavy vellum, vellum of the finest quality that practically begged a person to run a finger over its smooth surface. Resisting the urge to do so, since he didn't want to risk smudging what turned out to be an invitation, he set it on his desk, his smile widening with every line he read.

The pleasure of
Mr. Charles Dana's
company is requested aboard the yacht
Cornelia

in order to celebrate the engagement of
Miss Permilia Griswold
to
Mr. Asher Rutherford
Monday, June the fourth
at half-past four until half-past ten.
Responses delivered to
420 Park Avenue
Mrs. George Griswold

Shaking his head as he laid the invitation down on his desk, he leaned back in his chair, put his hands behind his head, and released a bit of a sigh. The sigh was no reflection of his happiness for the bride-to-be. It was more along the lines of an acknowledgment that even though Miss Griswold had given him exclusive notice about an event that was certain to be the talk of the town, he would never, no matter that the times were indeed changing, write what his readers would love to read—the story of a wallflower who'd defied all the odds by working behind the scenes she'd so carelessly been banished from, breaking free of the chains society had tried to bind her with, and in so doing, found her very own happily-ever-after.

Jen Turano, a *USA Today* bestselling author, is a graduate of the University of Akron with a degree in clothing and textiles. She is a member of ACFW and RWA. She lives in a suburb of Denver, Colorado. Visit her website at www.jenturano.com.

Sign Up for Jen's Newsletter!

Keep up to date with Jen's news on book releases, signings, and other events by signing up for her email list at jenturano.com

---

More From Jen Turano

When a fan's interest turns sinister, young actress Lucetta Plum takes refuge on a secluded estate owned by her friend's eligible yet eccentric grandson. As hijinks and hilarity ensue, and danger catches up to Lucetta, will her friends be able to protect her?

Playing the Part

You May Also Enjoy . . .

Millie and Everett are eager to prove themselves—as a nanny and a society gentleman, respectively. They both have one last chance . . . each other.

In Good Company by Jen Turano

Betsy Huckabee dreams of being a big-city journalist, but first she has to get out of Pine Gap. To that end, she pens a romanticized serial for the ladies' pages of a distant newspaper, using the handsome new deputy and his exploits for inspiration. She'd be horrified if he read her breathless descriptions of him, but no one from home will ever know. . . .

For the Record by Regina Jennings
reginajennings.com

Hope Irvine always sees the best in people. While traveling on the rails with her missionary father, she attracts the attention of a miner named Luke and a young mine manager. When Luke begins to suspect the manager is using Hope's missions of mercy as a cover for illegal activities, can he discover the truth without putting her in danger?

The Chapel Car Bride by Judith Miller
judithmccoymiller.com

More Historical Fiction . . .

After being unjustly imprisoned, Julianne Chevalier trades her life sentence for exile to the French colony of Louisiana in 1720. She marries a fellow convict in order to sail, but when tragedy strikes—and a mystery unfolds—Julianne must find her own way in this dangerous new land while bearing the brand of a criminal.

The Mark of the King by Jocelyn Green
jocelyngreen.com

After a night trapped together in an old stone keep, Lady Adelaide Bell and Lord Trent Hawthorne have no choice but to marry. Dismayed, Adelaide finds herself bound to a man who ignores her, as Trent has no desire to connect with the one who dashed his plans to marry for love. Can they set aside their first impressions before any chance of love is lost?

An Uncommon Courtship by Kristi Ann Hunter
HAWTHORNE HOUSE
kristiannhunter.com

Cassidy Ivanoff and her father, John, have signed on to work at a prestigious new hotel near Mt. McKinley. John's new apprentice, Allan Brennan, finds a friend in Cassidy, but the real reason he's here—to learn the truth about his father's death—is far more dangerous than he knows.

In the Shadow of Denali by Tracie Peterson & Kimberley Woodhouse
THE HEART OF ALASKA #1
traciepeterson.com
kimberleywoodhouse.com